J. 6·23-12

K 5 - 12

Bookplate Ink

Thomas Davies Clay

THE DEAD OF WINTER

RENNIE AIRTH

THE DEAD OF WINTER

VIKING

VIKING
Published by the Penguin Group
Penguin Group (USA) Inc., 375 Hudson Street,
New York, New York 10014, U.S.A.
Penguin Group (Canada), 90 Eglinton Avenue East, Suite 700,
Toronto, Ontario, Canada M4P 2Y3
(a division of Pearson Penguin Canada Inc.)
Penguin Books Ltd, 80 Strand, London WC2R 0RL, England
Penguin Ireland, 25 St. Stephen's Green, Dublin 2, Ireland
(a division of Penguin Books Ltd)
Penguin Books Australia Ltd, 250 Camberwell Road, Camberwell,
Victoria 3124, Australia
(a division of Pearson Australia Group Pty Ltd)
Penguin Books India Pvt Ltd, 11 Community Centre, Panchsheel Park,
New Delhi – 110 017, India
Penguin Group (NZ), 67 Apollo Drive, Rosedale, North Shore 0632,
New Zealand (a division of Pearson New Zealand Ltd)
Penguin Books (South Africa) (Pty) Ltd, 24 Sturdee Avenue,
Rosebank, Johannesburg 2196, South Africa

Penguin Books Ltd, Registered Offices:
80 Strand, London WC2R 0RL, England

First American edition
Published in 2009 by Viking Penguin,
a member of Penguin Group (USA) Inc.

1 3 5 7 9 10 8 6 4 2

Publisher's Note
This is a work of fiction. Names, characters, places, and incidents either are the product of the author's imagination or are used fictitiously, and any resemblance to actual persons, living or dead, business establishments, events, or locales is entirely coincidental.

LIBRARY OF CONGRESS CATALOGING IN PUBLICATION DATA

Airth, Rennie, 1935–
Dead of winter : a John Madden mystery / Rennie Airth.
p. cm.
ISBN 978-0-670-02093-5
1. Murder—Investigation—Fiction. 2. World War, 1939–1945—England—London—Fiction. I. Title.

PR9369.3.A47D43 2009
823'.914—dc22
2008054094

Printed in the United States of America

For Jonathan Randal

PROLOGUE

Paris, May 1940

DUSK WAS FALLING by the time Maurice Sobel reached Neuilly, and he walked the short distance from the Metro to his house in the cold, not quite earthly light of the blue-painted street lamps which were the city's sole concession to the war that was about to engulf it. His pace was brisk, and twice he glanced over his shoulder to assure himself that the street behind him was empty. The creak of the garden gate when he opened it was a welcome sound.

Only then did he relax his grip on the handle of the attaché case he was carrying. Since leaving Eyskens's office he'd been holding it tightly, and he felt the prickle of pins and needles in his fingers now as he shifted the case to his left hand and fumbled in his pocket for his house key.

Normally he would have been brought home by car, but that morning he'd paid off the last of the household staff, including his chauffeur, a blunt Breton by the name of Dugarry. Maurice had found the farewells upsetting and the sight of the darkened house as he walked up the gravel path to the front door was a reminder of the loss suffered by all parties. Florence, their cook, and a family retainer for the better part of a quarter of a century, had clung to his hand when they'd said goodbye. There'd been tears in her eyes.

'Tell Madame...' She had begun to speak three or four

times, but been unable to continue. 'Ah, but you'll be back . . .' It was all she could say.

Maurice had pressed her hand in return. 'Of course, of course . . .' Not knowing if it was true. Not knowing if they would ever meet again.

With a sigh he unlocked the door and switched on the lights in the hall. The emptiness around him seemed unnatural – he was used to the house being filled with people, loud with the voices of family and friends – and he regretted, not for the first time, his decision to postpone his departure, when he could have taken passage on the same ship that had carried his wife and their two sons across the Atlantic to New York a month earlier. Unwisely, deceived by the slow march of events in Europe following the occupation of Poland, he'd chosen to remain in Paris for a little while longer, taking time to dispose of his business and to attend to the many other details, such as the leasing of his house, which had required his attention. The delay had proved costly. He had not yet wound up his affairs when the long-threatened German invasion had been launched a week earlier, and with their armoured units advancing now with giant strides across the Low Countries and – according to as yet unconfirmed reports – about to encircle the French army entrenched on the Somme, he had been forced to take emergency measures, selling off the last of his stock at rock-bottom prices and, even worse, engaging in the kind of transaction he would normally have shunned in an attempt to salvage at least a portion of these assets.

On that last day – the last for him, at any rate – the city had worn an air of exhaustion. The soft breeze with its promise of spring had expired, like the hopes of so many, and it was the stifling heat of summer that hung in the air now and seemed poised to descend on streets already starting to empty as cars made their slow exit bumper to bumper from the capital in anticipation of the threat that daily drew closer. Although government spokesmen had said that every inch of French soil would be defended, Maurice knew from other sources – from the rumours that sped from mouth to mouth – that the German panzers were already moving south from the coast. He had glimpsed military lorries drawn up in lines outside ministries, prepared to cart away files and other vital equipment. And although no refugees had yet appeared in Paris, travellers arriving from the north-east spoke of roads clogged by those trying to escape the fighting; of whole families on the move pushing handcarts loaded with their possessions. More ominously still, there were even reports that French soldiers without their arms had joined the fleeing columns.

Although his appointment with Eyskens was not until the afternoon, Maurice had gone into the city earlier and after calling at his bank had paid a final visit to what had been until recently the store that bore his family's name: Sobel Frères. Furriers of distinction, the shop was located off the rue St Honoré, and although Maurice had relinquished the lease on the property he still had a key to the street door. Wandering about the deserted rooms, he had felt a deep sadness. It had taken his family years to build up the business – the company had been founded by his grandfather – and its loss felt like an amputation. He could think of no sight more desolate that day than the rows of empty hangers where only a few weeks before the finest furs had been on display, no sign more indicative of abandonment and flight than the thin patina of dust already starting to gather on the glass-topped counters.

Seeking an antidote to his depression, he'd chosen to lunch for the last time at a favourite restaurant in the rue Cambon, one he had patronized regularly over the years, where his face and name were known not only to the patron and waiters but also to some of the other clients, successful businessmen like himself, with whom he was accustomed to exchanging nods. No doubt some of them had heard of his decision to leave: he thought he detected sympathy in the glances cast his way. But for the most part they seemed preoccupied with their own affairs. (How could they not be?) They were taking stock of the new reality. And while there was little they could do to alter it, Maurice had nevertheless been distressed to observe the all too familiar hint of a shrug in their manner; that lift of the shoulders so peculiar to the French, signifying acceptance of a situation, however disagreeable.

Catching sight of his own image in a gold-framed mirror on the other side of the restaurant – wryly noting the elegance of his appearance, his silvered hair barbered to a millimetre, the distinction of his dark suit, one of several he'd had tailored in London, its sombre hue set off by a splash of red silk spilling from his breast pocket – he'd reflected on how little he differed from these pillars of the bourgeoisie, at least on the surface. How even now, he might have been pondering his country's future in the light of the fate that was about to overtake it: assessing what impact occupation by a foreign power would have on himself and his family, how best to protect his interests. In all probability the course of his life had not differed much from theirs. As a youth he had run up debts and made a fool of himself over women – to the despair of his father – but later redeemed himself by volunteering to serve in the war which only a generation earlier had bled his country white, and being twice decorated for gallantry. He had married well and raised a family.

But none of that mattered any longer, he knew, none of it counted. The future lay with the jackbooted conquerors whose armoured units even now were beating a path to the city's gates, and they would not be deceived.

A Jew was a Jew.

Willem Eyskens's office, or rather his place of business, since buying and selling were very much part of his day-to-day operations, was located off the rue de Rivoli. The brass plate beside the locked door bore his name, but gave no further information. Indeed, if you were not expected there in all likelihood you were not welcome, and beyond the door, which was only opened after the caller had adequately identified himself, access was further barred by a guard, presumably armed, who sat at a table in the small entrance hall with an alarm button close at hand. Maurice had been given Eyskens's name by a business associate, a dealer in costume jewellery and other fashion accessories with whom he did business from time to time.

'He's a diamond broker with connections in Amsterdam. Dutch originally, but he's been settled here a long time. He only deals in good-quality stones, I've been told, and he's discreet. He can certainly provide what you need – at a price, of course.'

The price, as it turned out, had been high. Eyskens had outlined the cruel economics of it at their first meeting. 'It's always the same in dangerous times. People try to save what they have. You can't take a factory with you, a business. So you turn it into something you know has value. Gold, if you can carry enough of it; otherwise stones. Diamonds. There's no need to explain what effect this demand has on the market.'

A thin-faced man with red cheeks and fair hair brushed back from his forehead, Eyskens had kept his gaze on the surface of his rosewood desk while he spoke. It was as though he was embarrassed to meet Maurice's gaze.

'Sufficient to say you are not the first to come to me with a request of this kind, Monsieur Sobel. These are, as I say, terrible times. Let us be businesslike. Your need is urgent, I see that. The short notice makes for difficulties, but I can provide what you want. However, I would prefer if this were a cash transaction.'

'You don't want a cheque?' Maurice hadn't been altogether surprised.

'It's not a matter of trust, I assure you. Your reputation is beyond question.' Eyskens had shown small signs of discomfort. 'But I will be forced to cut corners, if I can put it like that. And later on questions may be asked – I don't mean by the French authorities. Paris may soon be under new rulers, men who might wish to enquire into favours done for . . . for . . .'

'Jews?' Maurice had furnished the word he was trying not to utter.

'I am sorry . . .' Eyskens had spread his hands on the desk.

Their first meeting had taken place the previous week, and that afternoon, having earlier withdrawn the cash from his bank – Maurice had given Eyskens a round figure to work with – he had proceeded to their final appointment. Once again he'd been shown upstairs to the diamond broker's office, a small, windowless room, bare of decoration, where Eyskens was waiting. Before him on the desk was a black velvet bag tied with a drawstring. It lay on a piece of felt which had been spread across the desk. Beside the bag was a jeweller's loupe.

'I will leave you now.' Eyskens rose. 'You will want to examine the stones. Please take your time. I have made a list'

– he took a piece of paper from his jacket pocket and handed it to Maurice. 'The stones are marked by weight, but you will be able to tell by the size and the shape which is which. Taken together they match the sum we agreed on. Of course, if any of them doesn't meet with your approval, it can be discarded and we will make the necessary adjustment to the total.' He bowed and left the room.

Maurice had wasted no time. Uncomfortable though the transaction made him feel, he had taken a decision and meant to stick to it. With the start of the war, the movement of funds by more orthodox means had become increasingly difficult and the German invasion had brought even those to a halt. True, in the past few months he had managed to shift a good portion of his assets abroad, but he was reluctant to leave anything he possessed to the new masters of Europe, these brutal despoilers of his people.

Emptying the velvet bag on to the felt, he had examined the glittering contents. Though no expert, his experience as a furrier had made him familiar with all aspects of the fashion trade, including its most luxurious and costly items, and a few minutes' study with the loupe were enough to reassure him of the quality of the goods he was purchasing. The bag contained a score of diamonds – cut stones, as he'd requested – the biggest the size of his thumbnail, all of the finest water.

By the time the broker returned ten minutes later, Maurice had emptied the attaché case, which had been resting on the floor at his feet, and laid out the stacks of banknotes he had brought in a neat pile alongside the diamonds.

'You are satisfied, then?' Eyskens resumed his position across the desk.

'Perfectly.'

Maurice was relieved that their business was over. For

some reason – its hole-in-the-wall nature, perhaps – he'd found it distasteful. Nor had he warmed to the man who sat facing him. The Dutchman's pale blue eyes were unreadable.

'Would you like to count the money, Monsieur Eyskens?'

'Given who I am dealing with, that will not be necessary.' The broker had accompanied these words with a polite bow. They both rose.

'Goodbye, Monsieur Sobel. I wish you good fortune.'

There was nothing more he could do. Everything was set now for his departure the following morning, and as he wandered about the house switching on lights, Maurice went over the plans he'd made, plans which had grown in complication as the situation around him became more unstable. With sailings from Le Havre suspended, he'd been obliged to look further afield and had managed to book passage on a liner leaving Lisbon for New York in a week's time. This had still left him with the problem of getting to the Portuguese capital, and having considered – and discarded – the idea of trying to find a seat on the by now overcrowded trains heading south from the city daily, he had decided instead to make the long journey by motor car.

Dugarry's last job before departing to join his wife and children in Rennes had been to service the Sobels' Citroën cabriolet and to ensure that the tyres were in good condition and reserve supplies of fuel stowed aboard. Even so, Maurice might have felt daunted by the thought of the drive ahead – apart from the odd Sunday outing it was some years since he had driven a car – had it not been for a stroke of good fortune that had come his way a few days earlier. An acquaintance of his, a Polish art dealer called Kinski, long settled in France, had rung him out of the blue to ask, if it was not prying, if it was not an indelicate question, whether what he had heard was true – that Sobel was intending to quit Paris and would be travelling to Spain in his car? Before Maurice had time to get over his surprise – he had discussed his plans with only one or two people – Kinski had revealed the reason for his enquiry.

'I've been asked if I can help a young man whom the Nazis would like to get their hands on. A Polish officer. Jan Belka's his name. He joined the resistance soon after the Germans occupied Warsaw, but unfortunately his group was betrayed and he had to get out in a hurry. He's been in Paris for some time, without papers, of course, and now he's in danger again. He'd like to get to London, but Spain would be a start. I was wondering . . . would it be possible . . . ?'

While Kinski was speaking, Maurice had had time to reflect on the fact that it was not so surprising after all that his help should have been sought in the matter. The Sobels were Polish by extraction. They made no secret of it.

'You want me to take this man with me?'

'If possible. And his companion, a young woman, also Polish.' Kinski had hesitated. He said delicately, 'I understand she is Jewish.'

Ignoring the momentary prick of anger he felt just then – as if the fact that the girl was Jewish might sway him, as if he might be less inclined to help a mere gentile – Maurice had responded without hesitation.

'Of course, my dear fellow. I'd be happy to take them.' He'd spoken honestly. 'In fact, you're doing me a favour. I'd rather not make this trip alone.'

'I can't thank you enough.' Kinski's relief had been plain.

'Give them my address. Tell them we'll be leaving two days from now, on Thursday. I want to make an early start, so I suggest they spend Wednesday night with me. The house will be empty during the day – I'm paying off the staff – but I'll be home by six. I'll expect them then.'

He looked at his watch now. It was a few minutes after the hour. He reminded himself he must check the bedrooms on the floor above to make sure that the maids had prepared them as instructed before departing. Maurice had no idea whether his guests were a couple or not and had decided to offer them a room each and then leave it to them to settle their sleeping arrangements. For his own part he would be glad to have them as company on this last evening. The house was full of ghosts for him; full of memories. Although some of the furniture had already been dispatched across the Atlantic and other pieces put in storage, there were enough reminders of the life he and his family had shared here to weigh on his spirits and fill him with a sense of loss.

But he knew these were thoughts he must put behind him. The future was what concerned him now, the *immediate* future. Pausing by his desk to gaze dreamily at a photograph of his wife, which he'd not yet packed, Maurice delivered a silent reproof to himself. Léonie Sobel was a woman of character and her dark, emphatic features showed a strength he had come to rely on over the years. He knew very well if she were here now she would tell him to leave off wool-gathering. To focus his mind on the business in hand. In particular, there was the problem of the diamonds, which he'd taken out of the attaché case and placed on the desk beside his wife's photograph, to be resolved. How best to transport them? He'd be crossing two borders in the coming days, and quite possibly his luggage would be searched. It might be as well to remove temptation from the gaze of customs officers who'd be only too well aware of his predicament: of the threat that had driven him, and others like him, to take flight.

Even as he considered the question, weighing the velvet bag in his hand, he felt the beginnings of despair take hold of him, a feeling of hopelessness not rooted in the moment – he knew he could deal with the immediate problems facing him – but rather in the sense of destiny as a curse from which there was no escape. Despite the years of prosperity, his family had not forgotten their past. Dealers in furs for generations, the Sobels had fled the Pale of Settlement before the turn of the century, leaving behind them the bloody pogroms that had racked the western borders of the Tsar's empire. How many times, Maurice wondered, had he heard his grandfather, dead now these twenty years, tell of the night he had seen his parents' neighbour, a watchmaker, beaten to death in the street before a watching crowd while their own house went up in flames? Now, once again, the blood was flowing. Was there no end to it?

With a growl, he broke the spell. Enough! The dark street his thoughts had wandered down led nowhere. Frowning, he stared at the soft velvet bag resting in the palm of his hand, and as he did so an idea came to him. It concerned his street coat, which he'd taken off and hung up in the hall when he came in. Another Savile Row creation, its elegant folds contained an ample expanse of silk lining, and it had occurred to him that this might be put to some practical use as a place of concealment. It would require some skill in sewing, he saw that, but surely this young woman who was about to arrive could help him there. He didn't doubt he could trust her, she and her companion both, these brave young people, who even if they were fleeing with him now, surely meant to continue the fight against the loathed enemy. London, Caspar Kinski had said. That was where they meant to go, and Maurice wondered if he might not be able to help them achieve their aim. With money, certainly, but perhaps in other ways, too, once they had reached Spain. He had business contacts in many capitals.

Cheered by the thought – he was relieved to have shrugged off his dark mood – Maurice went out into the entrance hall where his coat was hanging. As he reached for it, he heard the creak of the garden gate followed by the sound of footsteps on the gravel path. Smiling a greeting, he opened the door to what he thought were his guests and received instead a blow to the jaw that sent him staggering backwards and then, before he had time to react, a second to the side of his head that knocked him to the paved floor. Crouched on his hands and knees, spitting out blood from a cut lip, he was aware only of a pair of trousered legs which moved swiftly around him and out of his blurred vision. Next moment his throat was encircled by something so thin it seemed to have no substance, but which burned like fire as it cut its way into his flesh, deeper and deeper. The pain was intense, but it lasted for only a few moments. Then sight and consciousness faded and his agony ceased.

PART ONE

1

London, November 1944

HANDS IN POCKETS, Bert huddled deeper in the doorway. Crikey, it was cold!

The wind that had got up earlier was still blowing, but not in gusts like before; now it was steady. It had force, and the power of it cut clean through his coat and overalls, and the jersey he was wearing underneath that, and went straight to his bones. And though his tin helmet, with the W for air-raid warden painted on the front, was safely settled on his head and hardly likely to fly away, even in the gale that was blowing, he clutched at it automatically.

'You'll catch your death, Bert Cotter, going out on a night like this,' Vi had warned him earlier when he'd been preparing to set off from the small flat in St Pancras where they lived. She'd insisted he put on an extra vest. 'And what's the use anyway? It's no good telling people to put their lights out. It don't make no difference to a buzz bomb.'

The advice was wasted on Bert. Hadn't he been saying the same thing himself for weeks? There hadn't been a proper raid on London since the summer. The Luftwaffe – the bloomin' Luftwaffe to Vi – had finally shot its bolt, or so they were assured. Now there were only the flying bombs to worry about. Those and these new V-2 rockets, which the government had finally admitted were falling on the city, though most people had already guessed it. After all, how many times could mysterious explosions be put down to gas leaks before people started asking questions?

'What do they take us for?' Vi had enquired of him in all seriousness. As though she thought he might actually know the answer. 'Bloomin' idiots?'

Fishing out a packet of fags from his coat pocket, Bert chuckled. She was right about the blackout, though. The whole of London could be lit up and it wouldn't change a thing. The bombs and rockets fell where they fell, and all you could hope was it wasn't your head they came down on.

He lit his cigarette and then used the flickering flame of the match to check his wristwatch. He was close to the end of his three-hour tour of duty and anxious to get home. Too old to enlist – he'd done his bit in France in the last shindig – Bert had opted to serve part time in civil defence, and since he worked in the area, being employed as a carpenter and general handyman at the British Museum, he'd joined a squad of wardens assigned to the Bloomsbury district. There'd been a time, back in '40, during the Blitz, when Jerry bombers had come over night after night, turning whole areas of the city into cauldrons of fire, when the job had been one to be proud of.

But now Bert wasn't so sure. The excitement he'd felt at the start of the conflict had long since faded. Truth to tell he was sick of patrolling the night-time streets, fed up with blowing his whistle and bawling up at people to 'put that bloody light out'. It was a feeling shared by many, and not least by his fellow wardens, if that evening's performance was anything to go by. When Bert had turned up at their rendez-vous point a little earlier – it was a pub in the Tottenham Court Road – he'd discovered that no fewer than four of the dozen-strong squad had rung in to excuse themselves. Two had bad colds (they said), one had twisted his ankle (a likely story) and the fourth had referred to some unspecified family crisis that prevented him from leaving home. Vi was right. Only a muggins like yours truly would venture out on a night like this.

His thoughts were interrupted by the wail of a siren. It sounded close by, coming from the area of Covent Garden, he guessed, and instinctively he glanced upwards, searching for the telltale finger of flame that would signal the approach of a flying bomb. During the summer they arrived day and night from across the Channel, and Londoners had learned to recognize the sinister drone of their engines and to dread the moment when the noise ceased and the craft, loaded with explosives, plunged to earth. Fewer fell now, it was true: the advance of the Allied armies in France and Holland had forced the Jerries to move their launching sites. But the threat was far from over. Only a few weeks before, returning home from work, crossing Tavistock Square, Bert had seen one pass overhead and heard its engine cut out. The tremendous explosion that followed had made the windows in the square rattle, and seconds later a huge buff plume of smoke had risen from the vicinity of King's Cross like a pillar into the grey October sky. Ears pricked, he waited now, but after a minute or so the noise stopped and the silence of the night was restored. A false alarm.

Bert put out his cigarette. It was time to get moving. The doorway where he'd taken refuge was in Little Russell Street, near the corner of Museum Street, and he needed only to walk over to Tottenham Court Road to reach the boundary of his allotted territory, a patchwork of narrow roads bounded to the north by Great Russell Street and to the south by Bloomsbury Way. The wardens usually patrolled in pairs, but because of the absentees that evening he was on his own and had already decided to shorten his route. Not two minutes from where he stood now, at the top of Museum Street, his place of employment loomed large and lightless, and although it seemed deserted he knew very well that the museum's doors would be unlocked and a squad of volunteer firemen would be on duty inside. (They'd been posted there as a precaution ever since a night back in 1941 when dozens of incendiary bombs had come through the roof during a Jerry raid and several of the rooms had been burned out.) What he planned to do was pop in there for a cup of tea, get the cold out of his bones, and then leg it home to St Pancras. (And two nights from now when he was next on duty he might just come down with a cold himself.)

As Bert slipped out of the doorway he heard footsteps, and next moment a dark figure came swinging round the corner from Museum Street.

'Whoops . . . ! Sorry, miss.'

If it hadn't been for the cry the figure let out as they collided Bert might not have known it was a young woman. She was wearing a coat which had a hood attached to it and was walking with her head down.

'It's this blinkin' blackout.' Seeing her shrink back, he tried to reassure her. 'You never see anything until it's too late.'

'I am sorry. It was my fault.' Breathless from haste, she spoke with a foreign accent. 'I should have looked where I was going.'

The face beneath the hood was a white blur. Bert noticed she had a bag in each hand.

'Bitter night,' he remarked, drawing his own coat closer about him, resettling the helmet on his head.

'Yes, isn't it?' The relief in her voice made him wonder if she'd felt nervous walking through the blackout on her own.

She'd put down one of her bags for a moment, and he saw now that in fact it was a basket, heavily laden, its contents covered by a cloth. He tested its weight and then held it ready for her while she wiggled her fingers to get the circulation back.

'Thank you so much.' She took the basket from him.

'I hope you haven't far to go with those.' He nodded at her burdens.

'No, it's only a short walk.'

'I'll give you a hand if you like.'

She looked over her shoulder. 'No, really. It's not necessary.' He caught a glimpse of her smile in the shadow cast by the hood. 'Goodnight, and thank you for your help.'

She plodded on, and as he watched her figure disappearing into the darkness Bert wondered if he shouldn't have insisted. She seemed like a nice girl. But his bones ached from the cold and whatever faint impulse he felt to follow her faded at the thought of the hot cup of tea awaiting him.

She would manage, he told himself as her figure grew faint and then vanished in the darkness.

She hadn't far to go.

Feeling a lot better after his break – the firemen were a friendly lot – Bert hurried down the museum steps into the buffeting wind and then tacked his way across the great forecourt like a ship under sail. The sirens he'd heard earlier hadn't sounded again. He was ready to call it a night. But while sitting in the warmth inside he'd felt the prick of conscience, and instead of going home directly as he'd planned he'd decided to return to where he'd interrupted his round earlier and make a final inspection of his area.

Pausing only to adjust his shoulder bag, he set off briskly

down Museum Street, using the road itself, rather than the pavement. Although the blackout restrictions had been relaxed in recent weeks – in some districts of the capital, street lamps were now permitted to show a glimmer of light, creating what was called a moonlight effect – inky darkness continued to prevail in many areas, and if you wanted to avoid barking your shins on unseen obstacles, or, even worse, collecting a black eye from walking into a lamp-post, it was best to keep to the middle of the street.

Bert had barely turned the corner and started down Little Russell Street, however, when he heard the sound of a car behind him. Looking back he saw its reduced headlights approaching, and moved off the roadway to give it passage. It went by slowly, the driver steering his vehicle carefully down the dark canyon created by the buildings on either side of the narrow street. Bert continued to walk along the pavement. He was keeping an eye on the car, ready to move back on to the road at the first opportunity, but before he had a chance to do so his foot caught on something and he tripped and fell headlong.

'Bloody 'ell!' Half-winded by the fall, he lay where he was for a moment, collecting his wits. 'What in the name of . . . ?'

Lifting himself up on one elbow he peered behind him. The darkness seemed impenetrable. But there was something there all right. He could feel it when he pushed his foot back; an obstruction of some kind. Bert levered himself into a sitting position. His shoulder bag had come off, but he quickly located it by feeling around in the dark, and having got the straps unbuckled his questing fingers found the torch which he carried inside it. He switched on the light.

'Christ Almighty!'

The whispered exclamation was involuntary. Revealed by the wavering beam, a pair of legs was protruding on to the pavement. They belonged to a woman, there was no doubt of that. Bert could see a knee-length skirt beneath the coat which the sprawled figure was wearing. He shifted the light. His hand was shaking.

'Ah, no . . . !'

He recognized the figure: it was the young girl he'd bumped into earlier. Her pale face was clearly visible now that the hood she'd been wearing had been dragged clear of her head. Bert could see the basket she'd been carrying lying beside her. It had tipped over and he caught a glimpse of some strewn apples and the remains of what looked like broken eggs. Although he knew instinctively that she was dead, he stirred himself to scramble to his knees and reach for her wrist, which lay close to him, the hand beneath it clenched. He found no pulse.

'Poor lass . . .'

Fumbling in the pocket of his overalls, Bert got hold of his police whistle, and as the wind gathered in strength, ascending to a high keening note not unlike a howl of grief, he blew a long blast on it. Then another . . . and another, piercing the enveloping blackness around him with its urgent summons.

2

'She was murdered all right, sir. There's no doubt of that. A possible strangulation. It seems an air-raid warden stumbled on the body. The first officer on the scene was a woman police constable. She was passing by and heard him blow his whistle. Bow Street has some men examining the site now. Because of the blackout, they weren't able to do it properly last night.'

Chief Inspector Angus Sinclair shifted uncomfortably in his chair. He'd spent a sleepless night, disturbed by the buffeting wind and also by an attack of gout, a malady that had begun to plague him in recent years. As Bennett watched he lifted one foot off the floor and set it down gently. Aware that the subject was a sensitive one so far as his colleague was concerned, the assistant commissioner kept a tactful silence.

Sinclair squinted at the page he was reading from. 'We don't have a name as yet,' he said. 'But she appears to be in her early twenties and ... er ... respectable.' He frowned at his own choice of word.

'Not a prostitute, then.' Bennett nodded. Thanks to the blackout, assaults after dark had become commonplace in London. Streetwalkers, in particular, had suffered in the upsurge of violence which the war years had brought to the capital. 'Do we know why she was killed?'

'Not as yet, sir. Bow Street rang in with this information overnight. They're sending other details over by hand. I expect to hear from them quite soon.'

Bennett grunted. 'What else?' He gestured towards the

typed sheets held together by a paper clip which Sinclair had laid on his knee. A summary of all crimes reported in the Metropolitan area during the preceding twenty-four hours, it was delivered to the chief inspector's desk each day in time for their morning conference, which took place in Bennett's office overlooking the Thames embankment.

'Just the usual. Balham organized a raid on a premises in Brixton last night. Two printing presses were seized. They were being used to turn out fake identity cards and ration documents. No arrests as yet.' The chief inspector paused. 'And we've had another report of looting in Stepney. They took a pounding over the weekend. Two V-2s came down in the district. The police are trying to keep an eye on damaged houses, but the looters slip in at night.'

'I want them caught.' Bennett's face darkened. 'Put the word out. If more men are needed, we'll find them.' In common with most policemen, he regarded looting as a particularly loathsome crime. It was taking advantage of others' misfortunes in the worst possible way and offenders could look for no mercy from the courts.

'One bright spot, if you can call it that.' Sinclair glanced up. 'The Stockwell police stopped a lorry they thought was suspicious in the early hours. It turned out to be filled with frozen carcasses of beef. Fresh from the Argentine, I've no doubt.' The chief inspector lifted a grizzled eyebrow. 'Two men were arrested. They're still being questioned.'

'It could be that hijacking gang we've been after.' The assistant commissioner tried to sound optimistic. 'Perhaps they'll lead us to the rest.'

'We can always hope,' Sinclair agreed, though without much conviction. 'So far all they've said is they were offered a tenner each by a man they'd never met before to drive the lorry to London. I doubt they'll change their story.'

He brooded on his words. Five years of war had brought a new dimension to lawbreaking, one which had stretched police resources to their limits. The thicket of regulations designed to control the distribution of food and other scarce resources issued by the government at the start of the conflict had opened fresh avenues for the criminal world, and it gave the chief inspector little satisfaction to know that several of the capital's most dangerous gangs, formerly employed in the business of extortion and notorious before the war for their violent conduct at race meetings, had long since moved into new spheres of activity linked to the flourishing black market. Even worse, the virus had spread to the general population. Prompted by shortages and driven beyond endurance by the tendency of authority to poke its nose into every corner of life, ordinarily decent citizens now broke laws they no longer respected without compunction, taxing the police still further.

The telephone on Bennett's desk rang and the assistant commissioner picked it up. While he was speaking, Sinclair allowed his gaze to stray to the windows, where a sky the colour of dishwater could be glimpsed through panes criss-crossed with tape to minimize bomb blast. Try as he might, he could no longer bring the same passion to his work he had once felt. In truth, he found it only a burden now, a duty he accepted as necessary for the good of the force he had served for half a century, but one he could hardly wait to relinquish. The mortal struggle which his country had been engaged in these past five years had demanded sacrifices from all, and Sinclair's own contribution had been to defer his plans for retirement, already in place when war had broken out, and answer the appeal which had come from Bennett's own lips.

'Angus, I need you. This war will be fought to the death, and it won't be over by Christmas.' This had been in late 1939, following the German invasion of Poland and before its assault on France, when peace had still seemed a possibility to some. 'The Metropolitan Police will suffer along with everyone else. We're already losing men to the forces and no fresh recruiting will be allowed until the fighting's over. It won't be long before we feel the pinch.'

Unable to refuse the request, or deny the necessity behind it, Sinclair had agreed to stay on, but with a sinking heart. By refusing several offers of promotion and clinging to his rank as chief inspector he had managed to prolong his career as an investigator beyond its normal span. His name was associated with some of Scotland Yard's most famous cases and his reputation, particularly among the younger detectives at the Yard, was close to legendary. But as he well knew, those days were over: he had turned seventy; it was time to retire gracefully and leave the world to others to bustle in.

The post he held now as special assistant to Bennett gave him supervisory authority over all criminal investigations, but no active role in them. With it had come yet another offer of promotion, to the rank of superintendent. As the assistant commissioner himself had pointed out, it might seem anomalous for a mere chief inspector to give direction to officers senior to himself. But at that point Sinclair had dug in his heels. Before the Met's plainclothes staff had been expanded in the years leading up to the war he had been one of only four chief inspectors on the Yard's strength, men who had been seen as an elite group, specialists assigned to handle only the most difficult cases. He had been proud of the distinction he'd earned, and the fact that there were now a round dozen men holding the same rank was neither here nor there to Angus Sinclair.

'I prefer to remain as I am, sir. And since I'll be speaking in your name, I don't imagine I'll encounter any problems.'

Left unsaid by him was the fact that many of those

promoted above him had learned their trade at his hands and it had become commonplace at the Yard to refer to him simply as 'the chief inspector' without further identification.

Beached at last, a slave to paperwork, to somehow making ends meet, Sinclair had quickly discovered the truth of the assistant commissioner's prophetic words. If the Yard had felt the pinch of war at the outset, it was now close to being trapped in a straitjacket of diminished resources. The Met's prewar strength of 19,500 had shrunk to a mere 12,000, and while the situation had been alleviated somewhat by the use of auxiliaries known as Specials, it had coincided with a sharp rise in crime. As though in response to some Malthusian principle, lawbreaking had increased in proportion to the number of laws added to the statute book. (Issued under the all-embracing Defence Regulations, there'd been no end of them.) Far too many policemen were engaged in pursuing petty offences, wasting both their own and the courts' time, adding to the store of national irritation and impatience with authority. It had been the chief inspector's aim throughout the war to counter this trend towards the trivial, to keep the plainclothes branch insulated from it as much as possible and engaged in the fight against genuine crime. But it was a battle he could never win entirely and the effort had exhausted him.

Nor was he alone in his suffering, Sinclair reflected, as he watched Bennett, who was saying little but still had the receiver pressed to his ear, stifle a yawn. As assistant commissioner, crime, Sir Wilfred was responsible for all CID operations in the Metropolitan area, a position he had held for many years and one that now hung like an albatross around his neck. Indeed, if the chief inspector sometimes mourned his own decline into bureaucratic impotence, he was able to spare more than a thought for his superior, who had nursed the ambition, even the hope, that he might one day ascend to the commissionership. The summons had never come. Throughout Bennett's career the government had continued its tradition of appointing a senior member of the armed forces to the post. (The present incumbent was an air vice-marshal.) And now that he, too, was preparing to retire – he'd already made it known that he was only waiting, like others, for the war to end before offering his resignation – he'd been forced to swallow a final irony. Word had come down from on high that the authorities had decided to make a break with the past: once hostilities were ended a new commissioner would be named, a civilian appointee.

The call over at last, Bennett replaced the telephone receiver in its cradle. He removed his reading glasses and rubbed the bridge of his nose. A slight, vital figure in his younger days, he had begun to put on weight lately and his dark hair, never abundant, was thinning to the point where what little of it remained barely covered his pale scalp.

'Well, Angus? Is there anything else?'

'Not for the moment, sir.' With an effort Sinclair brought his mind back to the business in hand. 'Apart from this murdered girl, of course.'

'What do you plan to do?' The assistant commissioner frowned. 'Will you make it a Yard investigation?' He was referring to a state of affairs relatively new in the capital, where in the past most serious crimes had been assigned as a matter of course to detectives stationed at the Yard, but where now, thanks to staff shortages, more cases were being farmed out to the various divisions.

'No, I don't think so, sir.' The chief inspector began to gather his papers. 'It sounds straightforward enough. Of course, it depends . . .'

He was interrupted by a knock on the door, which opened. Bennett's secretary put her head in. 'Excuse me, sir.

I've just had a call from registry. They've received some information from Bow Street which Mr Sinclair is waiting for.' She glanced at the chief inspector. 'It's a woman's name and address.'

'Come in, Miss Ellis.' Bennett gestured her forward and took the sheet of paper she was carrying from her hand. Slipping a pair of spectacles on, he studied it for a few moments.

'She's a land girl, I see. A Polish refugee.' He slid the piece of paper across the desk to Sinclair. 'You can bring in my letters now, Miss Ellis. And a cup of tea, if you would . . .' Bennett went on speaking to his secretary, but stopped when he saw the look of astonishment on the chief inspector's face.

'Angus . . . ?'

Sinclair seemed not to have heard. He was staring at the piece of paper in his hand.

'What is it, man?'

'I'm sorry, sir.' The chief inspector collected himself. 'It's this young woman who was murdered. I know her. Or of her, rather . . .'

'Are you sure? A *land* girl?' Bennett seemed unconvinced. 'Couldn't it be someone with the same name? What was it again? Rosa . . . Rosa something . . . ?'

'Rosa Nowak. No there's no mistake.' The chief inspector glanced across at his superior. 'You didn't notice her address, sir? The farm where she was working? The name of her employer . . . ?'

Wordlessly he passed the message back to Bennett, who peered at it through his spectacles for a moment, then shook his head in amazement.

'Well, I'll be damned,' he said.

3

'*JOHN MADDEN?*' Lofty Cook looked sceptical. 'I saw the name, of course, but it didn't ring a bell. Are you sure it's the same bloke?'

'It's him all right.'

'Your old guv'nor?'

Billy Styles chuckled. He'd just had a flash of memory: himself as a callow young detective-constable, pink-cheeked, and with a waistline that was now only a memory. And of the man he'd been assigned to then. All of twenty years ago it was now.

'I'd hardly call him that,' he said. 'We only worked together the one time and I was wet behind the ears.'

'Still, he gave you your chance, didn't he? Melling Lodge! What a case to kick off with. But then you always were a lucky devil.' Cook glanced down at his colleague, grinning. Recently promoted to detective-inspector, he stood a couple of inches over six feet and was called Lofty by his pals, of whom Billy was one. They had joined the force at the same time, right after the last war, but though Billy had advanced more quickly – he'd been an inspector for half a dozen years now – it hadn't affected their friendship, and Billy had been pleased to see his old chum's familiar hatchet face split by a grin when he'd climbed out of the radio car that had brought him from the Embankment up to Bloomsbury.

Although the gale had abated overnight, its icy claws could still be felt gusting down the narrow street and the pair of them had taken refuge in the doorway of a stationer's shop. Across the road from where they were standing, two detectives from Bow Street were busy searching the spot where the young woman's body had been found. The area, marked with tape, lay at the edge of a small unfenced yard that backed on to a bomb site, a building that had taken a direct hit at some time in the past and was now, like countless other tracts of ground all over London, a gutted ruin. An assortment of debris had been piled up in the cramped, cobbled space – bricks, mortar, sections of plastered wall – and the corpse had apparently been left on the fringe of this refuse, with the legs protruding on to the pavement.

'What happened to Madden, then?' Cook asked. He offered Billy a cigarette from his packet of Woodbines. 'After Melling Lodge, I mean? After he quit the force?'

'He got married to a lady he met while he was on the case. She was the village doctor.'

'Must have been something special,' Lofty observed. Cupping his hand, he struck a match and lit their cigarettes.

'Special . . . ?' Billy considered the remark, drawing on his fag. 'Yes, I reckon you could say that.' He smiled to himself. 'Anyway, he bought a farm down there, Madden did. Same farm where this girl was working. Which explains why I'm here. The chief inspector wants the full story. He and Madden are old friends.'

'Fair enough.' Cook pursed his lips, exhaling a plume of tobacco smoke into the frosty air. 'But there's not that much to tell. A case of being in the wrong place at the wrong time, if you ask me.'

It was an opinion Billy had already heard voiced, and by the chief inspector himself when he'd been summoned to his office not half an hour earlier.

'Odds on it was a casual assault, a crime of chance.'

Sinclair had shown him the initial Bow Street report. 'I've just spoken to John. The girl had only been with them for two months. She'd been given the weekend off and come up to London to see her aunt. Find out what you can. But don't spend too much time on it. Just determine the facts and report back.'

The chief inspector had not thought it necessary to refer to the case Billy had been working on, a tortuous investigation into the sale by a black-market ring of petrol and heating fuels stolen from military depots, which had ended only the week before in a successful prosecution; nor the few days' leave he'd been promised. With the shortage of staff that had prevailed for several years now, detectives were expected to put aside their personal lives as and when occasion demanded it.

'And just so you're clear in your mind, I'm not looking for an excuse to take this off Bow Street's hands. We've enough on our plate as it is. Just see to it there are no loose ends.'

These last words had been spoken with a scowl, as though his listener was known to be contemplating just such an outrage, from which Billy, armed with his sleuth's intuition, had deduced that the old boy's gout must be playing up. In spite of his awesome reputation, the chief inspector had his critics at the Yard and the suggestion had been made in more than one quarter that it was time he was put out to pasture. Billy, though, would have none of it. Having come under Sinclair's eye early in his career, and in circumstances where his inexperience might have cost him dear, he had never forgotten how the chief inspector, for all the sharpness of his tongue, had forgiven him his mistakes. And allowed him to profit from them.

He'd been more than content, too, with the orders he'd been given, particularly when he'd found out who was in charge at Little Russell Street. The Yard's habit of interfering in other divisions' business, of keeping plum cases for themselves, was often a sore point and he was glad he could tell Lofty that the investigation was still his to conduct. Given the rawness of the morning, neither of them had been disposed to dally and Cook had quickly shepherded him to the shelter of the stationer's doorway, where Billy learned that the body of Rosa Nowak had been removed to the mortuary at Paddington overnight after the pathologist called to the scene had examined it by torchlight.

'Who was the sawbones?' he asked.

'Ransom, from St Mary's. He thought it most likely she was strangled but said he'd give us a definite opinion later today after he's had her on the slab.' Cook stamped his feet to keep warm. 'It took us a while to discover who she was. We didn't find her wallet until it was light.' He nodded towards the two plainclothes men who were busy searching the rubble. 'She must have been carrying it in that basket.' He pointed to the object which was lying tipped over beside the white silhouette formed by the tape. Billy could see some apples lying loose there, mingled with the remains of broken eggshells. 'The wallet ended up under a piece of corrugated iron. It had her identity card inside.'

'What's your opinion, Lofty? Do you think it was a sexual assault?'

'Looks that way to me.' The Bow Street inspector nodded. 'She was lying on her back when we found her. Mind you, I don't think he got very far. Her coat was still buttoned up when we found her. It occurred to me he might have killed her by mistake.'

'Oh . . . ?' Billy lifted an eyebrow.

'Squeezed too hard, maybe. Then run off when he realized he'd topped her.' Cook shrugged. 'But that's only a guess.'

'I read it was a WPC who got here first.'

'That's right. Name of Poole. Lily Poole.' Cook grinned. 'She's stationed at Bow Street. Keen as mustard. She was walking back to the station after her shift when she heard the warden blowing his whistle and came over here to see what all the fuss was about. Didn't waste any time, either. Went straight up to Great Russell Street – there's a police call box there – and rang the station. By the time I got here she was already knocking on doors. But it didn't do any good. This isn't a residential street. Just shops and businesses. We spoke to one or two people who'd heard the warden's whistle, but nobody who saw anything.'

'Do we know when she was killed?'

'Almost to the minute. It was a little after ten o'clock. That's thanks to the warden. Name of Cotter. He'd bumped into her earlier. They had a chat. The last he saw of her she was walking down the street from that corner.' Cook pointed to his right. 'Twenty minutes later he came back – he was on his way home – and he tripped over the body.'

Billy nodded, taking it all in. He waited while a group of women dressed in dun-coloured overalls under their coats, and with their hair tied up in scarves or handkerchiefs, went by. They were trailed by a pair of WAAFs, who craned their necks to look at the two detectives bent double in the yard and at the uniformed constable who was standing guard there.

'Maybe all he meant to do was rob her?' he suggested.

'I thought of that. But it doesn't seem likely.' Cook blew on his fingers. 'Her wallet may have disappeared when she dropped her basket. But he didn't go through her things.' He gestured at a suitcase bound with cord that was lying on the pavement beside the yard.

'I understand she was on her way to visit her aunt. Does she live nearby?'

'Just round the corner, in Montague Street. A Mrs Laski.

She's a widow, quite an elderly lady. Naturalized. Been living here since the Twenties. She'd sat up all night waiting for her niece to arrive, then rang the station this morning. By that time we'd found the girl's wallet, so I had to take her over to Paddington to identify the body. Poor woman. Rosa was her only family. She got here soon after war broke out, but her parents were still in Poland, and they're gone now most likely, or so Mrs Laski reckons.'

'Gone?'

'They're Jewish,' Cook explained. He caught Billy's eye.

'Anyway, she worked for a couple of years in the Polish community, Rosa did. Looking after refugee families, that kind of thing. But she wanted to be in the country – she grew up in a village – so she joined the Land Army. Her first job was on a farm in Norfolk, but that packed up earlier this year when men invalided out of the services came home looking for work. That's when she was sent to Surrey. To Mr Madden's place. This was the first time she'd come up to London. She was planning to spend the weekend with her aunt and then go back on Monday.'

The inspector's face split in a yawn, and Billy wondered how much sleep he'd been getting. It was a problem everyone faced these days, a sort of national disease. After five years of war, five years of rationing and restrictions, a deep fatigue had settled like snow on the whole population. It could be dangerous, particularly in a job like theirs, his and Lofty's. It was easy to miss things.

'What about men friends?' he asked.

'None, according to the aunt. When she came here from France at the start of the war she travelled with a Polish boy, but he was just a friend, and anyway he joined up and was killed in North Africa. She was shy with men, Mrs Laski says. Old-fashioned when it came to the opposite sex.' Cook shrugged.

'In other words, she wasn't the sort of girl who would have picked up a man, say. Or let herself be picked up.'

'Out of the question. Or so her aunt reckons. I put it to her myself. Had to. Anyway, the girl was alone when the warden ran into her. That's for certain.'

Billy grunted. He trod on his cigarette. 'Are you done then?' he called out to the two men who'd been busy in the yard. One was named Hoskins, the other Grace. With more than twenty years on the force, Billy had made the acquaintance of just about every plainclothes man in London at one time or another, and worked with a good many of them.

'Finished, sir.' It was Hoskins who replied. Plump, and purple in the face despite the gelid air, he'd been making heavy weather of all the bending required by their task and stood breathing heavily beside the taped barrier that he and his partner had just erected at the edge of the yard with the help of a pair of iron stakes salvaged from the rubble. They were busy decorating it with a police notice on which the words KEEP OUT were printed in large capitals.

'Let's see what you've got.'

Trailed by Cook, Billy crossed the street and went down on his haunches to examine the objects the pair had retrieved and laid on a strip of cardboard. Besides the apples spilled from the basket they'd found two brown paper parcels, each containing a plucked chicken, three jars of homemade jam and a crock of honey.

'She must have brought those up from the country,' Joe Grace remarked. A thin, hard-faced man with the rank of detective-sergeant, he'd been one of a team of which Billy had been a part that the Yard had set up before the war to deal with the smash-and-grab gangs active in the capital at that time. 'There are two loaves of bread and a round of cheese jammed in at the bottom. We left 'em there.' He nodded at the basket which still lay beside the taped outline of the body. 'We also found these.' He indicated three matched buttons lying separate from the larger items, one of them still with a curl of thread attached to it. 'They were on the ground, near where her head was. Must have come from her coat.'

'No, they couldn't have.' Cook intervened. 'The buttons were all done up when we found her. There were none missing.'

'Where's it now?' Billy asked.

'At the mortuary. She was still wearing it when they took her away.' He turned to Grace. 'Is that all?' he asked.

'Pretty much.' The detective shrugged. 'The rest was just odds and ends.' He pointed to a handful of items deposited near the edge of the piece of cardboard which included an empty bottle of lemon rum, a broken comb, two hairpins and the chewed stub of a lead pencil, all coated with dust. Completing the haul were four charred matchsticks, which Billy examined with interest. He noticed that although their tops were blackened the stems beneath had hardly been touched by the flame.

'Looks like someone was trying to strike a match in the wind,' he remarked. 'And lately. The wood's still fresh. There's no sign of weathering.' He rose, stretching his cramped leg muscles.

Cook spoke to the two plainclothes men. 'You can put all this stuff back in the basket and take it to the station. Her suitcase, too. I'll deal with them later. We'll have to put up posters in the area. We need to know if anyone saw the girl earlier. Other than the warden, I mean.' Yawning, he glanced at Billy. 'Well, what do you think?'

Billy reflected. So far he'd heard nothing to suggest that Lofty wasn't right in his assessment. It seemed likely the girl had encountered her killer by accident in the darkness of the blackout. If so, it was a crime of chance, just as the chief inspector had supposed. But he wasn't ready to make his report quite yet. Sinclair's caution about leaving no loose ends was still fresh in his ears.

'What about slipping over to Paddington?' he suggested. 'I'd like a word with Ransom. He should be done by now.'

The corpse lay on a steel-topped table, hidden from sight except for the head and shoulders, which the orderly on duty in the mortuary had exposed by drawing back the white cloth covering it. Looking down at the lifeless face, so pale it seemed drained of blood, Billy recalled the photograph Lofty had shown him in the car coming over, a snapshot of Rosa Nowak which he'd obtained from her aunt. The dark-haired girl pictured in the snapshot had faced the camera with a remote and sorrowful expression, no trace of which remained now.

'Well, there she is, poor lass.'

An elderly man, one who'd either been retained like many past retirement age, or volunteered to do what amounted to war work, the orderly offered his opinion unprompted.

'Hardly looks dead, does she?'

It was true enough, Billy thought. Apart from a swelling on one side of her neck and a faint, livid mark in the same area the girl might have been asleep. As though it only needed a touch to awaken her. Glancing sideways at Cook, he saw the Bow Street inspector bending lower to peer at the white throat.

'Can't see that she was choked,' he remarked.

The two detectives had arrived at the hospital only to discover that the man they'd come to see wasn't immediately available.

'Dr Ransom's busy with another autopsy,' the receptionist informed them. 'A buzz bomb came down in Wandsworth last night, but they only dug out the bodies this morning.'

Left to their own devices, they had found their way downstairs to the mortuary, a grisly sanctum whose green-painted walls exuded a clammy cold unaffected by the change of seasons, where the orderly, at their request, had brought out Rosa Nowak's remains from one of the refrigerators built into the walls of the echoing chamber.

'You can wait if you like,' he told them. 'The doctor should be here any time now.'

Billy had been looking around. 'Are those her clothes?' he asked, pointing to a pile of women's garments on a table in the corner.

The orderly nodded. 'Dr Ransom said you might want to see them.'

Billy led his colleague over to the table and together they quickly solved the mystery of the loose buttons found at the scene of the murder. Examining the girl's coat, which was made of dark blue wool and might have had a naval past, they found it was fitted with a removable hood of the same material attached by buttons sewn on to the collar. Only two of these were still in place. Loose cotton threads showed where three others had in all probability been ripped off.

'I'd forgotten about the hood,' Cook admitted. 'We didn't see it at first. It was hidden beneath her body. I only noticed it when the ambulance men picked her up.'

Other signs of deft needlework were visible on the young woman's underclothes, which were undamaged but had obviously been darned and patched more than once. The embroidered blouse she'd been wearing, on the other hand, looked new, and to both detectives' surprise proved to be made of silk.

'What's that?' Billy's eye had been caught by a saucer standing on a shelf above the table. He took it down.

'Looks like a matchstick.' Cook peered at the charred fragment of wood which was all the saucer contained.

'Wonder what it's doing there.' Billy was still examining his find when the swing doors behind them opened and Ransom strode in, thrusting an arm into the sleeve of a white physician's coat.

'Sorry to keep you, gentlemen. We're like the Windmill Theatre here. We never close. I'm afraid there's another cadaver awaiting my attention, so this'll have to be brief. Hello, Inspector.' He nodded to Billy. 'I didn't know you were on the case.'

'I'm not, strictly speaking, sir.' Billy put down the saucer and went over to shake hands with the pathologist. 'Mr Cook's in charge. But the chief inspector has an interest in it. I'm to report back to him.'

'Sinclair, eh? Then we'd best be on our toes.'

Ransom blew out his cheeks. A heavy-set man with jutting eyebrows, he had a reputation in the Met as a joker, famous for his *bons mots*.

'You've seen the corpus delicti, I take it.' He moved over to where the wheeled table stood. The two detectives followed. 'There was little in the way of injuries to record. I dare say you noted the lividity on her neck and the swelling' – he pointed to the slight disfigurement on the slender column of the throat. 'The only real bruises I found were on her knees. She must have gone down when he grabbed her. See . . .'

He pulled the cloth off the girl's legs, showing the purple marks on her bare kneecaps.

'But that's all, really. There was no evidence of a struggle. She didn't get a chance to fight back. There was no skin under her nails, nothing of that sort. It was quick and clean.'

Billy glanced at Cook, thinking he might want to handle the questioning, but found that his colleague had chosen that moment to fall into a doze. Lofty's lack of sleep had finally caught up with him; he was swaying on his feet, his eyelids fluttering.

'No evidence of a struggle, you say?'

'That's right, Inspector.'

'He didn't sexually assault her, then?'

'Good heavens, no.' Ransom frowned. 'Why on earth . . . ? Oh, yes, of course.' He clicked his tongue. 'It did look that way last night when we found her. The inspector and I discussed the possibility.' He nodded at Cook, who'd come awake with a start. 'I checked for it, of course, when I made my examination, even though her underclothes weren't disturbed. But she wasn't touched. Not there, at any rate. In fact, she was virgo intacta. Not that it makes any difference now, I suppose.' He shrugged.

'But if he strangled her . . .'

'Strangled?' Ransom's bushy eyebrows rose in exaggerated amazement. 'Did I say that?'

'Yes, sir, you did.' Angry with himself for having drifted off, Cook spoke sharply. 'Last night, at the murder scene.'

'Then I apologize. It was a hasty judgement.' Ransom spread his hands in a gesture of appeasement. 'Put not your trust in pathologists. Particularly those called out in the blackout and made to examine bodies by torchlight. No, she wasn't choked. Her neck was broken. It's clear from the evidence. Let me show you.' He removed the cloth from the girl's head and shoulders again. 'Do you see the swelling on her neck and that mark on the side? It shows that the killer grabbed her from behind, slipped his right arm around her neck and snapped her spinal column. And to anticipate your question, yes, he was a strong man, but it wouldn't have required any special skill, particularly if she wasn't expecting it. Just a good wrench of the head. The whole business would have been over in a second.'

He covered the girl's head and shoulders again and then waited to see if the two detectives had any questions. A frown had appeared on Cook's face as he'd listened and he caught Billy's eye.

'So what you're saying is, he must have meant to kill her.'

'It would seem so.' Ransom shrugged. 'It's hard to see what other purpose he could have had in mind.'

'But ... but that doesn't make sense.' Cook spoke before he could stop himself.

'Possibly.' The pathologist looked owlish. 'But that's your department, Inspector, not mine. Now, if you've no more questions . . .' He stood poised to leave.

'One moment, sir.' Billy spoke up. 'That matchstick on the shelf over there. The one in the saucer. Where does it come from?'

'What matchstick where?' Ransom's eyes swivelled in the direction of his pointing finger. 'Oh, *that*. Yes, I found it tangled in her hair. Blown there by the wind, I dare say. She'd been lying on the ground for some time. Why do you ask?'

'We found others at the scene. It looked like somebody had been trying to light one.'

'The killer, do you mean?' Ransom showed renewed interest.

4

'SHE WAS A DEAR GIRL, very likeable. But so hard to get to know. Still grieving, I fear.'

Helen Madden mused on her words. Seated on a settee facing the fire that her husband had lit in the drawing-room a short while before, she turned her gaze on the flickering flames.

'She kept surprising us with her talents. Soon after she came I gave her a piece of parachute silk that had come my way and she made two embroidered blouses from it. They were quite beautiful. She was wearing one of them the day she went up to London, I remember.'

Helen glanced across at Sinclair, who was seated in an armchair on one side of the wide fireplace.

'And then we only discovered a week ago that she was a pianist. There was a call for volunteers to perform at a concert for the patients at Stratton Hall and Rosa came forward. She played two Chopin nocturnes and you could have heard a pin drop. I asked her afterwards where she had learned and she said her father had taught her. He was the schoolmaster in the village where she grew up. He must have been a remarkable man.'

Again she paused.

'But these are just odd details. We didn't really know her. She was so quiet. So withdrawn.'

Sinclair frowned. 'You said "still grieving". What did you mean?'

Helen looked at him. 'Are you aware she was Jewish?' she asked.

Sinclair nodded.

'It so happened she was in France when the Germans invaded Poland. Or perhaps it wasn't by chance. Her father had arranged the trip for her. He sent her to stay with an old university friend of his in Tours; it may be that he saw what was coming and wanted her out of the country. In any event she never heard from her parents again, nor her two younger brothers, though of course she kept hoping. For as long as she could. Until the truth came out.'

Helen regarded the chief inspector for a moment, then turned her gaze to the fire, where the heaped logs flamed and cackled, sending sparks flying up the chimney. Sinclair, too, remained silent. Two years had passed since the Foreign Secretary had risen in the House of Commons to confirm the reports that had been circulating for some time of the wholesale massacre of Jews in occupied Europe. He recalled a phrase from the joint declaration issued by the Allies, which had named Poland 'the principal slaughterhouse'.

'We only talked once, properly, I mean.' Helen put a hand to her brow. 'But I could see how much the thought of her family, and of what must have happened to them, had affected her.'

Madden stirred in his chair. He was sitting across the fireplace from the chief inspector, his face half-hidden by the deepening shadows in the room.

'There's not much more we can tell you, Angus,' he said. 'The last time I saw Rosa was at the farm on Thursday, just before Helen arrived to drive her to the station. She was weighed down with her bag and a basket of food I'd given her to take up to her aunt, and she kept trying to thank me for them. She wasn't a high-spirited girl. Reflective, rather, as

Helen says. But she seemed cheerful enough that day; she was looking forward to seeing her aunt.' He paused for a moment, then spoke again: 'Tell us a little more about the murder itself. From what you said first, it sounded like a chance crime. Is that still your opinion?'

'Yes and no. Which is to say, there's now a question mark hanging over the case.' The chief inspector grimaced. 'It all revolves around the injury she suffered, the manner in which she was killed. But it's a bit like trying to make bricks without straw. There just isn't enough evidence to be certain, one way or the other. But I'll lay it all out for you and you can tell me what you think. What you both think,' he added, with a glance at Helen. 'Just give me a moment to collect my thoughts.'

Though inured like all by now to the rigours of wartime travel, to the misery of unheated carriages, overcrowded compartments and the mingled smell of bodily odours and stale tobacco, he was still recovering from his trip down from London that afternoon when for two hours he had sat wedged in a window seat, gazing out at a countryside that offered little relief to eyes weary of the sight of dust and rubble, of the never-ending vista of ruined streets and bombed-out houses which the capital presented. Stripped to the bone by one of the coldest winters in recent memory, the fields and hedgerows through which they crawled had a lifeless air, while the sky above, grey as metal, had seemed to press on the barren earth. Scanning the paper he had bought at Waterloo, four pages of rationed newsprint filled mostly with war dispatches, his eye had lit on a single paragraph reporting the discovery of the body of a young Polish woman in Bloomsbury whose death was being treated by the police as suspicious. An account of the crime that Billy Styles had compiled and handed to him the day before was in his overnight case on the luggage rack above. The chief inspector had reviewed its contents a number of times without being able to come to any conclusion, an admission he had made to Madden when they had spoken on the telephone the previous evening.

'It's not exactly a puzzle, John,' Sinclair had told his old partner. 'To quote Styles, it's more of a conundrum. I'll tell you more when I come down tomorrow. I'm hoping you can help me with it.'

A frequent guest, the chief inspector's visit had been arranged some time before, and he'd been looking forward not so much to the break from his duties it offered, which would be brief, but to the prospect of spending a few hours with friends who over the years had become dearer to him than any. The knowledge that his stay would now be over-shadowed by a brutal crime, one to which they were con-nected, if only by circumstance, had darkened his mood, and it was not until his train was drawing into Highfield station and he glimpsed the familiar figure of his hostess waiting for him on the platform that his spirits had begun to recover.

'Dear Angus . . .'

The disagreeable image he retained of the past two hours had evaporated with the kiss of greeting Helen had given him. Still slender, seemingly ageless, and with the movements and gestures of a woman on happy sensuous terms with her life, she had the gift of lending grace to any occasion, even one as commonplace as this – or so the chief inspector had always thought – and the whiff of jasmine he caught as her cheek touched his brought with it the memory of happier days in the past.

'I've so many questions to ask you. But it'll be better if we wait. I know it's John you want to talk to about this.'

'Not only him. I want your thoughts, too.'

'Why, Angus, I'm flattered.' Her teasing smile had lightened the moment between them. 'I'm not used to being included in your old policemen's confidences.'

Though quite baseless, the assertion, as intended, had brought a flush to Sinclair's cheeks. John Madden's decision to quit the force, made twenty years before, had come as a keen disappointment to him, and for a while at least he had found it difficult to overlook the role his colleague's wife had played in bringing this about. Her remark now was an affectionate reminder of a time when they had not always seen eye to eye: his reaction to it a tacit acknowledgement of the power she continued to wield over him. A beauty in her day, and to Sinclair's eyes still a woman of extraordinary appeal, she had always had the capacity to disturb his equanimity; to unsettle his sense of himself. It was a measure of their friendship and of the deep admiration he had for her that far from resenting this he took it as a sign that age and an increasing tendency towards crustiness had not yet reduced him to the status of old curmudgeon.

The train of recollection set off by her words had continued to occupy the chief inspector's thoughts during the drive home. It had been a crime as bloody as any in the history of the Yard that had first brought him to Highfield, along with Madden, then an inspector, and his memory inevitably returned to that day as they drove past the high brick wall that hid from view the house where the outrage had occurred. Called Melling Lodge, it had lived under a curse ever since, or so it seemed to Sinclair. Though leased periodically to tenants, and used briefly to house evacuees at the start of the Blitz, it had more often stood empty, and the chief could seldom pass by the wrought-iron gates and the glimpsed garden beyond without a shudder. Today, however, the tremor he felt had more to do with the killing that had taken place in Bloomsbury two nights since and his concern for the effect it might have on the small community of which his friends were a part.

The early darkness of winter was drawing in by the time Helen turned into the long driveway lined with lime trees, bare of leaves now, but familiar to the chief inspector in all seasons, and drew up before the spacious, half-timbered house where she and Madden had lived since their marriage and which had belonged to her father; and his father before him. No lights were showing in the hall, but when they went inside they found Madden in the drawing-room with the curtains already pulled, kneeling on the hearth adding logs to the fire.

'We've had one burning in your room all day, Angus.' He had risen with a smile to greet their guest and shake his hand. 'Be sure and keep it going or you'll freeze.'

As he shed his coat and went closer to the blaze to warm his hands, Sinclair had cast a covert glance at his old friend, noting with envy his erect bearing and evident vigour. Unlike his wife's clear face, Madden's weathered features bore ample testimony to his age – he was past fifty – and to his past, as well, most notably in the shape of a jagged scar on his brow near the hairline that served as a reminder to those who knew his history of his time in the trenches.

Tall, and striking as much for his appearance as for his air of quiet authority, he was of all the colleagues the chief inspector had known during his long career at the Yard the most memorable.

And the one he had valued the most.

'As I say, there's no mystery about how she was killed, not according to the pathologist. Her neck was broken from behind. To be precise, whoever attacked her caught her in a headlock and snapped her spinal cord. She never had a chance to fight back. But that's part of the problem.'

Refreshed by a sip of the whisky his hosts had offered him, a precious wartime commodity, Sinclair was ready to go on.

'If the killer had an ulterior motive – rape, for example – it seems highly unlikely he would have seized hold of her that way. It's true he might have tried to silence her, even render her semi-conscious, but not like that, surely. It's far too dangerous.'

'I agree.' Helen interrupted him in a quiet voice. The crackling of the fire had died down in the last few minutes and as the flames diminished, the room, lit by a single table lamp, had grown darker. 'That's why boys are taught not to scrag each other when they fight. If he'd wanted to control her he'd more likely have squeezed her throat.'

'Precisely.' The chief inspector took another sip from his glass. 'And that was the pathologist's first guess. He examined the body by torchlight at the scene and guessed she'd been strangled. But there's no doubt now as to what happened. It seems the murder was deliberate.'

Madden grunted, but when Sinclair glanced at him, inviting him to speak, he shook his head.

'No, go on, Angus.'

Famous in his time at the Yard for his silences, for his practice, as Sinclair had once declared, in exasperation, many years before, of staying mum while others made fools of themselves, Madden's reversion to old habits left the chief inspector with no option but to continue:

'So with that in mind, we're faced with the question of motive. Why did he kill her? One theory is that he meant to rob her – her belongings, what she was carrying, were strewn all about – but of what? Not money, surely. But Styles found a number of charred matchsticks on and around the body indicating he'd been trying to strike a light in the wind: which in turn suggests he was looking for something. But there's no way of telling whether he went through her coat pockets, for example, or whether he found her wallet, which ended up under some corrugated iron and could either have fallen there by chance or been tossed away by the killer after he'd searched it.'

'Was there anything in it?' Madden spoke at last. 'Anything of value, I mean?'

Sinclair shook his head. 'Quite the reverse. It contained her identity card and a small amount of money. Nothing more. So it's possible he could have removed something from it. But these are all rational questions, and they may be the wrong ones to ask. It's possible we're dealing with a disturbed individual, someone who killed the girl for no reason at all, then set about trying to strike a light in order to examine his handiwork. But it's worth pointing out that lunatics of that sort usually have a weapon of some kind, often a knife, and they seldom attack with their bare hands. At least not in my experience.'

Sinclair sat back heavily in his chair. He'd already had a long day.

'You asked me earlier, John, if I still thought it was a crime of chance, and the answer is, yes, I do, on balance. But only on balance. We can't get away from the fact that the act itself was deliberate and that for all we know there may have been a motive behind it. A rational motive. We have to consider the possibility that she was killed by someone she knew.'

'Oh, no! Surely not.' The exclamation came from Helen.

She stared in disbelief at the chief inspector. 'You mean a man, don't you? Someone she was involved with?'

'As I say, it's something we have to consider, and it's where I'm hoping you and John can help me. Was there anyone here she'd become friendly with? Have you heard any gossip? I might add that her aunt, a Mrs Laski, scoffs at the notion. But she hadn't seen her niece for nearly two months and wouldn't necessarily have known of any new development in her life.'

'No, but she knew Rosa, and that was enough.' Helen's response was immediate. 'You never met her, Angus, but if you had you'd understand. It wasn't just that she kept to herself. She simply had no interest in . . . that side of life. In men. It was as though she had taken a vow: as if she was still in mourning. John . . . ?' She turned to her husband, and Madden nodded in confirmation.

'We can ask around tomorrow, if you like, Angus, but you'll find it's a blind alley. Anyway, it's hard to see some man following her up to London from here with the express purpose of killing her.'

'I agree. But I had to put it to you.'

The sigh that came from the chief inspector's lips then was partly one of relief. He knew better than most the distress a murder inquiry brought to any community, and his fear that the trail might lead back to Highfield had prompted him to ring the station commander at Bow Street that morning to inform him that he was going down to the village himself and would assess the need, if any, of extending the investigation outside the capital. Reassured now, he felt able to relax, and to let the wave of tiredness he'd been conscious of for some time wash over him. His stifled yawn caught Helen's eye.

'You must be exhausted, Angus. And though you haven't

mentioned it, I think your toe is bothering you. Why not go up to your room and have a rest before dinner.' She rose from the settee. 'I have to go out myself. We've an epidemic of whooping cough in the village, and there are some children I must look in on.'

Mildly put out to discover he'd failed to hide his discomfort from his hostess's all-seeing eye, the chief inspector waited until she had left the room. Then he rounded on Madden.

'You've been mighty quiet,' he accused his old colleague. 'Enough of that. Come on, before I go up, tell me what you think. I've given you the facts. What do you make of them?'

Emerging from the depths of his armchair, Madden leaned forward. His expression hadn't changed and the chief inspector was unable to gauge his reaction from his eyes, which were dark and deep-set.

'Not much, I'm afraid. Nothing that hasn't occurred to you already. But there is one thing. I'm still not clear in my mind what Rosa's movements were that night. How she came to encounter this man. Could you go through them again for me?'

'Willingly.' The chief inspector put down his glass. 'As well as I can, that is. We still don't know her exact route after she reached Waterloo, though it seems likely she came north to Tottenham Court Road by the Underground and then walked from there. Posters with her photograph are being put up along that route. We're hoping someone will remember seeing her. Once she got to Bloomsbury, however, the situation becomes much clearer. I think I told you about the air-raid warden she bumped into. After they'd exchanged a few words, the girl continued down Little Russell Street while the warden went the other way, up Museum Street towards the British Museum. It seems she was killed within seconds of the two of them separating. And no more than twenty paces from where they'd been standing. So it looks as though she met her murderer coming down Little Russell Street. He must have been walking in the opposite direction.'

'Or following her, surely?'

Madden's intervention brought the chief inspector up short.

'Well, yes ... I suppose so ... technically.' Sinclair frowned. 'But there's no indication of that. They stood there talking for a minute or two and according to the warden there was no one else about.'

Madden sat pondering.

'Yet you say they bumped into each other in the darkness?' he went on after a moment. 'Did she seem to be hurrying? Was she nervous, perhaps?'

'Because she thought someone was following her? John, I've just said there was no suggestion of that.' The chief inspector's puzzlement showed on his face. 'It wasn't only that the warden didn't see anyone. He didn't hear any footsteps either. The Bow Street detectives asked him. Mind you, that could be explained by the fact there was a strong wind blowing.'

'Or because the killer heard him speaking to Rosa and stopped.'

'Around the corner, you mean? In Museum Street? Out of sight?'

Sinclair stared at him, and as he watched, Madden got to his feet. The fire had burned down to a bank of smouldering embers and he stirred it, adding fresh logs to revive the blaze.

'Yes, but if he was following her with the intention of killing her, doesn't that suggest it was someone she knew?'

Sinclair resumed speaking, but this time his companion made no reply.

'And didn't we agree that the odds were against that?'

'True . . . But there's another possibility.'

Madden put down the poker and straightened, his tall figure casting a long shadow across the hearth. He looked down at the chief inspector.

'What if *he* knew *her*?' he said.

'John and I have decided. We're going up to London for the funeral. Do you know when it will be, Angus? Have the police released Rosa's body yet?'

Helen Madden sat back on her heels. She brushed a strand of fair hair from her eyes and regarded Sinclair, who was seated on a tombstone. Seeking to fill in time before the chief inspector's train departed, they had stopped at the church-yard, where Helen had a task to perform.

'I'm not certain,' Sinclair said. 'But I can find out for you. In any case, it won't be long. There's no reason for it to be held back. The pathologist has done his work.' He reflected for a moment. 'If you let me know what train you're catching I'll send your friend Billy Styles with a police car to Waterloo. The funeral will be at Golders Green, I expect. He can run you up there and collect Mrs Laski on the way. I dare say she'd be grateful for a lift.'

'That would be kind, Angus.' She smiled her thanks. 'And it means we can take Rosa's things with us and return them to her aunt. I know you looked through them today, but will the police in London still want to see them?'

The chief inspector considered the question. He had been watching while his hostess busied herself attending to her family's plot in the moss-walled cemetery, sweeping it free of dead leaves and branches and trimming the uncut grass with a pair of garden shears. The chore was a necessary one, Helen had explained. Highfield had been without a sexton since the death of the last incumbent the previous summer, and it was unlikely the post would be filled until the war was over. Buried side by side in the square plot were her parents and grandparents. But not her two brothers. Both casualties of the First World War, their bodies lay in cemeteries across the Channel, in what had been, until recently, enemy-held territory; one in France, the other in Belgium. The spot where they might have been interred was occupied by a relatively new gravestone, little weathered as yet, and inscribed simply with the name 'Topper' and beneath it the words 'Mourned by his many friends'. It marked the final resting place of an old tramp whose true name no one had ever discovered but who had been deeply attached to Helen and her husband and cared for by them in his last years.

'I'll have a word with the detective handling the case,' Sinclair replied, after an interval. He'd been remembering the old vagrant, and Helen's determination in particular that he should not end his days in solitude, abandoned by some path or hedgerow. 'But I don't believe so. There's a diary among her stuff, but it's in Polish, and the best thing would be for Mrs Laski to look through it and see if it contains anything unusual.'

The book in question, leather-bound and inscribed with its owner's name, had been among the effects which the chief inspector had examined earlier at Madden's farm. They had gone there in the late morning, and May Burrows, the manager's wife, had shown him up to the room where Rosa Nowak had slept. In her thirties now, May had been little more than a child herself when Sinclair had first come to Highfield. With her that morning had been her daughter, Belle, home on a weekend pass from an ATS barracks in Southampton, and with a dimpled face and a head of dark curls that had reminded the chief inspector of her mother twenty years before.

'Such an easy girl,' May had told him when she took him upstairs. 'Good-hearted, too. No trouble, ever. She'd do anything she was asked, and always with a smile. So different from the others we had before her.'

This last had been said with a knowing look and a shake of the head, and referred beyond doubt to at least two of the three land girls Madden had employed earlier in the war, both of whom had contrived to become pregnant during their time at Highfield. Of them, and their paramours, two signallers from a temporary training camp set up near the village, Helen had remarked that it was worse than trying to keep foxes out of a henhouse. The third, a wan creature from the London suburb of Ealing, had given up her job as a secretary to join the Land Army, seduced perhaps by the vision displayed by a poster put up early in the war in which a smiling girl stood beckoning, a sheaf of golden corn beneath her arm. 'You are needed in the fields,' the poster proclaimed, but made no mention of the work involved; of the grinding physical effort farm labour demanded, the backbreaking toil from dawn till dusk. The young woman in question had lasted less than two months before wilting under the strain and being shipped back to London. Thereafter, Madden had managed with the labour he had until the demands of the dairy, which fell more and more on May, had obliged him to look for outside help once more.

May's evident fondness for Rosa had been echoed later by her husband, George, when Madden and Sinclair found him in the tack room off the stable yard.

'She never said much, not even to us, but she had a sweet nature,' Burrows told them. He'd been busy repairing a broken harness: winter was a time for make and mend on the farm. 'Just ask our Tommy. She used to help him with his homework, though it wasn't part of her job. But she liked kids, you could tell. She was going to be a teacher one day, she said. Tom was in tears when he heard what had happened to her.'

Though not expected to appear that day – it was Sunday – the two farmhands Madden employed, a pair of middle-aged brothers named Thorp, had walked over from the cottage they shared a mile away to ask whether the grim news they had heard from other sources was true. And each, it turned out, had his own special memory of the young girl and the brief time she had spent among them.

'She were a worker, that one,' Fred Thorp, the older of the two, wistfully recalled when they came upon the two brothers drinking tea with May and her daughter in the farmhouse kitchen. 'You never had to go looking for her. After she'd finished with the cows she'd be there asking what she could do next. Once I caught her muck-knocking...' He chuckled. 'It were pouring rain and we'd all given up for the day, but then I spotted her down there – ' he gestured in the direction of the fields – 'still at it, soaked to the skin. So I told her, "Now you stop that", and I made her come in with me. Took her by the hand, I did, thought I might have to drag her, she was that set on staying.'

His younger brother Seth had a more personal souvenir which he proudly showed to Madden and his guest.

'She made this shirt for me, Rosa did.' He'd patted the well-ironed garment he was wearing under his patched tweed jacket. 'And another like it from a piece of material I had off our cousin Mabel when she went to Australia before the war. I'd never known what to do with it till Rosa said to leave it with her. It's a crying shame, sir. I hope you catch that bastard soon. Hanging's too good for him.'

The subject of Rosa's skill as a seamstress had come up again when the chief inspector examined the girl's belongings in what had been her bedroom. With Madden at his elbow, Sinclair had gone quickly through her clothes, few in number, but including one of the two embroidered silk blouses Helen had told him about and which he remarked on to his host.

'Oh, she could do wonders with a needle and thread.' Overhearing his remark, May commented from the doorway where she was waiting for them to complete their business. 'There was also that coat she made for herself, Mr Madden, do you remember? She was wearing it the day she went to London.'

Helen, too, had recalled the garment when she arrived at the farm later to collect the chief inspector, having spent the morning visiting patients in the area who for one reason or another were unable to get to her surgery during the week.

'It was an old coat of Rob's which he'd discarded,' she told him, referring to their son, who was a naval lieutenant. 'I was amazed when I took her to the station that day. She'd made a hood from some of the material left over after she'd shortened it. And not only that, she'd changed the whole cut. I hardly recognized it.'

With his precious weekend all but over, Sinclair had taken his leave then of Madden, who was committed to driving the tractor he'd been using for the past fortnight over to a neighbouring farm which had an urgent need for it.

'We're all sharing machinery now,' he'd remarked. 'And everyone's behind with the autumn ploughing as a result. But ours is done, thank God. We'll have a chance to catch our breath. Winter's usually a quiet time.'

The chief inspector had long ceased to wonder at the ease with which his old partner had been able to turn his back on the profession where he had found such distinction and settle into the life of a farmer. A countryman by birth, it had needed only the accident of his meeting with Helen and their subsequent decision to marry to provide the impulse necessary to return to his roots. But that morning Sinclair had sensed a change in the other man, an uncharacteristic tension in his manner, which had shown itself during a stroll they had taken in the garden together after breakfast.

Professing a wish to examine what damage had been done by the recent wind to his fruit trees, Madden had led the way down the long lawn in front of the house to the orchard that bordered a stream at the bottom of the garden. Beyond the brook lay a wooded ridge called Upton Hanger, which in summer glowed deep green but whose great oaks and beeches, stripped of their leaves, stood stark as skeletons in the leaden morning light.

'She worked mainly with the cows, you know, Angus.' Madden had spoken without preamble, taking the chief inspector by surprise. His attention had seemed to be fixed on the broken branch of a plum tree which he'd picked up from the ground and was examining. 'She had a gift for it. I'd hear her talking to them while she was milking. In Polish, I imagine. She called them by their names. I think she was happy here. Or less unhappy. I'll have to find someone local to take her place. May needs help in the dairy, but I can't face asking for another land girl. Not till this is settled.'

He had looked at Sinclair then.

'You will keep me informed, won't you, Angus?'

Though spoken in a quiet tone, the demand had brooked no refusal, and the chief inspector had been swift to reassure his friend. But he'd been struck as much by the depth of feeling evident in Madden's voice as by the look in his eye, which had seemed to reflect a stronger emotion; one, though, he was not used to seeing there: a cold, controlled anger.

'John's furious, though he tries not to show it,' Helen told him later that day when they were driving to the station. 'He never thought of Rosa as an employee. He saw the sadness in her from the first. The grieving. To him she was someone who needed help and comfort, as much a casualty of war as any wounded soldier. And now she's gone and there's nothing he can do about it.'

They had continued in silence for a few moments. Then she had spoken again:

'And something else. It's reawakened an old pain in him. Not that he's said so in so many words, but I can tell. The daughter he lost . . . you remember that?'

She was referring to an episode in Madden's life before he'd met her, an earlier marriage, which had ended in tragedy. A young detective at the time, he and his wife had had a daughter, but soon after her birth, the two of them had contracted influenza and died. Madden had witnessed the last hours of his child as she struggled for life, and the experience had left a wound in him which only the love he'd found later with Helen and the life they had made together had healed. Or so the chief inspector had always believed.

'He dreamed of her the other night for the first time in years and he wondered why. I think it's because of what happened to poor Rosa. She was in his care, you see. But he couldn't protect her.'

Her words had remained in Sinclair's mind until they reached the station, where, having elected to return to London on an earlier train than he might have rather than risk being delayed until all hours by the uncertainties of the rail schedule, he had discovered with little surprise that the early train was no longer early; that at the very least it would be an hour late. Preferring the company of his hostess to the cramped squalor of the waiting room, he had returned with her to the churchyard where he sat now, with his coat buttoned up over a thick scarf and his hat pulled down low against the persistent cold, watching while she attended to her self-imposed task.

'Poor Angus. It's been a miserable weekend for you. We haven't had a chance to talk about other things. For instance, I wanted to hear about your lunch with Lucy. Did you really invite her to the Savoy? That sounds far too grand for her.'

Busy raking the scattered leaves into a heap, Helen glanced up, smiling.

'I was the one who felt privileged.' The chief inspector grinned in response. Childless himself – and a widower – he had observed the Maddens' golden-haired daughter with fascination over the years, watching her grow from a strong-willed child, and via a stormy adolescence, into a beauty cast in the image of her mother. 'Not to say envied. She turned every man's head in the room.'

'If you think to please me by saying that you're making a grave mistake.' Helen's attempt at severity, contrived as it was, had little effect on her auditor. Sinclair's grin merely widened. 'Turning men's heads seems to be my daughter's sole ambition. And her only achievement to date. And no matter what she claims, I can't believe she's contributing to the war effort.'

On leaving school, and despite the opposition of her mother, who had wanted her to try for university, Lucy Madden had enlisted in the WRNS, a move which had enabled her not only to slip the parental leash, but to obtain a posting in London, much to the disapproval of Helen, who thought her daughter too young at eighteen for such an adventure.

'How she's managed to get herself assigned to the Admiralty is beyond me. She can't be remotely qualified for any sort of position there.'

It had been on the tip of the chief inspector's tongue when Helen had said this to him some months ago to point out that Lucy's qualifications were all too obvious and that men of rank, none of them spring chickens any longer, liked nothing better than to have youth and beauty in close proximity, the better to burnish the image they had of themselves.

'And any idea of Aunt Maud being a suitable chaperone is quite unrealistic. Poor dear, I doubt she knows what time of day it is, never mind what hour Lucy gets in at night. She may have survived the Blitz, but whether she can cope with the presence of my daughter under her roof remains to be seen.'

The lady in question, a spinster now in her nineties, lived in St John's Wood, and Lucy had lodged with her since moving to London.

'Still, at least I'll get a chance to talk to her when we go up,' Helen said, returning to her job of raking the leaves. 'And Lucy, too, if I'm lucky, though she'll probably claim that some crisis on the high seas requires her to be at her desk. If she has such a thing. It's a ploy she's discovered to avoid being interrogated, one she knows I can't get round. At least I used to know the mischief she was getting up to. Now I haven't the least idea, and I don't know which is worse.'

Unable to keep a straight face any longer, she began to laugh. But the change of mood was fleeting, and after a few moments her expression grew serious again.

'I didn't mention it earlier, Angus, but I rang Mrs Laski yesterday evening to tell her how shocked we were. I'll talk to her again when I see her at the funeral. I want her to know at least that we cared for Rosa. That we feel the loss of her.'

Unhappy with her thoughts, she stirred the mound of dead leaves with her rake.

'It's so wrong,' she burst out.

'Wrong?'

'Unfair, I mean. Undeserved. Without cause or reason. We've been living for years with death all around us. Violent death. First the Blitz and now these dreadful flying bombs. The knowledge that anyone might be killed at any moment. People we love . . . our children.'

Biting her lip, she looked away, and the chief inspector understood what it was she dared not say. A year had passed since the Maddens' son Robert had been posted to a destroyer assigned to the perilous Murmansk convoys. Out of touch for weeks on end, his long absences – and the silence that inevitably accompanied them – were a source of anguished concern to his parents.

'But this is different, somehow. It's got no connection to anything, not even the war. All poor Rosa did was go up to London to see her aunt. Don't you see – it makes a mockery of death?'

She turned and found the chief inspector's sympathetic gaze on her.

'It's meaningless. That's what I'm saying. All those others, her family, her people. Dead, all of them. And now her own life lost for nothing.'

5

TURNING THE COLLAR of his coat up against the driving sleet, Billy glanced at Madden, who like him was standing with his hands plunged in his coat pockets and the brim of his hat pulled down as protection against the tiny flecks of ice swirling about in the air around them. There were questions he wanted to put to his old chief, but now was not the moment.

Instead, he looked about him with curiosity. It was the first time he'd been in a Jewish cemetery and he was struck by how different it was from a Christian churchyard, how bare of decoration and adornment. Stretched out before his eyes were row upon row of flat, closely packed graves with hardly a headstone among them. Nor was any relief to be found in the gravelled pathways lacking any bordering tree or flower to soften their stony lines. Here the bleak reality of death was undisguised.

'Not much of a turn-out, is there, sir?'

He nodded towards the small group of mourners, most of them elderly women, who had gathered around the freshly dug grave at the end of one of the rows some distance from where they were standing. The sudden icy squall had driven them to seek warmth together and they stood huddled under their umbrellas with bowed heads like sheep caught in a blizzard.

'I doubt Rosa had many close friends,' Madden murmured. For some minutes he'd been standing with his eyes fixed on the ground before them, lost in thought. 'It was part of her sadness, the solitude she'd chosen.'

'No young man, either,' Billy remarked. 'Not that we were expecting one.'

Again he was tempted to probe Madden's mind, to ask him to enlarge on something he had said earlier, before they had reached the cemetery, but mindful of the occasion he kept his impatience in check, and instead glanced over his shoulder at a small brick shelter near the gates of the cemetery, hoping to see some sign of life within.

'I wish that rabbi would come,' he muttered. 'The sooner we get the old lady home, the better.'

Earlier, having met the Maddens at Waterloo station and driven them up to Bloomsbury to collect Rosa Nowak's aunt, Billy had been shocked to discover how frail the stricken woman appeared to be; how distraught at the loss of her niece. He had gone upstairs himself to knock on the door of the first-floor flat, and to give Mrs Laski the two suitcases containing Rosa's belongings which Madden and Helen had brought with them from Highfield. Though familiar with the statements she had made to the Bow Street CID, it was the first time they had met, and Billy's first reaction on seeing her had been to wonder whether she would be equal to the ordeal ahead of her. White-haired, thin to the point of emaciation, and with trembling hands, she had wandered about the small flat with slow steps, trying to get ready, but unable to remember where she had left her things. Watching her, he'd been put in mind of a wounded bird, one no longer able to fly, but dragging itself broken-winged along the ground. Her eyes, rheumed with age, seemed blind to the world around her. Until the moment of their departure, that was, when she had paused by a table where a number of framed photographs stood to direct her gaze at one in

particular, a family group composed of a man and a woman
with three children, two of them small boys and the third an
older girl whom Billy had recognized as Rosa. The picture
had been posed – it looked like a studio photograph, and the
figures had something of the lifelessness of waxwork models
about them. Mrs Laski had picked it up and, after studying it
for a long moment, had pressed the glass front to her lips in
a gesture of farewell.

'Enough. Let us go.'

They were the first words she had spoken to him. And the
last.

He'd escorted her down the stairs with a hand under her
arm and the other ready to catch her in case she fell. Outside,
in the road, Madden had already climbed out of the police
car Billy had brought with him to assist her into the back seat
beside Helen. Their greetings had been acknowledged by a
lowering of her eyelids and a slight dip of her white head, but
beyond taking Helen's hand in hers and pressing it for a brief
moment, she had shown no wish to speak or communicate.
Rather, she had seemed lost in whatever world of pain she
inhabited, and her frailty had been enough to excite Helen's
concern long before they reached Golders Green.

Finding that the shelter by the gates was furnished with
wooden benches, she had persuaded the old lady to rest there
with her until the arrival of the rabbi who was to conduct
the burial service. The two men had continued on into the
cemetery and waited now beside the main path, but some
way off from the rest of the mourners gathered at the
graveside.

Madden had said little in the interval, and Billy, too, had
remained silent for the most part. But his thoughts had been
occupied by what had occurred a little earlier that morning, before they had got to Mrs Laski's flat, when they had

stopped in Little Russell Street at the spot where Rosa Nowak had met her end.

It was Madden who had requested the detour, and Billy had been surprised. He'd already given the older man a brief account of the progress of the investigation carried out by the Bow Street CID during their drive up from Waterloo station and Madden had seemed satisfied. At all events he'd asked no questions.

'They've managed to pin down her route up to Bloomsbury,' he'd told him. 'She came up from Waterloo by tube. A guard on the Underground at Tottenham Court Road reckons he saw her go through the ticket barrier there, which makes sense. From there she would have gone on foot. He remembers a girl with a basket in one hand and a bag in the other; that's what Rosa was carrying. But the crowd was even thicker than usual, he said, because there'd been an alert just a few minutes earlier: the sirens had gone off. It turned out to be a false alarm, but a lot of people came down into the station from the street, they were milling about, and he only caught a glimpse of her as she went by.'

Madden had listened in silence, a frown grooving his brow, reviving Billy's memories of the brief span of weeks they had spent working together twenty years before, a period unmatched in the intensity it had brought to his life then, and the realization which came later that thanks to the man into whose company he had been thrown by chance he had found his own centre of gravity, the place from which he could embark on his future with confidence. That Madden himself had chosen another way of life soon after had never affected Billy's opinion of him. Even at that early age he had recognized qualities of character in the older man that set him apart from his colleagues: qualities that in time had become touchstones for Billy himself, standards against which he had come to measure himself.

But he'd made no comment during their journey in the car, and it was Helen who had taken up the conversation, pressing Billy for news of his family, chiding him in an affectionate manner for having been a stranger lately.

The warmth of her greeting and the kiss she had given him when they had met on the platform at Waterloo had brought a blush to Billy's cheeks, just as if he were still the same green young detective-constable she had first known years ago.

'But I'm cross with you,' she had said, her smile belying her words. 'It's been so long since you and Elsie brought the children down to Surrey to see us. And Lucy was saying only the other day that it's been nearly a year since she saw you last. You wouldn't recognize her in her uniform. She's grown up all at once.'

Billy had had to explain that his family had moved out of London temporarily. Elsie had taken their three children to stay with her mother in Bedford.

'It's these blasted doodlebugs,' he told her. 'They really put the wind up Elsie, and me too. You never know where they're going to land next. We had one come down on a house by Clapham Common, near where we live, and it killed the whole family. Folks we knew. The worst of it is you can hear them coming, the buzz bombs anyway, and you find yourself wondering whether this is the one that's got *your* family's name on it. Anyway, Elsie and I agreed it would be better if they stayed out of London, just for the time being.'

The traffic had been light that morning – petrol rationing had all but put an end to private motoring – and the radio car that Billy had brought with him to Waterloo on the chief inspector's instructions made rapid time through the bomb-damaged streets. But as they approached their destination – Mrs Laski's flat was in Montague Street, near the British Museum – Madden had requested the detour.

'I'd like to have a look at the spot, if you don't mind.'

Billy himself had not been back to Little Russell Street since his first visit, and on their arrival there he noticed that the taped barrier sealing off the rubble-filled yard had been removed. There'd been no need to tell Madden what it signified. With nearly a week gone by since the murder had occurred and no lead having come to light, the chances of a successful outcome to the inquiry were dwindling rapidly.

Leaving Helen in the car with the driver, they had got out and, at Madden's suggestion, walked to the spot near the end of the street where Rosa had paused to talk to the air-raid warden.

'She'd come around the corner, then?' Madden had asked, and Billy had confirmed it.

'That's what Cotter said. He'd been standing in this doorway here, out of the wind.' Billy indicated the recess.

Madden had walked the last few steps to the corner and looked down Museum Street, eyes narrowed. 'He might have waited there,' he had muttered. 'He would have heard them talking.'

'Sir . . . ?' Billy didn't understand what he was getting at, but as they walked back towards the car – and towards the spot where Rosa had been murdered – Madden had revealed what was troubling him.

'I talked to Mr Sinclair about this, but I'm still not clear in my mind. Can you remember exactly what the warden said in his statement? Did Rosa seem uneasy when she spoke to him that night? She was obviously hurrying, not looking too carefully where she was going, and I wondered if it was because she thought someone might be after her.'

'He said she seemed pleased to have run into him,' Billy had replied, after a moment's thought. 'That was in his statement, I remember. He reckoned she might have been nervous walking through the blackout alone. But she couldn't have been frightened, because when he offered to carry one of her bags and see her home she said it wouldn't be necessary, she was almost there.'

Madden had grunted. 'But she paused all the same for a minute or two, while they talked?'

'At least that. Why? Is it important?' Billy had cocked a curious eye at his old mentor.

'I don't know . . . but it might be.' Madden had shrugged. They had reached the yard and he stood staring down at the rubble, frowning. Then he'd nodded. 'All right, let's agree she wasn't frightened. She didn't think she was being stalked. But that doesn't mean she wasn't on edge. It would explain why the warden said she seemed relieved to have bumped into him. She may have wanted to reassure herself.'

'Of what?' Billy didn't understand. 'You've just said she wasn't afraid.'

'Afraid, no . . . but uneasy, perhaps.' Madden gnawed his lip. 'Look, there's nothing strange about a young woman feeling nervous as she walks through the blackout; especially if she hears, or thinks she hears, footsteps behind her. It probably means nothing, but she's still relieved to run into someone like an air-raid warden, a figure of authority, and to spend a few minutes chatting to him while she assures herself that the steps she thought she heard behind her were only imaginary. Or that whoever it was has taken some other route and isn't on her heels any longer. At that point she'd be happy to go on alone.'

Billy nodded. 'So it wasn't a case of her thinking some man was after her. Someone she might have cause to be afraid of.'

'No, I don't think so. She didn't feel she was in danger.'

'But this bloke *was* after her, all the same. He was waiting round the corner till she moved on. Is that what you're saying?'

'It's possible.' Madden had nodded slowly. 'After *her*. Rosa. That's the point.' He had looked up at Billy then. 'I know there's an argument for calling it a chance killing, but I don't accept that. It's already been established the act was deliberate, and I can't see it happening in a moment of rage, or insanity. It was too cold; too clean; too efficient. The killer knew what he was about.'

The silence that fell between them was broken by the sound of tapping, and they'd looked round to see Helen at the car window. She was pointing to her wristwatch.

'But as to *why* he murdered her.' Madden shook his head hopelessly as he turned away. 'That defies all reason.'

The service had ended, but the mourners still clustered around the rabbi, a young man with a bushy beard, whose voice as he intoned Kaddish had reached Madden only faintly where he was standing beside the cart that had carried Rosa Nowak's remains down the gravelled path to the graveside. More clearly heard had been the 'amens' which had punctuated his low, sing-song murmur.

As Madden watched, Helen detached herself from the group and crossed the path to where he was standing.

'I managed to have a word with Mrs Laski. She won't need a lift back to her flat. She's going to spend the rest of the day with friends in Hampstead. One of them is a doctor. He has a car.'

Helen slipped a gloved hand through her husband's arm. Although the sleet had stopped falling, a keen wind still blew across the open expanse of the cemetery and she had covered her head with a woollen scarf, tucking the ends into her coat, which was buttoned to the neck.

'I think we can slip away now. I'd like to stop off at St John's Wood for an hour before we go back. I must see how Aunt Maud's getting on. I'm sure Billy won't mind dropping us off. Where is he, by the way?'

The two men had been standing together, a little apart from the others.

'He's gone back to the car.' Madden nodded towards the gates. 'His driver said they were trying to get hold of him on the radio. Some message from the Yard.'

He watched for a moment as the group at the graveside began to break up. Two men armed with shovels moved forward to begin the task of filling in the grave.

'Do I need to say anything to Mrs Laski?' he asked.

'No, I don't think so. I told her we'd be in touch with her again soon. Let's leave it at that for now.'

They started up the long path towards the gates, soon overtaking the more elderly mourners ahead of them, and as they approached the exit to the cemetery they saw Billy appear. He was walking rapidly, and when he saw them he waved.

'Sir . . .' he called out to them as he came nearer.

'What is it?' Madden raised his voice in reply.

'A message from Bow Street . . .' Breathing hard, Billy came up to them. Madden halted, with Helen on his arm. 'They've got a lead, sir.'

'A lead?' Madden's voice was calm. But beside him, Helen felt his arm grow tense.

'I don't have the details. The message came through the

radio room at Central. But Bow Street have found a witness. A good one, too. She's at the station now.' Billy was still panting.

'Then you'll want to get down there right away.' Madden's response was prompt. 'Don't worry about us. We're going to stop off at St John's Wood. We'll find our own way there.'

'No, it's not that, sir. I can drop Dr Madden off if she likes. It's on the way. But I thought . . .' Billy paused. 'Well, you might like to come with me.'

'To *Bow Street?*' Madden's surprise was plain.

'That's right, sir.' A grin had appeared on the younger man's face.

'But why . . . ?' Madden glanced at Helen beside him.

'Because it seems only fair.' Billy's smile had broadened. 'After what you were saying only an hour ago.'

'What *I* was saying?'

'That it was odds on the man who killed Rosa was following her.'

'Yes . . . ? And . . . ?' Madden's gaze was piercing now. Billy gave a shrug.

'Well, it seems you were right.'

6

LOFTY COOK shook his head ruefully.

'This is a real stroke of luck, I can tell you.'

His remark was addressed to Billy, but he spared a glance for Madden, who was beside him.

'It came out of the blue, too. The first I knew of it was a call from Poole. She rang the station to say she was bringing Florrie in. That's when I phoned the Yard, looking for you.'

'Poole?' Billy asked.

'That WPC I told you about.'

'The one who responded to the warden's whistle? The first officer at the scene?' Billy nodded. 'I remember now.'

They were standing in the corridor outside the interview room at the Bow Street police station. Alerted by the desk sergeant, Cook had come out to meet them, shutting the door behind him. If he'd been surprised to see Madden there he gave no sign of it. 'I heard you were coming up for the funeral, sir,' he'd said, as they shook hands. 'It's a pleasure to meet you.'

He'd told them then who the witness was he'd been questioning.

'Florence Desmoulins is the name on her papers, but we know her as French Florrie and we've had her on our books since 'thirty-eight. She's got a pitch in Soho Square, but the night of Rosa's murder she was in Tottenham Court Road tube station taking shelter after the sirens went off and that's where she saw her. Saw Rosa.'

He explained how the streetwalker had come to their notice.

'When we started showing Rosa's photograph around, Poole made a point of checking with the tarts. It was her idea. She reckons they're more observant than most.'

'Yes, but why has it taken so long to find this Florrie?' Billy asked. He and Lofty had lit cigarettes and were dropping their ash on the bare wooden floor. 'The murder was a week ago.'

'She was off sick for a few days. With a head cold, she says. Poole spotted her this morning shopping in Oxford Street and showed her Rosa's photo. Florrie said it was the same woman she saw in the tube station.'

'And you're happy with that?'

'Oh, I think so, sir.' Cook nodded. 'Florrie saw her close up.'

'What about this man she says was following Rosa?'

'We were just getting into that when I heard you were here.' The Bow Street inspector eyed them both. 'But even from what little she's told me I'd say he was our bloke. What I suggest is I fill you in first on what happened earlier, how she spotted Rosa, then we'll go in and get her to tell us the rest.'

He trod on his cigarette.

'When the sirens sounded the first time, Florrie ran over to the tube station, but they went off again a few minutes later and no one seemed sure at first what it meant, whether it was the all-clear, or what. Actually, it was a false alarm, but people were milling about for a while. Florrie herself was at the bottom of the stairs, trying to decide whether it was safe to go out again, when this young woman went by her. She was carrying something in each hand, just like Rosa was, and as she worked her way through the crowd they came face to face. That's why Florrie's so sure it was her. Anyway, she went up the steps, this girl who must have been Rosa, and a few seconds later Florrie followed.

'When she got to the top, Florrie paused, still nervous, not sure whether it was safe to go back to her pitch. The blackout was on, of course, but she could still see the girl who'd gone past her crossing the Tottenham Court Road, heading east, which was the direction Rosa would have taken. Just then there was a disturbance behind her, a lot of pushing and shoving on the stairs, and a man came up, forcing his way through the crowd, obviously in a hurry, not caring who he elbowed. When he got to the top, he looked around, saw Florrie standing there and asked her straight out if she'd seen a girl with a bag in each hand go by.'

Cook paused, rubbing his nose. He looked reflective.

'Now it seems they had a conversation of sorts, Florrie and this fellow, and although I haven't got the sense of it yet it's pretty clear what happened, reading between the lines. She didn't want him chasing off after some other girl, she wanted to hook him herself: she was thinking it would save her the time and trouble of going back to Soho Square to look for a customer. But if that is what she had in mind, it didn't work out that way. What happened was he turned nasty.'

'How?' Billy killed his own cigarette. 'What did he do?'

'That's what I don't know yet.' Cook had his hand on the doorknob. He looked at them both. 'But what say we go inside and find out.'

The door behind them opened and a uniformed constable came in bearing a tray laden with cups of tea. He carried it carefully to the table, set it down, and with a nod to Cook left the room. Billy glanced at his watch. He'd promised Helen to have Madden at Waterloo station by half-past three when they had dropped her off earlier. The possibility of grabbing a bite of lunch had vanished, but they still had some time in hand. Not that there was much point in lingering. They had just about squeezed French Florrie dry.

Or she them.

He grinned as he watched the woman seated across the table simultaneously extinguish the cigarette she'd been smoking and refuse the cup of tea Cook was holding out to her with a disdainful gesture. Small in stature, and with sharp, catlike features, she was dressed in a tight blue skirt and a blouse cut to display the tops of her small breasts. Red hair shaped like a cap framed her carefully made-up face, to which she was attending now, applying lipstick and following this with a dab of powder to her nose from a compact she'd removed from her handbag a moment before. Then, having studied the result for several seconds, she snapped the compact shut.

'*Eh bien, c'est fini?*'

Billy's schoolboy French was just about up to understanding her words, though not a number of others she'd used in the course of the description she had just given of her brush with the man who in all likelihood had killed Rosa Nowak, an account laced with epithets and gestures which, though crude, had lent a compelling edge to her narrative. Listening to her, Billy had realized why Lofty was setting such store by her testimony, why he considered finding her such a stroke of luck. An experienced detective himself, he knew it wasn't often that you came across a witness as observant as Florence Desmoulins; one whose memory seemed so attuned to the finest detail; whose quick green eyes missed nothing. Talents she had no doubt honed in response to the demands of her profession, but no less valuable on that account.

A case in point was the description she'd given them earlier of the man she'd encountered at the top of the stairs outside the tube station. This was the first question Cook had put to her on returning to the interview room, and Florrie had responded without a second's hesitation.

'He was not young,' she had told Lofty. 'More than forty years, I think. Tall, but not as tall as you. Nor this gentleman.' Her glance had shifted to Madden. '*Mais peut-être comme toi.*'

The remark, which Billy didn't understand, had been addressed to Cook's colleague, Joe Grace, one of the detectives sent to Little Russell Street, who was standing with his back to the wall by the door, having given up his chair to Madden. Without warning Florrie had risen and walked over to where he was standing, checked her height against his and then returned to her seat, nodding.

'*Comme ça.*' She had gestured with a jerk of her red head. 'The same.'

Cook had noted it down as five feet ten inches and then quickly determined that the man's face and figure had been lean and his hair black and cut short.

'What about his eyes?' he had asked then, and Florrie had shrugged.

'At night in the blackout all eyes are dark.' She spoke with an accent, one she might even have exaggerated a bit, or so Billy thought, rolling her rs and saying 'ze' when she meant 'the'. 'Perhaps you already know zat, *Inspecteur.*' Her smile had been half taunting, half provocative, and Lofty had chosen to ignore it, staying bent over his notepad.

'And what was he wearing?'

'Wearing . . . ?' Florrie had considered the question for some time, gazing up at the ceiling as if the answer lay there. 'A dark coat and a hat is all I remember. He was carrying . . . how do you call it? A case?'

'A suitcase?'

'*Non . . . plus petite.* It was smaller.' She demonstrated with her hands.

'A briefcase, then?' Cook asked, and she nodded.

'*Exactement.*'

'Could he have been a businessman?'

She shrugged.

It was then that Cook had asked his witness to describe her brush with the man, and Florrie had launched into a graphic description of their brief encounter.

'I have come up the stairs, *oui*, I am standing there, and this man, *ce connard*, he asks me if I have seen a woman carrying two bags.' She had shrugged. 'I know who he means, it is the same girl who went past me, but I think maybe he would like to stop and talk, so I make a joke, I say, "What's your hurry?"' Her voice took on a droll note. 'I ask him if he want to spend some time with me. I am being friendly. *Tu comprends?*'

Out of the corner of his eye Billy saw a cynical smile flit across Joe Grace's thin, pockmarked countenance.

'But he only asks again about this girl, where she has gone, and when he speak a second time I change my mind. Even though he is smiling I know this is one I don't want. So I say, "What's it to you?" *Et sans rien dire il me prend par la gorge, le salaud.*'

'What's that? What did you say?' Cook struck the table with his fist in frustration. 'Speak English, damn it.'

'He grab me by the throat.' Florrie spat the words back.

'*Comme ça, tu vois.*' She clutched her own throat. 'And then he speak, but so softly only I can hear. He say, "Answer the question or I break your bloody neck." '

Flushed in the face, eyes bright, she stared at Cook.

'And I tell you, Inspector.' Her own voice had dropped to a hoarse whisper. 'This one . . . he means it.'

In the silence that followed, Cook caught Billy's eye.

'And so?'

'And so I tell him. I say she go that way . . .' Florrie waved her hand. 'And he leaves, walking fast, across the road, and when he is more than halfway I call after him. I shout, "*Tu n'es qu'un connard . . . une merde*", which is a big piece of shit, if you want to know.' Her voice had risen. 'I tell him I won't forget his face – "*Je n'oublierai pas ta sale gueule,*" I scream, so I know he will hear, and I am ready to run because he stops and turns and he looks at me and I think he is coming back. But instead he goes on and I don't see him again.'

She sat back, breathing fast, her breasts rising and falling beneath her blouse. Like her cheeks they were flushed. After a moment's pause, she spoke again, but in a lower tone.

'You are thinking he is the one who killed this girl? Maybe you are right. I wish now that I had not told him which way she go.'

She glanced down at her hands. Then, as though to rid herself of some memory, she shook her head, reaching for her handbag at the same time. Unsnapping the clasp, she plucked out her compact and while Cook was checking through his notes she repaired the make-up on her face.

'*Eh bien. C'est fini?*'

Cook glanced at Billy, who shook his head – he had nothing more to ask her – then at Madden, who was sitting a little back from the table, near the corner, with his arms folded and a pensive look on his face.

'Sir . . . ?'

Lofty's tone was respectful and it brought a grin to Billy's lips. He had watched the effect of his old chief's presence on both detectives with more than a little amusement. Even Joe Grace, as tough a nut as he'd encountered during his time in the Met, a man he'd once seen tackle a brace of thugs, enforcers for a smash-and-grab gang, and leave them both bloody and pleading for quarter, had moderated his usual abrasive manner and stood silent during the interview, as though out of deference to their visitor. And as for French Florrie, she had apparently decided from the outset that this was a male figure to whom she could relate, perhaps even flirt with, and had favoured him more than once with an inviting glance.

'Yes, thank you, Inspector. There is one thing . . .' Madden shifted in his chair so that he was facing the young woman. 'You've been very patient, mademoiselle. I know how tedious this must be for you. But I was interested by something you've just said and I wondered if you could explain it.'

'Something I said, monsieur?'

Florrie bestowed a smile on her new interrogator: not the faint, contemptuous curl of the lips she'd reserved thus far for Lofty and his two colleagues, men she was more usually inclined to view as her persecutors, but a generous parting of her wide mouth, offering a glimpse of white, pointed teeth.

'Yes, to this man when he was leaving.' Oblivious to the reaction he'd aroused, Madden pressed on. 'You called him a name.'

'*C'est vrai. Une merde.*' Unabashed, she repeated the words. 'I already explain what it mean . . .'

'Yes, yes, but you said it in French, am I right?' Madden leaned forward.

'Of course.' She spread her hands.

'Why?'

'*Why?*' She stared at him.

'Why not speak in English, so he would understand?'

For a full five seconds her face remained a blank. Then comprehension dawned in her eyes.

'*Mais oui.*' The smile returned. '*Vous avez raison.* But I speak in French because I know he will understand.'

'What was that?' Lofty Cook's glance shot up from his notebook.

'I forget to tell you . . .' She turned to him. 'When he talk to me first, this man, and he ask about the girl who is carrying the bags, I pretend not to understand. So he tell me she is wearing this thing on her head – ' Florrie cupped her hands about her hair – '*cette chose . . . je ne connais pas le nom . . .* how do you call it?'

'A hood,' Madden said.

'*Exactement.* An 'ood. This is a word I have not heard before and when he see that I don't understand he tell me what it is – "*un capuchon*" – and then he speak to me in French. He ask me again which way she go. *Voilà!*' She demonstrated with a flourish of her hand. 'This is how I know.'

Cook put down his pen.

'So what are you saying exactly?' he asked her. 'Was he French? Is that what you're telling us?'

'*Ah, non. . .*' Florrie waved her hand dismissively. '*Pas du tout.* He is English. I know from his *accent.*'

The Bow Street inspector made a final note. He glanced at Madden to see if there was anything further he wished to say.

'Just one last question.' Madden smiled at the young

woman. 'You said earlier – when you were telling us how you met this man – that you changed your mind about him?'

'Monsieur . . . ?' She seemed puzzled by his query.

'At first you tried to talk to him. But then you changed your mind; and quite suddenly, too. "This is one I know I don't want." That's what you said. And I wondered why.'

She nodded her head thoughtfully. 'It is true . . .'

'Up to then he'd been polite. Even friendly. You said he was smiling. Isn't that so?'

Again she nodded.

'Why then?'

Florrie sat silent. She seemed uncertain how to reply.

'*Ecoute* . . . it is hard explain.' She blew out her cheeks in frustration. '*Mais il' y avait quelque chose* . . . there was something about this man that was not right.'

'Not right?'

'All I can tell you is what I know.'

'Of course, mademoiselle.'

Madden waited while Florrie sat tapping one red fingernail on the table top, searching for the right words.

'Maybe it is his eyes, or maybe it is his smile – ' she glanced at Madden – 'but when I look at him I *know*.'

'Know what?'

'That this is one to stay away from.'

7

'I must say I had hopes after reading Miss Desmoulins's statement. I thought there was a good chance someone else might have spotted this man. That we'd have other sightings of him. But no luck so far, I'm afraid.'

Sinclair's sigh was lost in the static of the telephone line.

'I tell you, John, this case is as slippery as an eel. You no sooner think you've got a grip on it than it slides through your fingers.'

Three days had passed since Madden and his wife had returned from London, and true to his word the chief inspector had rung his old partner to bring him up to date on the progress of the investigation. His call had come while Madden and Helen were eating breakfast, a meal they took these days in the kitchen, where there was a wireless, so that they could listen to the news, even though lately it offered little in the way of comfort. The heady days of summer when the advance of the Allied armies across France after the breakthrough at Normandy had seemed irresistible were past. True, Paris had fallen without a fight, but the debacle at Arnhem had put a stop to further progress, at least for the time being, and if the reports published in the newspapers and broadcast on the radio were true, German forces were now digging in at their frontiers in preparation for the bitter fighting to come.

To Madden, scarred by his memories of the slaughter of the trenches – by the conviction bequeathed him that war was merely butchery under another name – the conflict had seemed endless, the years of peace a distant dream. Too old for active service, he had commanded the Highfield Home Guard until its disbandment a few months earlier; but only out of a sense of duty. Like others of his generation he had hoped never to put on a uniform again. And while he did not question his country's decision to take up arms – on this occasion its cause seemed manifestly right, its enemy an abomination – he could not blind himself to the suffering brought about by years of war, nor to the continuing sacrifice of youth it entailed. He needed only to listen to the voice of a news reader on the radio with its familiar litany of actions fought and casualties suffered to picture his own son, whose ship even now must be ploughing the icy waters off Spitsbergen and Novaya Zemlya, a prey to enemy submarines, battered by storms and wrapped in perpetual winter darkness.

It was from this hellish realm of the imagination that Sinclair's call had summoned him, and he'd had to struggle to adjust his thoughts to the cold reality of a young girl's life snuffed out, her broken body cast aside, as the chief inspector's familiar dry, clipped tones sounded in his ear.

'Not that Bow Street have been idle, mind you. A description of the man our lady of the streets so kindly supplied has been posted at all tube stations between Waterloo and Tottenham Court Road, together with a photograph of Rosa, but no one's come forward yet.'

Madden absorbed the information in silence. He'd taken the call in his study and was seated at the desk.

'Cook also tried to get an artist's sketch of this man with Florrie's help. She did her best. She's a willing witness. But it was too dark outside the tube station to make out his features clearly and they couldn't come up with an image that satisfied her. So he's going to have her look at some faces instead:

pictures of past offenders, men with a record of violence against women, rapists included. Anyone who fits the general description and isn't currently inside. They're expecting her at Bow Street this afternoon. I'll let you know if anything comes of it.'

Madden searched his memory.

'What about Rosa's diary?' he asked. 'Has anyone looked at it yet?'

'Cook has spoken to Mrs Laski. Apparently the girl kept one for years and there are several volumes among the possessions she'd left at the flat for safe keeping. They go back some time. Mrs Laski has promised to look through them, though I gather she doesn't fancy the task.'

'Why's that?'

'They're not about Rosa's daily life as such, or so she says. They're more a record of her thoughts and feelings, and Mrs Laski believes they deal particularly with the guilt she apparently felt at being the only one of her family to have survived. Poor child. Well, at least that pain is over for her.'

The chief inspector heaved another sigh.

'This is one of those cases I've come to dread, John. It seems unconnected to anything. All we know for certain is this man was after Rosa for some reason. But did he kill her on the spur of the moment, or had he learned she was coming up to London? Was he lying in wait for her?'

'My guess is the first,' Madden replied, after a moment's thought. 'I don't think he was prepared. He was on some business of his own; he had a briefcase with him. I think he spotted her on the tube, or at Waterloo. And it sounds as if he was taken by surprise: he was chasing after her, acting in haste . . .' He broke off and there was silence between them. Sinclair waited a few moments, then spoke:

'What is it, John? What's on your mind?'

'I've just had a thought . . . a strange one.'

'Yes . . . ?'

'If this man was so anxious to kill Rosa – if her death was a matter of such urgency to him – why hasn't he been looking for her? A young Polish girl . . . she wouldn't have been hard to find. He could have gone to a private enquiry agency. The Polish community would have been a good place to start. Why hasn't anyone been asking questions?'

His words brought a grunt of surprise from his listener. Some moments passed before the chief inspector responded.

'I've no idea,' he said, finally. 'But if he had, I think we'd know about it. Her aunt would have told us, or that farmer she worked for in Norfolk. You'd probably be aware of it yourself.'

'Quite . . . but don't you see – if he *hasn't* been looking for her, that suggests he wasn't expecting to find her. Not here in England, anyway.'

'Go on.'

'Assuming for a moment there was some earlier encounter between them, it must have happened abroad. In Poland – or France, when Rosa was there. Mind you, that would push the whole thing so far back in time . . .'

Madden fell silent. He could hear the rustle of papers and the mutter of another voice on the line.

'Well, it's something to think about, anyway.' Having waited to see if his old partner had any more to add, Sinclair spoke again. 'But let's see what today brings, shall we? What Florrie makes of our rogues' gallery. She may spot a face she recognizes. We're due some luck.'

With little to occupy him at the farm – the seasonal lull in work came as a welcome break – Madden spent the morning at home attending to odd jobs before walking in to Highfield after lunch and then making his way to Stratton Hall, on the outskirts of the village. A great-house since Tudor times, it was presently being used as a convalescent home for servicemen, but its owner, Lord Stratton, now in his late eighties, and a lifelong friend of Helen's, still lived there in a wing of the rambling edifice, and both she and Madden made a practice of calling on the old gentleman at least once a week so as to keep him up to date with news from the village and the wider world outside.

Crossing the great forecourt in front of the house, Madden was hailed by a uniformed figure who had just climbed out of a khaki-coloured staff car.

'Hello, John! What brings you to my lair?'

Although he was the commanding officer at Stratton Hall, with the rank of colonel, Brian Chadwick retained many of the attitudes of the country GP he'd once been, and on arriving at Highfield two years earlier had quickly formed a friendship with Helen which had later been extended to her husband.

'Come to see his nibs, have you?'

He joined Madden and they walked on together across the cobbles.

'By the way, have they caught the man yet?'

'Which man, Brian?'

'The one who killed that girl who was working for you?'

'Not yet.'

Madden glanced at his companion. The expression on Chadwick's face suggested there might be a reason for his question beyond simple curiosity.

'I ask because one of my young chaps is concerned. Well, not concerned, exactly. Upset, rather.' The colonel struggled with his vocabulary. 'He read a report on the inquest in *The*

Times, just a paragraph or two. It was the first he'd heard of it and he got on to me at once.'

'Got on to you? Isn't he here?'

'No, in Oxford.' Chadwick frowned. On the short side, and thickset, he was constantly bemoaning the size of his waistline. Helen had told him, in all seriousness, doctor to doctor, that he should put himself on a diet and have his blood pressure checked regularly unless he wanted his chronic shortness of breath to develop into something more sinister. 'We sent him to a hospital there that specializes in plastic surgery. He had facial burns. Perhaps you've seen him around. A young pilot officer. Tyson's his name.'

Madden shook his head.

'He was shot down over the Channel and picked up. But his plane caught fire before he could bale out, hence the burns. He had other wounds, too, but they've healed and he was recuperating here before having his face seen to.'

Chadwick paused for a much-needed breather.

'But why was he so concerned?' Madden asked, his curiosity piqued. 'Did he know her?'

'Oh, no. Nothing like that.' Chadwick dismissed the possibility with a wave of his hand. 'But he'd heard her play at the concert we had here – he's musical – and he actually spoke to her the day she went up to London. He was on his way to Oxford himself. They were in the same compartment. But you can ask him about it yourself, if you like. He'll be here in a few days.'

'He's coming back, is he?' Madden asked.

Chadwick nodded. 'He's already had the operation. But he'll need to convalesce for a while. Then it'll be hey-ho and off to the wars again. Unless, by some miracle, the whole ghastly business is over by then.'

They parted, Chadwick going to his office in what had

once been the butler's pantry, Madden heading for the wing where Lord Stratton had his apartments. His way took him through the great entrance hall. Hung with armorial shields when he'd first known it a quarter of a century before, the panelled walls now sported felt-backed boards thick with typed notices, while the maids and footmen of an earlier era had been replaced by white-veiled nurses. Passing through the dimly lit hall, he recalled the concert that had taken place there recently, remembering, with a stab of pain, the slight, dark-haired figure of Rosa Nowak as she bent over the piano keys, her expression rapt, the sorrow that dwelt in her eyes banished; for a few minutes at least.

The anger he had felt on hearing of the girl's death had not abated. But mixed with it was another emotion more difficult to isolate, a sense of failure unrelated to her violent end – there was no way he could have foreseen the danger into which she was heading – but having to do with the time she had spent in his care when he had seen her distress and been powerless to ease it. The link his subconscious had made with the death of his baby daughter long ago – so disturbingly vivid in his dream – had not occurred to him until Helen had suggested it, but he understood now why the old pain had returned to haunt him. He'd been unable to help either. His daughter had expired beneath his gaze, her faint breaths failing, while Rosa had died unhealed, grief claiming her for its own.

The sky was already paling when he left the hall an hour later and set out for home. His route took him through the village, and as he walked down the main street, past the pub, he heard his name called out and looked round to see a familiar figure in police uniform emerging from the side door of the

Rose and Crown. Highfield's bobby for the past thirty years, and something of a law unto himself, Will Stackpole felt no shame at being caught slipping out of the pub at half-past four in the afternoon.

'How are you, sir?' He waved to Madden.

'Will ...!' Checking his stride, Madden waited for the other man to catch him up. 'Helen tells me you've heard from Ted.'

'That's right, sir.' The constable crossed the road to join him and they walked on together. Almost as tall as Madden, he'd been putting on weight in recent years and now cut an imposing figure in his cape and conical helmet. 'First letter in two months. We were starting to get worried, Ada and I.' He was speaking of his oldest son. Captured during the fighting in North Africa, Ted Stackpole had been a prisoner-of-war in Germany for the past two years. 'They know we're winning the war, but they don't know how long it's going to take. Mind you, I couldn't tell him that myself.' Stackpole snorted. 'You listen to the news and you think everything's going well. We took Paris without much trouble, after all. But now our boys seem stuck. And those flying bombs keep coming over, don't they? It makes you wonder what's really happening.'

He stole a glance at Madden.

'Ted asked about Rob, same as he always does. Have you had any word, sir?'

'Not for a while, Will. But you know what it's like. Once they put to sea we don't hear anything.'

Acknowledging the constable's concern, Madden gripped his arm. Their long friendship, which dated from the murder investigation that had first brought him to the village, had been inherited by their sons. The two boys, with only a year's difference in age between them, and both taken with the natural world, had been inseparable in childhood. Together they had spent a string of summers exploring the woods and fields around Highfield, days which in Madden's memory now seemed bathed in perpetual sunlight.

'We're just praying he'll be home for Christmas.'

'Ah – now that would be something.'

Stackpole laid a comforting hand on his shoulder. After a moment he spoke again.

'Any word from the Yard, sir?'

'Nothing of note, Will. Mr Sinclair rang me this morning. They're working hard on the case, but they haven't made any real progress yet.'

His words brought a grunt from the constable.

'I've asked around like you suggested. But there's nothing to get a hold of here. It seems Rosa didn't have any close friends; she kept to herself. But everyone liked the lass, those that met her, and they keep asking me about her, wanting to know what's been done.'

The main street with its shops was behind them now and presently they passed by the church, and the moss-walled cemetery beside it. Ahead was a row of cottages, one of which belonged to the constable and his wife, and when they got there they found Ada Stackpole in the front garden with the elder of their two daughters, both in smocks, and with their hair wrapped in scarves, busy digging up carrots from a flower-bed that before the war had held a display of roses that were Will Stackpole's pride and joy. Pink from her exertions, Ada paused, leaning on her spade, to greet Madden and to inform him that he'd just missed Helen.

'She'd been over to Craydon to see old George Parker. Dropped a brick on his toe, he did, and broke it. His toe, that is. Silly old coot.' She chuckled. 'She came in for a cup of tea. Can I get you one?'

'No thanks, Ada, I have to get back.' Turning to the constable, he added, 'I'm expecting another call from Mr Sinclair. Do you remember me telling you about that street-walker the police interviewed?'

'The French woman?'

Madden nodded. 'Bow Street are showing her some photographs from records. I'll let you know if anything comes of it.'

Leaving the last of the cottages behind him, Madden walked on in the gathering dusk, and when he reached the high brick wall of Melling Lodge left the road and made his way through darkening fields to a footpath that ran alongside the stream at the foot of the valley and which, by a slightly longer route, would lead him home.

It was a way he loved to take, and treasured memories lay around him as he followed the winding path. The stream and its banks had been a favoured playground of his children, the wooded slopes above the scene of countless rambles with them. Not far from where he was now he had once sat unmoving with his young son by a badger sett for more than an hour before dawn so that they could catch a glimpse by torchlight of the dam with her cubs. Even closer, only a short way down the stream, was a patch of meadow grass hard by the bank and hidden by bushes which held a sweeter memory yet, one of which he never spoke but which still had the power to bring a warmth to his cheeks when he recalled it.

The afternoon light had all but faded as he unlatched the wooden gate at the bottom of the garden and walked up the long, sloping lawn to the house. The phone was ringing as he went in and he heard Helen answer it in the study. Thinking it might be Sinclair calling for him he went there and met her as she was coming out of the room into the passage.

'John, darling. I didn't know you were back.'

They kissed.

'That wasn't Angus, was it?' Madden asked. She shook her head.

'It was Gladys Porter. She says her Harold's come over all queer. Considering how much time he spends in the Rose and Crown I'm not surprised, but I'd better go over there and have a look at him.'

He accompanied her to the hall where her coat hung.

'Every time the phone rings now I think it might be Rob to say they're back in port. Safe.'

He helped her into her coat then turned her gently about and put his arms around her.

'It won't be long now.' He sought to reassure himself as much as her. 'Any day.'

'That's what I tell myself,' Helen said. 'Any day. But the awful thing is the closer we come to the end of the war, the worse it gets. If anything were to happen to him now . . .'

Madden tightened his hold, drawing her closer to him.

'I get so angry. It's so easy to hate. Then I think of Franz and try not to feel what I feel.'

The man she was speaking of, an Austrian psychiatrist named Franz Weiss, had been a lifelong friend of hers. Having fled to England from Nazi Germany, he had been planning to join his son and daughter in New York when he'd suffered a stroke that had prevented him from travelling. Soon afterwards war had broken out and Helen had brought the frail old man down to Highfield to spend what turned out to be the last months of his life with them. Though the full extent of the tragedy unfolding in Europe would not be known for another two years, there were already inklings of it, and Weiss had confided to his hosts that he did not expect to see or hear again from those he had left behind, including two brothers and a sister. During the final weeks of his life when he had been confined to bed he had spent many hours playing music on a gramophone he had brought with him from London. Bach cantatas for the most part, they had been the works of German composers exclusively, and it was Helen who had divined that it was their old friend's last wish to clear his mind of all bitterness and remember only what was dear to him.

'Sometimes, too, I wonder what he might have said to Rosa if he'd still been with us. How he might have drawn her away from thoughts of death and back to life. And then I think . . . but to what purpose?'

They stood locked in one another's arms for a moment longer. Then she kissed him again.

'I must be off. Perhaps you'll have heard from Angus by the time I get back. I hope so.'

'*Strangled, you say . . . ?*'

Madden stood stunned. He had heard the phone ringing from the drawing-room where he'd been laying the fire and had come to the study to answer it. As he picked up the receiver he had switched on a green-shaded lamp on the desk beside it, and now he found himself staring at his own reflection in the window, hardly able to comprehend what the chief inspector had just told him.

'That's correct. But not manually. The killer used a garrotte.' Sinclair spoke in a weary tone. 'I'm sorry, John. This is wretched news to be giving you . . .'

'When did it happen?'

'Some time overnight, it seems. She was due at Bow Street station this afternoon and when she didn't turn up they sent an officer to her flat in Soho. There was no reply when he rang her bell, but someone let him in the house and he found her body on the floor inside her flat. That was less than an hour ago.'

The reflected image of himself Madden was staring at faded: in its place he saw Florrie Desmoulins's lacquered red hair, her wide painted smile.

'She told him she wouldn't forget his face.'

'I'm sorry?'

'When he went off. She yelled after him and he looked back. It's in her statement.'

'Yes ... I see what you mean. But we can't jump to conclusions. She was a prostitute, after all. It's a hazardous profession.'

The chief inspector was silent. But the sound of a heavy sigh came faintly to Madden's ears.

'I'm waiting to hear more. Styles is at the murder scene now. Perhaps he'll learn something. I'll speak to you again later.'

8

'EITHER PIANO WIRE or a cheese-cutter. That's what Ransom reckons. He cut right through the skin and into the flesh. Bloody nearly took her head off, Ransom says. He put her on the slab right away.'

Lofty Cook screwed his features into a grimace. He had just returned from the mortuary at St Mary's where he'd accompanied the pathologist, leaving Billy behind at Florrie Desmoulins's flat with Joe Grace and a forensic team.

'And there were no other injuries?' Billy asked. Alerted by a call from Sinclair, he'd left his desk at the Yard and hurried up to Soho.

'None that he's found. She was topped, that's all. Just like the other one.'

Florrie Desmoulins's body had still been lying where it was found when Billy had arrived. Her flat was on the top floor of a narrow, three-storey house tucked into an alleyway called Cable Lane, off Dean Street, and he'd had to step over the corpse, which was curled in a foetal position in the narrow hallway and so close to the door it would only open a foot or two. The likelihood of a gar-rotte having been used had been mentioned in the report phoned from Bow Street, and when he crouched down Billy could see the red welt circling Florrie's throat from which blood must have leaked earlier – there were streaks visible on her pale skin above the nightdress she was wear-ing. Her green eyes were wide and staring. He recalled her

smile and the way she'd snapped her compact shut with a
flourish.

'*Eh bien! C'est fini.*'

That the flat had also been her place of business was
confirmed by her landlady – for so she claimed to be – a
woman named Ackers, who'd been convicted twice of running a bawdy house. Reassured by Cook, the first detective
on the scene, that she would not be prosecuted on the basis
of anything she told them she'd admitted it was Florrie's
habit to pick up her customers in Soho Square, only a few
minutes' walk away, and bring them back to the flat.

'Last night she wasn't busy. Said it was too cold out and
there weren't any men about. She brought one back at about
nine and he left half an hour later. Florrie came down and
told me she wasn't going out again. That's the last time I
talked to her.'

Middle-aged and skeletal, with cropped brown hair,
Mildred Ackers was being questioned by Cook on the
cramped top-floor landing outside Florrie's flat when Billy
had tramped up the linoleum-covered stairs to join them.
Wrapped in a brown cardigan that hung shapelessly about
her, she had stood with folded arms staring into space.

'A bit later Juanita came in with a man. He stayed for half
an hour.'

Juanita de Castro, the other tenant of the building, lived
on the first floor, Lofty had told Billy.

'Though if that's her real name, I'm the Queen of
Romania.'

Juanita was lying down in her flat below at that moment,
still recovering from shock – it was she who had let in the
bobby sent by Bow Street to fetch Florrie that afternoon and
had seen the body on the floor inside.

'The girls had keys to each other's flats. They sometimes

worked as a team. Or so Madam Ackers says.' Lofty had drawn Billy aside for a moment to bring him up to date. 'Juanita's bloke was a Yank airman. He took off about ten – we know that from her and from Ackers, who heard him leave.' He took out a packet of cigarettes and offered one to Billy, who shook his head.

'Ackers lives where? On the ground floor?'

Lofty nodded.

'Keeps an eye on the comings and goings, does she?'

'No question.' Cook put a match to his cigarette. 'That's what makes it strange. Whoever topped Florrie got in and out without being seen or heard. Normally anyone turning up here would ring the bell and Ackers would let them in. Besides the men they picked up, the girls had regulars, blokes who'd come round to see them by arrangement. But there were none last night.'

Billy grunted. He looked at the woman, who was standing a step or two away from them. Her attitude hadn't changed. She stood with folded arms, a vacant look in her eyes, waiting for this to be over so she could get on with whatever it was she called a life. Aware of his gaze she glanced up.

'So you didn't hear anything last night?' Billy asked her.

Ackers shook her head.

'What about the stairs? They creak, I noticed.'

The woman shrugged. 'I told you, I didn't hear any-thing.'

'Listening to the radio, were you?'

She viewed him with a leaden gaze.

'Yes or no?'

'I had it on some of the time.'

Billy turned back to Cook.

'Better have the forensic boys look at the lock on the street door. He may have jimmied it. And this one, too . . .'

He bent down to peer at the Yale lock on Florrie's door. Lofty joined him.

'I can see he might have crept in,' he said. 'But how would he know which flat was Florrie's?'

'By watching outside?' Billy suggested. He stood up straight. 'He could have followed her down from Soho Square and then waited in the alley to see which light went on. Even with blackout blinds you can tell. But he couldn't go in at once. She had a bloke with her, and then Juanita came back and she had a feller, too. He would have had a long wait. But once the girls' lights went out he could have slipped in. If Ackers had her radio on she wouldn't have heard him.'

'Still, she might easily have come out into the hall.'

Billy shrugged. 'Then he'd have done her too, this bloke.'

'Hmmm . . .' Lofty was still peering at the lock. 'But once he got up here, couldn't he have just knocked on Florrie's door?' he asked.

'Perhaps. But would Florrie have let him in? She wasn't expecting anyone. At the very least she'd have asked who it was. It's more likely she heard him working on the lock and came to investigate. That would explain why the body's where it is rather than in the bedroom.'

At that point Billy had gone inside, slipping sideways through the door and stepping carefully over the corpse, which he'd bent to examine. Beyond, in the bedroom, he'd found Joe Grace busy with two detectives from the forensic squad. It was after five, already dark outside, and the men had drawn the curtains and switched on two red-shaded lamps whose glow was reflected in a gold-framed mirror above the dressing table. Grace had been going through a chest of drawers filled mostly with underclothes, judging by the pile of lacy garments on the floor at his feet.

'Nothing so far,' he'd told Billy. 'She must have got up to go to the door.' He indicated the double bed behind him where the pillow was dented and the bedclothes pushed back. 'I'm not sure he ever got in here. There's no sign of it. Just did what he came to do and buggered off.'

Billy had looked about him. Hanging on the wall above the bed was a painting of a nude woman stretched out on a couch. Her cap of red hair suggested it might be an idealized version of Florrie herself, though Billy couldn't see much resemblance. There was a second mirror, attached to the ceiling and positioned above the bed, and as he craned his neck to look up at it he heard Grace's harsh cackle.

'Now that's what I call a bird's-eye view.'

On the bedside table were two framed photographs, one of the Eiffel Tower, the other of a woman wearing a white apron and the sort of cap favoured by bakers. She was holding a little girl by the hand, and this time Billy thought he recognized the shape of Florrie's catlike features in the small, grinning face.

At that point the sound of voices had signalled a new arrival and Billy had gone out into the short passage to find the familiar burly figure of Ransom crouched down over the body. As he'd watched, the pathologist had shifted on to his knees so as to peer more closely at the wound on Florrie's throat.

'Garrotted, beyond doubt. An expert job, by the look of it.' Raising his eyes he'd caught sight of Billy. 'Inspector! We meet again!'

'Hello, sir. Expert, did you say?'

Billy had joined him beside the body.

'That's my impression. But I'll want to look at her more carefully.'

Ransom had taken one of Florrie's hands in his and was testing the finger and wrist joints. He glanced under the nails.

'Rigor's receding. She's been dead more than twelve hours.'

'We think it happened during the night.' Billy glanced at Lofty, who was standing on the other side of Ransom in the half-opened doorway. 'What we're wondering is whether there's any connection to the Bloomsbury murder.'

'You're referring to the young woman whose neck was broken?'

Ransom rose to his feet, grimacing. He flexed his knees.

'I take it you've some reason to believe that. Apart from the medical evidence, I mean, which is far from conclusive.'

He stood pondering, his bushy eyebrows drawn together in a frown.

'I mean, the method's different, that's obvious. Strangulation in this case – that's assuming I don't find some other injury – a broken spinal cord in the other. Plus here the killer had recourse to artificial means, which wasn't the case in Bloomsbury. There the man used his bare hands.'

'Yes, but we think he was caught unprepared.' Billy continued to probe. 'He wasn't expecting to encounter Miss Nowak that evening.'

'And not even your habitual murderer walks around with a garrotte in his pocket just on the off chance. I take your point. He came here armed because he knew what he was going to do.'

Ransom mused a moment longer. 'Look, from a medical point of view I can't really help. There's not enough basis for a comparison. But there is one thing that strikes me: the efficiency with which these two young women were dispatched.'

The pathologist paused. He cocked an eye at Billy.

'Speaking as a doctor, I can tell you that's rare. It's much harder to kill a human being than you might think. I'm not speaking of bombs and bullets now. I mean by the use of one's hands, whether or not one employs a piece of wire. Much harder. Both physically and psychologically.'

'Unless you have the knack for it,' Billy said. 'Is that your point?'

Ransom shrugged. 'I don't want to mislead you. But if it does turn out to be the same man, then you'll be looking for an exceptionally cold-blooded individual, and in all likelihood one who has done this sort of thing before.'

He bent to pick up his bag from the floor.

'None of which, I hasten to say, will appear in my report, which will be business as usual. If you get her back to Paddington right away, I can do the post-mortem today.'

Leaving Billy to oversee things at the flat, Lofty had accompanied Ransom back to St Mary's. They had both wanted to be certain what they were dealing with – to be sure that Florrie's death, like Rosa Nowak's, was a case of murder pure and simple – before moving on to the next step in the investigation, which would have to include the possibility that the two killings were connected.

'The chief inspector's going to want some answers,' Billy had told his old pal. 'Which won't be easy, seeing as how we're still scratching our heads over the other business. I'll talk to Ackers again while you're gone. And Miss Castro. She's had long enough to pull herself together.'

Neither, however, had been able to add anything to the detectives' sum of knowledge, scant as it was. Mildred Ackers had stuck doggedly to the account she'd already given of the previous evening. Florrie had gone upstairs a little after half-past nine and had not been seen or heard from again. Juanita de Castro had returned soon afterwards with a client who'd departed in due course. Thereafter, as far as Ackers was aware, the house had been quiet.

At that point, however, there'd been a new development. Joe Grace had called down the stairwell to Billy to come up. He was on the landing with one of the detectives from the forensic squad, a man named Myers.

'Pete says this lock's been fiddled with,' Grace told Billy. 'Here, have a butcher's.'

He'd handed him a torch and Billy had got down on his haunches. With the aid of the beam he saw where a probe of some kind had cut grooves into the patina of grime coating the inner workings of the lock.

'Just what I thought,' Billy said. He was pleased with his stroke of intuition. 'Now take a look at the street door. I think he crept in here while her ladyship was listening to Billy Cotton at the Starlight Room. I wonder if Juanita heard any footsteps on the stairs.'

The answer was soon forthcoming. Roused by Joe Grace, who had banged on her locked door repeatedly until the dishevelled woman appeared, she had denied hearing any sound at all after she'd gone to bed. Dark-haired, with a mole on one cheek and a small, crescent-shaped scar on the other, Juanita de Castro had emerged still fumbling with the cord of her robe, offering glimpses of a well-fleshed body beneath it. Her cheeks, smeared with mascara, had shown the tracks of the tears she'd undoubtedly been shedding.

'It's a bleeding shame,' she'd said to Billy, with a glare at Grace, who had ogled her nakedness, grinning. 'She was a nice girl, Flo was. She had a good heart. What are you lot doing to stop this sort of thing, that's what I'd like to know. Bugger all's the answer.'

'Here, that'll do . . .' An outraged Grace had shaken his finger at her, but she'd ignored him.

'So why'd it happen?' she'd demanded of Billy. 'You tell me that.'

'I can't,' he'd replied quietly, looking her straight in the eye, letting her know he was different from other coppers, a trick he'd learned during his time with John Madden all those years ago, the way *he'd* talked to people, only with Madden it hadn't been deliberate. It was just the way he was. Different. 'But I mean to find out and I'm hoping you can help me. Did you hear anything last night? Even the slightest sound . . . the stairs creaking . . . ?'

But she hadn't, she told him. Once her customer had departed she'd gone to sleep and only roused herself at midday to go out for an hour or two. Soon after her return the constable sent by Bow Street had arrived in search of Florrie and she'd been persuaded to let him in to the flat above hers.

'I saw her lying there. Poor Flo. She never did no harm to anyone. All it takes is one rotten bastard . . .'

Billy had let her go back into her flat and soon afterwards Lofty had returned from Paddington with a more detailed account of how Florrie had met her end and an assurance from Ransom that she had not been assaulted in any other way.

'Same as the Nowak girl,' Lofty said. 'It's got to be the same bloke.'

Myers, the forensic man, was just finishing his inspection of the front-door lock.

'You guessed right,' he said to Billy as he went out. 'This one's been fiddled, too.'

Billy told Cook about the upstairs door.

'Either he followed her down here to Cable Lane, or he was waiting. It would have been easier to do her outside in the alley, but she had a man with her. He had to wait.'

'Some nerve, though,' Lofty said. 'Tiptoeing up the stairs.'

In the darkness of the narrow alleyway all Billy could see

of his lanky colleague was a glimpse now and again of his hatchet features as he drew on his cigarette. The air was freezing and their frosty breath mingled with the smoke they expelled. Footsteps approached from the black pit at the end of the street.

'I've got him, guv.' The voice was female, the accent pure Cockney. 'He was in the Black Cat, trying to sneak out the back. Must have heard we were looking for him.'

Billy caught a glimpse of a peaked cap. Then the caped figure of a WPC emerged from the darkness.

'Where's he now?' Lofty asked.

'In the back of your car.' She nodded behind her. 'I left him there with Hoskins. Told him we wanted a word with him down at the station. He's asking for his brief.'

'Well, he can whistle as far as I'm concerned.' Cook trod on his cigarette. 'This is Poole,' he told Billy, who'd guessed as much – he remembered the name of the officer who'd been first at the scene when Rosa Nowak's body was discovered. 'I sent her off to pick up Florrie's pimp. He's a Maltese called Ragusa. Lil, this is Inspector Styles. He's from the Yard.'

'Guv.' She touched her cap.

'Now let's all get inside. It's perishing out here.'

In the dimly lit hallway WPC Poole was revealed to be a fair-haired young woman, still in her twenties, but with a strong, determined face that made her seem older. Short and stocky, her slightly protruding lower jaw gave her the look of a bulldog, one you'd think twice about crossing, Billy thought. Her glance took him in briefly before her eyes, blue as periwinkles, settled into a neutral gaze.

'Did Ragusa know about Florrie?' Cook asked her.

'Yes, he'd heard all right. But he's not saying much.'

'What do you know about him?' Billy asked. 'How does he treat his girls?'

'Do you mean, would he top one, like what happened to Florrie?'

The bluntness of her question took Billy by surprise; he was accustomed to more deference from the lower ranks of the uniformed branch. But he nodded, after a moment.

'Yes, that's what I mean.'

Poole pursed her lips, weighing the question.

'I wouldn't put it past him,' she said. 'But they're his living and you can't get money from a corpse. Besides, he's got another way of keeping them in line.'

'What's that?'

She shrugged. 'You can usually tell one of Tony's girls. Like as not she'll have a scar on her cheek, just a nick.' She touched her own with a fingertip, and Billy recalled the mark he'd seen on Juanita de Castro's face. 'That's what he does to them if they make trouble, or he thinks they're being lazy. Not enough to ruin their looks, just enough to make them think how bad it could be if he really got to work on them. Dago bastard,' she added, for good measure, causing Billy to blink once more.

'Is that it, then, Lil?' Lofty caught Billy's eye and winked.

'Not quite.' She turned to him. 'I've just heard about a bloke who may have been looking for Florrie.'

'Oh, yes—?' Cook's tone sharpened.

'He was in the Three Stars the other day. Said he was trying to find a red-headed French tart. Didn't know her name, but thought she had a pitch somewhere up near Tottenham Court Road tube station. He spoke to Ma.'

'The Three Stars is a café the toms use,' Lofty told Billy. 'In Peter Street. It's run by an old girl called Ma Hennessy. Did she get his name?' He put the question to Poole, who shook her head.

'Ma never asked him. She gave me a description, though.

Said he was a skinny bloke with small eyes, like a weasel. She didn't take to him. Reckoned he'd been inside.'

'Why was that?'

'No special reason. But Ma can usually sniff 'em out. He didn't get anything from her. She told him she didn't know who he was talking about: didn't know any red-headed French tarts.'

Lofty clicked his tongue. 'Skinny? Doesn't sound like our man, worst luck. Still, you'd better ask around, Lil. Have a word with some of the other girls. See if they know this bloke.'

'Will do, guv.' She touched her cap.

'And find out if any of them gave him Florrie's address,' Billy added.

Poole turned her blue gaze on him: though her glance remained neutral, Billy had the impression he was being weighed up.

'Her address? Right, guv.'

She turned on her heel and went out, shutting the door behind her.

'Good officer you've got there,' he remarked to Lofty. 'Got her wits about her. She ought to be in plainclothes.'

Cook grunted. 'Don't let Lil hear you say that. She's put in three times for the CID and been turned down. You know how the Met brass feels about the fair sex. Some of them, anyway. The fewer the better. She's been warned to stop bellyaching. Told to put a sock in it. She's not best pleased.'

'Got a mind of her own, has she?' Billy had guessed as much.

'That and more.' Lofty chuckled. 'She's a right tartar when she's roused, our Lil. Bloody good copper, though.'

*

It was seven by the time Billy got back to the Yard, and as he stepped out of his car he could see in the distance, to the south-east, searchlights probing the night sky, illuminating the barrage balloons that floated like giant moths above the darkened city. They were there to hinder the approach of flying bombs, though few believed they were of any use, any more than the ack-ack guns that blazed away furiously whenever the strange craft with their fiery tails appeared in the skies. (Rumour said they had yet to hit one.) And neither were they any defence at all against the V-2s, which descended without warning like thunderclaps and which Londoners had come to fear more than any other weapon used against them. Only a few weeks before, one had landed on a Woolworths in New Cross Road, killing more than 150 people, housewives mostly, and Billy could only thank his lucky stars his own family was safe and living out of range of this new sky-borne peril.

He had spent the last hour at Bow Street police station going over the details of Florrie's murder with Lofty and Grace after the latter had returned from Cable Lane with the news that the forensic squad had completed their examination of the house and had nothing further to report.

'He must have come in and out like a cat,' Grace had commented. 'Didn't leave a mark apart from a few scratches on the locks. And a dead body, of course.'

He had returned just as Cook and Billy were interviewing Florrie's pimp, an unrewarding exercise made more difficult by the Maltese's reluctance to answer any questions except in the presence of his lawyer, whom Lofty had refused to have called.

'Can't you get it into your head? We're not accusing you of anything. We just want a word.'

Dark and dapper, with plastered-down hair and a thin

moustache, Ragusa had stayed mum at first. His eyes, moist and motionless as a lizard's, were fixed in an unblinking stare, and when at last he'd responded it was only to advise them in a heavily accented voice that any attempt to link him with the death of 'this young lady' would result in a charge of harassment being laid against the police. These final words had been overheard by Grace as he'd joined them in the interview room, and they brought a swift response from the irascible detective.

'Harassment? Why, you miserable Maltese insect, you don't know the meaning of the word. Let me tell you something. You can't breathe in this country now without breaking the law. I could step into that sewer you call a club and find half a dozen violations of the emergency regulations without blinking an eyelid. We can have you up in court from now until Christmas, that's next Christmas I'm talking about, and in the meantime we'll arrest every one of your girls any time she sets foot on the street. They can keep you company in the dock. Harassment . . . ? Don't tempt me.'

He had leaned closer, his grin unpleasant.

'Now be a good little pimp and answer Mr Cook's questions. And we'll have no more lip out of you – is that understood?'

Shaken by this verbal assault, Ragusa's tongue had been loosened at last, but to no avail. He had spent the previous evening at his club and had not learned of Florrie's death until that afternoon. As for the incident in which she'd been involved on the night Rosa Nowak had been murdered, he acknowledged having heard about it – it seemed Ackers had reported the matter to him – but he knew no more than that she'd been questioned by the police.

'Did you speak to Florrie about it?' Lofty had asked him.

'Only once. I told her she must do what the police say.'

'Did you think of protecting her?'

'From what?' Ragusa had spread his manicured hands. And then, 'Did you?'

His shaft, though it brought a hiss of anger from Joe Grace's lips, had gone home, at least as far as Billy was concerned, and he acknowledged as much to Sinclair when he knocked on the chief inspector's door and found him still at his desk.

'It never occurred to me she might be in danger, sir. Maybe it should have.'

'So you also feel it's the same man?' Sinclair had listened in silence to Billy's account of the murder scene. 'For what it's worth, John Madden seems to agree with you. I spoke to him earlier. He suggested Florrie might have died because the killer believed she could identify him.'

'Lofty and I had the same thought, sir. And if we don't connect them then we've got two murders with no explanation for either.'

Sinclair grunted. 'Let's not overlook the obvious,' he said. 'She wouldn't be the first streetwalker to end up this way.'

At the back of the chief inspector's mind, Billy surmised, was a notorious case that had occurred in London before the war when a number of girls managed by a Paris gang had been strangled for refusing to hand over their takings.

'That's true, sir. But there's a difference here. Florrie didn't fit that pattern. For one thing her pimp was a Maltese, for another she was valued property. His best girl, Ragusa told us. He's a nasty piece of work. Nicks his tarts' cheeks with a blade if they don't behave. Florrie didn't have a mark on her.'

Sinclair frowned. He was still not satisfied.

'I'd be happier if we had something more solid to go on. A link of some sort. Evidence to show there's a connection between these two crimes.'

'Well, I can't give you that, sir.' Billy shrugged. 'There's no obvious link between them. But there is a common factor.'

'Is there?' Sinclair's tone was deceptively mild. 'I seem to have missed it.'

'It's something Dr Ransom put his finger on. The way these two girls were topped. Cold-blooded doesn't begin to describe it. They were disposed of, simple as that. The evidence points to a certain kind of killer being responsible, and the question then is could there be two of them? We don't think so, Lofty and I. We reckon it's the same man.'

Billy sat back. He'd made his case. It was up to the chief inspector now, and as yet he had given no hint as to how he wanted the investigation to proceed. Nor could any clue be deduced from his manner. Sealed by the blackout blinds fixed in the window, his office had taken on the aspect of a cave and the single lamp set low on his desk that of a fire over which he bent like some tribal shaman, his face unreadable in the shadows. After a minute he stirred and looked up.

'Very well. I'll go along with your judgement. From now on we'll treat these two cases as one.'

Billy breathed a sigh of relief.

'But there'll have to be some changes. This will become a Yard inquiry. Cook can stay on the case, but you'll be in charge. Will that be a problem?'

'Not for us, sir.' Billy smiled. 'We're old pals.'

'Is there anyone else you want?'

'Joe Grace, if he can be spared.'

The chief inspector signalled his assent with a nod.

'Now, you're to keep me informed,' he continued. 'Every day, if you can. That means all developments, no matter how minor. Speaking of which, just where do you propose to start? It seems to me you've precious little to go on.'

'With this fellow who was asking about Florrie a few days ago.' Billy had his answer ready. He felt more relaxed now that the decision had been made. 'At least, we think it was her he was after. He's got to be tracked down.'

Sinclair nodded.

'And there's another line of enquiry we want to follow up. Rosa's murder didn't give us any leads, but it's different this time. Whoever killed Florrie jimmied two locks, and according to Myers it was expert work. It's likely this bloke is a villain, a professional. We're going to have to go through the records in detail.'

'And what will that involve?'

'It's hard to say, sir.' Billy grimaced. 'Up to now we've been concentrating on men with a history of violence towards women. But that could be a mistake. These crimes aren't sexual. But whoever this bloke is he's likely got a record. If we look carefully enough we may find him.'

'And equally you might not. The image of a needle in a haystack springs to mind.' Sinclair scowled. 'And there's another problem. From what the Desmoulins woman said it seems this man's fluent in French, which suggests he may well have been active abroad, which in turn might explain why we've no record of him here. If that's the case we're not likely to find out any more about him till the war ends.'

He sat brooding.

'You realize what you're asking for? It could prove a huge waste of time. I don't want either you or the Bow Street CID tied up doing this, and I can't spare another detective. But if the job's going to be done properly it'll require someone who's familiar with both cases. Someone with a sharp eye, what's more.'

Billy nodded sagely. 'I was thinking the same thing, sir.'

'Oh, you were, were you?' Sinclair eyed him with suspicion. 'You'll be telling me next you've got someone in mind.'

'Well, yes, sir – as a matter of fact I have.'

Billy grinned. He didn't know if he could get away with this, but he was going to try.

'It's a uniformed officer stationed at Bow Street. Could be just the person we need.'

9

'WE KNOW HIS NAME now, sir. It's Alfie Meeks. But so far we haven't been able to lay hands on him.'

'And why is that?' Bennett snapped. He was in a testy mood.

'Because we don't know where he's living. Not at this moment. He's been moving about in the past couple of months. Renting rooms here and there for a week or two.'

The assistant commissioner had been away – off sick with a dose of flu – and Sinclair was devoting a good part of their initial meeting to bringing his superior up to date on the inquiry into the murder of Florrie Desmoulins.

'But for some days now he hasn't been seen in his usual haunts.'

'Which are?'

'An open-air market in Southwark, for one. He's got a stall there, but hasn't appeared lately. The same applies to the café where he usually eats.'

'Are we sure he's still in London?' The assistant commissioner looked sour. 'Come to that, do we know he isn't dead?'

'Yes to both questions, sir. He's been spotted, glimpsed, I should say, but not by a copper, as yet. One of our snouts saw him coming out of the tube station at Chancery Lane yesterday, but by the time Bow Street was alerted Meeks had disappeared. The snout said he seemed to be on his way somewhere; he was in a hurry. By the look of it he's up to something and as soon as we get hold of him we'll find out what it is. And who he's working for.'

'Ah—?' Bennett showed a flicker of interest at last.

'That's only an assumption, but a reasonable one. It's just not conceivable that a character like Meeks could be behaving this way on his own account.'

The chief inspector was giving voice to a judgement made by Billy Styles and Cook after they had learned the identity of the man who, it was clear from the enquiries Bow Street had pressed, had been looking for Florrie Desmoulins and no other.

'He talked to several girls in Soho and described Florrie to them,' Billy had reported. 'He asked first for her address. They wouldn't give it – they never do, to a stranger – but they told him where her pitch was, in Soho Square. That would have been enough. Whoever killed her could have followed her home. It wasn't far, just a short walk down Dean Street.'

Meeks's name had come from another source.

'He was spotted talking to one of the girls by a character called Clive, who has a business supplying them with cosmetics. He's been in trouble with us in the past for black-market dealing and so has Alfie Meeks, and Clive thought he was trying to move in on the trade. Told him to shove off, apparently. Anyway, that's how we got his name.'

Sinclair had already passed on this information to the assistant commissioner, together with a photograph retrieved from police records. It showed a thin, lined face with narrow eyes topped by a receding hairline. According to the details on his arrest form, Meeks was in his mid-forties.

'He's an habitual criminal with a record as long as your arm. But it's all small stuff, petty thieving. He was sent to a borstal for breaking and entering when he was a boy and has been inside four times since then. Twice for receiving stolen goods, once for fraud and once for forging petrol coupons. That was his last stretch: he did two years in the Scrubs and only came out three months ago. What's interesting from our point of view is that he's never engaged in violence. Though that's odd.'

'Why odd?' Bennett's tone remained terse.

'I was thinking of his family background,' Sinclair had replied, pretending not to notice his superior's grumpy mood, whose cause he'd already guessed. 'His father was Jonah Meeks. Deceased, I'm happy to say. There's no reason you should remember him – it's all of thirty years ago now – but he was one of the worst we had to deal with then. A thug with a taste for violence that scared even his own kind: the terror of Bethnal Green in his day. We put him inside twice for assault with intent to do grievous bodily harm, and it was only by the grace of God they weren't murder charges. Alfie's the fruit of his loins, but hardly his father's son – not in that respect at any rate. To judge by his record he hasn't the nerve, which makes his present behaviour all the more peculiar.'

'So you think he's acting for someone else?' Bennett asked now.

'That's what it looks like.'

'Someone who wanted to know the whereabouts of this French girl?'

'And who wasn't prepared to go wandering about Soho inspecting tarts till he found her. A man who apparently doesn't want his face seen and remembered. The same might explain whatever it is Meeks is up to now. He could be running other errands for him. Chancery Lane's a long way from his usual stamping ground. He's an East Ender.'

Bennett remained silent. He'd been sitting half-turned in

his chair, staring out of the window at the sky, which that morning was unseasonably blue.

'Well, this is interesting as far as it goes, I suppose,' he said, after a few moments. 'But what's it got to do with the other girl who was killed? Rosa Nowak? What's your justification for linking these two cases?'

The question was a delicate one and the chief inspector paused to consider his reply.

'I wish I had a better answer, sir. But all I can tell you is I thought long and hard before deciding. It's virtually certain that the man who killed Rosa is the same one Florrie Desmoulins had words with. Now she's dead, and we don't know why: unless we assume that their encounter had something to do with it. We can't prove there's a connection between the two crimes. But the possibility's too strong to be ignored.'

'All right. I'll accept that for now.'

Sinclair barely had time to get over his surprise at the mildness of his superior's response before Bennett had swung round in his chair to face him.

'But I can't say the same for this other step you've taken – and without consulting me, either.'

'I'm not sure I follow you, sir . . .'

'Did it have to be a woman?' Bennett glared at him. 'Were you being deliberately provocative?'

'Good lord, no.' The chief inspector contrived to look shocked.

'I ask, because there are a good many people in this building who won't see it that way.' The assistant commissioner shook a warning finger. 'Why on earth is a WPC being dragged into this? That's what they'll say. And they'll have a point.' He shook his head. 'I'm aware of your feelings about women in the force, Angus. As a matter of fact, I share them. But this is a question that won't be tackled properly until the war is over, if then. For the present it's understood that their role is to handle domestic disputes in the main and to deal with prostitutes. Apart from traffic duties, that is. I hate to say it, but they've no place in an investigation of this kind.'

'I'm aware of that, sir. But it's a special case.'

'Is it?' Bennett's tone was disbelieving. 'You say you need this young woman to go through the records. Is that really so important? So urgent?'

'I believe it is.' Sinclair spoke firmly. He was not surprised to find his decision challenged and had come prepared to defend it. 'Even though we think this man we're seeking is implicated in both murders, we've absolutely no idea who he is, or even what kind of a criminal he might be. Neither of these assaults was sexual in nature. So what was his motive? This applies particularly to Rosa Nowak's killing. One place we can look for an answer is the records. But it won't be obvious, otherwise we'd be aware of it already. It'll take fine combing, and that means giving someone the sole job of going through files, possibly stretching back years.'

Bennett frowned. 'All right, let's say I accept that for now. But even taking it for granted, isn't this a job for the CID? For a detective?'

'In normal times, yes. But we simply haven't the man-power any longer. I've already assigned three detectives to the case and I'm reluctant to add another, particularly one who'll be trapped in what's essentially a clerk's job. A clerk with a very sharp eye, mind you.'

'But why a WPC?' Bennett remained unconvinced. 'And why from Bow Street? This is a question that's bound to be asked, Angus. Why not someone from the Yard? We've more than enough uniformed officers of our own, if that's what you were looking for.'

'Ah, well, that's the crux of it, sir.' Sinclair nodded wisely. 'I wanted someone who was familiar with the case, and as it happens Poole was the first officer at the scene in Bloomsbury when Miss Nowak's body was discovered. She was also instrumental in identifying Meeks. Cook recommended her to Styles, who's been equally impressed by her. They say she's alert, intelligent and persevering. All qualities I associate with good police work. And she'll know what we're looking for – that's the key point. I felt she was the obvious choice.'

'Well, if you insist . . .' Weary of the argument, Bennett yielded finally. 'But don't imagine you've heard the last of it. The commissioner will require an explanation. Can I at least assure him this is not some attempt on your part to put one over on him?'

'Perish the thought, sir.' The chief inspector chuckled. 'You can tell him that in all honesty the sex of the officer in question had no bearing on my judgement. I have only one standard in these situations.'

'And what, pray, is that?'

'Why, to pick the best man for the job.'

'Very droll. I only hope the commissioner shares your sense of humour.'

Bennett sat back in his chair and watched as Sinclair gathered his papers into a folder, preparing to leave. He studied his colleague's face.

'This case bothers you, doesn't it?' he said.

The chief inspector glanced up, surprised. 'Yes, it does,' he replied after a moment.

'Why?'

Sinclair gave some thought to his answer.

'Well, mainly because we're in the dark, I suppose, and that's rare,' he replied, finally. 'Crime and mystery don't go together nearly as often as authors would have us believe. Usually we've got a good idea of the whys and wherefores of a murder and can even make an educated guess as to the likely perpetrator. But that doesn't apply here at all, and it's disturbing. Something else, too . . .' His brow darkened.

'Yes . . . ?'

'You'd think two murders were enough, but I've a nasty suspicion we've only scratched the surface so far. That there's more to come. I feel like the skipper of the *Titanic*: I can see the tip of the iceberg all right. But it's what's hidden underneath the water that worries me.'

Bennett grunted. 'He didn't see it, actually. As I recall, he was asleep.'

'Well, there you are.' Chuckling, the chief inspector picked up his file. 'Still, I don't want to sound too pessimistic.' He paused at the door. 'We may well be able to clear this up quicker than I thought. It all depends on what Alfie Meeks has to tell us, and it won't take long to find him. A matter of hours, I would guess.'

His words proved to be prophetic. Returning to his own office, he found Billy Styles waiting for him with fresh news.

'We're on to him, sir. Meeks. Cook's just had a call from Wapping police station. He was spotted in a pub on the river called the White Boar last night.'

'Last night?' Sinclair fumed. 'That's no good to us. Where's he now? That's what we want to know.'

'I couldn't say for sure, sir.' Billy grinned. 'But I can tell you where he'll be this evening. He's reserved a room at the back of the pub for a private party.'

'A *what?*'

'A meet of some kind. Must be. That's what the landlord keeps it for. He's an old lag called Jewell. We put him away twice for burglary before he went straight. If he ever did. The pub's well known to the Wapping police. They keep an eye on it through a cellar-man Jewell employs. Another ex-convict called Barrow. He's one of their snouts. Knows Meeks by sight. He said Alfie fixed to rent the room and paid Jewell a tenner in advance.'

'A tenner, you say? I wonder where that came from.' Sinclair sat down at his desk.

'Not out of Alfie Meeks's pocket, that's for certain. We may have struck lucky, sir. Our bloke could be there this evening.'

'And who else besides, I wonder.' Sinclair fingered an earlobe. 'This is a strange business, and it doesn't seem to be getting any clearer.'

He was distracted by a faint creak that came from a small room adjoining his. Little more than a cubbyhole, it was separated from his office by a glassed partition.

'What is it, Constable?' he barked.

In response, the door opened and Lily Poole appeared, blushing.

'You weren't eavesdropping, I hope.'

'Sir—?' Her cheeks turned a brighter shade of red.

Sinclair regarded her with a flinty expression. Billy watched. He'd warned the young policewoman not to take any liberties in her new assignment.

'This is a feather in your cap,' he'd told her when she'd reported to him the day before, ready to be introduced to the chief inspector. 'But don't let it go to your head. Mr Sinclair will oversee your work, and I'm warning you now he's a

hard man to please. Old school, too. Know what that means?'
Poole had shaken her head. 'It means you speak when you're
spoken to, not before. And whatever you do, don't go calling
him "guv".' Billy thought he'd better set her straight on that
point. 'He's "sir" to you, and don't you forget it.'

'Well, what is it, Constable?'

Sinclair's tone was sharp and Billy remembered from his
own experience – from the time he had worked with Madden
– how disconcerting he had found it. Many months had
passed before he had realized, in retrospect, that the chief
inspector had been testing him. Seeing whether he could take
criticism and harsh treatment and still function. Not buckle
under pressure.

'Sir . . . sir, you told me when I started that if I had any
ideas I should come to you.'

Lily Poole, in a crisp white blouse and blue skirt, stood to
attention like a soldier on parade.

'That's perfectly true.' Sinclair's gaze was expressionless.

'Well, sir, I've got one . . .'

The chief inspector regarded her in silence. Watching,
Billy saw the young woman's neck muscles twitch in a
nervous spasm. But her blue eyes held steady.

'Very well. Let's hear it.'

Poole swallowed. 'This idea of Meeks working for someone else, maybe even the bloke who topped those girls . . .'

'Yes . . . ?' Sinclair kept his eyes on her.

'Couldn't he be someone he came across in prison? In the
Scrubs? A real villain. Someone he might have met up with
afterwards . . . ?'

She broke off, unsure what effect her words were having.

The chief inspector made no reply. Instead, he shifted his
gaze to Billy, who was grinning now.

'Well, couldn't we find out, sir?' Her strong jaw had set in a dogged look. 'The warders would know. Who did he mix with inside? Did he have any special friends?'

'That's a good idea, Constable,' Sinclair responded at last. 'But as it happens, Inspector Styles has already thought of it. I'm expecting to hear from the prison governor today. He'll have a list of names you can check against the records.'

Her face fell.

'But don't be discouraged. You were right to bring it up.'

He nodded, dismissing her, but she stayed where she was, standing in front of his desk.

'Sir . . . about this meet at the pub this evening . . .'

'So you were eavesdropping?' His gaze narrowed.

'No, sir, I just happened to hear . . .'

'Take care, Constable. Don't play the innocent with me.'

Lily Poole paled.

'What about this meeting?' he snapped.

The young woman swallowed. 'I was wondering, sir, if I could . . . if I might . . .'

'You'd like to be there? Is that what you're saying?'

'Yes, sir.' She nodded her blonde head eagerly.

'Not a snowball's chance in hell.' The chief inspector's scowl was ferocious. 'Now get back to work.'

Poole's brow darkened. For an agonizing moment it appeared to Billy that she was about to answer back, and he feared the worst. But then, as though thinking better of it, she made a smart about-turn and went out, shutting the door behind her.

'Well, well . . .'

His scowl banished, Sinclair observed her departure with a smile. He seemed to have enjoyed their exchange. He turned to Billy.

'Right, Inspector, what's your plan?'

'I'm going to pick up Cook at Bow Street now and we're going down to Wapping to have a look at this pub.'

'You're not going to speak to the landlord, are you? This man Jewell?'

'Oh, no, sir. We don't want to tip him off,' Billy reassured him. 'In fact, we won't show our faces inside in case we're recognized. We just want to have a look at the place, get the lie of the land. Once this meeting's under way we'll move in. We'll detain whoever's there on suspicion, and if our bloke's among them, so much the better.'

'What time will this be?'

'We don't know that. But we'll be there when the pub opens, out of sight. It shouldn't be hard. The blackout'll help.'

'What about men? Have you got enough?'

Billy nodded. 'We'll have Joe Grace with us and Wapping are going to supply a couple of detectives and as many uniforms as we need.'

'Good . . . good.'

The expression on Sinclair's face was one Billy couldn't recall having seen there before, and if he hadn't known him better would have termed it wistful. He realized that the chief inspector was probably wishing he could be with them. Word at the Yard was that Bennett had him well tethered now. He wasn't supposed to involve himself actively in investigations, or so it was rumoured.

'Just so you know, I'll be working late this evening.' Sinclair settled himself at his desk. 'You're to ring me as soon as it's over. Here or at home.'

Billy buttoned his coat.

'And Inspector . . .' Sinclair looked up. 'Take care, all of you. Remember – you're dealing with a killer.'

10

Joe Grace came up the steel ladder panting, blowing out plumes of frosty breath.

'Two blokes, one older than the other and well-dressed. Pruitt said he had a silk scarf. Carrying a briefcase. The other's short and squat. Swarthy. Pruitt reckons he had something under his coat.'

'Something?' Billy asked.

'Something he was trying to keep hidden.'

Grace hauled himself up the last steps of the ladder and joined Billy and Lofty Cook, who were waiting with the senior of two detective constables supplied by Wapping in the ruins of what had once been a warehouse overlooking the Thames. From where they were they could see one side of the White Boar across a narrow lane that led down to the river from a flight of stone steps, but not the front of the building where the entrance was; nor the door through which Alfie Meeks and whoever else was attending the gathering would enter. That was on the other side of the pub.

'No sign of Meeks yet. Pruitt's sure. Only these two blokes. But they went in the side door all right.'

Grace took a packet of Woodbines out of his coat pocket and offered them around. Cook accepted a cigarette; Billy and the Wapping detective – his name was Hornsby – shook their heads. A match flared in the darkness. Billy looked at his watch. It was coming up for eight o'clock. They'd been there for more than three hours. Freezing their knackers off, as Joe Grace had picturesquely put it. Unable to position themselves where they could watch for the arrival of Meeks and whoever came with him, they were forced to rely on a signal from Pruitt, the second of the Wapping plainclothes men and only a recent appointee to the CID. Nevertheless, it was him Billy had chosen for the job.

'I'm counting on no one knowing his face,' he'd told Lofty after hearing that Pruitt, a uniformed officer until only six months before, had been transferred from Ealing. The young detective was presently hanging around a vendor who was selling roasted chestnuts in a paved area between the pub and the river bank, acting as though he was expecting to be joined there, by his girlfriend perhaps, checking his watch and clicking his tongue with impatience (at least Billy hoped so), meantime keeping an eye on an even narrower alley that led to a door on the far side of the building not used by the patrons. According to Wapping's informant, Barrow, the cellar-man, it was through this door that anyone using the back room would enter. He'd explained the layout to Billy and Cook when they had visited the scene with Hornsby earlier that afternoon.

'You come in and there's a short passage with a door off it to the bar and another at the end that leads to the back room.' A skinny, balding man, with a nervous tic, Barrow had slipped away during his lunch break to meet them in the ruined warehouse which Billy had already decided would be their observation post that evening. 'Anyone using the room comes in there. That way they don't have to pass through the bar.' Unhappy in their company, he'd paused only long enough to tell them they wouldn't be seeing him later. 'I've got a job to do, and anyway I'm not sticking my neck out any further, not for you lot.'

The problem of how to keep watch on the side door had

occupied Billy for the rest of the afternoon. To post even a single man in plainclothes anywhere near it, with no good reason for being there, was bound to arouse suspicion, and by the time his forces assembled in the early evening, the best solution he'd been able to come up with was to have each of them slip out of the warehouse in turn and walk past the pub upstream for a short way and around a bend that would take them out of sight, before turning and retracing their steps. This route took them past the alley and also covered the approach to it from upstream, where the walkway continued for fifty yards or so, ending at another set of steps. After some thought Billy had posted two uniformed officers supplied by Wapping in the street above with orders to remain there, out of sight, unless they heard the blast of a police whistle. In which event they were to descend the steps and make their way to the White Boar as quickly as possible, detaining anyone they ran into on the way who might be seeking to leave the scene.

This arrangement had been in effect for more than two hours, with the detectives taking it in turn to walk up and down the riverside, before the chestnut seller had appeared, hauling his brazier and other equipment down from the street. He'd had to make two trips, but the effort appeared to be worth it since he was soon doing brisk business with the pub's patrons, both arriving and leaving, as well as other passers-by, and seeing this Billy had dispatched Pruitt to take up his post there. He'd had orders to signal them by removing his hat if anyone entered the pub by the side door. Should he recognize Meeks he was to run his fingers through his hair. He'd given the first of these signals a few minutes earlier and Grace had gone down to investigate.

'What now?' Lofty asked.

'We wait,' Billy said. 'I'm not going in till I'm sure Alfie's there.'

'And whoever's with him?'

Billy shrugged. 'We can but hope.'

He stamped his feet. His toes had gone numb and the rest of him felt sluggish, too, his limbs dulled by lack of movement in the near-freezing air. At least there was no wind that night, which was lucky, since the warehouse – what was left of it – offered little protection from the elements. It wasn't only the roof that had been demolished but the floors above them, and while sections of the walls remained here and there, they offered little more than cover for the detectives who were huddled together in the shadow of one of the larger bits left standing, unable to move about freely since the floor on which they stood was an unstable surface riddled with holes and broken masonry. The port of London had been one of the Jerries' main targets during the Blitz and the whole area had taken a pasting. How the White Boar itself had escaped destruction was a mystery, since the buildings on either side were in ruins. But it didn't seem to have suffered from its isolation, judging by the steady stream of customers arriving. Although the detectives couldn't see in – the window facing the warehouse was covered with a blackout blind – they could hear the babble of voices coming from inside and the noise had mounted steadily as the evening wore on.

'It's always had a name,' Hornsby had told him. He and Billy hadn't worked together before, but they were acquainted. 'Always been a thieves' pub, but the locals use it too, and that doesn't bother Stan Jewell. Good for camouflage. More than one job's been set up there, I can tell you. If that back room had ears . . .'

Billy yawned. He was growing sleepy and he moved a few steps away, to the corner of the warehouse, so as to flex his knees, which were starting to stiffen. No trace of a wall remained there and he was able to gaze out over the river, which in peacetime would have mirrored the lights on both banks but now reflected only the faint glimmer of a new moon. The sky was clear – the day had been sunny – but there was bad weather on the way according to a long-range forecast he had heard on the wireless that morning. A depression was moving in from the Atlantic and snow was predicted for Christmas, now little more than a fortnight away.

It was news that might once have brought cheer to the population, but that year Billy sensed little joy in those around him at the approach of the festive season. The war had gone on too long. People were worn out. Only that morning, along with the news of the weather, had come a report of a new German offensive in a region called the Ardennes, in Belgium. It was clear that the fighting was far from over and normal life still a long way off. He himself had not seen his family for more than a day or two at a time in over three months, and he wondered whether they would even manage to spend Christmas together. Although the chances of him getting any leave looked remote, he was reluctant to bring Elsie and the kids down to London. The fear of flying bombs still loomed large in his mind.

Just then, like a ghostly echo to his thoughts, he heard the faint wail of a siren and a second later a searchlight pierced the sky downriver, in the direction of Woolwich. Then another, and another, lending an eerie beauty to the velvety darkness.

'What odds it's another false alarm?'

Joe Grace was at his shoulder, a cigarette glowing at his lips.

'We had three the other night. The wife was going up and down from the bedroom to the basement like a yo-yo.'

Billy grunted. Since the Luftwaffe had stopped coming over it was only the V-1s that put the capital's defences on alert – the V-2s descended from a great height and without warning – and the number of their attacks had declined in recent weeks. It was reported that the batteries that fired them had been driven out of France. But rumour also said the Jerries were now launching the unmanned craft from planes, and Londoners remained nervous and on edge.

'Billy!'

Lofty Cook's urgent call brought their heads round.

The Bow Street inspector was pointing down, towards the front of the pub. Billy looked that way and saw that Pruitt had taken off his hat. He was running his fingers through his cropped fair hair.

'Right! Let's move.'

The only way down was by a steel ladder that went to the warehouse basement. Cook led the way, stepping backwards. Billy followed. A doorway at the foot of the ladder gave on to a flight of steps that ascended to the cobbled lane beside the pub. In no time the three detectives had joined their colleague by the charcoal brazier where the air, warmer by a few degrees, was rich with the smell of roasting nuts.

'It was Meeks, all right, sir,' Pruitt murmured to Billy as they came up. Erect and square-shouldered, he still had something of the beat bobby about him. 'I recognized him from his photo. He was with another bloke. They came that way.' He gestured upstream.

'What did he look like?' Billy eyed the alleyway. 'The other man?'

'Couldn't make out his face. He had his coat collar turned

up and his hat pulled down. They went straight in. Didn't hang about.'

Billy glanced at Cook, who was at his elbow.

'We could go in ourselves now, or we could wait, see who else might be coming. What do you think, Lofty?'

Cook pursed his lips, considering. Beside him, Joe Grace had turned his gaze away from the pub and was staring into the darkness downriver. Billy followed the direction of his glance and saw the night sky lit up, not only by searchlights now but by the flash of anti-aircraft shells exploding. It seemed they were too far off to be heard, but then he caught the faint pop-pop sound of the guns firing. The sirens continued to wail in the distance.

'Why not wait?' Lofty said. 'See what develops. This is the only way out.'

'Joe?'

Grace shook his head. 'I say go in now. We're sticking out like sore thumbs standing around here.' He caught the chestnut vendor's eye: the man, bundled up in a coat and balaclava, was cocking an ear to their murmured conversation. 'What's your problem, sunshine?' His smile was unfriendly and the man looked away quickly.

Grace hawked and spat.

'The thing is, guv –' he spoke to Billy – 'if we wait for them to come out, one or two may make a run for it and we might not catch 'em all. In that back room they're cornered. Rats in a trap.'

Billy thought for a moment longer, then nodded. 'We'll move in now. We'll detain them on suspicion.'

'Suspicion of what?' Grinning, Grace threw his cigarette into the river.

'Conspiracy to commit a crime. Or anything else that

takes your fancy. We can sort it out at the station.' He turned
to the two Wapping detectives. 'The three of us will go in –
it's our case. You stay out in the alley, by the door. If any of
them makes a break for it, nab him. Have you got a whistle?'
he asked Hornsby.

The detective nodded.

'If things look like they're getting out of hand, give a blast
and those bobbies will come running.'

He paused for a moment, looking at the circle of faces
around him.

'I don't want to be an alarmist, but watch yourselves,
specially with this pal of Meeks's. We don't know how
dangerous he might be. Stay on your toes.'

While he was speaking a piano had struck up inside the
pub and it was soon joined by a number of voices. The song
was 'Run, Rabbit, Run' and Joe Grace could only shake his
head in disbelief.

'A bunch of villains having a sing-song? What next . . . ?'

His words were lost in the sudden wail of a siren. Coming
from close by, the long keening note rose swiftly in pitch and
volume until the air around them throbbed with its urgent
clamour. The singing inside the pub stopped; the piano, too,
fell silent. As one they looked downriver. It was Billy who
spotted it first.

'There—!' He pointed.

'Crikey!' The whispered word came from Grace's lips.

Suspended above the city, a thumb of bright orange flame
glowed in the night sky. It appeared to hover motionless,
but after a few moments they saw it was coming nearer,
the stationary effect due to the lack of any solid background
against which to gauge its movement. As they stood there,
transfixed by the sight, the siren was cut off – the sudden loss

of volume hinted at an electrical flaw – and in the silence that followed they heard the familiar stuttering drone of the flying bomb's engine.

'Coming our way, do you reckon?' It was Hornsby who put the question.

'We'll soon know,' Grace muttered.

The lottery was understood by all. Even the chestnut vendor stood riveted, his eyes fixed on the approaching craft. It was a question of when the doodlebug's motor cut out: that would determine where it would fall.

The flame of its engine had grown brighter and it seemed to Billy it would pass over them, but then, all at once, as though a switch had been pushed, the fiery glow in the sky went out. There was a pause. The motor coughed ... once ... twice ... and went silent.

'Down!' he yelled. 'Get down.'

Dropping to his hands and knees, he was about to throw himself flat on the stone pavement when he saw that the vendor was still staring at the sky, open-mouthed. Reaching up, he grabbed the man's arm and pulled him to the ground where his four colleagues were already spread out on their stomachs, faces pressed to the stone.

The hush was unearthly now. To Billy it seemed that the whole world was holding its breath.

But the next sound he heard was not the explosion he was expecting. It was a single gunshot, muffled, but unmistakable: then two more in rapid succession.

'Christ Almighty!'

Joe Grace reared up from the ground, Lofty with him.

'Get down!' Billy yelled again, and at that moment he felt the ground beneath him shudder as the air was rent by an ear-splitting explosion followed at once by a blast of hot air that swept across the open pavement where they were lying.

In its wake came a shower of stones and broken brick enveloped in a cloud of smoke and dust that swirled about them, filling the air and blinding them. Covering his head and neck with his arms, Billy waited till the rain of debris had ended, then looked up. To his right, in the middle of the warehouse, angry red flames burned in the midst of a black cloud that was ascending through the open roof. In front of him, the pub doors had been flung open. Although the smoke was still thick, Billy could make out the figures of two men who had come staggering out, one of them holding a bloody handkerchief to his head. Beside him, on the ground, Hornsby groaned.

'Jack . . . ?' Billy lifted his head to peer at him. There was a gash on Hornsby's neck that was bleeding freely. 'Hold still,' he said.

Cook's face appeared like a ghost's in the billowing smoke. 'Did you hear those shots?' he gasped.

'Yes . . . three.'

'No, the others . . . three more.'

'What—?'

Billy looked up. He'd bent over Hornsby to examine the wound in his neck, which didn't seem too bad. A nasty gash was all.

'Right after the bomb went off. Joe heard them, too.'

Grace, on the other side of Cook, was already on his feet. He was batting his hat against his leg, knocking the dust out of it.

'We'd better get in there, guv.'

Billy clambered to his feet. He saw the backs of his hands were bleeding from the rubble that had come down on them. 'Pruitt . . . where's Pruitt?'

'Here, sir.'

The young constable was bare-headed. The sight of his

cropped hair made Billy realize his own hat had gone missing in the blast.

'Stay here with Hornsby. See to him.'

He blinked at the chestnut vendor beside him. The man was sitting up. He seemed unhurt. There was no sign of his brazier and pan.

'Three more shots, you say . . . ?' He struggled to get a grip on his scrambled wits. 'Come on, then. Let's go.'

The smoke had thinned and a stream of people, a few in uniform, but most in civilian dress, was issuing from the pub's doors. Though there was blood to be seen on faces and hands here and there, they didn't look to be too badly hurt. Just shaken up. Billy saw Grace was ahead of them, making for the alley at the side.

'Sir . . . sir!'

Two bobbies had appeared as if from nowhere, out of breath and panting. Billy recognized their faces. They were the men he'd posted up in the street. He realized they must have run down when they'd heard the bomb go off. He looked about him. There was quite a crowd in front of the pub now. One or two had sat down on the paving stones; they were shaking their heads, probably surprised to find themselves still alive, he thought. Then he noticed that others were drifting off, leaving the site.

'Did anyone go by you?' he asked the constables. 'When you came down?'

'Sir . . . ?' The older of the two answered him. 'I'm not sure, sir. We couldn't see, not with all that smoke.'

'Never mind. Wait here. Come if we call.' Billy looked for Grace and Lofty, but they'd vanished: gone inside. He started down the alley himself and came to the door, which was open. As he moved to enter it, Lofty Cook's tall figure materialized out of the dust-laden gloom inside.

'Jesus. Billy . . . ! You'd better come and see.'

Lofty's eyes were wide, his face pale. Without saying more he turned and led the way back down the unlit passage to the door at the end, which was open and where there was a light burning. As they went in he moved to one side, giving Billy a view of the interior, where the bodies of two men were sprawled on the floor close to a table in the centre of the room. Joe Grace was on his haunches beside them.

'We've a couple over here, guv.' His eyes seemed unnaturally bright. 'Old friends, these are. But guess who that is . . .'

He pointed and Billy saw a third body propped against the blood-spattered wall near the door, head askew, eyes empty and staring. The narrow features looked familiar.

'It looks like Alfie Meeks,' he said.

'It's him, all right.' Grace rose to his feet. He caught Billy's eye and grinned. 'Bastard made a clean sweep. He topped 'em all.'

'Solly Silverman, did you say? Well I never.'

Sinclair bent down to look at the body, which was that of a man in late middle age whose forehead, lightly coated with dust, bore the blackened circular mark of a bullet fired at close range. Silver-haired and distinguished-looking, he was dressed in an expensive woollen coat of prewar cut belted in front, and the chief inspector had to peer closely before he could make out the bloodstained patch in the dark material which showed where a second shot had been fired into his chest. A navy blue silk scarf hung loosely about his neck. His face wore a surprised expression.

'When I think of the years I spent trying to put that old villain away . . .'

A second body lay close by, face-down, and the chief

inspector turned to examine the back of the skull, which had been shattered, white bone showing through the mat of close-cut black hair.

'Costa, I take it?' he said to Billy, who nodded.

'You can't see his features too clearly, sir, but it's Benny all right.'

Billy could feel himself starting to sway on his feet and he collected himself quickly. A feeling of exhaustion had descended on him in the past twenty minutes, the after-effects of shock, he reckoned, and he was having to grit his teeth to keep going. He watched as Sinclair bent lower.

'That looks like a shotgun,' the chief inspector remarked, peering under the body.

'It's a sawn-off,' Billy told him. 'Benny usually brought one with him on a buy. Been doing it for years, by all accounts.'

'A buy? So you think that's what this was about?' Sinclair straightened.

'It's only a guess,' Billy admitted. 'But Silverman's a fence, after all, and I can't think what else would have got him out and down here on a cold winter's night. Also, he had a briefcase with him – Pruitt saw it – and it's not here now, so whoever shot him, shot them, must have taken it. If it was a buy, Solly would have brought cash with him. That'd be the drill. And he'd have had Costa with him as a bodyguard.'

Relieved to see Sinclair's nod – he seemed to agree – Billy shook his head to clear it. He'd rung the chief inspector from a telephone in the pub within minutes of their discovery of the three bodies, only to find he'd already left for home, and thereafter had hardly drawn breath as he'd struggled to bring order to the chaos that had soon enveloped the riverside when the rescue services, alerted to the explosion, had begun to pour down the steps on to the narrow embankment.

Firemen trailing hoses had jostled with ambulance crews and air-raid wardens, their passage delayed by the White Boar's customers, who had thronged the terrace, themselves unable to leave the area easily due to the steps being blocked. As it happened, the pub had survived the blast relatively unscathed. The V-1 had come down in the middle of the neighbouring warehouse, rearranging the debris there but causing little other damage. Only one window had been broken, and though it had been blown in with considerable force the combination of taped panes and the blackout blind had cut the amount of flying glass to a minimum. Medical teams who had arrived with the ambulances left on the street above had treated a dozen or so patients, but only two – Hornsby one of them – had been taken to hospital. Firemen had inspected the tiled roof and pronounced it safe. Gradually the crowd on the embankment had thinned.

Meanwhile Cook and Grace had secured the murder site and prepared it for the forensic squad which Billy had called for when he'd telephoned the Yard. With the aid of two lamps borrowed from the rescue services and set up in the corners, the room was lit now like a stage set; it was possible to make out every detail down to the peeling wallpaper and the thin patina of dust that had fallen from the ceiling in the aftermath of the explosion, covering the table and dulling the pools of blood lying on the bare floorboards beside it.

Presently Ransom had arrived, summoned from St Mary's, and Billy had cleared the room so that the pathologist could make his examination undisturbed. In the meantime he'd instructed Grace and Pruitt to interview whatever customers they could find in the hope that one of them might have laid eyes on Alfie Meeks's companion earlier and to question the landlord of the White Boar, Stan Jewell. But the effort had proved fruitless. A good many of Jewell's patrons, aware by now of the police presence, had made themselves scarce, and although some of the others recalled hearing the shots that had preceded the detonation, none had witnessed the arrival of Meeks and his associate. As for the landlord himself, in Grace's words he'd proved, not surprisingly, to be a 'wise monkey'.

'He didn't see who went into the back room with Meeks. Doesn't know what happened there. Says he rents the room for private parties. Private parties . . .' Joe had snorted in derision. 'He even tried to pretend he'd never heard of Silverman, though it's odds on he moved half the stuff he lifted through Solly when he was a second-storey man.'

'What about Meeks?' Billy had asked. 'He's the one who rented the room. Did he know him?'

'He admits they were "acquainted".' Grace curled his lip. 'I could tell Jewell didn't think much of him, though. He all but said he couldn't understand what Alfie was doing there. But he won't help us, that's for certain. Like I say, he's a wise monkey.'

Grace had also had a word with Barrow, but learned nothing from him. The cellar-man had been below broaching a fresh keg of beer when the bomb had gone off.

Feeling the need for a breather, Billy had gone outside at that point, and it was while he was leaning against the stone parapet overlooking the river, smoking a cigarette, that he'd caught sight of a familiar figure advancing briskly, though with a slight limp, along the paved walkway towards him. It was after ten; he hadn't expected to see the chief inspector that night.

'I rang the Yard before I went to bed,' Sinclair informed him. 'It seems you've had a busy evening.' He had looked at Billy closely. 'How are you feeling, Inspector?'

'Oh, I'm all right, sir.' Billy had grinned, though the truth was his legs still felt wobbly. In the few moments he'd had to himself since the explosion he'd found himself thinking about his family: wondering how they would have managed without him. 'We were lucky. It could have been worse. Apart from Hornsby's cut, none of us was hurt.' Seeing the direction of Sinclair's glance, he held up his hand, wrapped in a bloodstained handkerchief. 'It's just a scratch, sir.'

Nevertheless, he'd taken a grip of himself then. There was something he had to tell the chief inspector and there was no point in delaying it.

'I'm sorry, sir, but if I'd had my wits about me we could have nabbed this bloke. He took off right after he'd shot them. Ran along the bank to the steps, I'd guess.' Billy pointed in the direction Sinclair had just come. 'We heard the shots. We should have grabbed him then and there.'

Sinclair had said nothing, but Billy could see he was paying attention.

'The two bobbies I posted up on the street missed him, too. I don't know how that happened, except they were reacting to a buzz bomb coming down, not to a police whistle. They must have thought anyone going by them was trying to get away from the explosion. And then there was the smoke and dust . . . clouds of it. I don't want to lay any blame on them.'

'Nor do I, Inspector,' Sinclair had responded briskly. 'And you're not to hold yourself responsible either. You'd just had a close call. I doubt you were thinking clearly. We're not machines, any of us.'

'I suppose not.' Billy had been reluctant to agree. He still felt he'd come up short. 'But it didn't seem to bother *him*, did it – that bastard? The buzz bomb wasn't part of his plan, but he went about his business just the same. Even took advantage of it, I reckon. He shot them just after the siren had sounded – when they must have been waiting like the rest of us to see what would happen next – and then after-wards, when we were trying to gather our wits, he finished the job. Didn't blink an eyelid.'

'You paint a disturbing picture,' Sinclair had remarked drily.

His words returned to Billy now as he watched him slowly scan the room, his glance eventually coming to rest on the third body – that of Meeks – which was partially hidden by the burly figure of Dr Ransom, who knelt beside it peering closely at a wound in the dead man's temple.

'Chief Inspector . . . !' Sensing Sinclair's gaze on him, the pathologist looked round. 'A little late in the season to be out . with a gun, wouldn't you say, but a good bag nonetheless. It's one corpse after another with you fellows these days. I'm tempted to remind you there's a war on.'

'Thank you, doctor.' Billy could see his chief was not amused. 'In the meantime, perhaps you could tell me some-thing about the wounds?'

'The wounds . . . ? Ransom pursed his lips.

'And spare us your wit this once.'

The pathologist flushed. He peered at Sinclair from beneath his bushy eyebrows. 'Well, they were caused by bullets, which is plain enough. Small calibre. From a pistol or revolver, I'd say. Each man was shot twice. First in the body – in the chest – and then in the head. At least, I assume so.'

'You assume . . . ?' The chief inspector scowled.

'I mean, I assume that was the order in which the shots were fired. The ones to the head were all from close range – the powder burns are visible. It looks as though he put them down with body shots first, then gave them the *coup de grâce.*'

'And what do you deduce from that, doctor?' Sinclair regarded him, head cocked to one side.

'Why, the same as you, I dare say.' Ransom shrugged. 'What was done was quite deliberate. It was an execution, pure and simple.'

11

'Sir, I can't express my concern about this case too strongly. It's clear now that we're dealing not only with an extraordinary situation, but with a very special kind of criminal. Unusual measures are called for; unusual arrangements.'

Sinclair paced the carpet in front of Sir Wilfred Bennett's desk. Detained at the crime scene in Wapping until after midnight, he had arrived at his office that morning later than usual to find a message on his desk saying the assistant commissioner wished to see him at once.

'I'm not trying to "commandeer" this investigation. Styles and his team are doing all that can be done. But there's a degree of complexity here that can't be dealt with by the detectives on the ground, who in any case have enough to occupy them. I can't say yet how far this inquiry will stretch, but there are already strong indications that the answers we're looking for won't be found here. In England. An overall view of the situation is required, and with all due modesty I feel I'm the person best placed to supply it.'

The chief inspector paused, as much to assess how well his argument was going down with his superior as to catch his breath. He had found Bennett in a testy mood, quietly fuming over the fact that he seemed to be the last man at the Yard to have learned about what he was pleased to term 'this massacre in our own back yard'.

'Three men shot dead. Our officers put at risk. Yet if it wasn't for my secretary I'd still be in ignorance of the whole affair. Miss Ellis heard about it in the canteen. I had to ring down to registry for the detectives' report. It seems that no one could take the trouble last night to pick up a telephone and let me know what was going on.'

This last shaft had been aimed at Sinclair, whose attempts at an apology so far had fallen on deaf ears.

'I'm not trying to excuse myself, sir, but when I heard about the flying bomb I rushed over there. I was concerned for our men. I didn't know if any of them had been hurt. By the time I got to Wapping and discovered what had happened it was already too late to ring you. I thought it best to wait until morning when the situation would be clearer.'

'By the time you got to Wapping . . .'

Bennett glared at him. It had not escaped his notice that exposure once more to the raw surroundings of a murder scene seemed to have had an invigorating effect on his old friend and colleague. Despite his long night, the chief inspector's eye was noticeably brighter that morning, his step more lively. In fact, observing the way he continued to pace up and down, Sir Wilfred was tempted to enquire innocently if his gout had yielded to some miracle cure.

'This is precisely the point, Angus. You're effectively my deputy, and it was made quite clear when you took the position that you were not to involve yourself in actual investigations. You were to exercise a purely supervisory role. Now I find you've been in the thick of it. And, as I say, too busy to carry out your primary duty which is to keep me informed at all times.'

The assistant commissioner ended his harangue with a muttered phrase inaudible to his listener and then turned in his swivel chair to stare out of the window. But he was unable to maintain his air of displeasure. Before long curiosity got the better of him and he swung back.

'A special kind of criminal, you say? What do you mean, exactly?'

'I mean a man who doesn't fit into any of the categories we're familiar with. Before last night all we could say about him with any certainty was that he was a cold-blooded killer; now we know he's a thief as well. But he still doesn't match the profile of any criminal we have on record. Not remotely. He seems to have appeared suddenly from nowhere, but that can't be so. He must have a past.'

Bennett grunted. He leaned back in his chair and stared at the ceiling.

'Let me see if I've got it straight ... This whole business began with the murder of that Polish girl – am I right?'

The chief inspector nodded.

'Then there was the French prostitute ... she was his next victim. Or so we assume?'

'Correct.'

'Now you're telling me he's killed three men, one of them a notorious fence, shot them in cold blood, and in all probability stolen a large amount of money?'

'That's the sum of it, sir.'

'Then I have only one question.' Bennett eyed his colleague. 'Are you absolutely certain, beyond any reasonable doubt, that it's the same man?'

Sinclair let out a long sigh. His smile was rueful.

'Until last night, I'm not sure how I would have answered that,' he admitted. 'Starting with the murder of Rosa Nowak, we've had difficulty making any sense of this. But things have changed since we last spoke. Clever as this man is, he seems to have made a mistake and it's given us a lead of sorts, a foothold anyway. You recall the name Alfie Meeks, I'm sure?'

'Certainly.' Bennett nodded. 'He came to your notice because he'd been looking for that French girl. I see he was among last night's victims.' He gestured towards the typed report lying on his desk.

'It's become clear now this man hired Meeks. We believe he was paid to seek out Florrie Desmoulins, for one thing, and to set up last night's meeting for another.'

'You say "clear". But isn't this merely supposition? How can you be so sure?'

Sinclair had paused in his pacing, and before replying he seated himself in a chair in front of Bennett's desk.

'There's been a new development, sir. It has to do with a sum of money that was found in Meeks's pocket. Sixty pounds, to be exact. The bodies weren't searched until quite late, after the pathologist had done with them, which explains why it's not in the report you have.'

'Sixty pounds?' Bennett's eyebrows went up. 'A tidy sum. But why is it significant?'

'Because rightly speaking, it shouldn't have been there. Not in Alfie Meeks's pocket. We already knew from the enquiries we've been making that when he came out of prison three months ago he was flat broke. Since then he's been scratching a living out of a small stall he set up in an open-air market at Southwark. All he sold were cigarettes and the odd bottle of spirits: sixty pounds would have seemed like a fortune to him.'

'And you think it was payment for services rendered?'

'It's hard to imagine where else it could have come from.' Sinclair frowned. 'But you have to put all the pieces together, sir, that's when the picture becomes clear.'

He shifted in his chair.

'Meeks abandons his stall without warning and next thing he turns up in Soho looking for Florrie Desmoulins, whom he doesn't know, incidentally, not even by name. A day or two later Florrie is murdered and when we start searching for Meeks we hear he's been spotted in Holborn, not far from Leather Lane, which is where Solly Silverman had his jeweller's shop. Styles and Grace are there now and I'll wager they'll be able to confirm that Meeks paid a call on Solly not long ago. And since we know for a fact he rented that room at the White Boar it's reasonable to assume he also set up the meeting that took place last night. On instructions. Because whatever else, one thing at least is certain: Meeks wasn't acting on his own account. He was being used. First used, then discarded.'

Bennett had listened with a sombre expression, and when he spoke finally it was with a heavy frown.

'You make a good case, Angus, and I won't quibble with you. What was it you called this man – a special kind of criminal? I can think of some other names that might fit better, and I've no doubt some of them will occur to the popular press once they get hold of this, which will be soon enough. They like nothing better than a break from war news. Let's see . . . how does the Grim Reaper strike you?'

'As only too apt, sir.' Sinclair smiled wanly. 'If there's one common note in all these killings it's the apparent ease with which this man deals with his victims. He seems born to it. In all my years I've never come across a criminal quite like him. Let me give you an example of what he's capable of; you can judge for yourself.'

The chief inspector's smile had vanished while he was speaking; a scowl had taken its place.

'The third man shot last night was Benny Costa. I take it you're familiar with the name?'

'Certainly.' Bennett nodded. 'We put him away twice, didn't we? The last time for assault with a deadly weapon. It should have been attempted murder, but the prosecution felt their case wouldn't hold up.'

'Precisely. He was a dangerous individual: a strong-arm man, one of the few who was ready to use a gun if necessary. Among other things, he was often employed as a bodyguard – we know for a fact that Silverman used him in the past – and his reputation went before him. So long as you had Benny at your side with his sawn-off you had nothing to worry about. That's how the legend went.'

'I remember now. It was always a shotgun.'

'Well, he had it with him last night, Costa did – he was lying on it – and he must have been ready to use it, because when they finally moved the bodies to take them away they found that not only was it loaded, no surprise there, but Benny had it cocked and his finger was on the trigger. He was primed, on his guard, but it didn't do him any good. This man took him down – took *Benny Costa* down – and that tells us something.'

Bennett had been studying the ceiling while he listened. Now he shrugged.

'Well, so much for Costa. But I was surprised to see Silverman's name in the report. I was under the impression he'd retired – from that line of business, at least.'

'So he had, sir. And that's another mystery we'll have to unravel. As far as we know Solly hasn't handled stolen goods for the past five years. The last job he was involved with was that burglary at Staines Manor just before the war: the Countess of Stanmore's jewels. We almost had him then, but a key witness died on us and he got away with it. However, it seemed to have put a scare in him and his name hasn't come up since.'

'So why did Meeks approach *him*? Why not some other fence?'

'I've no idea, and unfortunately it's too late to ask him. But he may simply have been following orders.'

'You mean this man, whoever he is, gave him Silverman's name?'

'It's the likeliest answer, and if that's what happened it would tie in with a theory I have – well, actually it's an idea of Madden's – that this killer may have been active abroad. In Europe. He thinks that whatever prompted this man to kill Rosa Nowak may have occurred sometime in the past.'

'On the Continent. Before she arrived here . . . yes, I get your drift, Angus . . .' Bennett's frown deepened. 'But how does that tie in with Silverman?'

'Ah, well, this is where my theory turns into guesswork, but we know Solly had a partner abroad. It was one of the reasons why we were never able to charge him: he didn't sell any of the stuff he fenced in this country. So if this man does have European connections he might have got hold of Silverman's name that way.'

'Yes, but since he wasn't active any longer – Silverman, I mean – what was he doing in Wapping last night?'

'Again, I can only guess.' Sinclair shrugged. 'But off the top of my head I'd say he was made an offer he couldn't refuse. And since it's Silverman we're talking about, I'll stick my neck out and say it involved sparklers – diamonds most likely. They were always his speciality; and he did have a jeweller's loupe on him.' The chief inspector frowned. 'The trouble is, there's nothing on the current list of stolen gems, nor in the recent past, that fits the bill. Nothing that would get Solly Silverman out of his slippers and down to Wapping on a freezing winter's night. So what was the bait, I wonder – because that's what it was, I'm convinced. This man wanted to lure Solly down there with a large sum of money and he used Alfie Meeks for the purpose.'

'And then killed them both, and Benny Costa into the bargain, to cover his tracks.' Bennett growled. 'You're right,

Angus. You must keep an eye on this. But only from your desk, mind. I don't want to hear again that you've been gadding about.' He wagged an admonishing finger. 'Where do we go from here, then? What's next?'

'That rather depends on what Styles finds out this morning,' Sinclair replied. 'He and Grace will be talking to whoever's in charge at Silverman's shop. Wapping will take care of the crime scene. They'll question the landlord again and see if they can get any names of customers out of him, those we didn't interview last night. Cook's going down to Southwark. We need to find out how this man came to pick on Meeks to do his dirty work, and the market where Alfie had his stall is a good place to start.'

The chief inspector prepared to rise from his chair.

'And what of your fair helper, Angus?'

'My what, sir . . . ?' In the act of getting up, Sinclair checked himself.

'WPC Poole. This building is abuzz with rumours of her presence in your office. Is it a sign of things to come, I am asked.' Bennett's eye had taken on a roguish glint. 'The commissioner's wondering the same, especially since he's the one who lays down policy. He wants a report from you: an explanation of why you have decided to go outside established guidelines on staffing and employ this young woman in a job usually reserved for a member of the CID. In writing, that is.'

'Sir, really . . .' The chief inspector started to protest.

'No, no, Angus. You must put pen to paper.' The assistant commissioner rubbed his hands. 'I look forward to reading the results myself. In the meantime, though, if it's not impolite to ask, just what is she doing for you?'

'A good deal, as it happens.' Nettled by this inquisition, Sinclair spoke sharply. 'Up until yesterday evening she was going through a list supplied by the governor of Wormwood Scrubs, names of felons who were in prison at the same time as Alfie Meeks and with whom he would have come in contact, violent criminals, in case one of them might be the man we're looking for. She spent all day yesterday checking their records.'

'Without success, I imagine, or you would have told me?'

'That's true. But it was a job that had to be done.'

'Excellent. Then I take it she can return to her normal duties now?'

The assistant commissioner wasn't done with his ribbing yet, but Sinclair had regained his poise and he rose with a smile and a shake of his head.

'Not for the present, sir. There's something else I want her to do: it's equally important. As I said earlier, I'm increasingly of the opinion that if we're going to pick up this man's tracks anywhere it will be abroad. I've told Poole to get hold of the International Police Commission files. Since the war began they've been gathering dust in the basement, but I want her to go through them. There's a chance we may discover some trace of him there.'

His instructions to the young policewoman a little earlier had been more precise. Finding her already at her desk when he'd arrived that morning, he had called her into his office. Bennett's summons, brought by hand, lay on his blotter, but he had delayed some minutes to explain exactly what it was he required of her.

'This is an area of policing you're probably not familiar with, though I'm sure you've heard of it. Before the war the commission acted as a clearing house for its members. It enabled them to communicate with one another easily and also kept a register of certain types of offenders, mainly sexual, who had a tendency to move about from one country to another. Unfortunately it was based in Vienna and staffed by Austrian police officers, so the war brought a halt to all cooperation. Nevertheless, we have copious files dating back years, which include routine advisories sent out by the commission to all its members dealing with crimes that might involve more than one country – fraud, for example – but also requesting information about criminals who were being sought. It's these I want you to look at carefully.'

Standing stiffly before his desk, Poole had received her orders in silence, but her eagerness had been palpable and the chief inspector was put in mind of a greyhound trembling in the traps, poised to be off.

'Before you go down to records, though, I want you to read this.'

A copy of the same report Bennett had secured from registry had already been delivered to Sinclair's desk and he handed it to Poole.

'It's an account of the shooting in Wapping last night. Study it carefully. I'm convinced this man we're seeking is an experienced criminal, and it would be strange if he hadn't left his mark elsewhere. It appears he's also a thief, and the presence of a well-known fence at this get-together suggests that jewellery might have been his line. Keep all these factors in mind when you go through the files. Look for similarities.'

At least one of the chief inspector's assumptions was confirmed a little later when Billy Styles with Grace in tow returned from their visit to Solly Silverman's shop in

Holborn. The two detectives had been waiting there when Silverman's sole employee, a middle-aged woman named Mrs Delgado, arrived to open the store.

'She went to pieces when she heard what had happened, sir,' Billy told him. 'It was genuine shock. And when we told her what Solly had been up to in his wicked past she threw another fit. I don't think she had the first idea what sort of bloke he was. Or had been. Mind you, if we're right about him and he's been straight since before the war, that would make sense. She's only worked there for the past two years.'

Their experience the night before had left its mark on both detectives, whose drawn faces showed signs of fatigue and lack of sleep, and Sinclair had Poole bring in an extra chair from next door so that they could sit down and then ordered the young officer to remain while they made their report.

Once she'd collected herself, Billy told him, Silverman's employee had proved to be a good witness with a memory for details. She had confirmed Alfie Meeks's visit four days earlier – he had used his own name – and recalled that he'd asked to see Silverman 'on a matter of business'.

'According to her, Solly used to spend most of the day in his office at the back of the shop. He'd only appear if he was needed. When she told him about Meeks wanting to see him he took a look at Alfie through his peephole and instructed her to get rid of him.'

'Do you think Silverman recognized him?' Sinclair asked.

'I doubt it, sir. Alfie Meeks wasn't in his league: I'd be surprised if their paths ever crossed. But he probably spotted him for what he was and didn't want him on the premises. Anyway, Mrs Delgado went back with the message, but instead of shoving off Alfie produced a small velvet box – the kind you keep a piece of jewellery in – and asked her to show it to Silverman. Said if he still wasn't interested he'd leave. So she did that, went back into the office and gave it to Solly, who told her to wait outside.'

Billy grinned. 'I don't know what was in the box – Mrs Delgado says she didn't look – but whatever it was it made Solly change his mind. He had her send Meeks in and they spent the next twenty minutes together, and when Alfie left, Mrs Delgado said he was looking pleased with himself. Like a cat that had swallowed a canary was how she put it.'

'So . . .' Sinclair sat back in his chair, fingers laced across his stomach. 'It looks as though Meeks had a piece of jewellery to show Solly. Something calculated to capture his interest. But there must have been more to it than that.' He looked for confirmation to Billy, who nodded.

'That's what we thought. Meeks must have been showing him a sample of the goods on offer. Then Grace had an idea . . .' He turned to his colleague, who'd been sitting silent in his chair beside him. 'Go ahead, Joe. Show the chief inspector what you've come up with.'

With seeming reluctance, Grace gathered himself. Never one to seek the approval of others, his harsh manner had antagonized many over the years and promotion had been slow in coming. But none questioned his sharpness, and Billy was among those who had learned to turn a blind eye to those traits of his personality, including a sheer bloody-mindedness, which had made him a burden to many of his superiors.

'It was something I found in Solly's wallet last night, sir.' Grace spoke gruffly. 'It didn't mean much at the time. Just some sort of list with figures and letters. But after what we heard at the shop today it gave me an idea, and Mr Styles and I went by forensic to collect it on our way here.'

He passed a folded sheet of paper across the desk to Sinclair, getting to his feet as he did so.

'We reckon it's a list of jewels. Stones. Diamonds, maybe.'

Grace twisted his head to squint at the paper upside down as the chief inspector unfolded it and Sinclair beckoned him round the desk.

'Show me what you mean,' he said.

'There's a column of numbers –' Grace pointed – 'with ct after each, which must be carats, and then some other stuff, letters that don't make much sense, but might be descriptions of the stones.'

He bent over Sinclair's shoulder as the latter emitted a humming sound, his eye running up and down the neatly penned column.

'Eight, ten, twelve . . . there's one of twenty-five carats at the end of the list. That's a fair-sized stone.' The chief inspector grunted. 'A score in all. If they're good-quality diamonds they'd be worth a pretty penny. So you think this is what brought Solly down to Wapping with his loupe in his pocket?'

'It looks that way, sir,' Grace agreed, with a glance across the desk at Billy, who was sitting back, allowing him his moment of glory. 'Meeks must have given him these details when they met. Solly could have copied them down.'

'No, no . . .' Sinclair tapped the piece of paper which lay flat on his blotter. 'This wasn't penned by Silverman. The ink's old for one thing and the numbers are continental. Do you see that seven – it's crossed? And the ones have a little loop on top. That's not how we make them. The paper's expensive, too . . . prewar, I'd say.' He turned in his chair and held it up to the light. 'I can see a watermark. I'll hang on to this. I've a friend in Bond Street who'll decipher those letters for us. And we'd better let the lab have a look at it, too.'

While he was speaking, Grace had returned to his chair, and the two detectives waited while their superior sat ruminating; gnawing at his lip.

'We're on to something.' Sinclair spoke at last. 'Just what, I'm not sure. Was this man actually in possession of these stones, or was he spinning Solly a line? And how did he get hold of this list?'

'He must have had one stone at least,' Billy suggested. 'The one Meeks showed Solly.'

'One which must have been on this list.' The chief inspector weighed the piece of paper in his hand. 'And that tells us, too, how Solly Silverman was lured down there. If these stones were stolen in Europe they wouldn't necessarily be on the lists we've circulated, and that might have been enough to tempt him back into business.'

His glance fell on Lily Poole, who'd been standing all this time behind the two men, wordless, but with a rapt expression on her face.

'How far have you got in your researches, Constable?' he asked her.

'Up to 1933, sir.'

'Jewel thefts. What about them? Has anything caught your eye?'

'Not really, sir.' Lily Poole frowned. 'Quite a few were reported, but the IPC messages don't say much about them. They just give details of the stuff that was stolen and ask member countries to keep an eye out for it.'

'But those would be pieces of jewellery, wouldn't they? Not individual stones like those on this list?'

Poole nodded.

'No matter. Stick to it. We're looking for a jewel thief all right, but one who may be a little different from the general run. Keep that in mind.'

Not wishing to leave his superior in the dark a second time, Sinclair paid a further call on Bennett in the late afternoon.

'I thought with the weekend nearly on us I'd better bring you up to date, sir,' he said as he took his accustomed seat in front of Sir Wilfred's desk. Outside, the early darkness of winter had already set in and the assistant commissioner's windows, like his own, were blackened by blinds. 'All in all, it hasn't been a bad day. We've made some progress.'

The information acquired that morning at Silverman's jewellery store made up the bulk of the chief inspector's account, but there were other items to relate and he wasted no time in imparting them to his superior.

'The post-mortems have been done. Ransom sent his report over. The bullets he retrieved from the bodies were all thirty-twos, as you might expect. There's no way of telling what make of pistol was used, nor whether it belonged to this man or was acquired locally. The country's awash with unlicensed firearms at present thanks to the war.'

The chief inspector had brought his file with him and leafed through the pages contained in it.

'Styles and Grace collected Mrs Costa at her home in Stepney this afternoon and took her to Paddington to make a formal identification of her husband's body. They were hoping the sight of her Benny lying stiff and cold might loosen her tongue for once – we've questioned her in the past, she's as hard as nails – and they struck lucky. She told them Costa hadn't heard from Solly Silverman in years. Like us, he thought he'd retired. And one other thing. When she saw Benny get out his shotgun she asked him if he was expecting trouble and he said no, not necessarily. But Solly didn't know the man he was dealing with and it would be best not to take chances.'

'The man he was dealing with . . .' Bennett mused on the words. 'He wasn't referring to Alfie Meeks, obviously.'

'Obviously.' Sinclair tugged at an earlobe. 'And that tells us something. There was no prior connection between them. We still don't know how this man got hold of Silverman's name.'

He returned to his file.

'The Wapping police have found a witness who says he got a glimpse of the man who arrived with Meeks at the White Boar last night. He was relieving himself in the alley and saw them go in the side door. He says the man had a moustache, something Florrie Desmoulins didn't mention in her description of him. I'm inclined to believe them both.' Sinclair glanced up. 'It's entirely likely he's done something to alter his appearance since killing those two young women. The more I think about him, the cooler he seems to be. There's no hint of panic in his behaviour: if he's grown a moustache then he knows we're after him. He may even have guessed that we've already connected those two early killings: that we have a description of him. But he's keeping ahead of us. We still have no clue as to his identity.'

The chief inspector closed his file and sat back.

'There's where we stand, sir. All we can do is keep at it. I've issued a statement to the press. You'll see it in the papers tomorrow. It deals with the Wapping shooting only. I've not mentioned the two earlier murders, and until we're sure of the link I intend to leave things that way. Last night's events should be enough to keep them occupied. I'll be at my desk tomorrow and I'll keep you abreast of any new developments.'

'What about Sunday?' Bennett looked at his watch. 'You must have some time off, Angus.'

'Styles has volunteered to remain on duty here.' Sinclair rose. 'I shall be spending the day in Highfield. I want to talk to John Madden again. We're accumulating a lot of information and it's a question now of making sense of it. That was always John's strong point.'

'Let me know what comes of it.' The assistant commissioner began to tidy his desk. 'Oh, by the way –' he glanced up – 'I can't help but notice that you've been silent on the subject of the International Police Commission records. Am I to take it this initiative of yours has drawn another blank?'

'Not at all, sir.' The chief inspector smiled serenely. He'd been waiting for the question. 'Constable Poole is still pursuing her task with commendable energy.'

In fact, he had left the young policewoman seemingly prepared to stay at her desk all night and had felt obliged to put a halt to her labours and order her home. In the course of the day she had made three separate expeditions to the record depository in the basement, returning on the first two occasions weighed down with the dusty files clutched in her arms and on the third wheeling a tea trolley, heavily laden, which she'd acquired from the canteen on some pretext.

Apparently unaware of the comments her presence in his office had aroused, she'd treated all she encountered – Sinclair excepted – with a jaunty self-assurance that had brightened the chief inspector's days, particularly when he had seen it extended to one of a group of elderly constables still on the Yard's strength, all of them well past retirement age, to whom the war had given the opportunity to cling like barnacles to their jobs. Congregated in a room a short way down the corridor from his own, they were available in theory for whatever duty might be required of them but in reality dwelt in an idleness that was virtually undisturbed, thanks to their uselessness for all but the most trivial of errands.

One of them, PC Mullet, had long since designated himself as Sinclair's special creature and would bring him his tea and newspapers at the start of the day and respond thereafter, though with reluctance, to any further demands made on his time provided they came from the chief inspector himself. Ordered the previous day to bring a second cup of tea and a plate of biscuits for 'the WPC', he had dragged his heels in silent protest, returning only ten minutes later with the desired articles, to be greeted by a brisk 'Thanks, Alf, but next time no milk' from the young woman, who had hardly looked up from her files. Pausing only to cast an outraged glance at Sinclair, he had departed down the corridor, boots creaking in indignation.

Lost in pleasurable recollection, Sinclair walked down the same passage now, his own heels echoing on the uncarpeted boards, returning to what he thought would be an empty office, but which proved to be still occupied, despite his instructions to the contrary.

'Constable!'

Not entirely displeased to find Lily Poole still at her desk, the chief inspector nevertheless felt it was time to remind the young woman that orders were there to be obeyed. He stood in the doorway frowning.

'I thought I told you to go home.'

'Sir . . . ?'

Bleary-eyed from hours of scanning smudged type, her cheek smeared with carbon, she was slow looking up from the open file in front of her.

'Why are you still here?'

She swallowed. She seemed uncertain how to reply. She glanced down at the folder.

'Sir, I looked at all the jewel thefts reported, but there was nothing, so I started going through other stuff, other crimes . . . murders and so on . . .' She broke off, gnawing at her lip.

'Yes . . . ?' His tone was encouraging.

'Well, I think I've found something, sir . . .'

Sinclair stepped through the doorway into her small office.

'Go on,' he said in a calm voice.

'It was a case in France . . . back in 1937 . . . before the war.' She saw that he was paying close attention and began to speak more confidently. 'A break-in at a house near Paris. There were three people topped. But it was the *way* it happened, *how* they were killed. As soon as I read it I wondered if maybe it was him, our bloke . . .'

'In France, you say. It wasn't in Fontainebleau by any chance?'

She stopped speaking. Her jaw dropped.

'You know about it, sir?'

By way of reply the chief inspector held out his hand for the file. He opened it and studied the contents in silence. The seconds ticked by. Lily Poole stared at him, her eyes wide.

'Well I never . . . !'

Sinclair shook his head in astonishment.

'I'll be blowed!'

He looked up. His gaze met Lily's.

'Well done, Constable,' he said. 'Well done, indeed.'

12

'FOR A GIDDY MOMENT I had visions of the case being resolved at a stroke. I felt like that fighter pilot. I was ready to carry WPC Poole off in triumph on my shoulders and present her to Bennett, wreathed in laurels. But then reason reared its head. It's only a lead, after all. But do you know, I've a sneaking feeling this is our man.'

The chief inspector blew on his fingers. A few seconds before, he and Madden, their gaze drawn upwards by the sound of a low-flying aircraft, had seen a Spitfire speeding by overhead perform a slow victory roll, a manoeuvre greeted by rude hand signals and a round of ironic applause from a group of young officers engaged in a scratch game of football not far from where they were standing in the gardens of Stratton Hall.

'What she'd spotted, my young Artemis, was an advisory sent out by the commission in 1937 in response to a request from the Paris police. It concerned a triple murder that took place at a house in Fontainebleau, not far from the city. As soon as Poole mentioned the case I remembered it. You probably do, too. It made quite a splash at the time. The owner of the house was a wealthy businessman. He and his wife were both killed, as was their fourteen-year-old daughter.'

Sinclair paused while they negotiated a muddy spot in the yew-lined path. On arriving by train from London earlier that morning he had learned they were all to lunch with Lord

Stratton, and it was thanks to Helen that he'd been given this chance to discuss the case with his old colleague. Closeted at that moment with their host, she'd contrived to kill two birds with one stone and use the occasion of their invitation to make an examination of a patient of hers who, now that he was past eighty, had grown increasingly fractious and prone to dismiss any fears she might have for his health as being of little consequence in the eye of eternity. At her suggestion the two men had delayed their arrival at his lordship's apartments, and Sinclair had used the time to acquaint Madden with the details of the Wapping shooting and to tell him about the disturbing new direction the investigation had taken.

'They say the devil is in the details, and fortunately Poole took the trouble to go through this rather lengthy message we received from the IPC carefully. The killer broke in just before midnight when most of the household was asleep – he'd cut the telephone line first – but the police were able to piece together what happened from the position of the bodies as they were found afterwards. The businessman – his name was Lagrange – was strangled in his study; he'd been up working late. His wife had gone to bed earlier but she must have been disturbed, since her body was found on the stairs. It seems she spotted the intruder, perhaps as he was leaving the study, because she screamed and he shot her from below, hitting her in the stomach. The noise brought the Lagranges' daughter out of her room and she, too, was shot, hit in the leg, but able to drag herself a short distance away from the top of the stairs down the passage.'

The chief inspector paused once more. He eyed his companion, who'd been listening in his customary silence, a frown creasing his brow.

'Now bear in mind that Madame Lagrange's scream had

been heard in the servants' quarters at the top of the house – the police determined that later – and was followed by two shots which must have roused them all. But did this man panic? Did he flee? Not a bit of it. He walked calmly up the stairs and put a bullet in the back of Madame Lagrange's head, then did the same to the daughter, who was still trying to drag herself away, as shown by the bloodstains on the carpet.'

The two men had reached the end of the yew alley, where there was a fish pond, and for a few seconds they stood gazing into its weed-choked depths before Sinclair continued.

'By any measure his behaviour was extraordinary – and the resemblance to what happened at Wapping remarkable. But there's more. Lagrange wasn't just strangled; he was garrotted, and according to the police report it was the work of an expert; just what Ransom said about the Desmoulins woman.'

Sinclair stole another glance at his companion.

'Fourteen years old, you say?' Madden was still gazing down, but he caught the chief inspector's nod. 'Why was the report circulated. What were the French after?'

'Initially, any indication that this killer might have been active elsewhere. Later, they were more specific. They were after a particular man, one who'd been sought for years all over Europe and had a score of murders attributed to him.'

'A professional, do you mean?' Madden stared at him.

'That's right. A paid assassin. Highly expert. One you may even have heard of, though he's never been active in this country. Does the name "Marko" ring a bell with you? That's with a "k".'

Madden shook his head.

'The popular newspapers have written him up once or twice. He was said to be a Serb—'

'A Serb?' Madden scowled. 'But our man's British. Florrie Desmoulins was positive on that point.'

'So she was. But that's not the end of the story. Far from it. Bear with me.'

Sinclair paused for a moment as they turned to walk back the way they had come, waiting until they were pacing side by side again before resuming.

'Now do you recall that big fraud case we had before war – it was in 1938 – involving a City firm? Astrid Holdings? There was a French bank mixed up in it and the Sûreté sent one of their men over here to help, a detective called Duval. A first-rate man. It turned out he'd also been in charge of the Fontainebleau investigation, and since he spoke good English I heard all about that, in particular what lay behind the crime. According to Duval it was what they call a "règlement de comptes" over there: a settling of accounts. The businessman, Lagrange, had got mixed up with some shady characters in the Paris underworld and let himself be lured into investing in an opium deal. But at the last moment he pulled out of it and threatened to go the police, which was tantamount to signing his own death warrant. One of the principal figures involved in the deal was a Dutch gangster called Hendrik Bok, who had control of the drugs trade in Holland at that time. He was importing opium from the Far East into Europe via Rotterdam and he saw his business threatened, so he sent a killer to Paris to deal with Lagrange. It was the sort of crime the police usually got nowhere with, Duval told me; their sources of information would dry up. But in this instance the "milieu" had felt that the murder of the daughter went beyond what was regarded as permissible, even in that world, and the police were tipped off as to who had done the killing. The wife and daughter weren't part of the contract, but apparently this man Marko had a reputation for leaving no witnesses behind.

'At that point the French police pulled out all the stops. They began pressing the Dutch police to move against Bok and also set out to discover all they could about this mysterious "Serbian". What they learned was quite extraordinary. I must say I was spellbound listening to Duval.'

The chief inspector shook his head. He pursed his lips in a silent whistle.

'The trail they followed led back to Belgrade, which is where he first came to notice and where he was thought to have committed several murders in the early Twenties: political assassinations, all of them. You'll recall the Balkans were a most unstable area then: it was after the break-up of the Austro-Hungarian Empire. The only name the Yugoslav police were able to provide Paris with was Marko Pilic, but they stressed it was false: the real Pilic had emigrated to America; somehow this man had got hold of his papers. They had no idea who he really was, or where he came from. Now, as it happened, the real Pilic had been a member of the Black Hand in his youth. Remember them – that Serbian secret society that was behind the assassination at Sarajevo? The society was broken up after the war and its leaders executed, but some of the smaller fry escaped and set up in business on their own. Extortion and bank robberies were their staples but they also hired themselves out to do the odd killing, and for a while this man who was calling himself Marko Pilic joined up with them. Eventually the Yugoslav police cornered the gang in Belgrade; there was a gun fight and most of them were killed.'

'But not Marko, obviously.'

'No, he escaped. Perhaps he was tipped off. Anyway he

disappeared after that – at least as far as the Yugoslavs were concerned – and wasn't heard of again until he took up with Hendrik Bok. This would have been in the mid-Twenties, at a time when Bok was engaged in a struggle with other gangs for control of the Rotterdam docks. How they got together isn't known, but soon after Marko was hired, Bok's enemies began turning up dead, and he let it be known he had a killer working for him who had once been a member of the Black Hand. It was a crude piece of psychology – Bok was obviously bent on creating a climate of fear – but that was when the myth about Marko began. No one ever set eyes on him. He wasn't part of the gang Bok had about him; he was invisible, appearing only when needed, and almost invariably disposing of his victims by garrotte, which only added to his legend. After all, it's the true assassin's weapon, isn't it? The wire? Silent; bloodless. And it takes a certain kind of man to use it, wouldn't you say?'

They had retraced their steps up the yew alley and had come to a long terrace flanked by empty borders with a path running parallel to it. At the far end of the terrace the football game was still in progress, and after a moment's pause the two men continued their stroll, taking the path in the opposite direction.

'Of course, once Bok had established his position in Rotterdam he had less need for Marko's services. But by then he must have realized what a valuable asset he'd acquired and in due course he let it be known that his killer was available for hire. It's hard to be certain just how active he was – legend has a way of inflating reality – but over the next few years Marko seems to have employed his talents quite widely. He was sought for murders in several other countries – Austria and Spain among them – though on scant evidence. There's no known photograph of him; only descriptions that more or less fit the one we got from Florrie Desmoulins. He was given to altering his appearance, too. His hair was sometimes longer or shorter and he was glimpsed wearing a beard and spectacles. I mention that because a witness at Wapping said the man who went into the pub with Alfie Meeks had a moustache, which is something Florrie didn't mention.'

'Was there any indication as to his true identity? His real nationality?'

The chief inspector shook his head. 'But based on what we know, he could well be British. Assuming he's our man, he seems to have chosen to sit out the war here. And the fact that we've found no trace of him in our own records might even support that premise. For some reason hired killers, political or otherwise, don't figure much in our way of life. They're more of a Continental phenomenon. Maybe that's why Marko took his skills elsewhere. The one person who might have known where he came from was Bok. But if so, he never let on, and for a good reason. It was to his advantage to keep the fairy story about the Black Hand alive. Bok himself was well known to us, incidentally, by name at least, and not only for his role in the opium trade. He had his finger in a lot of pies – prostitution, extortion, the white slave trade – and something else that might prove significant: the disposal of stolen goods. Since Poole's brainwave I've been wondering if that might not be relevant to this investigation.'

'How so, Angus?' Head down, hands clasped behind his back, Madden kept his naturally longer stride in check, matching it to the other's shorter steps.

'I told you about Solly Silverman and his chequered past. What I didn't mention is that we always suspected he had a European outlet for the stones he fenced – it was why we were never able to charge him. If Bok was his contact then that would help to tie up at least one loose end. It would explain how this Marko figure – if he is our killer – got hold of Solly's name, and why, since Bok could only have given it to him years ago, before the war, he didn't know he'd retired.'

Pausing for breath, Sinclair glanced over at his companion. He was still waiting for some reaction from Madden, whose brow remained knotted in a frown.

'That's the sum of what Duval told me when he was over here, and soon afterwards the war started, since when we've been in the dark. There's been no communication with the Continent: we don't know what's been going on over there. But now that Paris has been liberated we can at least get in touch with the French police again, and I've sent them a message.'

Madden's scowl lifted. He looked at Sinclair in surprise.

'Oh, not by the usual channels. Those aren't functioning yet. I did try to telephone the Sûreté but I was told that the lines were reserved for government use. I had to scratch my head, but I came up with an idea. I asked our colleagues in the Military Police to help. You may not know it but we've had a detachment of them stationed at the Yard throughout the war, and apparently the service has a pouch that goes by air almost daily to their headquarters in Paris. They agreed to deliver my message to the Sûreté. It went yesterday and I marked it for Duval's attention.'

'What exactly are you asking them?'

'Well, for a start if they've any fresh information about Marko. For all we know, he may have been arrested years ago. He may be dead. I don't want to start a search for him over here then find out it's been a wild-goose chase. But I gave them an account of the Wapping shooting, pointing out the similarities to Fontainebleau, and also told them about the gems we think might have been the bait that got Silverman down to that pub. I haven't mentioned this yet, but there was a list of stones in his pocket described in detail as to weight, colour, clarity and cut. Diamonds, according to a contact of mine in Bond Street. He says the gems listed could be worth upwards of £30,000 on today's market. The piece of paper on which the list was written as well as the figures are of European origin. The Paris police may know something about them.'

Sensing his companion was about to speak at last, Sinclair fell silent.

'The Fontainebleau murders were in 1937, you said.' Madden shook his head. 'That's too early.'

'Too early for what?'

'For Rosa to have been there. She didn't arrive in France until the summer of 1939, when her father sent her.' He saw Sinclair's look of bafflement. 'I'm not suggesting she had anything to do with that. I'm just trying to imagine where she might have run into this man. Marko. As far as I know she never went to Holland, so France seems the most likely place. But as I say, the dates don't fit.'

The chief inspector grunted. 'Yes, but wouldn't it be better to concentrate on Wapping for now?' He was surprised by his old colleague's train of thought: after what he had just told him he'd expected him to be looking at the questions raised by the case with a different eye. 'Assuming Marko's our killer, it offers the best chance of tracking him down. We can deal with the question of Rosa's murder later, when we catch up with him. After all, other than the fact that these crimes seem to have been committed by the same man, there's no obvious link between them.'

He paused, seeing the expression on Madden's face.

'Or is there?' he asked.

Madden shrugged. 'It depends on what you mean by a

link. Don't forget, all this began with Rosa's murder. Immediately afterwards this man got in touch with Alfie Meeks. Why? Not simply to locate Florrie Desmoulins, surely. What he really needed him for was to set up the Wapping robbery. Apparently he wanted to lay his hands on a large amount of money in a hurry and was willing to take the risk that entailed. We still don't know why, but whatever the reason was I've a feeling it had something to do with Rosa. It was killing her that got him started.'

The path along which they'd been wandering had come to an end at a ruined folly with a stone bench beside it. Noticing that the chief inspector's limp had got worse, Madden suggested they sit down. At the other end of the terrace the football game had come to an end and the young officers, some of them in their uniforms, others in heavy sweaters and scarves, were moving in a straggling line back towards the house.

'Isn't it strange, though, how all this keeps coming back to Alfie Meeks?' Busy flicking dirt from the seat with his handkerchief, Madden looked up. 'Ever since you mentioned his name I've been wondering how on earth he came to be mixed up in it, and nothing you've told me today makes it any easier to understand. Assuming for a moment that Marko's our man, what's a criminal of his kind doing associating with the likes of Alfie Meeks? Why choose him as his jackal?'

'Him of all people, you mean?' The chief inspector sat down.

'Yes, and how did Alfie come to accept the job?'

'Oh, well, that's easily answered. I told you, he had sixty

pounds in his pocket. It wasn't money he could have earned any other way.'

'Still . . .' Madden pursed his lips. 'It's hard to believe he would have let himself be used so easily. Not unless he and Marko were already acquainted. I know that's unlikely, but have you looked into it?'

'In detail, I assure you.' Sinclair heaved a sigh. 'All the way back to when Meeks was fifteen and was sent to a borstal for breaking and entering. We've checked the names of the people he was banged up with, then and later, but we haven't found one worth following up, never mind a killer of this kind. He was a petty criminal all his life and the people he associated with were just the sort you might imagine. Nobodies like himself.'

Madden acknowledged his words with a grunt.

'Well, that's no surprise, at least. He was only a lad when I knew him, twelve or thirteen, but he was timid even then.'

Sinclair said nothing. Earlier, in the course of their leisurely stroll, he'd been brought up sharply by a mental lapse, the thought of which still irked him. It had entirely escaped his memory that early in his career his old partner had been stationed at Bethnal Green and had known the Meeks family.

'It was when I was a young copper,' Madden had reminded him. 'Still in the uniform branch. The first thing I was told when I got there was to keep an eye out for Jonah Meeks, Alfie's father. He gave us more trouble than the rest of the borough put together. He had a violent streak – he'd been inside twice on assault charges – and we reckoned it was only a matter of time before he went over the edge and killed someone in a fit of rage. I was there when the firemen recovered his body.'

'I remember it all now.' Sinclair had shaken his head in chagrin. 'In fact, correct me if I'm wrong, but wasn't there some question as to how Jonah met his end? A suspicion of foul play?'

'A suspicion, perhaps. But nothing more than that. Jonah had his share of enemies all right, but most of them were too scared to go near him. He was a great hulking brute, strong as an ox, and though he was drunk the night he died it's doubtful anyone would have had the nerve to tackle him. He'd spent the evening in a pub and then set off home, taking a short cut through the yard of an abandoned soap factory. Next morning his body was spotted floating in a cistern with a severe head injury. Blood was found on a stone at the edge of the tank and it was reckoned he tripped and fell on it, then tumbled into the water unconscious, or semi-conscious, and drowned.'

'I take it he wasn't robbed?' Sinclair had found himself silently marvelling at his old friend's tenacious memory, a quality he had always displayed and one that the chief inspector now had cause to envy.

'No, he had money on him, I remember. His wallet was in his pocket. In fact, the only thing missing was his false teeth. He had an upper set. They must have come out when he went into the water.'

'It sounds like an accident. Why was there any doubt?'

'Only because of Jonah himself.' Madden had shrugged. 'When a villain like that meets a violent end there are always questions asked, but there was no real basis for calling it murder. Still, I did wonder once or twice . . .'

'Wonder . . . ?' The chief inspector had been curious.

'Going about later, speaking to people. They're a close-mouthed lot down there, they don't care for the police, but I got the impression there were people around who knew more than they were saying. That was one thing; and the other was they didn't bother to hide their satisfaction: you could almost taste it. No one had a good word for Jonah, and that included his wife, Alfie's mother; stepmother, rather. She didn't even pretend to any regret. Meeks was a brute: he'd made her life hell, by all accounts. Alfie's, too.'

Considering that they'd gone over the matter in such detail earlier, it surprised Sinclair to find his old partner still nagged by the same questions.

'There must be some way of getting to the bottom of this,' Madden insisted now. 'How did their paths cross? Where did Alfie encounter this man? Were they spotted together anywhere before the shooting?'

'Not so far as we know,' Sinclair replied. 'Meeks disappeared without explanation from the market in Southwark where he was working ten days ago. We only found out the other day where he'd been living; it was a room he'd rented in Bermondsey. His landlady said he'd been there for three weeks and was already owing her rent. But then all of a sudden he'd paid up. She said he was acting chipper, full of himself. Told her he wouldn't be staying much longer and implied he was moving on to better things. Obviously he'd met his new employer by then, but why such a nonentity should have been taken on by our man remains a mystery. Even in the short time they were together Alfie managed to make two mistakes that may turn out to be critical in the end. Surely Marko could have found someone more reliable.'

He was interrupted by the sound of a voice calling out their names: looking up, he saw Helen standing at an open window in the house above. She was waving to them.

'She's calling us in,' Madden said. He returned her wave, and they rose from the bench. 'What mistakes?' he asked.

'Well, first there was the trail Alfie left from Soho to the

White Boar via Solly Silverman's shop. That enabled us to tie all these killings together.'

The chief inspector trod gingerly as they set off across the lawn.

'And second was that list of stones. I'd lay odds Meeks was ordered to bring it back with him from Leather Lane and either forgot or was bullied into leaving it with Solly. The irony is, if we do crack this case it'll be largely due to Alfie's slip-ups, and that brings us back to the question you've just asked. How did this man come to pick *him*? Now, if we knew the answer to that . . .'

It was with a feeling of a day well spent that Sinclair boarded the train for London later that afternoon. Not only had he had an opportunity to discuss the investigation with his former colleague, something he set great store by; he had also learned that Madden would be in town the following week.

'There's a problem at Aunt Maud's,' he'd explained. 'Her boiler's giving trouble and Helen's asked me to go up and deal with the problem. She also wants me to cast an eye on Lucy and find out what she's up to. I'll probably have to spend a day or two there, so with any luck we can get together again.'

As so often, the ideas they'd exchanged had given Sinclair a fresh perspective on the problems before him, and even the familiar sense of regret he had felt as he and Madden had ambled around the gardens together had done no more than remind him of the time, now long past, when they had worked together as one.

Nor had he been alone in this exercise in nostalgia. Their luncheon host, Lord Stratton, had been equally affected. Greeting the chief inspector warmly, he'd been moved to recall the circumstances of their first encounter, which had taken place two decades earlier during the murder inquiry that had brought both Sinclair and Madden to Highfield. Albeit with a wry smile.

'Do you know, I can recall those days as if they were yesterday,' he'd remarked on welcoming the chief inspector. 'It's yesterday I have trouble remembering, though my doctor assures me this is nothing to be concerned about.' He caught Helen's eye and smiled. 'A slow erosion of the faculties is a small price to pay for the blessings of old age, she says. Blessings indeed!'

Though a frail figure now, he had lost none of the grace and old-world courtesy that Sinclair recalled from previous encounters, and if the changes which the war had wrought to his way of life weighed on him at all he showed no sign of it, speaking instead of the satisfaction it had given him to see his family seat transformed into a convalescent home for wounded soldiers and airmen.

'I like to watch them through my window,' he had declared at one point. 'Though Lord knows they tear up the lawn with their games. They seem so young to me ... so carefree. One has to remember what they've been through. What they've survived. Somehow it makes my four score years seem trivial by comparison.'

Listening to the old gentleman, Sinclair had been moved to consider his own mortality and to wonder how and where he might spend his last years. It had always been his intention to retire to his native Scotland, where he still had family. But as the time drew nearer he felt a growing reluctance to make the necessary preparations and now, once again, found uncertainty nagging at him as he contemplated this thorny question.

As ever, much of the conversation at lunch had concerned

the war and the depressing news of the latest German counter-attack in the Ardennes that was threatening to extend the conflict still further; and at a time when many had hoped it might be drawing to an end. The matter was naturally of deep concern to both Maddens, who still had no word of their son, or of the whereabouts of his destroyer, and who dreaded a continuation of the dangerous convoy duty on which he was engaged. But it also weighed heavily on Lord Stratton, who had seen neither *his* eldest son and heir, an officer serving on Mountbatten's staff in India, nor his daughter, who was married to a diplomat in Washington, for nearly two years, and was beginning to fear that time was running out for him.

'Medical opinion notwithstanding,' he had declared drily, though with a smile at Helen, 'I feel my days are numbered and would like to have my family around me when I make my adieus.'

Nevertheless, in spite of his own preoccupations, he had not allowed the lunch to end and his guests to depart until he had asked Sinclair about the investigation he was conducting.

'I had no idea who the child was, not until John told me, but I remember how beautifully she played the piano at the concert we had here. What a waste of a young life! As if enough have not been cast away already.'

In response, Sinclair had spoken perhaps too encouragingly of the progress being made in the inquiry. Or so Madden had seemed to feel when they were pacing the platform a little later that afternoon, waiting for the train.

'Don't be too sure you're closing in on him, Angus,' he had cautioned, reverting to the subject that had occupied their morning. The chief inspector had used these same words a little earlier in replying to their host. 'If you're right about the link to that Fontainebleau business – if it really is Marko

– then it's worth remembering he's never been arrested and that can't just be down to luck.'

'He's taken pains to stay out of sight, you mean? And made sure there were never any witnesses to identify him. Yes, I'm aware of that. But the war has changed everything. It's almost impossible for a man to go to ground now. We're all hemmed in by regulations. Identity cards, ration books. They're unavoidable. All we need is a clue to his identity and we'll track him down.'

Madden's shrug had been noncommittal, his closing words all but drowned by the whistle of the approaching train.

'Well, I hope you're right,' he had said. 'But bear in mind he'll be aware of that. And he may have other surprises up his sleeve.'

13

PADDINGTON POLICE STATION was quiet that Sunday evening, and the desk sergeant, an elderly Ulsterman named Paddy McDowell, was dozing quietly on his size elevens, swaying from side to side like a horse in its stable, Lily Poole thought, as she rapped smartly on the counter with her knuckles.

'What ... what ... ?' Paddy woke with a gulp and a splutter. 'Here now ... what do you think you're doing, young lady ... ?'

The glare he fastened on her lasted for only a second or two. Then a broad grin took its place.

'Hello, Lil.' He regarded her with affection. 'Didn't recognize you out of uniform. Not in that get-up.'

'What? This piece of haute couture?'

Lily indicated her coat, a shapeless, dun-coloured garment furnished with narrow lapels and a single pocket. Produced under government regulations designed to save precious material and with the depressing description of 'utility' attached to it, it was an article shunned by many of her sisters, but not by Lily Poole, who cared little for her appearance.

'I'll have you know it's the latest style, Sarge. Fresh from Paris.'

'If you say so,' Paddy grinned. 'You'll be looking for Fred, I dare say. He came in ten minutes ago for his break. Try the canteen.'

He hooked his thumb at the door behind him and watched with a smile as she went by.

'It's good to see you again. You've been missed.'

Lily was pleased to hear him say it, even if the accolade had been hard won. She'd spent her first two years in the force at Paddington before being posted to Bow Street, and with female officers still a rarity in the Met had faced more than her share of hostility, both silent and acknowledged. But she'd won them round at last – or so she liked to think – and when she stepped into the canteen a minute later it was to a muted rumble of greetings and one or two friendly waves.

'There you are, lass.'

Fred Poole rose from a table in the corner where he was sitting with a cup of tea, a pie and his conical helmet parked in a neat line in front of him. Broad-shouldered, and with cropped sandy hair that only now was starting to grey, he'd been a police constable for thirty years. And Lily's Uncle Fred for twenty-five of them.

'Sorry I wasn't home,' he said. Shy of showing his feelings, he slid a hand across the table to press hers. 'I got called in sudden.'

'Aunty Betty told me. Are you short-staffed?' Lily asked.

'That and the usual colds and flu.' Fred brushed the matter aside. 'But I wasn't best pleased since it meant missing you. How've you been, love? We've not seen you for a while, and you know how worried your aunt gets, the way she starts imagining things. "When I think of that young girl all on her own out in the blackout patrolling the streets..."' His imitation of Aunty Betty's anxious voice brought a grin to Lily's lips. 'I tell her, look, any bloke with mischief on his mind runs into our Lil, he'll wish he'd stayed at home.'

Again he reached for her hand and Lily returned the

squeeze he gave it. Fred wasn't just like a dad to her: he was the elder brother of the father she had never known, who'd been killed in the last weeks of the Great War before Lily was even born and whom her mother had mourned for only two years before she herself had died in the great influenza epidemic that had followed. It was Betty and Fred who had raised her and whom Lily loved as much as if they were her true parents. Her earliest memory was of a large blue-uniformed figure bending down from what seemed like a great height to sweep her up in his arms. And she firmly believed it was the sight of Uncle Fred preparing to leave for work each morning, slipping his silver whistle into his pocket and donning his helmet, weighing his heavy truncheon in his hand, that had fixed her heart on following in his footsteps. Even though he'd tried to dissuade her.

'Believe me, love, it's no job for a lass. There are things you don't want to be doing, ever, stuff you don't want to see.'

But that was just what had drawn Lily to the job. Knowing there were things she might never see or know about if she went the way of other girls. The ones she knew, her friends even. All they seemed to care about was clothes and make-up. All they talked about was boys. Lily knew she wanted something else.

'And don't count on getting a warm welcome, either,' Fred had counselled her. 'There's plenty of blokes in the force don't like the idea of policewomen. You'll be up against it from the start.'

Fred hadn't said whether he was one of those blokes, though Lily thought most likely he was. But once he knew she'd made her mind up, he'd taken her part, and from then on he'd been the one she had turned to for advice; and for encouragement when his predictions as to what might lie in wait for her once she'd donned a police uniform were borne out.

'Sorry I haven't been in touch lately,' she said now. 'But I've been busy. And I've got a surprise for you.'

'Oh, yes—?' On the point of taking a bite out of his pie, Fred paused. He looked at her, narrow-eyed. 'Is this about the job?' he asked, and Lily nodded.

'I've been working at the Yard these last few days. Straight up.'

'Well, blow me!' Fred beamed. 'But doing what?' he asked. 'Paperwork?'

'In a way.' Lily's blue eyes shone. 'It's this Wapping business. Biggest murder case in years. And I'm smack in the middle of it.'

'Well, now . . .' His pie still untouched, Fred drew back, as if to take her in. 'So . . . so what does that mean, Lil?' he asked. 'Are you plainclothes now? Is that your surprise? Have they finally given in?' He knew how long she'd been knocking on the door.

'Nah . . . no such luck.'

Lily's smile faded as her jaw set in the bulldog look that was so familiar to Fred. Just like Winnie's, he was wont to remark, referring to the Prime Minister. Same cut of the jib. Same sort of determination, too.

'But it's CID business. And you'll never guess who I'm working under.' The light had come back into her eyes. 'Chief Inspector Sinclair, no less.'

'Crikey!' Fred was impressed. 'The old man himself? You'd better mind your Ps and Qs, girl. They say he's hard to please.'

'Oh, he's all right.' Lily spoke airily. 'His bark's worse than his bite. But he keeps me at it, I can tell you.'

'At what, Lil?' Peering at his niece, Fred saw her hesitate. 'Look, I'm not prying, lass . . .'

'No, it's not that.' Lily rubbed his hand. 'It's just it's confidential for the moment. It hasn't been put out. So keep it to yourself for now, that's all.'

'Message received and understood.' He nodded solemnly.

'It's to do with the man who shot those blokes in the pub. They don't know who he is. I mean, they haven't got a clue, even. So I was told to read through the files, and that's what I've been doing, going through them, one after another, file after file, till I was cross-eyed, looking for a name, someone with a record who might fit the bill. But there didn't seem to be anyone. That is, till I got my hands on this foreign stuff . . .'

'*Foreign* stuff?' Fred's brow darkened.

Lily explained about the IPC advisories. 'It was in one of those. A report about a man who broke into a house in France before the war and topped the owner and his wife and daughter as well: three of them. Same modus operandi as at Wapping. Lots of similarities. Soon as I saw it I knew – this was the bloke. And Mr Sinclair agreed. He's getting in touch with the police in Paris.'

Basking in the warmth of her uncle's proud smile, Lily sat back.

'Modus operandi, is it?' Fred chuckled. 'I knew you'd show them if you ever got the chance.' He regarded her fondly. 'But . . .' He bit his lip. 'Now don't take this wrong, love, but how did you come to get this job? Why you?'

'Ah, well, that's another thing. I haven't even told you about that yet.' She paused, her glance teasing. 'But aren't you going to eat your pie, Uncle Fred?' She nodded towards the unappetizing-looking object still lying untouched on the table between them. 'It's getting cold sitting there.'

Fred growled. 'Never mind my pie,' he said. 'You bite into one of those things these days, you never know what you'll find inside. Come on, lass. What haven't you told me yet?'

Lily hesitated. 'You remember that girl who was killed in Bloomsbury?'

'When you were first at the scene?'

'That's right. Well, it seems this bloke they're looking for topped her as well. *And* the tart who was strangled in Soho last week. You'll have heard about that.'

Fred nodded. He whistled in amazement.

'Well, I had a hand in both cases. Mr Cook let me help. He's a decent sort and I reckon he put in a word for me with this inspector from the Yard who's taken over. Bloke called Styles. It was him who sent my name up.'

'Well, good for both of them.' Fred Poole thumped the table with his fist in approval. 'And about time, too. But will it lead anywhere? Does it mean you'll get a crack at plain-clothes?'

'Hard to say.' She sucked at her teeth. 'Depends what Mr Sinclair thinks. He's the one I have to impress.'

'Seems to me you've done a good job so far.'

'So far . . .' Lily echoed his words. Then her face bright-ened. 'But the good news is, when I dug out the report about the murders in France I thought that'd be it. I'd be on my way back to Bow Street, directing traffic and playing nurse-maid to tarts. But Mr Sinclair told me I could stay on for the time being. So I'll be back at the Yard tomorrow first thing.'

'That's my girl.' Fred didn't hide his satisfaction. 'Once they've had a good look at you they'll see what they've been missing.'

'Well, I don't know about that . . .' His niece blushed.

'Still, from what you've told me, it's a rum business. I

can't make head or tail of it.' He scratched his head. 'You're saying the same fellow who did the Wapping job killed those two girls?'

'That's what they reckon. But it's the first one that's really puzzling. Seems he killed her for no reason. She'd been working as a land girl, living on a farm in Surrey, minding her own business. Didn't have a boyfriend, never been in any trouble. There was nothing to explain it. Nothing about her that was unusual.'

Lily sat frowning.

'Except she was foreign, of course,' she added.

'Well, maybe that was it,' Fred responded, anxious to be of help. 'Maybe that's the reason. I remember you telling me now. Polish, wasn't it?'

PART TWO

14

'So he wasn't a policeman at all?' Mary Spencer said. She was standing at the sink, peeling potatoes and looking out of the window into the stable yard where her five-year-old son Freddy was pretending to be a Hurricane. Arms outstretched, he circled the cobbles, now and then emitting a high-pitched staccato noise meant to sound like a machine-gun. 'Eh-eh-eh-eh-eh . . .'

'Then what on earth was he doing here?'

'That's still a mystery,' Bess Brigstock replied. Bess was a volunteer postal worker; she delivered mail to outlying farms and houses in the Liphook area and was an invaluable source of information and gossip. 'Bob Leonard rang Petersfield in case they knew anything about it, but they didn't. They certainly hadn't sent anyone, and anyway they pointed out it wouldn't have been a policeman enquiring about that sort of thing; it would have been someone from the Ministry of Agriculture, or the Board of Trade. They have their own inspectors.'

'Yes, but he showed Evie a warrant card,' Mary insisted. Tired of his circling, Freddy had zeroed in on Bess's pony Pickles, who stood harnessed between the shafts of her trap in the middle of the yard. 'Eh-eh-eh-eh . . .' He swooped down on Pickles, who disappointingly showed no reaction but continued to chew thoughtfully on the contents of his nosebag. 'He told her he was a detective.'

'Annie MacGregor said the same.' Bess frowned. 'He

turned up at Finch's Farm before he came here and he flashed his card at her, too. She said he was a greasy little man.'

'Evie couldn't bear him. According to her he just pushed his way into the house.'

Mary brushed the pile of peelings off the edge of the sink into a bucket that already held discarded bits of leaf vegetables, some of them in the first stage of decay, as well as other food fragments, all of them destined for the porkers Hodge was fattening in the pigsty behind the stables. She wiped her brow with the back of her wrist.

'They tell you to cook them in their skins,' she murmured, peering at a well-thumbed booklet published by the Ministry of Food that was lying open by the sink. 'It's supposed to keep the goodness in. Too late now. Potatoes au gratin? We've still got some mousetrap. Freddy will hate it. But he hates potato soup even more.'

She turned to look at Bess, who was sitting at the kitchen table with a cup of tea in front of her, taking comfort as always from her burly, reassuring figure, clad that day in a brown, hairy sweater that made Mary think of Mama Bear from the book of children's stories she read to Freddy every evening. The cup of tea Bess was cradling in her large callused hands might easily have been a plate of porridge.

'What did he say to Annie MacGregor, this man?'

'The same as he told Evie, so far as I can gather.' Bess's face darkened. Heavy in the shoulders, and with thighs like oaks, her leathery complexion testified to a life lived out of doors. 'That there'd been reports of illegal slaughtering of livestock in the area and what did she know about it. Annie said she'd never heard of such a thing and if he was trying to insinuate that she and Alec had been killing off their animals on the sly he must be out of his mind. He might not have noticed but they had a *dairy* herd. But it didn't seem to faze him; he insisted on taking their names and the names of their two farmhands.'

'That's what he did with Evie. Took her name and got her to tell him mine and made a note of Hodge's, too. I only wish I'd been here. Policeman or not, I'd have sent him off with a flea in his ear.'

Mary began to fill a saucepan with water from the sink, and as she did so she caught sight of her son's nanny, who'd gone out a few minutes earlier to collect eggs, emerging from the barn with a basket on her arm. Spotting a fresh target, Freddy sped across the cobbles towards her. 'Eh-eh-eh-eh . . .' Smiling, Mary watched as Evie dropped the basket and caught him in her arms. She swung him around, her long red hair, in plaits that morning, airborne for a moment as she pirouetted on the spot, and while Freddy wriggled, trying to escape, she whispered something in his ear. Her words, whatever they were, seemed to work the desired spell and when she put him down and collected her basket from the ground he took the gloved hand she offered him and together they walked to the end of the stables and then disappeared from sight behind the long, low building.

Mary carried the saucepan to the other end of the kitchen and placed it on the old iron range which stood there radiating heat. Unhitching the gate to the fireplace beneath the stove, she took two logs cut to size from a wood bin and added them to the bed of embers before returning to clean the sink.

'But is that all Bob Leonard could tell you?'

Leonard was the Liphook bobby. Bess had undertaken on Mary's behalf to find out all she could about the mysterious man who had called at the Grange a few days earlier brandishing what now seemed to be a bogus warrant card. Mary herself had been in Petersfield that day: she'd gone to the market that was held there once a week, leaving her son in Evie's care, and had returned to find the girl clearly upset by what had occurred. It appeared from her account that the man had behaved in a menacing way, warning her that the authorities were well aware of what was going on, which had made no more sense to Evie than apparently it had to the MacGregors, who were their closest neighbours.

'Bob's only contribution was to wonder whether you had anything worth stealing.' Bess snorted.

'He *what—?*'

'He said it sounded like this man, whoever he was, might be on the lookout for places to rob. How do they put it in American films? Casing the joint?'

Mary had started laughing even before she finished speaking.

'Well, if he thinks the Grange is worth casing, he must be even dimmer than he sounds.'

Mary herself had been combing the house for anything that looked remotely saleable since coming to live there, but her rewards had been scant. On the same day the greasy little man had appeared she'd gone to Petersfield with the last of her gleanings: two gilded picture frames discovered in the cellar and an old set of cutlery missing only a carving knife and fork. She'd returned with a sweater and gloves for Evie, some boots for Hodge, whose own were now past mending, six pork chops slipped to her surreptitiously (and quite literally) under a table, and, best of all, a set of lead soldiers of the Napoleonic era complete in number and only slightly damaged.

'The odd lance is bent and some of the shakos have lost their plumes,' she'd told Bess, who, ever reliable, had been waiting at the station with Pickles and her trap to take them home. 'But Freddy will love them. He's become very martial of late. I was beginning to despair of finding him anything for Christmas.'

All in all the expedition had been a triumph. But Mary's elation had been short-lived when she'd discovered on returning to the Grange what had happened in her absence. Evie had been so upset by the experience that Mary had asked Bess the following day to find out all she could about the incident.

'Well, at least I can tell her it's got nothing to do with the police,' she said now. 'Poor Evie. She worries enough as it is.' One of the reasons Mary had felt drawn to the girl – why she'd employed her in the first place – was that they both shared the same anxieties. Mary's husband Peter had been posted with his regiment to North Africa in 1942 and was now in Italy. Evie's was serving with the Allied forces in France.

'It was all right when he was in hospital over here. But he was returned to his unit last week, so she'll have to start worrying all over again. She's such a dear girl. And a great help to me. I don't want her upset. Not when things are going so well.'

She smiled at Bess.

'We've settled down at last. I've never seen Freddy so happy. He simply loves it here. He wouldn't be back in London for anything. And it's all thanks to you, dear Bess.'

'Oh, good Lord! Don't exaggerate.'

Bess snorted. Scowling, she buried her nose in her teacup. Mary regarded her with affection. Though they'd known each other for only a few months it had taken less time than that to discover that her new friend's gruff manner was little more than a mask; that her generosity was in fact limitless. Nor, in consequence, had it surprised her to learn later that Bess had spent the better part of her life ministering to others:

first as an ambulance driver during the First World War; later as a Red Cross worker in distant parts of the world, a career that had been cut short when her mother had fallen seriously ill and she had had to return to England to nurse her. The old lady, bedridden in her last years, had finally passed away the previous Christmas, at which point Bess, looking around as always to see where else she might be needed, had answered a call for a volunteer to deliver post in the Liphook area.

'Mind you, I did worry when you first arrived,' she allowed, running her fingers through her cropped hair, scrunching up her face into a frown that no self-respecting bear would be ashamed of – or so Mary told herself. 'You'd had your whole life turned upside down, and it's not easy getting over that sort of thing.'

What Bess was referring to had happened six months earlier when Mary's house in London – the home she and her husband had bought in Maida Vale when they'd got married – had been destroyed by a V-bomb. Terrible though the event had been, however, it paled beside another memory of that day which continued to haunt Mary's dreams.

After they had moved into the Grange and she and Bess had got to know each other, she had told her the whole story. How she had left Freddy with his nanny for the afternoon and gone out to keep a dental appointment and how, while travelling on a bus to Portland Road, she had heard the sound of a distant explosion and wondered, with the other passengers, whether it was one of the new flying bombs the newspapers were talking about. And how, an hour later, coming home, she had turned into her street to find a fire engine blocking her way and the road full of men in uniform: air-raid wardens, firemen, police officers. Still vivid in Mary's recollection had been the sight of the hoses extended like black snakes along the length of the pavement and the smell hanging in the air, which she hadn't recognized at first but then realized was the scent of freshly turned soil.

'My heart stopped, Bess. I couldn't breathe.'

A glance had been all it took her to see that her house had disappeared: the slate roof and the chimney that leaned to one side and the window boxes she had bought that spring and filled with geraniums. All had vanished. In their place was a pile of smoking rubble, and as she'd stood there unable to move, an icy calm had descended on her like a shroud.

'Then I saw them, Freddy and Evie. They were standing on the pavement hand in hand looking at this awful heap of bricks and plaster.'

Later she had learned that his nanny had taken her son out for a walk only minutes before the bomb had landed. They had gone down to the canal to feed the ducks and had seen the cigar-shaped craft, its tail glowing brightly, pass by overhead.

'Only *minutes*, Bess . . .'

Although it had been days before Mary had been able to think clearly, their move to Hampshire had been inevitable in the circumstances and dictated by logic. Short of looking for a flat in London to rent, the Grange had offered the only roof immediately available to her. An old stone mansion situated a mile or two from the village of Liphook, it had belonged to a bachelor uncle of hers and been left to her in his will when he died at the end of 1938. Something of a white elephant – it was too big for a weekend retreat – the house had remained empty during the war apart from a brief spell in 1942 when it had been occupied by a company of sappers on a training exercise. All but settled on the idea of selling it, Mary and her husband had put off a final decision until after the war and in the meantime had arranged with an estate agent in Petersfield to keep an eye on the property, which was left in the day-to-day care of an elderly couple named Hodge who had worked for Mary's uncle for many years and had a cottage nearby.

A week after losing her home, Mary had taken the train down to Liphook with Freddy and his nanny. Weighed down by suitcases – she and Evie had spent hours picking through the rubble salvaging what they could – they had clambered off the train to find Liphook's only taxi already commandeered and were sitting in the station waiting for it to return, Freddy growing more fractious by the minute, when the door had opened and a large woman wearing an old army greatcoat and a fur-lined cap with earflaps had put her head in.

'I'm told you want to go to the Grange,' she had growled at them. Her heavy frown had seemed to dispel any idea that she might be doing them a favour. 'I'm headed that way myself. Can I give you a lift?'

Only later had Mary realized that Bess had not been going in their direction at all. She'd finished her round for the day and was about to return home in her trap when she'd heard from the station-master, Mr Walton, that a party from London was camped in the waiting room looking lost.

'I thought for a moment you were refugees,' she'd confessed long afterwards, weeks later. 'You looked so forlorn sitting there with your suitcases.'

15

'COME NOW, ANGUS. It's no use getting upset. These things take time. We must be patient.'

Bennett removed his glasses and rubbed the bridge of his nose.

'Paris was an occupied city until a few months ago. Heaven only knows what the police are having to deal with there. Apart from anything else there's the matter of wartime collaborators. From what I hear, a lot of private justice is being exacted. It's not something they can turn a blind eye to. I'm sure they'll get around to our problem in due course.'

'No doubt they will, sir. But it matters how long they take. It's vital to know who we're chasing, and time isn't on our side. It's already been a week since the Wapping shooting and we've had ample evidence that he's bent on covering his tracks. I only hope by the time we hear from Paris there's still a trail left to follow.'

Sinclair sat scowling. He knew he was being unreasonable: barely four days had passed since his message had been dispatched to the Sûreté. But his gout had chosen that morning to return with particular venom and he sat shifting miserably in his chair, his toe throbbing.

'Is there anything more we can do from this side now? Have we exhausted all avenues?'

Fully cognizant of his colleague's discomfort – and equally aware that he would not wish it referred to – the assistant commissioner sought to be sympathetic.

'For the time being, yes. What we're doing now is waiting on Paris, hoping they can tell us first whether or not this is Marko we're dealing with and if so, what they know about his movements before the outbreak of war. They would surely have stayed on his trail as long as they could.'

The chief inspector sought to control his impatience. While awaiting a reply from Paris he had used the time to pursue what few leads seemed to offer any prospect of progress, and it was their failure to produce even a gleam of light that he'd been recounting to Bennett that morning, and which had contributed to his gloomy mood.

'There were two areas I wanted covered,' he'd declared. 'The first was to do with Alfie Meeks. We're still faced with the mystery of how he came into contact with this man, and I've had detectives scouring the market at Southwark trying to find someone who might know – or have spotted – something that would be of use to us. Styles and Grace have been organizing that with the help of the Southwark police, and between them they must have talked to every stallholder there as well as a lot of the customers. But all to no effect: it was the same story wherever they went. One day he simply packed up and disappeared. His stall was only a folding table and his goods fitted into a suitcase. He asked one of the other traders to look after them for him and she put them with her stuff in a shed she uses for storage. They've been lying there ever since.'

Sinclair had ground his teeth in frustration.

'His landlady was no help, either, other than telling us that Meeks had been able to pay the rent he owed her and seemed pleased with himself. It's clear this man put money in his pocket. But he doesn't seem to have had any friends, not close ones, anyway. Just people he would chat to when he went to the pub. We asked there, naturally, but no one could tell us anything; nor at the café he frequented. Just that he hadn't been in for a while. He'd vanished.'

Bennett had listened to him in silence. Then he, too, had shrugged.

'That sounds like a dead end. Two areas, you said?'

Sinclair nodded. 'I decided to approach Mrs Laski again. She rang up a week ago to say she had read through Rosa Nowak's diaries and there was nothing in them that would help us. As she'd suspected they weren't a record of Rosa's life, as such, or of the people she'd met. Just a young girl's thoughts and dreams. Upsetting for her aunt, poor woman, but she did it, and I thought we might ask for her help again.'

The chief inspector had paused, frowning.

'Unfortunately, we learned yesterday she'd been admitted into University College Hospital with severe bronchitis. She can't clear her lungs. It's a common cause of death among the old at this time of year, and according to the hospital she's in poor health anyway and unlikely to recover. I don't want to bother her again, particularly with a subject that's bound to upset her.'

'What did you want to ask her exactly?'

'Whether she knows anything about the time Rosa spent in France. This is all very speculative, but it springs from John Madden's idea that there might have been some prior encounter between Rosa and this man – something that prompted him to kill her – and in view of what we now know about him we wondered whether that might have occurred in France. At present our only information on that score comes from a conversation Helen had with the girl. Rosa told her she'd got there shortly before the war started and stayed with a friend of her father's in Tours. However, she did visit Paris shortly before the Germans invaded France and it was from there that she left to go to England.'

'Madden's wife told you this?'

Sinclair nodded. 'That was the time of the "phoney war", and from what Rosa said, Helen gathered she was hoping like others that things would be resolved; that there might be peace after all and she would be reunited with her family. The girl had some contacts in Paris among the Polish community, and she went there to talk to them, and perhaps get some news of home. In the event, the Germans invaded soon after her arrival and then it was a matter of getting out of France herself. At some point she'd joined up with a friend, a young Pole she knew, but they left it late, apparently, and in the end had to escape via Spain. They managed to get passage on a boat from Lisbon. Unfortunately this young man's not available for questioning; he enlisted in the army soon after they got here and was killed in action. That's all I remember of what Helen told me, but I'm seeing Madden later – he's up in London for a day or two – and I'll check with him in case I've forgotten anything.'

The chief inspector shifted uncomfortably in his chair. Sighing audibly, he assembled his papers and prepared to depart. Bennett eyed him.

'I spoke to the commissioner yesterday. He's been pressing me on the Wapping shooting. Wants it cleared up quickly. Well, don't we all? I was able to tell him of the possible link we've made to those French murders, and how it came about. He allowed that he was impressed.'

'You mentioned Poole's name?' For the first time that morning a smile crossed Sinclair's lips.

'I did more than that. I told him exactly how she'd unearthed the IPC message; the hours of work she'd put in. He still wants that report in writing from you. But you might put a different slant on it now. He's in a receptive mood.'

Bennett, too, was smiling.

'Cheer up, Angus. I'm sure we'll get a response from Paris soon. What do you hear from the Military Police? When do they expect another pouch?'

'There was one due this afternoon, but it goes to the Military Police headquarters in Chichester first. If there's anything in it for us it'll be sent up to London by courier tomorrow. We can only wait and see.'

'Still, we'd better be prepared. The reply will be in French. Have a word with Registry. Make sure they have one of their people on hand who can do whatever translation's needed. We don't want to waste any time.'

He watched as the chief inspector gathered himself.

'You say Madden's up in London. See if you can persuade him to pay us a visit. It's been a while since I saw him last and I'd be interested to hear his views on all this.'

The suggestion was one Sinclair had already acted on, though for a different reason. Knowing that Madden would like to see him while he was in town, he had invited Billy Styles to join them for lunch, and it had been agreed they would all gather at the Yard before setting off.

'We might look in on Bennett afterwards,' he said when his former colleague appeared shortly after midday, having been escorted upstairs to the chief inspector's office by one of the commissionaires. 'That is, if you can tear yourself away from Aunt Maud's boiler.'

'Oh, don't worry about that.' Madden looked wry. 'The matter's out of my hands. Lucy's taken charge. I think her mother underestimates her. But as for her comings and goings – I'm supposed to enquire into them – well, they're a complete mystery.'

'Ah, the joys of fatherhood!' Sinclair chuckled heartlessly.

'Well, here's another one for you. We've got a little time to waste. You might care to cast an eye on it.'

He tossed Madden the file, and he was still leafing through its pages, his brow creased in a familiar scowl, when Billy knocked on the door and came in.

'I've been reading about your exploits, Inspector.' Madden rose with a smile to greet him. 'That was a nasty business at Wapping; you must tell me all about it. Something else, too.' He tapped the file with his finger. 'I've spotted a familiar name, someone I want to ask you about. But it'll keep till lunch.'

The restaurant Sinclair had chosen was in Westminster, within walking distance, and on the way over he warned his guests not to get their hopes up.

'It used to be a decent place. But the food's appalling wherever you go now. One can only pray for a miracle.'

In vain, as it turned out. The fish pie they chose from the menu materialized as glistening, whitish lumps, barely edible, and the chief inspector was the first to push his plate away.

'I was given an American magazine the other day,' he said gloomily. 'It was the issue before Thanksgiving and the cover had a picture of a table groaning with food. Turkey, ham, pumpkin pie; fruit and nuts. I tell you I was close to tears.'

Billy caught Madden's eye. 'A name you said, sir?'

'That's right. I spotted it when I was going through the statements you took down in Southwark. Nelly Stover . . . ?'

'Oh, her?' Billy emptied his glass of beer. 'She's a tough old bird. I interviewed her myself. She's got a stall in that market where Alfie Meeks worked. Claims she knew him. She was the one he asked to look after his stuff when he went off.'

'Knew him? From before he came to the market?'

'She said she'd remembered him from when he was a kid. Over in Bethnal Green. That's where Alfie grew up.' Billy cocked an eye at his old mentor. 'Is that where *you* knew her, sir?'

'If it's the same Nelly Stover. Tell me, did she mention having a husband? Bob was his name, I think. A merchant seaman.'

Billy grimaced. 'Then it's her, all right. She told me her old man copped it in '42. His ship went down in the Atlantic. Torpedoed. I'd asked about him because I thought with them both coming from Bethnal Green one or other might have known something more about Meeks. Who his friends were, for example. But she said they'd moved away from there years ago and she hadn't seen Alfie again until he turned up one day at the market with his folding table and a suitcase of goods. She didn't recognize him, but when she heard his name she went over to say hello and tell him who she was. That's how he came to leave his stuff with her.'

Madden mused for a moment. 'Did she happen to mention her son?' he asked.

Billy shook his head.

'Why?' Sinclair asked. He'd been listening to them with interest.

'It's coming back to me now.' Madden smiled. 'He was a handful. Not a bad boy, just wild. In with the wrong lot. I caught him trying to break into a tobacconist. I knew if I charged him he'd end up in a borstal, so instead I dragged him off by the scruff of his neck and put him in Nelly's hands. She had a fish and chip shop then, and the way I heard it she walloped him so hard with one of her saucepans he had bruises for weeks. But he never put a foot wrong again so far as I know, and the last I heard he'd got himself a job.' With a sigh he turned back to Billy. 'I'm sorry to hear about her husband. Tell me, how did she strike you? Is she well? She must be on her own now.'

'Not quite. She's got a couple of grandkids living with her. I know, because she shut up shop while we were still talking and went off to collect them. Told me if I had any more questions I'd have to come back another day.' He grinned. 'A tough old bird, as I say. But I liked her.'

'So she knew Alfie when he was a boy . . .' Madden was looking thoughtful. 'I might have guessed. It was a close-knit community.' He caught Billy's eye. 'Alfie's father was a villain called Jonah Meeks. He was the worst kind of bully; hated by all. His body was fished out of an abandoned cistern one day. It was ruled an accident.'

'Yes, I got that from records. And his mother died when he was ten. Nelly Stover told me. There was a stepmother later, but she's gone, too. He didn't seem to have any family. Nor friends, come to that.'

'Did she know about the Wapping business?' Sinclair asked. 'Before you told her, I mean?'

Billy nodded. 'She said she couldn't understand what Alfie was doing in that sort of company. Said he was a sad little man.'

While he was speaking, the head waiter had appeared beside their table. He bent to whisper in Sinclair's ear and the chief inspector rose to his feet.

'Would you excuse me? I've a call.'

He was back after only a minute, and it was plain to see from his expression that something momentous had occurred. He signalled at once for the bill.

'That was Bennett,' he said, glancing at Madden. 'Do you remember me telling you about that French detective who came over here before the war to help us with a case?'

'The one who'd been in charge of the Fontainebleau case?'

Sinclair nodded. 'Commissaire Duval. Well, he's just been on the phone from Paris. Don't ask me how he got through, but it seems our guess was right. It's Marko we're after. Duval says there's no mistake.'

'How does he know?' Madden's voice carried an edge of excitement. 'How can he be sure?'

'I've no idea.' Sinclair rose and his two guests followed suit. 'But we'll find out soon enough. Bennett wants us back right away.' He touched Madden's arm. 'You, too, John. He made that clear. He's got something to tell you.'

'Angus . . . at last!'

The assistant commissioner looked up from his desk as Sinclair came in. Several sheets of paper covered with his scrawl lay on the blotter in front of him; he'd been peering down at them.

'Madden, how are you?' He had just caught sight of the chief inspector's companion. 'Come in, please.' He rose and they shook hands.

Bennett gestured to the chairs that were already lined up, facing his desk. His face was a little flushed.

'Duval asked for you first, Angus, but you were out, so the switchboard sensibly put him on to me. He'd been trying for a couple of days to get through. Said in the end they'd "gone to the top", whatever that means, but it'll give you some idea of how important they think this is. Unfortunately we only spoke for five minutes before the telephone people cut us off. However . . .'

He paused to catch breath, and as he did so he sought Madden's eye.

'Angus will have told you already. It's the same man.'

Madden nodded. 'We were wondering how they knew.'

'It was that list Solly Silverman had on him. They're diamonds that were stolen in Paris on the eve of the German occupation. From a furrier, Duval said. I've got his name here . . .' Bennett scrabbled among the scattered sheets of paper. 'Sobel . . .' He peered down through his glasses. 'He'd bought them that same day from a dealer. He meant to make a run for it to Spain. He was Jewish, you see . . .' Glancing up, he found the chief inspector's gaze on him.

'*Was* you say—?'

'Yes, he's dead. Murdered. Garrotted.'

'By the man who stole the jewels?'

Bennett nodded. 'The one they call Marko. They've sent us a copy of their dossier on the case, which will explain how they know it was him. That and a lot besides. It's in the MP's pouch that came over today. We should have it by tomorrow. There's not much more I can tell you. The line was bad. Duval kept having to repeat himself. He sent you his regards, by the way. I asked him how things were in Paris. He said "bloody awful".'

Bennett took off his glasses. He rubbed the bridge of his nose.

'There was one other thing he mentioned; it's of special concern to you, Madden. I believe it answers your question.'

Their eyes met.

'This furrier who was murdered in Paris. Sobel. He was Polish by extraction and he'd offered to give two young Poles a lift to Spain in his car. They wanted to escape as well. Duval doesn't know their names, but one of them was a young woman, and it seems she arrived at Sobel's house minutes after he was murdered. It's possible she saw the killer, Duval says. She may even have come face to face with him.'

Bennett brooded for a moment.

'He didn't finish telling me about it – we were cut off then – but I gathered she fled from the scene and the police were unable to locate her afterwards. They had to assume that she and her compatriot, whoever he was, managed to escape from France by some other means. At all events they've never been found. We'll learn more about it when this dossier arrives. But it struck me at once: she must have been the same young woman you had working for you.'

'So that was it!' Madden, his face in shadow now that the afternoon light was dying, sat stunned. 'I always knew there had to be a reason why he killed her.'

'He must have caught a glimpse of her the other night . . . the killer . . . this Marko. In the Underground, perhaps. If he recognized her then it's odds on they did come face to face in Paris, and that would have been enough . . .'

'Enough?'

Still dwelling on what he'd heard, Madden's attention had strayed.

'Enough reason to kill her.' Bennett explained, and after a momentary pause Madden dipped his head in silent agreement.

'Being the man he is.'

16

INFORMED BY THE Military Police headquarters at Chichester that it would be mid-morning before the package sent from Paris the day before reached London, Sinclair elected not to alter his accustomed routine and went to see Bennett as usual at half-past nine, leaving Lily Poole behind with orders to let him know the moment it arrived.

'Tell Inspector Styles to stand by, too.'

His deepening involvement in the inquiry that had started with the murder of Rosa Nowak had not relieved the chief inspector of his other duties, and as ever he brought with him the crime report for the preceding twenty-four hours to run through with his superior. But the now familiar litany of pilfering and black-market dealing compiled by the various metropolitan divisions held little interest for either man that morning, and before long Bennett reverted to the subject that occupied both their minds.

'I couldn't get to sleep last night. I kept thinking of that girl coming up to London to see her aunt, never dreaming . . . but why didn't she report it? What she witnessed in Paris? Why stay silent all these years?'

'John was wondering the same thing. We discussed it before he went off yesterday.' Sinclair settled himself in his chair; his gout had eased somewhat and he was thankful for the break from nagging pain. 'But it's not that hard to understand. If she'd stayed on in Paris to give a statement to the police she might well have ended up being trapped there. They would almost certainly have held her as a material witness. And once the Occupation was in force, what would have become of her then? She did the human thing: she saved herself. Perhaps the man she was travelling with helped to make up her mind. But whatever the explanation, I can't find it in my heart to blame her.'

'Granted, but when she'd reached safety here – when she was settled in England – why not go to the police then and tell them everything? It's not as though we would have taken any action against her.'

'I suppose that's true . . .' The chief inspector's tone belied his words. 'But could *she* be sure of that? After all, she'd committed a serious offence: she'd left the scene of a murder. And she was here on sufferance, remember. She was an alien in wartime, with all the sense of insecurity that brings. It would have been tempting simply to forget what had occurred, or at any rate push it to the back of her mind. To tell herself there was no way she could help the French police, not with Paris under German occupation.'

The assistant commissioner thought for a moment.

'And that's Madden's view, too, is it?'

'I believe so.' Sinclair frowned. 'But he was going to ask Helen her opinion. Neither of them got close to the girl while she was working for them, but of the two, Helen probably knew her better. It was her impression Rosa's melancholy sprang from the tragedy that had overtaken her family, and though it's tempting now to think it might have had another cause, I very much doubt it. After all, whatever she witnessed in Paris had happened four years before. There's no reason to think it still loomed large in her mind. Not with all that has happened in the world since then. But it's unlikely we'll ever get to the bottom of that. If Rosa told anyone about it, it was most likely her aunt, and I'm afraid that road's closed to us now.'

'Has she gone then?' Bennett asked.

'Yesterday afternoon. We rang the hospital before Madden left. We were told she'd fallen into a coma some time earlier, so we couldn't have spoken to her even if we'd wanted to.'

The chief inspector bit his lip.

'It may seem cruel to say so, but at least we can put Rosa's death to one side now. We know why this man killed her. It was because she could identify him. He knew that if ever he was arrested she could send him to the guillotine – for the murder of Sobel at least, if not for any of his other victims. The same applies to Florrie Desmoulins. He knew we were bound to interview her – that we'd make the link between the man she had words with and Rosa's murderer – so the sooner he cut that thread the better. His pattern doesn't change. Fontainebleau ... Wapping. It's the same wherever you look. He leaves no witnesses behind.'

'Yes, but still...' The assistant commissioner stirred unhappily behind his desk. 'He was in no danger of arrest when he murdered Rosa Nowak. We had no idea he was here. All he's done is stir up a hornet's nest. It makes no sense to me.'

'I agree. Until you look at it from *his* point of view.' Sinclair eyed his superior meaningfully. 'To begin with there was no way he could have guessed that Rosa Nowak never made contact with the French police, never offered herself as a witness. He would have assumed the opposite, and that with Paris liberated now there was every chance the Sûreté was back on his trail. And since Britain was one of the countries he might have fled to, they were either already in touch with us, or soon would be. He was safe enough during the war years, but if a hunt for him was launched here then Rosa's presence, her very existence, became a threat that he couldn't ignore, especially as the French were bound to pass on her name to us. Or so he'd assume. So his action was pre-emptive. In effect, he was cutting the chain of evidence before the links could be joined. It's his actions after that that are harder to read. Killing Rosa seems to have forced him into further action. Immediately afterwards he set up the Wapping robbery, and while we can't be sure what his motives were it suggests he wanted to be ready to leave the country at the earliest possible moment once the war was over.'

'With money in his pocket?' Bennett asked, and Sinclair nodded.

'He set out to lure Silverman to that pub with a case full of cash and he succeeded. Now he has both the money and the diamonds. He's ready to run. At least, that's the theory we're working on. But John has raised an interesting question. Why was he in such a hurry? Granted Rosa was a threat he had to deal with. But once she was dead he was under no pressure: he could have planned his next move carefully, chosen someone more reliable than Alfie Meeks to do his bidding. He was safe for the time being. So why the rush?'

The assistant commissioner had been listening closely. 'So he's still giving this some thought,' he remarked. 'Madden, I mean.'

'Sir . . . ?'

'I would have thought he'd got the answer he was looking for. Why that girl was murdered.'

'That's true, certainly.' The chief inspector chuckled. 'But John's got more of an old copper's instinct in him than he's prepared to admit. He doesn't like letting go. But you're right – there's nothing more he can do. This is a purely police matter now: a question of tracking this Marko down. We're having a drink later, by the way. John's going back to Highfield tomorrow, but he wants to know what's in that dossier before he leaves.'

'A question of tracking him down . . .' Bennett was reflecting on the other's words. 'Just how difficult do you think that will be?'

'Well, it rather depends.' Sinclair scratched his head. 'Granted, we know *when* he arrived: it must have been in the days, or at most weeks, following the German occupation of Paris, and if he entered the country under an alias – as a foreigner – we can probably get on to him quickly. His name would have been noted and placed on the official register of aliens. His whereabouts now would be a matter of record.'

'You say "if".'

The chief inspector nodded. He began gathering his papers.

'Unfortunately we've every reason to believe he's British, and if so it's more than likely that he arrived here under his own name – his real name – which he may have been keeping in reserve for just such an eventuality; and if that's the case, finding him could prove a lot harder.'

Bennett watched as he rose to his feet.

'Perhaps the French can help us there,' he suggested. 'That information might be in the dossier.'

'It might.' Sinclair stood poised to go. 'But I doubt it. If Duval was aware he was British he would have said so yesterday. And if he knew his real name, he would have told us.'

In the event, it took the chief inspector very little time to discover he was right on both counts. On returning to his office he found a package wrapped in brown paper delivered by a military courier only a few minutes earlier lying on his desk, and before the hour was out, with the help of a translator, he learned that in spite of the wealth of new information it contained, the one piece of knowledge they sought more than any other was still to be unearthed.

'All the French could tell us was what he was calling himself when he passed through Paris,' he told Madden when they met that evening. 'Klaus Meiring. He had French papers, and later it turned out he'd been living under the same name in Amsterdam. But there's no Meiring listed as having entered this country in 1940, and although there are a couple of men with the same surname on the aliens register, neither one of them is our man. By the time he stepped ashore here he was someone else. British, at a guess, but that still doesn't help. He came over at a time when the ferries had all been suspended: so anyone who crossed the Channel then must have hired a French fishing boat to bring them over. As a number of people did, the Coast Guard tells us, and the proper procedure would have been for them to report their arrival both to the police and to Customs and Excise. However, I doubt our friend Marko did either. It's far more likely he slipped ashore unnoticed, and if that's the case it's quite possible there's no record of his arrival, no name we can trace.'

Somewhat to the chief inspector's surprise, his old colleague had suggested they meet in Bloomsbury – he had left a telephoned message with the switchboard to that effect – and when Sinclair reached the designated rendezvous, a pub in Museum Street, he found it was little more than a stone's throw from the spot where Rosa Nowak had been murdered.

'I went over to the hospital where Mrs Laski was admitted,' Madden told him when he arrived. He had already ordered a beer and was standing at the bar gazing into his glass (like a fortune-teller studying his crystal ball, Sinclair felt). 'I wanted to be sure arrangements were in hand for her funeral. She had no family over here; no one other than her niece. But I found a Polish couple had got there before me and were taking care of things. Then I thought since I was in the area I'd have another look at the spot where Rosa was killed. I've only seen it by day. But it turned out to be a waste of time. That street's pitch-dark. If he came up on her from behind, he must have eyes like a cat.'

'Perhaps he had a torch,' Sinclair suggested. Finding that the pub was out of whisky – an occurrence all too common these days – he had settled for a gin flavoured with bitters.

'No, I don't think so. You remember those burned-out matches Billy found by the body? It sounds as though Marko was fumbling around in the dark himself.'

The chief inspector ordered a fresh drink. Around them the pub was filling up, growing noisy, as a steady stream of customers, many of them in uniform, drifted in from the street. A ripple of notes from a hidden piano proved to be the prelude to a chorus of 'Happy Birthday'. It was followed by an even louder rendition of 'Why Was She Born So Beautiful?'

The two men eyed each other.

'Shall we . . . ?' The chief inspector picked up his glass.

In search of quiet they found a small 'snug' bar at the back of the smoke-filled taproom separated from the public area by a half-glassed partition and as yet unoccupied. Commandeering the single table it contained, Sinclair sat down with their drinks, and while Madden went in search of something to eat – they had decided to forgo dinner in favour of a sandwich – the chief inspector assembled his thoughts. It had been an exhausting day. The translation of the dossier had only marked the beginning of his labours; later he had had lengthy meetings, first with the detectives assigned to the case, then with Bennett. But tired as he was, he had much to relate, and as soon as Madden returned, plate in hand, he set out to enlighten him.

'It's too bad about the name. But we've not come up empty-handed. Duval's compiled a long report separate from the evidence they've collected and he only gave us the bare bones yesterday. For one thing it's clear now how the Wapping robbery came about. The same kind of trick was played on that furrier Marko murdered. First he was sold the diamonds, then he was robbed of them. The aim was identical in each case: to get both the money and the stones.'

Sinclair paused as a chorus of voices burst into song next door. Forced to wait until the noise died down, he sampled one of the cheese sandwiches his companion had brought from the bar. They were sitting facing each other across the table, and as the last notes faded, Madden leaned forward.

'Was it Marko's idea?' he asked.

The chief inspector shook his head. 'It was cooked up by a Dutch diamond dealer called Eyskens. Although he was based in Paris, he had links with Hendrik Bok going back years, and was part of a diamond-smuggling operation which Bok started after he got control of the Rotterdam docks. He brought in illegal stones from West Africa and Eyskens used his business to feed them into the European market. The French police knew he was crooked, but what they didn't know was that he was effectively Bok's man in Paris. Nor that he'd been instrumental in setting up the Lagrange murder. He'd provided Marko with a plan of the villa at Fontainebleau which he'd acquired somehow. He was one of the few people who'd actually met him.'

'How did the French police come by this information? Did they arrest Eyskens after the Sobel robbery?'

'They meant to. But when they went to pick him up they found him dead. Marko had got there first. Most of what I'm telling you now came from Bok's wife. Widow, rather. Bok himself died in 1941, of natural causes. He had cancer. She made a long statement to the Dutch police which they sent to Paris. It fills in some of the blanks.'

A burst of loud laughter from beyond the partition interrupted him again, and Sinclair took advantage of the moment to finish his sandwich, stifling a yawn as he did so. Madden waited patiently until he was ready to resume.

'Bok's wife was also his book-keeper, and after he died the Dutch police got hold of some of his ledgers, which were in her hand. It gave them a lever to use, and she was persuaded to tell them what she knew about her husband's activities and his relationship with Marko. We don't know for certain how they met, but Bok had dealings over the years with a number of other European gangs, and at a certain point when he was battling for control of the docks he went looking for help. His wife was clear on that point. He was shopping for a killer. Where he found him – how they were put in touch – she didn't know, but towards the end of 1927 Marko turned up in Rotterdam. Strange to say, there's a record of their meeting, a photograph no less. They were only snapped by chance – they happened to be in the picture – but the Dutch police managed to get their hands on a copy of the photo and I've brought it along for you to look at. Not that it'll be of any use to us.'

While he was speaking, Sinclair had been searching in his pocket, and, having fished out a photograph, he passed it to Madden, who held it up to the light and squinted at the glossy print. The subjects of the snapshot were a young couple sitting hand in hand at a table in a café. But it was the pair of men behind them that Madden fixed his gaze on. They were seated at another zinc-topped table, this one bearing a bottle, half-empty glasses and an overflowing ashtray, and the head of one of them had been circled with a pen. He was the least visible of the duo, appearing to have turned away at the moment when the photograph was taken, and only one side of his face could be seen; the image was further marred by the hand which he had raised to his temple. His companion, fair-haired, and with a thick moustache, sat sprawled in a careless pose, legs thrust out, and there was more than a hint of aggression in the way he held himself. Not so the other. Lean and alert-looking, he had not been taken by surprise, Madden saw. The lifted hand, the quickly turned head – everything about his pose suggested a swift reaction.

'The one with the moustache is Hendrik Bok,' Sinclair explained. 'He had a bodyguard called Graaf, who ended up in prison, and Duval arranged with the Dutch police to interview him. According to Graaf, the snapshot dates from the day Marko arrived in the city. He said he'd accompanied Bok to the café where the rendezvous took place, but was told to wait outside and keep watch. He didn't actually set eyes on Marko, but quite soon after this meeting, the cull of Bok's enemies started and word spread about a Serbian killer he had working for him.'

The chief inspector took the photograph back from Madden and returned it to his jacket pocket.

'Bok's wife never met Marko, incidentally, though she knew all about him, and she believed the story Bok put about – that he'd been a member of the Black Hand. And she said an interesting thing. She thought her husband was afraid of him.'

'Even though Marko worked for him?'

'And even though Bok must have come across some bad actors in his time. He was one himself. It makes you wonder whose idea it was to keep Marko out of sight; to produce him only when he was needed. Perhaps it suited them both. Marko didn't want his face known and Bok may have been relieved not to have him around.'

'One to stay away from.' Madden murmured the words to himself.

'What was that?' Sinclair cocked an ear.

'Something Florrie Desmoulins said. Men were her business; she knew he was dangerous.' Madden was silent for a moment. Then he asked, 'What about the Sobel robbery? What did Bok's widow have to say about that?'

'Very little. Only that when Bok heard about it later – when the Dutch police questioned him – he had laughed and said that some people were too greedy for their own good. Later he told his wife he'd had nothing to do with it. It was Eyskens's own idea. Marko himself had quit Holland some time earlier. The war had put an end to his partnership with Bok, who was dying anyway. Although he didn't say where he was going, his only escape route lay through France, and he must have got in touch with Eyskens as soon as he reached Paris. I say "must have" because what follows is supposition on Duval's part, though it seems to hang together.'

The chief inspector emptied his glass. He took a deep breath, trying to shake off his drowsiness.

'Eyskens had already agreed to sell Sobel the diamonds: he'd done the same for other émigrés who needed to leave in a hurry, and made a handsome profit out of it. But before the deal went through, Marko appeared, and that seems to have given him the idea of going one better: of doubling his money, so to speak, by stealing the stones back from Sobel after he'd paid for them. But what he didn't stop to ask himself was why a man like Marko should have sought him out in the first place. Their only connection had been over the Fontainebleau affair, and that ought to have warned Eyskens. Apparently it never occurred to him that Marko might be set on wiping out whatever tracks he'd left before moving on: that he was one of the few people who could identify him. What seems certain is his plan to rob Sobel merely postponed the inevitable. Marko must have seen it as a windfall, a way of lining his own pockets before attending to his main business.'

Sinclair paused to reflect on what he had said.

'Whether Sobel's murder was part of Eyskens's plan, or whether Marko was simply following his instincts, we'll never know. But the scheme misfired. It seems Rosa turned up at the critical moment. She may actually have seen the murder take place. What's certain is she screamed and ran from the house out into the street and Marko pursued her. Given his usual pattern of behaviour, there's not much doubt he would have killed her as well if he'd caught her, but before he could do that he ran into a pair of gendarmes who were patrolling in the district and had to turn tail. Shots were exchanged and they chased after him, but he managed to escape. However, in the interim Rosa had disappeared. The gendarmes had seen her come out of the house and one of them called to her to wait for them there, but when they returned she was gone. Later, after Sobel's body had been found, it was learned from his desk diary that he'd had an appointment that same afternoon with Eyskens. Since his name was already known to the police, a pair of detectives were dispatched to bring him in for questioning, but they found him dead in his office. Strangled. Presumably his plan had called for Marko to return the stones to him after robbing Sobel, so he would have been expecting him. Later, when their pathologist examined his body they found signs of torture on it.'

'Torture—?' Madden shot him a look.

'He'd used his wire on Eyskens's neck before killing him . . . the marks were plain to see. The police thought it likely he was trying to persuade him to open his safe; that he was after the money Sobel had paid for the stones earlier. We're back with greed. He must have been interrupted though, because he had to run for it again when the police arrived – this time over the rooftops. But he took the diamonds with him and that list Eyskens had made. The police found a copy of it on Sobel's body: that's what alerted them to the theft. They also found a large sum of cash in the safe when it was eventually opened. The equivalent of about £25,000 according to the figures Duval gave us.'

'But Marko got away?'

Sinclair nodded. 'By the skin of his teeth. But the police had a stroke of luck. They got hold of the name of the hotel where he was staying. He'd rung Eyskens when he'd arrived and left a number which Eyskens's secretary had made a note of. So they got to the hotel before he did and found he'd left a briefcase in the safe there with a large sum of money in it. About £40,000 in various currencies, Duval said.'

'Good grief!' Madden was struck dumb with surprise.

'The wages of sin, one assumes.' The chief inspector cocked an eyebrow. 'All this took some time to put together, needless to say, but eventually the Dutch police discovered the identity he'd been living under in Amsterdam and they located a safe-deposit box in the same name at a bank. It was empty; he must have cleaned it out before leaving.'

Sinclair paused to swallow what remained of his drink.

'They also provided the French with some details about him, what they'd gathered from people who'd come in contact with him. It made interesting reading. The name he used for a start – Meiring. As I say, he had French papers, acquired for him by Bok most likely, but he claimed to come from

Alsace, of German stock, which would have explained his less than perfect French. He let it be known he was a dealer in rare stamps and actually had a collection, though there's no record of him having done any business. Or none the French have been able to come up with. But it gave him an excuse to travel whenever he needed to.'

'How did the Dutch police know he had a stamp collection?' Madden had been paying close attention.

'From a woman who knew him. A prostitute. She used to visit him once a week. His tastes were . . . how shall I put it . . . unusual.'

The chief inspector raised an eyebrow.

'He liked to be punished . . . whipped or beaten with a cane. The woman in question was a specialist in these matters, but although she was accustomed to dealing with clients of his kind, she claimed she was never at ease in these sessions. There was something about this man that alarmed her, and although the drama they played out required her to assume a dominating role, in fact it was she who was afraid of him, and she only continued with the arrangement, which lasted for a few months, because he paid her well.'

Sinclair drained his glass for a second time.

'That apart, his life was unremarkable, excessively so. He seems to have lived at the same address in Amsterdam for six years without catching anyone's eye. He'd obviously come a long way since his Balkan days. There he'd been little more than a cheap thug. By the time he joined up with Bok he was a much smoother article, and he must have put some thought into how others saw him. Though he made no friends, he had a number of acquaintances and he let it be known that he'd been married in the past but lost both his wife and young son in a motor accident. He was thought by some who knew him to be still in the grip of melancholy, and he seems to have used this perception as a means of keeping them at bay, not that anyone seemed to regret this. None were ever easy in his company.'

The chief inspector was silent for a moment.

'There was something else the Dutch police learned – they found out he'd been a member of a chess club and used to play there regularly. He was better than average, according to other members, but they knew little about him. He would arrive, play a game or two, drink a glass of schnapps and then depart. When he first joined, one or two tried to engage him in conversation, but they gave up. It seems he had nothing to say for himself. All the same, the police were told an interesting story . . .'

'What was that?'

'It came from one of the members of this club, a lawyer who played quite often with Meiring. He said that once in the mid-Thirties – he thought it was in 1934 – he had travelled to Brussels on business and while he was there had caught sight of his chess opponent. At least he had thought it was him, though Meiring looked different. He was wearing spectacles and his hair seemed to have greyed somewhat. The encounter was fleeting. This lawyer was hurrying to board a train to return to Amsterdam and he only caught a glimpse of the man he took for Meiring.'

'Took for him, you say?'

Sinclair nodded. 'When they met again a few weeks later at the chess club, the lawyer remarked that he thought he'd seen him in Brussels, but Meiring said he was mistaken. He hadn't been away for some time.' The chief inspector grunted. 'Our friend Duval was intrigued by this and went through the records – their own collection of IPC messages – and found there'd been an unsolved murder in Antwerp in June of 1934. The director of a shipping firm had been shot dead in his office late one night. There seemed to be no motive for the killing other than the fact that he'd threatened to expose one of his partners for embezzlement. Duval recalled what Bok's widow had said about her husband hiring out his pet killer from time to time and wondered if this was another of Marko's victims.'

'It sounds as though they had a financial arrangement,' Madden remarked. 'Bok arranged the contracts and Marko executed them.'

'And given the amount of cash he was carrying when he left Holland, he must have been well paid. His life's savings lost at a stroke! That may explain why he set up that Wapping business. He needed the money – for when he makes a run for it.'

'Yes, but that's what bothers me . . .' Madden stirred unhappily in his chair.

'You mean the haste he acted with? What you said before?'

'It was a strange way to behave. Rosa was dead. She wasn't a threat to him any longer. He could afford to take his time. Yet he acted at once, setting up the robbery and using an accomplice he normally wouldn't have touched with a barge-pole. Something was goading him on. But what?'

Gnawing at his lip, Madden peered into the dregs of his beer, as if the answer might lie there. Then he shook his head again, this time in frustration. 'You were saying – they missed him at the hotel, the French police?'

'He must have realized they were waiting for him; the trail went cold after that. Mind you, the fact that the first German units entered Paris the day after Sobel's murder didn't make things any easier. Though policing continued as normal during the Occupation, there must have been a hiatus which Marko may have used to his advantage. Duval says they weren't sure at that stage who he was, but they already suspected he might be the same man who had killed the Lagrange family because of the link with Eyskens and through him to Bok. Later, when they received a copy of Bok's widow's statement from the Dutch police, they could be certain. By that time, of course, it was clear Marko had left the country, and since they had no idea of his destination, they checked with the Spanish and Portuguese authorities and also got in touch with the FBI in Washington. We know now it was England he came to, and since it seems unlikely he travelled via Spain and Portugal, he must have found some way of crossing the Channel.'

Sinclair stretched in his chair. He was feeling his years.

'His details had been noted at the hotel where he stayed in Paris. That's how the Sûreté got hold of the name he was using. Later they were sent to the Dutch police, who used them to ferret out the identity he'd been living under. The point is, Marko seems to have been in possession of papers and probably a passport that to all intents and purposes looked genuine, and he could have used them to enter this country if he'd wanted to. There was no way we could have learned they were bogus: not with France and Holland occupied. He could have sat out the war here as Klaus Meiring and no one would have been any the wiser. But instead he chose to abandon the name, which suggests he had another ready-made identity to step into. One that was clean.'

'And most likely his own.' Madden nodded his agreement. 'He was coming home.'

'That's what it looks like. But unfortunately we can't dismiss the possibility he arrived here under another alias, so we're going to have to check on all foreigners who entered the country in the weeks following the occupation of Paris. The same goes for British subjects, the ones who bothered to report their return. It's going to be a long job, I'm afraid, which means Marko will have all the time he needs to cover his tracks, something he's had plenty of experience doing. I should have listened to you, John. I was too cocksure. I thought we'd catch him easily once we had him in our sights. I was wrong.'

He looked at his watch at the same moment that Madden glanced at his.

'So you're going back to Highfield tomorrow – is that right?'

Madden nodded as they rose from the table.

'We've been hoping Rob will be with us for Christmas. But it's only a week away now and there's still no word from him. The trouble is they won't tell you when his destroyer is due back. They won't tell you anything.'

Sinclair pressed his arm: there was little else he could offer in the way of comfort. But once they were outside, making their way down the dark street towards the tube station at Tottenham Court Road, he turned to a more cheerful subject.

'And what of Lucy? You haven't said a word about her.'

'She'll be home for Christmas. I can tell you that much. They've given her a few days' leave. But the fact of the matter is I've hardly set eyes on her since I came up. She's never in. I don't know what I'm going to tell Helen.'

'You arrived with instructions, did you?'

'You might put it that way. Helen wanted me to have a serious talk with her. Father to daughter. I'm supposed to find out what she's been doing since she came up to London.'

'Dear me.' Angus Sinclair contrived to look grave. 'No easy task, I imagine.'

'I told you – I haven't been able to sit down with her, even for a minute. She's always in a rush. But try explaining that to Helen . . .'

The hint of self-pity in his old friend's tone brought a gleam of mischief to the chief inspector's eye. He was finally deriving some enjoyment from the evening.

'She expects you to be firmer, does she?'

'In a nutshell. Though I don't think she holds out much hope. She says Lucy has always known how to get the better of me. Like most daughters with their fathers, according to Helen.'

He meditated on his own words in silence as they walked on. Then he sighed.

'It seems I'm putty in her fingers.'

17

THE TRUTH OF THIS judgement, harsh though it seemed, had been only too evident to Madden during his stay in London. Anxious to see his daughter before she went on duty, he had caught the early train from Highfield, but as often happened nowadays the service was delayed – this time by a breakdown in the signalling system, or so the passengers were told as they sat motionless for more than an hour in Guildford station – and it was not until mid-morning that he'd reached his destination, only to discover that Lucy was still asleep.

'Poor dear – they work her something dreadful,' Maud Collingwood's maid, a woman he had known for twenty years but only by her first name, which was Alice, had confided to him on his arrival. 'Until all hours. She has to catch up on sleep as best she can, poor child.'

Not entirely surprised – it was Helen's contention that Lucy's vagueness on the subject of her working hours arose from a confusion in her mind (she was unable to distinguish the Admiralty from Quaglino's and the Stork Room) – Madden had offered no comment. He intended to get this matter, and others, sorted out when he sat down with her later. Instead he had enquired after Aunt Maud, only to be told that she seldom came downstairs before one o'clock.

'She and Miss Lucy usually have breakfast together in her room, and that can be any time,' Alice had informed him. Well into her sixties now, she had acquired a benign motherly look that reminded Madden of the pictures of

Mrs Tiggywinkle he had shown Lucy when she was little. 'It depends . . .'

'Depends on what?'

'On what time Miss Lucy wakes up. We don't like to disturb her.'

Forced to bide his time, Madden had set about carrying out the instructions he'd received from Helen before departing.

'Look over the house, would you, darling. Aunt Maud's far too old to keep an eye on things and Lucy's a scatterbrain. Make sure all the doors and windows are secure and see that everything's in working order, not just the boiler.'

A quick tour of inspection had proved reassuring. He had found nothing that required immediate attention apart from the boiler, which Alice confirmed had been 'playing up', adding that arrangements were already in hand for its repair.

'Since when?' This was news to Madden.

'We had a man come in yesterday,' Alice had told him. 'He said it needed some part which he'd have to get hold of. He'll be back tomorrow.'

'What man? Who is he?'

'Ah, well, you'll have to ask Sid that. He's the one who sent him round.'

'*Sid*?'

'Miss Lucy's friend. Have you met him, sir?'

Madden had not. Nor had he ever heard of him. But the omission was soon repaired. At eleven o'clock – just as the first faint stirrings could be heard on the floor above – the doorbell had rung and Alice had admitted a young man wearing a sharp-looking suit and sporting a pearl-grey fedora which he'd doffed on being introduced.

'Morning, squire,' he'd greeted Madden.

Sid's black hair, plastered flat on his head, had shone with brilliantine. His wide smile revealed a gold tooth.

'Luce up?' he'd enquired of Alice, and on being told she had not yet appeared had placed a parcel wrapped in brown paper on the kitchen table.

'Nice bit of fillet, that,' he'd confided to Madden in a low voice. 'Trouble is there's no one here to eat it. Luce is never in and as for Miss C . . .' He had raised his eyes to the ceiling. 'Well, she don't seem to consume. Isn't that right, love?'

His last remark, directed at Alice, had brought a giggle from her lips.

'I've told you before, Sid, Miss Collingwood eats like a bird. It's no use bringing all this food. It's just going to waste.'

'Well, you never know . . .' Sid had sounded philosophical. 'Squire . . .'

Saluting Madden with a further flourish of his hat, he'd departed.

Not averse to gossip, Alice had told him that Sid had knocked on their door one day to enquire if they needed any coal and that from that moment on his relationship with the household had blossomed.

'Do anything for Miss Lucy, he would.'

Shortly afterwards the subject of their discussion had appeared, still in her pyjamas and dressing gown, and with her long hair uncombed. Catching sight of her father as she burst into the kitchen, her face still flushed with sleep, she had flung herself into his arms.

'Daddy, why didn't you tell me you were here? Why didn't you wake me?'

She had hugged and kissed him, and paused only long

enough to inform Alice that Aunt Maud would like toast and tea but that she herself would do without breakfast that morning.

'I'm in a rush,' she confided to them. 'I've been late on duty twice this week.'

The transformation between the rumpled child he had held in his arms for a brief moment, so familiar, so deeply loved, and the poised young woman who appeared not ten minutes afterwards, elegant in her navy blue coat and with her golden hair coiled neatly under a Wren's hat, had robbed him of all words.

'It's so lovely you're here, Daddy. I'll try not to be late this evening.'

She had kissed him warmly and departed.

Later he'd discovered, when he ascended the stairs to pay his respects to Aunt Maud, that the old lady had been only too happy to hand over the running of her household to her great-niece.

'She's such a dear girl. So full of surprises. Do you know what she found for me to eat the other day? A jar of caviar. And now she's having the boiler repaired. Such a treasure.'

Aunt Maud had received him propped up by pillows in her bedroom. Shrunken by age, she retained a bright eye, but although she took a lively interest in all matters relating to the family, she'd been unable to enlighten him on the subject of Lucy's activities outside the house.

'The poor child works till all hours,' she had said, repeating the theme Madden had already heard voiced by Alice. 'But she comes in to see me whenever she can and we have such lovely talks. She's so like her mother. Sometimes I forget it's not Helen sitting there on the end of my bed.'

With the repair of the boiler now out of his hands – at least for the time being – Madden had been reduced to pottering about the house, and though he'd had no intention of prying further, nevertheless found another shock awaiting him. Conscious of the relative good fortune all country dwellers shared when it came to the matter of food rationing, he'd arrived laden with produce from the farm, and having deposited the butter, eggs and cheese he had brought with him in the conspicuously crowded fridge, had looked for a place to put the pork pie May Burrows had made at his request, eventually settling on one of the cupboards in the pantry.

'Good God!'

Its contents revealed, he had stood aghast.

'What on earth . . . ?'

Stacked up before his eyes was an assortment of delicacies now little more than a memory to most. Tinned pheasant, pâté de foie gras, preserved truffles; yet another jar of caviar. Three tins of olive oil marked 'extra vergine' and bearing the name of a Genoese manufacturer. Two bottles of champagne; two of cognac. On the shelf below were bars of chocolate laid one on top of the other beside expensive prewar condiments – chutneys and sauces with exotic names – and beside them a noble Stilton, its cloth wrapping as yet untouched.

And what were these?

'Oranges!' Madden had exclaimed out loud.

'Ooh, yes.' Alice had been standing behind him, watching. 'They were a surprise. I did squeeze one for Miss Collingwood yesterday morning to have with her breakfast but she said it was too acid for her stomach.'

Though resolved to get some explanation from his daughter, Madden had been thwarted when Lucy had rung during the afternoon to say she would not be home until very late – an emergency had arisen at the Admiralty – and he was not to wait dinner for her. When midnight had come and gone with no sign of her he had gone to bed, but the following morning when she appeared downstairs already dressed in her uniform and in the same hurry to be off he had moved to intercept her.

'Daddy, I can't stop now,' she'd implored him.

He had never found it easy to resist her appeals, and the uncanny resemblance she bore to her mother, not only in looks, but even in her gestures and the tone of her voice, only added to his difficulty. But on this occasion he had steeled himself.

'No, wait, Lucy. I must have a word with you.' He had stood in the doorway of the kitchen barring her exit. 'This man . . .'

'What man?' For a moment panic had flared in her eyes.

'This Sid!'

'Oh, *Sid*?' Her smile pierced his heart. 'Have you met him? Isn't he an angel?'

'No, he's not an angel. He's a spiv. All that food in the cupboard – where on earth do you think it comes from?' And when she'd failed to reply. 'You can't imagine he got hold of it legally?'

Two tears had appeared in her sapphire eyes.

'Lucy . . . !'

'It's not for me. It's for Aunt Maud. She never eats anything, but I keep hoping we can find something she wants. Sid's doing his best.'

'I'm sure he is. Have you any idea what it must be costing her?'

She had stayed silent. But her glance had been accusing.

'My darling, it's quite normal for old people to behave this way. They lose interest in eating.'

'That's easy for you to say,' had been her riposte. 'But if you like I'll speak to him. Poor Sid. He'll wonder what he's done wrong.'

Unable to detain her any longer – she'd warned him she would be 'disciplined' if she was late again – he had had to let her go without fixing a time for the talk he meant for them to have, and sure enough, when he'd returned after his long afternoon at Scotland Yard it was to discover yet another telephoned message to the effect that she would be working a double tour of duty that evening and would be spending the night with friends, two other Wrens who had a flat in Victoria not far from the Admiralty.

'Does this happen very often?' he had asked Alice when she served him what proved to be an excellent dinner. (Only after Madden had sunk his teeth into one of the tender slices of beef put before him did he realize it must be the piece of fillet Sid had brought the day before that he was eating.) 'Surely they can't expect these young girls to work double shifts?'

'Oh, I wouldn't know about that, sir.'

Alice's pursed lips had suggested she did not think the subject a suitable one for discussion. But on the topic of the illicit hoard of food Madden had discovered, and which continued to trouble him, she had proved surprisingly sympathetic to his point of view.

'I do wish Sid would ask first. There are all sorts of things Miss Collingwood can't digest nowadays. Chocolate, for example. Nor those oranges. I'm sure I don't know what I'm going to do with most of it. You couldn't help, could you, sir?'

'Take it away, you mean?' Madden had frowned at the idea. 'But it's all been paid for, Alice. By Miss Collingwood.'

'And a pretty penny it's cost her too, sir, I can tell you. But it's not doing any good sitting there.'

'Well, I suppose I could take some of it. There are plenty of children I know down in the country who'd love a bar of chocolate. And some of them have never tasted an orange. I'll have a word with Miss Collingwood before I go.'

'At least I'll return bearing gifts,' Madden told Helen when he rang her at her surgery the morning after his drink with Sinclair to say he would be taking the train back to Highfield later that day. 'And the boiler's purring like a kitten, though no thanks to me. I keep thinking of that advertisement you see in all the railway stations. "Is your journey really necessary?"'

As always, his first question had been about their son. He'd been hoping she might have heard from Rob since they last spoke, but Helen told him there was still no news.

'I'm sure his ship should have been back by now. It's weeks since they sailed.'

Since pursuing the subject would only have added to their worry, Madden had quickly moved on to other topics, reassuring her first that funeral arrangements for Mrs Laski were in hand – the thought had been causing Helen concern – then relating to her the gist of what Sinclair had told him the night before.

'I've heard of criminals like him, paid assassins, cold killers, but in all my time as a policeman I never had to deal with one and I'm afraid Angus has his hands full. This man's clever. He thinks ahead. The worst of it is, by rights the police ought to know his real name by now. It's quite extraordinary that they don't.'

'Why extraordinary?'

'Because of Alfie Meeks. I told you about him. He was just a petty criminal, but for some reason Marko took up with him. Used him, rather. Used him then killed him. But Meeks was a lead that ought to have paid off. Somehow he and this man were connected, but though the police have combed through Meeks's record they can't find any link between them. The answer *ought* to be there, but it's not, and it makes no sense.'

Helen made a humming sound. In the background Madden could hear a man's voice speaking in a monotone. She was listening to the lunchtime news with one ear while they talked.

'I know what Miss MacFarlane would have said. She was our maths teacher at school. "Girls" – ' Helen mimicked a Scottish accent – ' "Remember Occam's razor." '

'What's that?' Madden chuckled. 'Some fiendish surgical device?'

'Not at all. It's a medieval concept. Roughly speaking it says, when the solution to a problem isn't clear, look for the simplest answer. Oh, and I've just remembered, darling, I won't be here when you get back. I've got to go over to Farnham this afternoon. I've promised to help Jim Oliver with his rounds. He's on crutches at the moment. So I can't pick you up at the station. Can you manage? I'll tell Mary you're coming home. She'll have tea ready . . .'

She paused for few moments, expecting a response, and when one failed to come:

'John . . . ! You've gone silent. What is it?'

She received no reply. For the last few seconds Madden had been staring at a watercolour of Westminster Bridge with the Houses of Parliament behind it which hung in the hall above the telephone. But his gaze had lost focus: he was staring at nothing.

'Look, dear, I've changed my mind.' He found his tongue. 'I'm not coming home this afternoon. I'm going to stay up another day. There's someone I have to talk to.'

'What did I say?' She was laughing.

'Something very interesting . . . the simplest answer . . .'

'And why is that so interesting?'

'Because it's been there all along, staring me in the face, and I didn't see it.'

Obliged to inform the household of his change of plans, he knocked on Aunt Maud's bedroom door and, as usual at that late hour of the morning, found her up and dressed and sitting in front of a brightly glowing fire fuelled by a substance which these days was as rare as hen's teeth: real coal.

'He's a resourceful young man, that Sid,' Madden observed, after he'd poured them each a glass of sherry. 'But I'm not sure you should have any more dealings with him. Or you might find the police knocking on your door.'

'An alarming thought, to be sure, though less so for me than for others.' Aunt Maud's bright eyes twinkled. 'Old age has its advantages. One can always claim senility as an excuse. But thank you for the advice, my dear.'

Needle-sharp in spite of her advanced years, she had the reputation of a tartar in Helen's family and few had escaped her barbed tongue unscathed. But for reasons unknown to him, Madden had always been a favourite of hers, and during his stay in London their talks had centred largely on family gossip, a passion of Aunt Maud's, whose interest these days was focused on the youngest member of the Madden clan.

'I'm beginning to wonder if she has a young man,' she announced before he took his leave, having arranged to spend a further night under her roof. 'You can usually tell with girls. They get a look in their eye. But it's no use asking her. She's as deaf as a post when she wants to be. Mind you, her mother was just the same.'

In the course of their conversation that day, Madden had

also enquired about the hoard of illicit foodstuffs downstairs and received Aunt Maud's permission to plunder it at
will. After conferring with Alice, he filled a shopping bag
borrowed from her with a selection of items from the cupboard, to which he added the chunk of homemade cheese
he'd brought up from the country – it could hardly compare
with the Stilton – and the pork pie May Burrows had made
at his request but which Alice assured him, apologetically,
she could find no possible use for.

Though anxious to be on his way – he had something of
an expedition ahead of him – he delayed his departure long
enough to ring Billy Styles at the Yard to ask him for
directions to the open-air market in Southwark where Alfie
Meeks had had his stand.

'Are you planning to go down there, sir?' Billy asked after
Madden had made a note of its location.

'Yes, I am. But you'd better not tell the chief inspector.
He might think I was taking things into my own hands.'

'You're not actually doing that, are you, sir?'

Billy's concern was so naked it made Madden laugh.

'Of course not. It's just an idea that's come to me;
something I can only do myself. But on second thoughts you
can tell Mr Sinclair I may have a surprise for him later.'

'A surprise—?'

'And ask him if he's ever heard of Occam's razor.'

18

THE MARKET WASN'T hard to find. Though it had no address as such, the piece of waste ground on which it was located, fronting a derelict warehouse by the Thames, in the shadow of Southwark Cathedral, was visible from some distance off.

'You'll see it upriver to your right when you cross London Bridge,' Billy had told Madden when he'd learned that his old mentor was planning to travel down from St John's Wood on the Underground. 'It's only ten minutes' walk from Monument.'

In the event, the light rain that had been falling when he set off from Aunt Maud's house had turned to driving sleet by the time he emerged from the tube station, and crossing the bridge, at first he caught only a glimpse of his goal as he clutched at his hat, turning his face away from the stinging pellets of ice, harbingers of more bad weather that was moving in from the Atlantic, according to a forecast he had heard on the wireless that morning.

But even before he reached the further bank the squall passed and he was able to pause and take stock of the scene. Being near the docks, it was an area that had suffered heavily in the Blitz four years earlier, and while Madden could recall the dramatic newsreel footage of the destruction wrought by the bombing and of the damage left in its wake, it was the first time he had seen for himself the gutted buildings lining the river, their walls charred by the nightly rain of incendiary bombs, and the near-mystical sight of the great dome of

St Paul's, floating calm and serene above the devastation surrounding it, miraculously untouched.

It was not a part of London he knew well – he had never been posted to Southwark during his time as a policeman – but on the journey down he had found his thoughts straying to an episode from his past, before the Great War, when as a young detective he'd been assigned with a more senior colleague to investigate a double murder that had taken place in the borough. Two bodies had been found in a house not far from the river, one of them that of a postman who had gone missing. Like the second victim, a drayman's wife, he'd been battered to death, and detectives later discovered he had called at her house the day before with a registered letter and, finding the door ajar, had stepped inside – no more than that – most likely announcing his presence as he did so, only to be struck on the head with a heavy lamp stand swung by the already dead woman's enraged husband, who had just beaten his wife to death after a furious quarrel.

Although the case had been easily resolved – the husband had tried to drown himself in the Thames, but lacking the nerve, finally, had struggled ashore and lain sprawled on a stretch of bank exposed by the tidal ebb until he was spotted – Madden had never forgotten it. The casual manner of the postman's death – the terrible power wielded by chance in human destiny – had struck a chord in him that was to sound over and over again in the years ahead when his own life had hung by a thread in the charnel house of the trenches while those of so many others around him had been blown away.

Only that morning he had put the same thought into words while relating to Helen what he had learned from Sinclair about Rosa's tragic encounter in Paris with the man who would later kill her.

'They might so easily have missed one another in the Underground. He wasn't stalking her. He had no idea she was here. But he saw her by chance and her fate was decided in a moment.'

The market site, when he reached it, proved to be a stretch of muddy ground cobblestoned in places and crammed with stalls whose owners were still busy removing the protective strips of canvas and other makeshift coverings they had used to shield their goods from the rain. One of many that had sprung up all over the country in response to the shortages that were now a part of everyday life, it had the air of a temporary encampment hastily pitched and liable to vanish at any moment, an impression heightened by the chestnut vendors whose mobile braziers, glowing like campfires, had been set up at whim about the site.

'Between you and me, we tend to turn a blind eye to them,' Billy had told him that morning. 'A lot of the goods on sale are black market, and then there's the stuff that's been pilfered from bomb sites. We come down hard on looters when we catch them, but once the stuff they've lifted has been put back in circulation, there's not much we can do about it. And there are always people looking for household goods these days – stoves, pots and pans, cutlery – folks that might have been bombed out themselves and lost everything. So as I say, we tend to look the other way.'

Whatever else, there seemed to be no lack of customers, Madden noted wryly as, despairing of finding any easy way through the tightly packed stalls, he chose one of the roughly marked avenues between them and started to forge a path through the dense throng of shoppers, most of them women, and some of whom were still in their dressing gowns and slippers, suggesting they must live locally. The row he had picked was devoted to kitchenware and the trestle tables lining it on either side were heaped high with crockery, little of it matched, as well as an assortment of second-hand cooking utensils and mounds of cheap-looking cutlery. At the end of the line were some smaller tables where a variety of goods were on display: cigarettes, lipstick, pocket combs. One bore a stack of American magazines beside a bottle of men's hair oil.

'There are blokes really scraping the bottom of the barrel down there,' Billy had told him. 'And Alfie was one of them. I was told he had the odd bottle of scotch for sale and sometimes a few bars of decent soap. But mostly it was cigarettes and tinned food. It's a mystery how he made a living at all.'

During his slow passage along the crowded avenue, Madden had been scanning the faces behind the banked tables. What he could see of them. With a cold wind still gusting up the river, most of the stallholders, both men and women, had wrapped themselves in heavy coats with scarves that were not just wound about their necks but in many cases pulled up to cover their mouths so that few of their features were visible. Having reached the end of the row, he paused, and as he did so his eye fell on some wooden planks that were lying stacked one on top of the other near to where he was. Stepping up on to the low platform they provided, he stood still, scanning the whole expanse of the market, letting his gaze move slowly up and down the rows of trestle tables, studying the faces of the stallholders. Towards the edge of the market, not far from the river, was a section where clothes were being sold, and as his glance wandered along the row, his eyes narrowed and he began to stare hard at one stall in particular, a long trestle table piled high with various articles of clothing, behind which a woman stood stamping her feet and slapping her gloved hands together. Clad in a coat and scarf like others, she also wore a knitted woollen cap pulled down low over her forehead, but even so there was something familiar about her stocky figure, and Madden smiled in recollection.

Two minutes later, having ploughed his slow way along another avenue packed with shoppers, he approached the stall where Nelly Stover was busy with a customer, a housewife by the look of her: she had a shopping bag not unlike the one Madden himself was toting, which she had parked on the table in front of her. He paused a short way off – now that he was closer he could make out Nelly's craggy features more clearly, the jut of her lantern jaw – and waited patiently while the prospective purchaser chose a dress from a number hanging on a rail behind the stall. Holding it up to her body, she examined her reflection in a mirror which Nelly had produced from beneath the table, and, having nodded her approval, paid for the garment with a banknote and some change. As she moved away, Madden edged forward until he was standing in front of the stall. Nelly had bent down to return the mirror to its place under the table and he waited until she stood up before he addressed her:

'Hello, Nelly,' he said.

The slate-blue eyes beneath the woollen rim of the cap narrowed with suspicion. She gave him a long hard look. Then, without warning, a harsh cackle of laughter burst from her lips.

'Well, strike me pink!' she declared. 'If it isn't Officer Madden!'

'I heard about you,' she told him later. 'Cos I asked, see. That sergeant at the station in Bethnal Green, what was his name –

Callahan – he said you'd left the force. That you weren't a copper no more. That was before the war. The last war. And I told him it was a pity. That we could do with a few more like you.'

'I came back afterwards,' Madden told her. 'I rejoined the police. But not for long. I'm a farmer now.'

'Garn . . .' She was disbelieving.

'It's true. I got married and my wife and I bought a farm in Surrey. I'm hardly ever in London any more.'

By good fortune he'd arrived shortly before Nelly shut up shop for the day.

'It's too bad I have to close early. I lose a bit of business. But the kids come first.'

She left the market every day at half-past three, she told him, so as to collect her two grandchildren from the woman who looked after them during the morning and gave them their lunch.

'They've been living with me for the past three years, them and their dad, when he's here. Bloke called Denny Miller. He married my Margie. You never knew her. She was just a nipper when you was in Bethnal Green.'

'I remember your son, Nelly.'

'You mean Jack?' She smiled. 'Him that you kept out of stir?'

'He wouldn't have gone to prison. Not at his age.'

'Maybe not, but they'd have sent him to a borstal for sure, and I've seen many a boy come out of there after a year or two and never the same again. Anyway, he turned into a good bloke, my Jack, thanks to you. Got himself a proper trade – he's a fitter and turner. Works in an airplane factory up in Birmingham.'

She had glanced at Madden as she spoke: he was helping her clear her stall. They were loading the clothes into cardboard boxes and the boxes on to a trolley – the kind used by railway porters to shift luggage.

'What happened to Margie, Nelly?'

'Copped it in the Blitz, that's what.' She bit her lip. 'I heard their house had been hit, they were living just down the street from where we were, her and Denny, only he was often away, being a merchant seaman, so I ran down there and when I saw the house, what was left of it, I thought it was all up with them. Margie and the kids. Both floors had caved in. But when the firemen dug down they found them in the basement, Tom and little Sally. Covered in dust, they were, but not a scratch on them. Margie must have taken them down there when she heard the sirens and then gone upstairs to fetch something. Anyway she was in her bedroom when the bomb hit, so that was that. And then a month later I got the telegram . . .'

'The telegram?'

'About Bob . . . you remember him? My old man?'

Madden nodded. He had put his own bag on the trolley.

'I was told he was lost at sea. I'm sorry, Nelly.'

She grunted something and was on the point of turning away when a thought seemed to strike her and she paused to peer at him; more keenly now.

'*Told* was you? It wouldn't have been by that copper who was down here the other day, asking questions about Alfie Meeks?'

'Yes, I heard it from him.' Madden nodded. 'Billy Styles. We're old friends.'

Nelly Stover absorbed the information in silence. Then she cocked an eye at him.

'So you turning up here – it's not just a coincidence then?'

'Hardly.' Madden met her glance and she guffawed.

'Fancy that.' She chuckled to herself. 'Well, if you've come down here to ask me about Alfie, you're wasting your time. I told that copper everything I knew, which wasn't much. And you've left it a little late, what's more. I've got to go off now. I can't stay here.'

'I know. But I thought I might come with you, Nelly.' Madden smiled. 'I'd like to meet your grandchildren.'

'Oh, you would, would you?' She produced the same harsh, cackling laugh. 'Well, if you like . . . I've got no objection.' But she shook her head as she turned away. 'My grandkids . . . my eye!'

Still chuckling to herself, she grasped hold of one of the handles of the trolley, Madden the other, and together they set off, pushing the clumsy vehicle over the cobbles, skirting the market and the line of chestnut vendors, pursuing a course set by Nelly that took them away from the river and up the side of the ruined warehouse into a street lined with houses, several of which were only bomb sites now, yawning holes from which the debris had long since been removed. It was in front of one of these that Nelly paused, and at her direction they steered the trolley down a narrow alley into what must once have been a small back garden where a potting shed still stood undamaged.

'I managed to get hold of the key for this,' she told Madden after she had unlocked the door and they had begun to move her goods inside. 'Bloke who owned the house sold it to me for a fiver. It's been worth its weight in gold.'

Inside the dark, unfloored structure there was a suitcase lying on the ground, and Nelly gave it a kick.

'I don't have to tell you who that belonged to, I reckon,' she remarked. 'In fact, if I'm not mistaken you knew Alfie when he was a lad. Back in Bethnal Green. Him and his family.'

Madden nodded. 'I was talking to Billy about him the other day.'

She digested his statement in a silence that lasted for several seconds.

'And you're still telling me you ain't a copper no more?'

'That's right, Nelly.'

His words produced another cackle of laughter from her.

'Well, if you say so . . .'

What light there was in the sky was already dying as she locked the door behind them and they set off through the deepening dusk. In the distance the faint wail of an air-raid siren sounded, but faded quickly into silence. Across the river a searchlight probed the darkening sky. Paying no heed to either, Nelly plodded on, talking as she walked, offering Madden a brief account of her life in the years that had passed since they had last seen one another.

'We left Bethnal Green, Bob and I, back in '20, after the war. He'd been at sea since he was sixteen and he was in one of the first ships that was torpedoed – bet you didn't know that. When this lot started he told me not to worry: said it couldn't happen to him twice. Anyway we came over here, south of the river, and we never went back. I told that friend of yours, that copper, I hadn't seen Alfie since he was a lad. But I heard he'd got himself sent to a borstal. Poor little sod. Never had a chance in life, not with a father like that.'

'When did you go into the clothes business, Nelly?' Madden paced along beside her.

'A year ago come Christmas. With Bob gone I had to do something, and then I thought of these markets that had started up all over. I get hold of old clothes and do 'em up. Sell 'em like new. Well, not new, but you know what I mean. That's what I did when I was a lass. Sewed. I was a seam-stress. Bet you didn't know that neither.' She chuckled. 'But then who would have guessed you'd turn into a farmer. Officer Madden . . .'

They had been walking through narrow streets in a darkness so dense Madden had been able to make out little more than the dim outlines of the terrace houses on either side. Here the full blackout was still in force and only the occasional faint glow at the edge of a blind or curtain signalled the presence of life inside. With little sense of where they were any longer – he knew only that the river lay to their left – he had allowed Nelly to guide them, and when she came to a halt outside a front door he checked his own stride.

'Wait here. I'll just be a sec.'

She knocked on the door, was quickly admitted and in less than a minute was back again with two small figures who tumbled out into the dark of the street holding on to her hands.

'This one's Tom.' She indicated the taller of the two figures. 'And this here's Sally. Say good evening to Mr Madden,' she commanded them and they mumbled some words. 'Our house is just down the road. I'll have to give these two a bite of supper before I put them to bed. Then you and I can sit down together and have a quiet cup of tea.'

Her smile glinted in the darkness.

'And maybe then you'll tell me the real reason you came down here.'

Nelly Stover's kitchen shone like a new pin. Though there was nothing in it – nothing Madden could see – that wasn't old and well used, every surface from the rough pine table they were sitting at to the enamelled sink and the glass-fronted cabinet that housed Nelly's best china showed the effects of repeated washing or polishing. Even the linoleum-clad floor had a sheen to it.

'We bought this house twenty years ago, Bob and I,' Nelly had told him when they came in off the street. She'd gone ahead to the kitchen, which was at the back, to fix the blackout blinds and switch on the light before inviting him to follow. 'Lucky we didn't lose it in the Blitz. There was three others in this street that copped it.'

Stripped of her coat and scarf and the woollen cap, her face was revealed as more bony than Madden remembered it, the craggy features accentuated by the shedding of what little surplus flesh had once covered them, and seen in repose her thrusting jaw combined with a flinty gaze gave her the look of someone to be reckoned with. But when her tight-lipped mouth broke into a smile, which it did at the sight of the crayon drawing of a cat which her little granddaughter had been clutching, waiting to show to her, her face took on a quite different aspect.

'I don't know what I'm going to do when the war's over,' she had confessed to Madden while the children were out of the kitchen for a few moments washing their hands. 'I've got used to taking care of these two: I won't fancy giving them up. But I dare say Denny'll get married again one of these days and then he'll want a home of his own.'

Before long the smell of frying bacon filled the kitchen as Nelly bustled about preparing supper for her two charges, who on returning had been urged by their grandmother to take their seats at the table. Tommy, a wiry six-year-old with straw-coloured hair cut close to his scalp, placed himself opposite Madden, obliging his little sister, whose own fair hair hung in ringlets, to clamber on to a chair beside him, where she seemed uncomfortable, her chin barely clearing the rim of the table, until Madden, with a smile, scooped her up and placed her on his lap. 'There – isn't that better?'

'Well, look at you,' Nelly said, seeing the beaming smile

on her granddaughter's face as she brought their plates from the stove and then set about spreading margarine on the slices of bread she'd cut earlier.

When the two children had munched their way through their sandwiches, Madden reached for his shopping bag, which had been resting on the floor at his feet.

'What's this, then?' Nelly demanded, her eyes sparkling, as four bars of chocolate appeared from its depths as if by magic. They were followed by a tin of biscuits and then three oranges which Madden produced from the bag one by one with the air of a conjuror drawing rabbits from a hat and laid on the table in front of them. 'Bribery and corruption?'

She caught her granddaughter's eye.

'You've never seen an orange, have you?'

The little girl shook her head. She gazed in wonder at the fabled objects.

As her brother reached for one, Nelly checked him.

'Not so fast.' She seized the orange herself. 'One's enough for the two of you. The others'll keep for later. But who's going to peel it – that's the question?'

She made a show of looking around the table.

'I know – Mr Madden!'

She passed him the fruit, then sat back with folded arms to watch as he plucked at the rind.

'Now you see what you've let yourself in for.'

Tommy, too, had been eyeing him from across the table.

'Was you a copper once, mister?' he asked, bolder now that he and his sister were getting used to the tall stranger's presence.

'Yes, I was, Tommy. But that was a long time ago. I've got a farm now. It's not far from London.' He caught Nelly's eye. 'You must bring them down,' he said. 'When the weather gets warmer. Let them come and spend a week with us. Helen's always saying the house seems empty without children.'

'Well, we'll have to see about that.' Nelly was at pains not to show any undue pleasure at the invitation, but the flush in her cheeks betrayed her true feelings.

'Have you got a horse, mister?' Tommy had been paying close attention.

Madden nodded. 'An old mare called Daisy. I use her for getting about the farm.'

'Can I ride 'er?'

'You certainly can.' He nudged the small figure on his lap. 'What about you, Sally? Do you want a ride on Daisy?'

She shook her head, still too shy to speak.

'We've got other animals. Rabbits and dogs and cats . . .'

'What about piglets?' She spoke up at last.

'Oh, we've got lots of those.'

His task complete, Madden divided the orange in two and handed half to Tommy. Then he began to separate the other half into individual lobes, popping them one at a time into Sally's open mouth. She chewed luxuriously, oblivious of the juice running down her chin. Nelly watched for a minute, shaking her head, then got up and went to the sink, returning with a damp cloth which she handed to Madden.

'Here – you're going to need this.'

She studied him while he mopped the little girl's face and then took care of her hands, one finger at a time.

'You've done this sort of thing before, Officer Madden.'

'We've got two of our own, Nelly. They're grown-up now. Rob's in the navy. He's serving on a destroyer. Lucy joined the Wrens this year.'

Madden bent his head to look at the small face below his.

'There now. Is that better?'

Nelly guffawed. She clapped her hands.

'Right, now. Off to bed, the two of you. I'll be up in a minute to say goodnight and if you're good there'll be a piece of chocolate for each of you.'

Tommy scampered off obediently, but Sally lingered on, leaning back against Madden's chest, head tilted to look up at him.

'She wants you to carry her upstairs. That's what her dad always does when he's here.'

Madden rose at once and, hoisting his small giggling burden on to his shoulder in a fireman's lift, he bore her up the narrow stairway to the children's room at the top of the house, which he found papered with daffodils and decorated with a poster of a Spitfire speeding through a sky darkened by the smoke of exploding anti-aircraft shells, its guns blazing. Tommy had already slipped into his pyjamas – he was lying beneath the bedclothes – but it quickly became apparent that the process would take longer with his little sister, who was in no hurry to dispense with the services of the willing slave she'd acquired.

'What? Not in bed yet, young lady?'

Nelly had dallied in the kitchen to clear the table before coming up. She stood in the doorway now with a fierce frown.

'Someone doesn't want their bit of chocolate.'

Sobered by the threat, Sally abandoned her delaying tactics and, helped by Madden, who was sitting beside her on the bed, struggled to push her hands through the narrow sleeves of her flannel pyjamas.

'Come on,' he coaxed her, as he'd once coaxed Lucy when she'd been little. 'Let the dog see the rabbit.'

'What rabbit?' Tommy shot up in bed.

'Now see what you've started.'

Laughing, Nelly shooed him out, and a few minutes later she joined him in the kitchen downstairs.

'They'll be looking for that rabbit all night.'

In her absence Madden had emptied his bag on to the table.

'That's a bit of home-made cheese, Nelly, and some butter, too. And I can vouch for this pork pie. Nobody makes a better one than May Burrows.'

Nelly Stover ran her hands over the greaseproof-paper parcels. She sighed.

'I reckon it's time we had that cup of tea.'

Silence fell between them as she busied herself with the kettle. At the table, Madden sat lost in thought. Nelly glanced at him over her shoulder.

'I used to wonder what happened to you,' she said. 'After you left Bethnal Green. After I heard you'd quit the force. I've never forgotten what you did for my Jack. It might have seemed a small thing to you, bringing him home to me instead of taking him down to the station. But it's small things like that can make a difference to a boy's life.'

She poured boiling water into a teapot, emptied it, spooned tea-leaves into the heated interior and then refilled the pot.

'Take Alfie Meeks now. He never had a chance, poor lad. Not with a father like that. Jonah used to hit him with his belt, and he made a point of using the buckle end. You could hear Alfie yelling up and down the street. But Vera couldn't do nothing. She was too scared.'

'Vera—?'

'His step-mum. Jonah used to beat her too. I'd see her down the high street often enough with a black eye or a cut lip. Once he broke her arm. It all came back to me when I heard about Alfie and that business at Wapping. I couldn't understand what *he* was doing there. A bloke who never amounted to nothing. Scared of his own shadow, he was. Mixing with the likes of Benny Costa. It didn't make sense.'

She brought the teapot over to the table and sat down. Madden waited while she filled their cups.

'The police thought the same,' he said. 'They've been wondering how Alfie came to be there. Who got him involved.'

He was watching her expression closely. But she seemed to take no special note of what he'd said.

'And what about you, then?' she asked. 'What are you doing down here? You still haven't said.' She peered at him over the rim of her teacup. 'Did the Old Bill ask you to come and talk to me? If so, you're wasting your time. Like I said, I told that other copper everything I know. I hadn't seen Alfie for years till he turned up at the market that day. I'd forgotten he even existed.'

Madden sipped his tea. He hesitated, choosing his words.

'I came on my own account, Nelly. I wanted to talk to you. But not about Alfie. Not directly, anyway.'

'Oh . . . ?' She sounded wary. 'What then?'

'I've got a question for you. It's about something that happened thirty years ago, and I'm not even sure you know the answer. But if you do you're going to have to decide . . .'

'Decide what?' She paused with her cup at her lips.

'Whether or not to tell me.'

He met her gaze with his own steady glance.

'Go on then,' she said.

'Who was it cracked Jonah Meeks's skull and pushed him into that tank? That's what I want to know. Who murdered Alfie's father?'

'Crikey!'

She stared at him.

'You're asking me *that*?'

Madden nodded.

'Now? After all this time?' She seemed bemused. '*Why*?'

'There's a killer loose in London. He's murdered several people: not just Alfie and those others at Wapping. Two women besides. I think it may be the same man.'

'Same bloke as murdered Jonah?'

'So you know about that?'

'I didn't say so.'

Nelly scowled and Madden saw he'd caught her off balance. She sat staring at the cup which was clutched in her fingers. He spoke again:

'Nelly, I think you know the answer.' He paused. 'Won't you tell me?'

She kept her eyes from his, refusing to meet his gaze.

'I seem to recall the law saying it was an accident,' she muttered.

'That was how it looked at the time. But I've begun to wonder. And remember . . .'

'Remember what?'

'How the people down there behaved afterwards, some of them. Ones I talked to. Oh, they didn't say anything, but I saw it in their faces.'

'Saw what?'

'Satisfaction. Only I didn't know then what it meant. I thought they were just pleased to have seen the last of Jonah. But now I'm not so sure. I think they knew something. Or they'd heard it . . . a story maybe . . . ?'

Madden cocked his head to peer at her.

'A story . . . ?' She laughed harshly. 'Well, you hear plenty of those.'

'Yes, but did you hear the one about Jonah?'

There was a long pause. Then at last she looked up.

'I might have . . .'

Madden warmed his hands on his teacup. He saw from her face that she was still undecided and he waited patiently.

'This feller . . . the one you say topped Jonah. What makes you think it's the same bloke as killed Alfie?'

Her flinty gaze had hardened; she challenged him to reply.

'We know Alfie was working for someone; that's why he quit his stall at the market. He had money in his pocket when the police found his body and with no explanation of how it had got there. Even before he went down to Wapping that night he was in deep, and that could only have happened through someone he was familiar with. Someone he trusted, perhaps. Someone who was also a killer.'

'Which didn't leave too many possibilities. Is that what you're saying?' Her voice was toneless and Madden nodded.

'There's nothing in Alfie's record to suggest he'd ever mixed with violent criminals; that he was acquainted with anyone like that. You said yourself he was a nobody. So it had to be someone from his past . . . his childhood even.'

'Someone who only had to lift a finger for him to come running? Is that what you mean?' She looked at him bleakly

'I suppose so.' Madden shrugged, and as he did so saw a shadow pass across her rugged features.

'Someone like his brother?'

'Alfie Meeks had a *brother*?'

Madden was thunderstruck.

'Not really, no.' Nelly grimaced. 'Not a proper brother. He was Vera's son by some other bloke. She had him before she married Jonah.'

'So he was Alfie's *stepbrother*?'

'I suppose . . .' She shrugged. 'But he only lived with them, with Jonah and her, for a little while. Then Vera had to send him away. She parked him with a sister of hers who lived out Romford way.'

'What was his name?'

'Raymond. Ray, Vera called him.'

'Ray . . . ?' Madden scowled. 'I don't recall ever hearing that name.'

'No reason you should have.' Nelly smiled bleakly. 'Especially after Jonah copped it. Anyone who knew what had happened wasn't going to breathe a word. Like you said, they was all that pleased to see the last of him.'

Still shaken by the revelation, Madden paused for a moment to order his thoughts.

'You said Vera had to send him away. Why? Jonah must have known she had a child when he married her.'

'Oh, he knew, all right. I told you: at first Ray lived with them. Alfie's mum had died a year or so before – pneumonia it was – and Vera took care of them both. But it didn't last. After a few months she had to send Ray away. Vera told me herself. It was when I had that fish-and-chip shop. She used to come in of an evening to get their supper. She said those two – Ray and Jonah – they couldn't live under the same roof. Jonah had started out trying to treat him the way he treated Alfie; knocking him about when he felt like it; clipping him round the ear. But that soon stopped. Ray wasn't the sort you could do that to. Once when Jonah hit him he grabbed a kitchen knife and went for him, Vera said. Jonah threatened to wring his neck, but that was just bluff, she reckoned. The fact was he was scared and so was she. She was afraid Ray would take a knife to Jonah one night when he was asleep. Cut his throat maybe. That's what she told me.'

'Good God!' Madden was appalled. 'How old was he then?'

'Ray?' Nelly screwed up her face as she searched her memory. 'Thirteen, fourteen . . . ? I couldn't say for sure. A couple of years older than Alfie, anyway.'

'You're telling me Jonah Meeks was afraid of a fourteen-year-old boy?' Madden shook his head in wonder.

'All I'm telling you is what his mum told me. Mind you, if you'd met that boy you might think different. Sometimes he'd come over from Romford when Jonah was away; when he was off working on the coal barges, which was the closest thing he ever had to a job. I was there once or twice when Ray turned up – by then he was older, sixteen maybe – and I remember how he'd sit in Vera's kitchen, not saying a word while she kept chattering on; smiling to himself as if there was some joke only he could see. Thinking his own thoughts. He had this way of staring at you, staring through you, like you weren't there. It gave me the shivers.'

'Would Alfie have been present?'

'Oh, yes. He was there, looking at Ray with these big eyes. I reckon Ray was who he wanted to be himself. Someone who wasn't afraid. Not of Jonah, not of anything.'

'He hero-worshipped him? Is that what you thought?'

'Maybe.' Nelly shrugged. 'But what he couldn't see was that Ray didn't care for him one bit. He didn't care for anyone. Not even his own mum. She knew it, Vera did, poor soul. I reckon it broke her heart.'

Nelly shuddered involuntarily. Clasping her elbows, she hugged herself tight.

'Still, if Ray had suddenly turned up now, after all these years, Alfie might have been pleased to see him?'

'He might.' Again she shrugged. 'Like I said, he never understood the sort of bloke Ray was. Mind you, he'd have been surprised. We all thought he was dead.'

'Why?'

'Well, he went off to the war, didn't he, like all the other lads?' Nelly gestured with her hands. 'That was the last I heard of him. Mind you, by then Vera had moved away – she went to live with her sister in Romford after Jonah copped it – so we didn't know for sure what had happened to Ray. Only that he never came back.'

'What about Alfie? What became of him?'

'Vera took him with her, but he got into trouble quickly, ended up in a borstal, I heard. By then Bob and I had left Bethnal Green, we'd come south of the river, and I didn't hear any more about them, except that Vera had caught the flu soon after the war and died. After what she'd been through, I reckon it was a blessing.'

In the silence that followed, Madden heard the faint sound of a clock striking in the distance. He counted seven chimes.

'Tell me about Jonah,' he said. 'What happened that night? How did he die?'

Nelly ran a hand across her brow.

'I don't know nothing for sure. All we heard was a story. Bloke who told it to us – and this was a while afterwards, maybe a year later – was a pal of Bob's, someone he'd known since they were boys. He'd heard Bob was back ashore for a spell and he dropped in to see him.' She laughed shortly. 'You probably remember him. Feller by the name of Charlie Mort.'

'Charlie Mort, the burglar? I helped send him up.'

'Not for long, you didn't, because he was fresh out of stir when he came to see us. Him and Bob had been lads together and Bob always liked him, though he thought he was a fool for doing what he did and told him so often enough. Not that it made any difference. Anyway they went down the pub, the two of them, and when they came back Charlie had

had a few and he told us about Jonah. What he'd heard. He'd got the story from a bloke he knew in stir, he said.'

Nelly paused. A crease had appeared in her forehead.

'Now you'll also know who I mean by Seamus Slattery?'

Madden nodded. 'That Irish thug. He was responsible for most of the crime in the borough. He and his gang. They went in for thieving mostly, and extortion. But they had a tie to one of the big race-course mobs, I remember. They'd go down to Newmarket to lend a hand whenever there was a fight in prospect.'

'That was them, and they reckoned Bethnal Green was their patch. Their manor. No one was allowed to take liber-ties.' Nelly laughed. 'Except they forgot to tell Jonah, or maybe he wasn't listening. He'd worked for them early on; Seamus had him as his bodyguard for a while. But it didn't last. Jonah never took orders from anyone and when he got drunk he was a holy terror. He'd been inside twice for assault, and that's not counting all the other times he got into fights. Nor the time Seamus sent two of his boys round to a bookie who hadn't paid his insurance and they found Jonah there and for some reason, or maybe no reason at all, he took against them and gave one of them a cracked skull and threw the other out of a window. Lucky it was only the second floor, but the bloke still ended up with a broken leg.'

'I remember that . . .' Madden nodded his head in recollec-tion. 'We heard about it. But there were no charges pressed.'

'Well, you wouldn't expect any, would you, not with Seamus Slattery. But you can imagine how it looked. There was him saying it was his manor and nobody was allowed to step out of line, and there was Jonah tossing his blokes out of windows. It couldn't be allowed to go on.'

Nelly bit her lip.

'Course, what would have happened normally was he

would have sent some of his fellers round with orders to make a right mess of Jonah. But they'd already tried that, and each time he was given a seeing to he'd find the blokes who'd done it later on and give it back to them, only worse. So Seamus decided enough was enough and one night when they were all at the old Ship's Bell, which was the pub they used, he laid a hundred quid in notes on the table and said it was for whoever got rid of Jonah for him.'

'He wanted him killed?'

'He never used the word, according to Charlie – though Charlie wasn't there – but everyone understood what he meant. And it seems the news got out. I didn't hear it, but some must have, because by Charlie's account there were bookies taking bets on how long Jonah would last, while others were offering odds on him turning the tables on Seamus and topping him. But less than a week later, while people were still thinking about it, Jonah's body turned up in that tank.'

Madden grunted. 'I was there that morning. At the soap factory. We'd heard about him getting drunk the night before and staggering off home. The detectives were already thinking it was most likely an accident. What really happened?'

Nelly gave a sigh.

'What happened was that Seamus and his lot were sitting in the back room of the Ship's Bell around lunchtime drinking toasts or what have you to the news when Vera's Ray shows up and says he's come to claim his hundred quid. Well, of course they just laugh at him, but then he tells them he's got proof, and before they know it he's pulled out a set of false teeth with a nick in one of them from his pocket and dropped it on the table in front of Seamus. "There you are," he says. "That's your proof."'

'Jonah's missing bridge?' Madden shook his head. 'We

noticed it was gone. We thought it must have fallen out of his mouth and sunk to the bottom of the tank. And I remember now – one of the teeth was chipped.'

'You'd run into him, had you?' Nelly was curious.

'Several times. Twice to break up disturbances in pubs.' Madden laughed. 'I used to look at him and hope to heaven he wouldn't take it into his head to have a go at me. He was a big brute and he had hands like shovels. All of which makes me wonder . . .'

'Wonder what?'

'How that boy got the better of him. Did Charlie tell you that?'

Nelly nodded. She paused to refill their cups.

'The bloke he'd got the story from had been in the Ship's Bell that day and had heard what Ray had to say for himself. Seems he'd learned about the hundred quid and come over from Romford. Either he knew where Jonah would be drinking or he followed him to the pub, and he must have guessed what route he'd take home because he was waiting for him in the soap factory. Right by the tank, in fact. It was the only way through the yard; you had to walk past it.'

'I remember it well. The path narrowed at that point. There was a wall running alongside it.'

'There was and all.' Nelly bared her teeth in a grin. 'And guess who was up on top of it when Jonah came by. With a bleeding great rock in his hands.'

'Ray dropped a rock on his head?'

'So Charlie said. Knocked him out cold. Then he hopped off the wall, hit him a couple more times with it just to be sure, then rolled him into the tank, not forgetting to take his teeth out first.' She shook her head. 'And him all of sixteen years old.'

Madden sat silent. He was staring into his teacup.

'But here's the bit that really surprised Charlie; not me though.' Nelly's thin lips parted in another bitter smile. 'Seamus paid him! He gave Ray the money. Charlie said he couldn't believe it. Here was this lad, this boy who was still wet behind the ears, trying to get a hundred quid out of Seamus Slattery! Even if he'd done what he said he'd done there was no reason Seamus shouldn't have just given him a kick up the backside and told him to bugger off. But instead he paid him like he'd promised.'

'And why weren't you surprised?' Madden was still gazing into his teacup.

'Because I knew him, that Ray, and Charlie didn't. I'd looked into his eyes the same way Seamus Slattery must have done. I'd seen his smile. I never exchanged a word with that Irish pillock, not in all the years we lived in Bethnal Green, Bob and me, but I can tell you what he was thinking. He knew Ray had done what he'd said he'd done, and just by looking at him he knew that if he didn't pay him it was odds on he'd be next, and he didn't want to spend the rest of his life looking over his shoulder.'

She put down her cup.

'So now you know. But that still don't explain why it's you that's come asking me all these questions instead of the law. Is it because we used to know each other? Did you tell them I owed you a favour because of what you did for Jack?'

Madden shook his head. 'No, it's not like that, Nelly, though I did think it might be easier if you and I talked alone. But I was already involved in this business. I told you this man had killed two women here in London. One of them worked for me on the farm. She was a Polish girl, a refugee.'

'Why'd he kill her?'

'At first we didn't know. There seemed no explanation for it. But now it appears she saw him kill a man in Paris. That was years ago, just as war was breaking out, but then he ran into her here by chance a few weeks ago . . .'

'And topped her? Just like that?' Nelly shuddered.

'Whoever did it – and whoever murdered Alfie and those others, because it was the same man – has made a living out of it. He's an assassin, Nelly; killing's his trade. The French police know all about him, though they never found out his real name, or even where he came from.'

'And you reckon it's Ray?'

'I do now.' Madden's nod was final. 'The man I'm talking about never worked in this country. He plied his trade in Europe and you've just told me Ray didn't come home after the war. Other things seem to fit, too. The early contact with Alfie Meeks. Jonah's murder. But mostly what you said about him.'

'What *I* said?'

'The feeling you had.' Madden met her gaze. 'What you sensed about him. What you saw in his eyes.'

She shook her head; her distress was plain.

'I always knew he had a black heart. But killing people for a living . . . !'

Madden waited until she had collected herself.

'I'm going to have to tell the police what you've told me, Nelly. I've no choice. I'm going to give them his name. He's been living in Europe all these years under aliases. But it's likely he's using his own name now because he's kept it clean. The police can start looking for a Raymond Meeks.'

'That'll keep 'em busy,' Her bleak grin had returned. 'From now until Judgement Day, if you ask me. Seeing as how he never called himself that.'

'What do you mean?' Madden stared at her.

'He wouldn't have taken Jonah's name, that boy, he wouldn't have called himself *Meeks*, not for anything. Vera never married his dad, so it was her name he used always. Ash. That's what he called himself. And that's who you should be looking for.'

She shook a finger at Madden.

'Raymond Ash.'

PART THREE

19

'OH, DEAR – what a nasty business this is. I'm so sorry to bother you with it, Bess dear.'

Mary Spencer spread her hands in a gesture of apology.

'But I want your advice. I've told Evie she must make a clean breast of this. It's the only sensible thing to do. But she doesn't want to, poor thing. She's afraid it might mean trouble.'

Shivering, Mary drew closer to the small fire that was burning in the grate. Bess had lit it when she'd arrived; unexpectedly. Mary had walked into Liphook from the Grange to do some shopping, and seeing Bess's pony-and-trap standing in the road outside her cottage had knocked on the door. Bess, it turned out, had only looked in for a moment to collect an extra sweater before continuing with her postal round, but on discovering that Mary wanted to talk to her had insisted that she come in for a cup of tea.

'It's a strange story.' Bess Brigstock sat frowning, nursing her cup in her hands. 'She came to you on her own, did she? You had no idea . . . ?'

'None at all,' Mary assured her. 'It was a complete surprise.'

'I wonder what made her do it. Tell you, I mean.'

Mary shrugged. 'She hasn't been herself for some time. Not since she went up to Norfolk to see her husband. You remember he was wounded and in hospital there? I thought she was behaving oddly when she came back. I could see she had something on her mind, but though I asked her once or twice if there was anything bothering her, she always said no, and I just assumed it was her husband she was worrying about. She knew that once he was better – he just had a minor shrapnel wound – he'd be sent back to France to rejoin his unit, so it was only natural.'

She paused to stare into the flames that were starting to catch and spread in the fireplace. A frown creased her brow.

'When did she come to you?'

'Last night. After we'd put Freddie to bed. I didn't know what to say at first. It was so . . . so *unexpected*. And I couldn't think what to advise her. After all, it's not as though she hasn't had time to decide herself. She and her husband. So I told her I'd sleep on it and speak to her again this morning.'

'Which you did?' Bess frowned. Mary nodded.

'As soon as Freddie had had his breakfast and gone outside. I told her there was no rush, but once Christmas was over she must talk to the police. I said I'd go with her to Petersfield and that seemed to cheer her up.'

Bess made one of her rumbling bear-like noises; a sort of low growl that always brought a smile to Mary's lips.

'You don't want to do it through Bob?' she asked, meaning Bob Leonard, the Liphook bobby.

'No, I don't think so. He's a good sort, but he's an awful old gossip, and I don't want people talking about Evie. Pointing a finger at her. I'm sure it's something that can be cleared up easily. What do you think?'

'Oh, I imagine so. The thing, as you say, is to make a clean breast of it. You must tell her not to worry.'

Bess patted her hand and Mary smiled in relief.

'Dear Bess. Thank you for listening. I feel so much better now. You're such a comfort to me.'

Uncomfortable as always at being singled out for appreciation, Bess dismissed her thanks with a wave of her large paw. She rose, collecting the tea tray as she went, and disappeared into the kitchen. With a sigh Mary sat back and let her eye wander about the small sitting-room, which was decorated for the most part with souvenirs of her friend's earlier life. Framed snapshots of Bess in exotic locales stood on side tables. In one she was seated on a camel with a great sweep of desert behind her; in another, ankle-deep in the mud of some narrow alley with two small black children clinging to her hands. Pride of place, though, had been given to a larger photograph, handsomely mounted, which hung above the fireplace. It showed a much younger Bess – and a strapping girl she'd been – dressed in a voluminous leather coat and khaki puttees, standing with arms akimbo between two similarly attired women, all three of them smiling broadly. Behind them, serving as a backdrop, was an ambulance of First World War vintage marked with a red cross.

'They were happy days,' she'd told Mary once, 'though the war was dreadful. But we were such friends, all of us. And it was an adventure, driving into areas where the battles were still going on, something women had never done before. The men used to cheer when they saw us.'

Soon Bess was back, bustling in with their coats.

'It's time I was off. I'm heading out towards Devil's Lane, but I can give you a lift as far as the crossroads.'

'Will we see you out to the Grange?' Mary asked a few minutes later when they had both mounted on to the sprung seat of the trap and Bess was unhitching the reins.

'Yes, but not for an hour at least. I've all this Christmas post to deliver first.' She nodded at the pile of packages in the trap behind her, smiling as she did so. 'There's something for you. I was keeping it as a surprise. It's a parcel from Canada.'

'Oh, Bess...' Mary was delighted by the news. She screwed round on the seat and peered down at the heap of parcels. 'It must be from my cousin Jenny. They live in Toronto. I was starting to think she'd forgotten us this year.'

Bess clicked her tongue and the trap gave a lurch as Pickles set off.

'It's right at the bottom,' she said. 'Dig around and you'll find it.'

Mary did as she was told, and having delved among the packages found the one she was looking for. She lifted the canvas-sewn bundle up by its stout binding, but quickly set it down again.

'Goodness, it's heavy. She always sends us jam and marmalade. And a big tin of biscuits. They're just what I need for Christmas.'

'You can take it with you now if you feel strong enough.'

'Oh, no, that would never do. Freddie loves the ritual of you arriving and then the excitement of seeing whether you've got anything for us. This will be a red-letter day. There's nothing he likes better than opening parcels from overseas. There's nearly always a bar of chocolate in them.'

Mary turned and faced the front, her cheeks flushed by the cold air as they rattled along at the brisk trot Pickles had settled into.

'I'm so glad we had this talk. Now all I have to worry about is Peter. I had a letter from him a few days ago – but of course you know that. He said it's absolutely foul in Italy. Cold and wet and miserable. He never mentions the fighting. All he hoped was that our Christmas would be better than his, and I'm determined to make it so, especially for Freddie. It's lovely that you're coming to us, Bess. It'll make all the difference to the day.'

She chattered on.

'Did I tell you we've got a turkey? I've been on tenter-hooks about it. At first the MacGregors weren't sure they would have one for me; it seems they'd all been spoken for months ago. But then one of their customers dropped out. I went over to the farm yesterday to inspect it. I couldn't resist the temptation. It's a splendid-looking bird.'

'But one not long for this world, alas.' Bess sighed windily and Mary laughed.

'I knew you'd say that. And I did feel awful for a moment, watching it gobbling down its food and thinking: yes, go on, keep eating, the fatter you get the better. Thank goodness Annie will take care of the slaughtering and the plucking. At least I won't recognize it when I put it in the oven.'

She looked up at the sky. The clouds had been piling up for days; thickening, or so it seemed to her; growing dense and heavy with the burden they bore.

'Oh, I wish it would snow,' she said. 'Freddie's longing for a white Christmas and so am I.'

Mary shook the blanket she was holding vigorously and then paused to look up at the sky through the tall sash window. The clouds seemed a trifle lower and still heavy with promise. She wondered where Freddie and Evie had got to. The house had been empty when she'd returned, cheeks flushed red from her walk, but forsaking the warmth of the kitchen where the old iron range was kept burning day and night, she had gone upstairs where it was always colder, to start pre-paring the room that would be Bess's when she came to them for Christmas.

The house wasn't an easy one to manage. Old and ram-bling, it was an uneasy mix between the farm it had started out as and the country villa it had become thanks to additions made in the last century. These Victorian touches had given it a somewhat gloomy aspect seen from the front, where high eaves overlooked an elaborate garden now run wild. At the rear, however, the less formal surroundings of the stable yard and the stalls behind it made for a more cheerful picture, particularly now that it had become Freddie's playground, and Mary never tired of watching her small son as he scampered about the cobbles.

Discovering on their arrival that the house was without a central heating system – the uncle from whom she had inherited it had spent his winters in the south of France – Mary had decided at the onset of the cold weather to restrict their living quarters to as few rooms as possible. Apart from the kitchen, where an oak table with matching chairs provided ample space for family meals, and where by far the greater part of her time was spent, the only room she had made use of downstairs was a small sitting-room reached via a passage that ran the length of the house, where she and Evie would sit together in the evening listening to the wireless while they read or sewed. She had abandoned the spacious drawing-room beyond it completely, finding it cold even in late summer; likewise the dining-room that lay on the other side of the kitchen at the far end of the passage.

Upstairs there were six bedrooms, two of which were occupied by Mary and Evie, while Freddie was accommodated in what must have been a dressing-room adjoining his nanny's living quarters. Luckily the single bathroom still supplied hot water, thanks to a wood-burning furnace in the basement whose mysteries Hodge had explained to Mary once he was assured that her unexpected arrival at the Grange held no threat to himself.

Again it was Bess who had come to her aid when Mary found her initial advances to the elderly couple rebuffed.

Employed by her uncle during his lifetime, they had been left to take care of the house after his death.

'Old Hodge is afraid you'll put a spanner in his works,' she had explained with a chuckle. 'Don't forget, he's been lord of the manor for the past few years. Monarch of all he surveys. He keeps two cows in the stalls there, as you've probably noticed, besides his dray horse, and raises porkers in the pigsties. What's more he and Mrs H have taken over the old kitchen garden. They do a thriving business at the village market and he's wondering if they'll be allowed to continue.'

'Well, he needn't,' Mary had protested. 'I'm perfectly happy for things to go on as they are.'

'I should tell him that then, and also offer to buy milk and cheese off him and a side of bacon next time he slaughters one of his pigs. Chances are he'll offer them to you for nothing, which strictly speaking he ought to, seeing they're your facilities he's using. The important thing is to make the gesture.'

Mary had wasted no time in following this advice, with the result that her relations with the couple had improved to the point where Mrs H now came in three mornings a week to help with the housework while her gnarled husband, unasked, delivered fresh milk and butter, as well as vegetables from the garden, to their doorstep, assuring Mary meantime that he was ready to help with any problems that might arise.

Chief among these was the amount of wood needed to keep them warm, and here Hodge had proved his value, supplying them with logs gleaned from the woodland that was part of the twenty or so acres that went with the house. Mary herself had become adept at chopping up these large pieces into smaller sections for use in the stove, though not nearly as skilful as Bess, who wielded an axe and saw with all the aplomb of a lumberjack and who apparently liked nothing better than to round off her working days with half an hour of brisk exercise by the woodpile in the yard.

She had seemed happy, too, to join with Mary in picking out a few acceptable items of furniture from among the mass of heavy, ornate pieces with which the house was stuffed. Together they had rummaged through the cold, empty rooms and the attic above, accompanied always by Freddie, who had enjoyed these expeditions. A man of some means – and as far as Mary could remember, one little inclined towards work of any kind – the uncle who had left her the house, and whom she had barely known, had spent much of his life abroad. Not an explorer exactly, rather a wanderer, he had accumulated a bizarre collection of souvenirs from his travels: tiger-skins and hookahs from India; puppets from the Indonesian archipelago; Maori carvings and other totems that hailed from the South Sea islands. Some they had discovered hanging on the walls, others relegated to the attic or the basement. A Red Indian headdress found hanging on a hook in what had once been the gun-room had been appropriated by Freddie and now decorated the wall above his bed. His attempt to take possession of a Zulu shield and assegai that came to light in the attic, however, had been blocked by Mary and his pleas had moved her only so far as to agree to allow the objects to be mounted on the wall in the sitting-room well out of reach of his eager hands.

Having shaken out the bedclothes, she left the bed stripped to air and went downstairs to the warm kitchen, where a stew made of scrag ends, the only meat available in the butcher's that week, had been simmering on the iron range all morning, and where Hodge's wife – known to all as Mrs H – was busy peeling potatoes and chopping up carrots and parsnips to add to the pot. A cheerful woman with a face as red as a lobster, she'd become a great favourite of Freddie's once he'd discovered she had a glass eye.

'There'll be snow before the day's out,' she remarked to Mary. 'You'll see. And once it starts it'll go on. That's what they say.'

The topic had been much discussed between them, Mary's romantic wish for a white-clad countryside countered by Mrs H's countrywoman's dislike of the stuff because of the disruption it brought to everyday life, a dislike tempered now by her realization of how much it would mean to Freddie. She had had two sons herself, she had told Mary, both killed in the last war, and within only a few weeks of one another, a tear rolling down her cheek from one eye as she spoke, while the other had remained fixed and staring.

Having lingered for a moment longer to inspect her stew and give it a stir and a cupful of water, Mary went to the other end of the room, where the latest proof of Ezra Hodge's now well-established benevolence towards her household was on display in the shape of a Christmas tree. A week earlier the old boy had knocked on the kitchen door and presented her with the object, which he had dragged from his cart.

'Spotted it in Foley's Copse a month ago,' he had said, referring to a small wood at the edge of the property, his weathered countenance split by a toothless grin. 'Been keeping an eye on it.'

Together he and Mary had filled a wooden tub unearthed from a pile of junk in the barn with soil and set up the tree in a corner of the kitchen. Later that same afternoon, when Freddie had returned from a walk with Evie to the neighbouring MacGregor farm, he had found his mother down on her knees stringing fairy lights on the pliant branches and had watched open-mouthed as she crawled behind the tree to plug the set in and then sat back on her heels with a sigh.

'I noticed these in a box when we were going through the attic,' she told them both. 'I've no idea if they still work.' (A small fib; she had already tested the circuit.) 'Freddie, why don't you switch them on and we'll find out.'

Holding his breath, eyes popping with suppressed excitement, her son had found his way under the branches to the switch and a moment later, like magic, the score of brightly coloured bulbs had come alight. Red, blue and gold, they had twinkled amidst the branches while the little boy gazed in wonder at the sight.

Further embellishments had since been added to the tree, thanks to Bess, who had produced several yards of silver string to drape on the green branches and an angel with hands folded in prayer to perch on top. But although Mary loved seeing it lit up, she was conscious of the need to save electricity and only turned on the switch after dark.

Pausing for a moment to set the angel straight, she went to a door beside the tree which gave access to the cellar beneath the kitchen. Steep steps led down into darkness, but there was a light at the top, and, having switched it on, she descended to the dank depths and, before pursuing the mission that had brought her there, attended first to a task that by now was almost second nature: checking the wood-fired furnace that occupied a corner of the basement to see if it needed feeding. Maintaining a supply of hot water for the house was one of her principal worries: both the furnace and the water tank above it were relics of an earlier age and Mary lived in dread that one or the other, or perhaps both, would fail, leaving the household deprived of this basic amenity.

Relieved, as always, to find all well, and having added some logs to the fiery mass within, she turned to scan the cellar's varied contents, which included old wine racks, discarded pieces of furniture and crates of books too mouldy to put in shelves but which Mary hadn't had the heart to throw out. She had not found the item she was searching for when she noticed that the door which gave access to the yard had been left unlocked yet again. The culprit was undoubtedly her son, who, though he'd been told countless times not to play down there, persisted in exploring the stored rubbish whenever he got the chance, safe in the knowledge that a swift escape was always possible should his presence be detected.

Having rebolted the door for the umpteenth time – and reminding herself to speak to Freddie yet again – Mary resumed her search and almost at once spotted what she was looking for: a full-length mirror that was standing propped against the wall beside an empty wine rack. Grasping hold of the glass on either side, she retraced her steps and ascended to the kitchen, pausing at the top to switch out the light and delaying a few seconds more when she saw her own reflection close up: her brown eyes (which Mary secretly had always thought of as her best feature) now showing the first faint creases at the corners that one day – one day all too soon – would turn into crow's feet; her cheeks still unmarked by age but grown thinner and browner these past months, a development she ascribed to the healthy outdoor life she'd been living, and last of all her hair, which she hardly dared look at. Deprived of the services of a beauty salon – the nearest one was in Petersfield – she'd been forced to rely on the combined efforts of Bess and Evie to keep her thick brown hair trimmed and manageable, and though they had done their best (she was sure) the results had not been happy, and for several days after each barbering session Mary had gone around feeling like a shorn sheep. She wondered what Peter would say if he saw her: she wondered what he would feel when they met again after so long. (It was more than two years now since he'd been posted abroad with his regiment.) Would they have to get to know each other again? Would something have been lost between them? Shuddering at the horrid thought, she thrust it from her mind.

The mirror was destined for Bess's room, which for some reason was lacking one, but as Mary reached the top of the stairs with her burden and stepped into the kitchen she heard the creak of wheels outside and saw through the window above the sink that Hodge's cart, drawn by his old dray, had appeared in the yard and was moving slowly across the cobbles. The mystery of Freddie's whereabouts was solved at the same moment; she spied her son sitting perched on the driver's seat beside its owner, holding the reins while Evie, buttoned up in her coat and with a woollen shawl shielding her head and ears, walked alongside them.

'Keep an eye on this, would you, Mrs H?'

Leaving the mirror propped against the sink, Mary went outside into the freezing afternoon air. She waved to Freddie, but he gave no sign of seeing her, being far too occupied with managing the reins. Hodge, however, lifted his cap in a salute.

'Lad's getting the idea,' he called out.

Evie waved her free hand. She was carrying a basket of pine cones from the wood, where they must have gone with Hodge, and Mary watched as she took off her shawl, shaking her head and letting her red hair fall free; smiling as she did so. It seemed the talk they had had that morning had lifted her spirits, and thinking over the events of the past few weeks Mary thought she understood better now how the girl's worries must have been accumulating until they reached the point where she felt the need to share them. She walked across the yard to join them, smiling herself as she saw Freddie, with his mentor's help, bring the cart to a stop. Still bubbling with pleasure as his feat, he sprang off the seat into his mother's arms.

'Did you see me, Mummy? Did you see me?'

Before Mary could reply, the clip-clop of trotting hoofs sounded from the lane outside and next moment Bess swept into the yard, the wheels of her trap rattling on the uneven cobbles.

'Whoa, Pickles!'

She pulled back on the reins, drawing to a halt beside the cart.

'Just the man I'm looking for.' She peered down at Freddie. 'I've got a parcel in the back for you all the way from Canada. I wonder what's in it.'

Turning, she hoisted up the package from the bed of the trap and lowered it into his waiting arms.

'Careful! It's heavy.'

Bundled up like a parcel himself in a tweed coat and scarf, Freddie's short arms offered little in the way of purchase, but somehow he managed to hang on to the precious object, and ignoring his mother's offer to take it from him he turned and set off on a weaving path towards the kitchen door. Evie hurried after him, still clutching her basket of pine cones, ready to catch the package if it fell.

'Hodge, thank you for all this lovely wood.' Mary turned to the old man, who had climbed down from his seat and was starting to unload the logs from the back of the cart. 'Here, let me help you with those.'

'Oh, don't you worry, Missus. I can manage.'

Gnarled and gnome-like though he was – Mary could only guess at his age, but she thought he must be seventy at least – Ezra Hodge still possessed surprising strength, and it took him only a few minutes to haul the logs he'd brought out of the cart and carry them to the stall that served as a woodshed. Bess, meanwhile, had jumped down from the trap and she shooed Mary back towards the house.

'You'll catch your death of cold standing out here without a coat.'

'It's freezing, isn't it.' Mary hugged her elbows as she obeyed, turning to go back to the kitchen. 'But I love it here in the country. I'm so pleased we're not in London. It's going to be a wonderful Christmas. I feel it in my bones.'

And just then, as she spoke, she felt a touch light as a feather on her cheek, and looking up she saw that the air was filled with spiralling shapes, countless numbers of them, drifting down in their hundreds from the low clouds above.

'Freddie ... Freddie ...' She called to her son. 'Come outside. It's starting to snow.'

20

'Damn it!'

Bennett stood with his hands thrust in his pockets looking out of his office window over the Embankment and the muddy Thames beyond. Not that there was much to see. Snow had been falling since early that morning and the spiralling flakes blurred the buildings on the farther bank to faint outlines in the gathering dusk.

'It's frustrating, isn't it? I thought after Madden's stroke of good fortune we'd get on to him quickly. So did the commissioner. He asked this morning whether we were doing everything we could. Pointed out that the newspapers were asking the same question, though less politely. And they only know about Wapping.'

He looked over his shoulder.

'Well, Angus – what should I tell him?'

Sinclair muttered to himself. He shifted in his chair, wincing. His gout was playing up again and he was beginning to suspect there might be a psychological element to his malady. The pain in his toe seemed to wax and wane according to the progress being made in the investigation, and that day it was feeling particularly tender.

'Firstly, it's kind of you to call it a stroke of good fortune, sir. But as I've already admitted, John made a connection I should have made myself. Right from the start we were looking for a link between Alfie Meeks and this killer, and his father's death was the one event in his past that might have explained it. If I'd realized that myself and acted sooner we might have had Ash in custody by now. By all means pass that along to the commissioner. If he wants a sacrificial victim I'm ready to offer him my head. To tell the truth, I'm beginning to think I'm too old for this job.'

'Now, now, Angus . . .' Bennett spoke soothingly. 'There's no need to take this personally.'

Billy Styles, who was sitting in a chair beside Sinclair, eyed his chief with concern. He and Cook had been invited to join in what amounted to a council-of-war in the assistant commissioner's office, and he could see from Lofty's expression that he, too, didn't like the turn the conversation had taken.

'It's no more than the truth, sir. To use a sporting metaphor, I took my eye off the ball and we've paid for it as a result.'

The chief inspector's regret was heartfelt. The discoveries made in the past thirty-six hours – the span of time that had elapsed since Madden had rung him late in the evening to recount what he'd learned from Nelly Stover's lips – had left him burdened with a sense of what might have been had he acted sooner.

The search, begun in earnest the following morning, had seemed at first to promise success. Although a man of Ash's age would have been too old for military call-up – Sinclair calculated their quarry must be in his late forties by now – he would still have been liable for national service of some kind, and the chief inspector had ordered a check made of all Civil Defence rolls in the capital, his reasoning being that if Ash's aim on returning to Britain had been to avoid notice he almost certainly would have abided by the rules and regulations.

'He'd have been a fool not to volunteer for something,

and we know he's no fool,' he had told Billy on issuing his orders. 'If you draw a blank there try the Fire Brigade and the railways. They would all have been taking on older men at the start of the war. Filling the gaps.'

In the event, Ash's name had come to light in less than an hour. Billy, with both Cook and Grace in tow, had brought the news to the chief inspector's office.

'His name's on the list of fire-watchers in Wandsworth. He was one of a team of volunteers that stood duty in the Blitz and through 1942 on top of a waterworks near the river, and he stayed on their reserve roll when the service was reduced. They've got his home address. It's a street off Wandsworth Common.'

'Are we sure he's our man?' Sinclair had asked. 'The Raymond Ash we want.'

'It sounds like it, sir,' Billy had told him. 'I rang the Civil Defence headquarters there and spoke to someone who told me that the Ash he had known spoke French. They'd had to get him to interpret once when they had a Frenchy who'd volunteered for duty but couldn't speak English.'

'Anything else?'

'He said he remembered the blokes who served with this Ash saying that although they usually went for a drink after their spell of duty he never would. He'd buzz off home once they were done. Never talked much to anyone.'

'That's good enough for me.' Sinclair had hesitated no longer. 'Unless or until proved otherwise, we'll assume it's him. Find out if he has a job. I want him picked up at once. We can't charge him as yet, but we'll detain him on suspicion. I'll arrange for a search warrant. I want his flat or wherever he lives turned upside down. Look for the tools of his trade; a gun perhaps, or a length of wire. I doubt we'll get much by questioning him, but if we find those diamonds we can hold him for the Sobel robbery while we build a case against him over here.'

It was an aspect of the investigation he had not given much thought to previously, but one that now increasingly occupied his mind, as he confessed to Bennett when he went to the assistant commissioner's office later for their morning conference.

'We've been so bent on finding this man we've forgotten how difficult it's going to be to bring him to court. Grotesque though it seems, we've no evidence against him. There's not a single witness living who can place him at the scene of any crime, either here or in France. As things stand, the most we could come up with is hearsay evidence twice removed that he once claimed to have topped a villain called Jonah Meeks thirty years ago. Some case that would make.'

'Isn't it curious though how he boasted about that?' The assistant commissioner had been listening closely. 'It seems out of character.'

'I'm not sure "boasting" is the right word, sir.' Sinclair was dubious. 'If Nelly Stover's story is to be believed, he had to convince Slattery of what he'd done before he could collect the reward. And it was the only time he spoke out of turn, so far as we know. But you've got a point: that may have been one of the reasons he never returned to England after the war. He'd left himself at risk with that little prank. There was no saying it might not come back to haunt him one day. As indeed it has. He may have decided at that early stage to make his career elsewhere, and under another name.'

'His career . . .' Bennett had brooded on the words. 'So you think he actually chose his profession? Sat down one day and said to himself: "This is what I'm best at?" '

The chief inspector shrugged. 'Who knows? Perhaps he fell into it by chance. But he seems to have opted for a criminal life early on. I'm not talking of Jonah Meeks now. You might just argue that was an aberration. I'm thinking of the curriculum vitae the French sent us. What took him to the Balkans, do you imagine? Could it possibly have been because law and order had broken down there and he saw a chance to exercise his talents? And why would that gang have taken him on unless he had something special to offer? He was always a killer, if you want my opinion, and I think Nelly Stover would say the same.'

His meeting with Bennett was still going on when the first results of the enquiries he had set in motion reached him. They brought no comfort.

'Bad news, sir. He's hopped it.'

Billy Styles had rung the assistant commissioner from his own desk and Bennett had handed Sinclair the receiver.

'We got the name of his landlady from the Wandsworth police. She owns the house where he had his flat. I've just spoken to her. She said he left nearly a month ago. That would have been right after Rosa Nowak was murdered. He told her he had a new job and was moving to Manchester. We got the name of his employers in London from her: they're a City firm dealing in office supplies and Lofty's spoken to them. Ash was one of their travelling salesmen. He'd had the job for three years, but he resigned a month ago; same time as he left his flat. But he gave them a slightly different story. Said his mother had died unexpectedly and his father who was ill himself had been left on his own. He said he had to go up to Manchester to take care of him. I reckon he made that up because he wanted to quit right away and not work out his notice. They weren't best pleased, his employers, but they let him go.'

'That's unfortunate.'

Sinclair had caught Bennett's eye and grimaced.

'Lofty's gone over to talk to them to see what else he can find out.' Billy had continued with his recital. 'I'll take Grace to Wandsworth with me. We'll have a word with the landlady and look at his flat. It's not rented yet. He may have left something there. And we'll take a forensic team with us and dust the place for prints. They could come in handy later.'

Before Billy rang off, he and Sinclair had agreed that while the Manchester police would have to be alerted to the possibility that Ash might be there – remote though it seemed – the search should be concentrated on London for the time being, and it was decided that Ash's name should be circulated to all stations in the Metropolitan area and a systematic search made of lists of guests and tenants at hotels and boarding houses.

'When all's said and done, and in spite of his wanderings these past twenty years, he's still a Londoner,' Sinclair had told Bennett after he'd hung up. 'He'd be more at home here than anywhere else. Less noticeable, too.'

He had sat silent then, staring out of the window, until the assistant commissioner had interrupted his reverie.

'What's the matter, Angus? Why so down in the mouth? It would have been nice if he'd fallen into our hands like a ripe apple, but that was probably expecting too much. We've picked up his tracks now. Sooner or later we'll catch up with him.'

'I do hope so, sir. What puzzles me, though, is why he's acted this way. Quit his job and moved out.'

'Surely it's obvious. He's on the run.'

'Yes, but *why*? What's he afraid of?'

The chief inspector had turned his gaze away from the leaden sky outside.

'He can't know we're searching for him. For Marko, I mean. Or Raymond Ash. There's been nothing in the papers.

Yet he acted as if we were already hot on his trail. Madden made the same point, but in a different context. He wondered why he'd set up the Wapping robbery in such haste. We still don't know the answer to these questions, and that worries me.'

Later that same day the chief inspector paid a second visit to Bennett's office, taking Billy with him and bringing a sheaf of typewritten reports compiled by the various detectives in the course of the day. The sketchy accounts of Ash's life in London obtained earlier had been amplified by means of extended interviews with his landlady in Wandsworth, a widow named Mrs Fairweather, and the office manager of the company he'd worked for, an old-established firm called Beddoes and Watson. In addition enquiries had been made with the Home Office in the hope that a passport might have been issued to Ash at some time in the past. This proved to be the case. Records showed that he had applied for and received a travel document in the summer of 1919, but that the passport had never been renewed thereafter.

'So he did come home after the war, but didn't take the trouble to visit his mother,' Sinclair had observed. 'He must have set out on his travels after that. But there's no record of a Raymond Ash returning here in 1940. It would certainly have been noted if his passport had expired. So he must have done what we supposed – got some French fisherman to ferry him across the Channel and not bothered to inform the authorities.'

On a more positive note, the Home Office had been able to supply Scotland Yard with a copy of the photograph affixed to Ash's original passport, and this had been sent up to the photographic department.

'We're distributing copies of this to all police stations in London for a start,' the chief inspector said after he'd shown one of the prints to Bennett. 'Then we'll extend it nation-wide. He could be anywhere. But what we have to decide is whether to issue it to the press as well. As you can see, he was in his early twenties when it was taken. I dare say he's changed somewhat.'

The assistant commissioner had gazed for a full minute in apparent fascination at the face portrayed in the grainy print. As Sinclair had said, the features were those of a young man, but beyond that there was little to remark in them. Raymond Ash's dark hair was cut short and neatly combed on either side of a straight parting. His brow in the snapshot was pale, as were his slightly sunken cheeks. He had been snapped with his head raised a fraction – perhaps the photographer had told him to look up just then – with the result that the lids of his dark eyes were lowered, giving him a wary look.

'Is there any reason we shouldn't publish it?' Bennett had asked.

'Well, if it's not a good likeness of him now it won't help with the search. What it will do is alert him. Even if we make no reference to Wapping, just say we want to speak to this man, he'll know we're after him.'

'But judging by what you said this morning, he seems to know that already,' Bennett had pointed out.

'True . . .'

The chief inspector had glanced at Billy, who was seated by his side.

'What's your opinion, Inspector?'

'I think we should use it, sir.' Having had time to think about what he was going to say, Billy replied at once. 'Even if he's changed, there must be some resemblance. We'll show it to Mrs Fairweather and to Ash's fire-watching team and at his place of work and see what they say. Grace could get cracking on that right away.'

'Do it then.' With a glance at Bennett, Sinclair had given his consent.

The assistant commissioner had wanted to know what else had been discovered in the course of the day, and Billy had responded with a brief summary of all they had learned.

'Basically, it's what we expected, sir. He was a lone wolf. Didn't mix with others. No friends. Mrs Fairweather told me he never had visitors. She lived on the ground floor, below his flat. He'd come and go pretty well to a fixed pattern. Off to work in the mornings and then back at night. Not always at the same time. It would depend on where his work had taken him during the day. We know from the office manager at Beddoes and Watson, a bloke called Badham, that his routes were all in an area south of London. In Kent and Sussex and Surrey. He'd visit customers they had or hoped to get in various towns, taking samples with him. Pens, pencils, paper clips, what have you. That's what he would have had in his sample case, the one Florrie Desmoulins said he was carrying. The day Rosa Nowak was murdered he was visiting a firm down in Guildford. Badham checked it for us. The train Rosa caught would have stopped there. Ash spotted her either on the train, or later when they got to Waterloo.'

'He'd obviously decided to lie low during the war and he'd found a job that suited him.' Sinclair had let his younger colleague speak uninterrupted before offering his own view. 'He was on his own all day. He didn't have to mix with others. He's not at ease in company. That seems to be the lesson of his years in Amsterdam and it was no different here. I wonder what he did about women, though. You might put out a query, Inspector. Ask the various divisions to check with the ladies on their books, particularly the ones who cater to deviant tastes. We know what his are and one or more of them may be able to help us with a lead.'

Billy had also been able to tell them about a further avenue of information that was being pursued. Earlier that day he had telephoned the War Office with a request for information about Raymond Ash's military career, and been told by an official in the records department that a man of that name had served with the West Kent Regiment from March 1916 until the end of the Great War.

'I got Lofty to ring the regimental headquarters for more information and we struck lucky,' he told his two superiors. 'One of the officers at the depot, a major, actually remembers Ash. He was his commanding officer for a short spell in 1917 before he got wounded and sent home.'

'And he can remember one soldier in particular after all these years?' Sinclair had been impressed.

'He remembers Ash all right.' Billy had looked grim. 'According to Lofty he reacted to the name at once. Asked what had become of him, "What's he been up to now?" were his actual words, and when Lofty asked him why he had put it like that, he said Ash had been a bad lot. "A cold-hearted devil" was how he described him. He said he knew almost for a fact that he'd murdered three German prisoners.'

'He what—?' Bennett had been shocked into silence.

'He said although it happened after he'd been invalided home, he'd got the details later from the bloke who succeeded him as Ash's company commander. It was near the end of the war and the Allied side had made an advance and captured some German trenches. Ash was detailed to take these three prisoners back to his own lines, but when he got there he reported they'd tried to escape and he'd had to shoot them. His commanding officer didn't believe him and he tried to have him court-martialled. But they couldn't get the evidence they needed. While he was supposed to be bringing the fellows back, the Jerry artillery got going again, and what with the shelling no one could say for sure what happened. Lofty asked why he thought Ash had done it, killed those men, and this major said he'd put the same question to the officer who told him the story, and this bloke had said most likely for convenience's sake.'

'Convenience . . . ?' Bennett had found it difficult to comprehend what he was hearing.

'He reckoned Ash couldn't be bothered bringing the men back through the shellfire. It was easier to shoot them.'

Billy had closed his file.

'One last thing, sir. Cook asked what sort of soldier Ash had been, and this major said he was the sort you didn't want in your company. Not a troublemaker, but someone the other men didn't like. A cat who walked by himself, was how he put it, but there was one thing he was good for; something he even seemed to enjoy.'

'And that was . . . ?'

Billy had shrugged.

'Seems he was always ready to volunteer whenever there was a night raid into no-man's-land. A party would slip out of the trench and crawl across to the German lines. The idea was to spy out their positions and take a prisoner if they could. Sometimes they had to deal with sentries, and that's where Ash came in. It was his speciality; he could do it quicker and quieter than anyone else. And he always did it the same way.'

Billy saw the question in Bennett's eyes.

'Yes, always with a garrotte.'

Recalling now the look of distaste that had appeared on his superior's face at that moment, Sinclair prepared to rise.

'So here's where we stand, sir, if the commissioner should

ask. We're still checking hotels and boarding houses in the capital and the same process will be extended to the rest of the country shortly.'

'You're looking for a "Raymond Ash", are you?'

'That's correct.'

'And if he's changed his name? Got himself a new identity card?'

'Then there's still this photograph of him which will appear in the national press tomorrow morning. Some of the people we've shown it to say there is a resemblance to Ash as he is now. But only a resemblance. Whether anyone else could pick him out from it only time will tell. We must just hope someone spots him.'

The chief inspector got slowly to his feet. His earlier, half-jocular remark to the effect that he was getting too old for the demands that a major police investigation made both in time and energy were starting to sound hollow in his own ears.

'But if it would help to pacify the commissioner, you might explain to him some of the difficulties we're facing. Normally a criminal like Ash would be tracked down through his associates. But it seems he has none. He's a cat who walks by himself, as that army officer so picturesquely put it, and all places are alike to him. He'll adapt to his new circumstances. Change his name; change his appearance. He's done it before. That's why he's never been caught. But he's still in a trap and as long as the war goes on he can't escape it – he can't leave the country – and there are all sorts of tripwires that exist now, thanks to the emergency regulations.'

'So you believe that we'll get him.' Bennett looked keenly at his colleague. 'I can tell the commissioner that.'

'Indeed you can, sir.' Sinclair nodded to Billy, who had also risen to his feet. 'But what I can't say is when.'

21

'So all in all you're the hero of the hour! I'm surprised they haven't given you a medal. Or something to hang round your neck.'

Helen directed a fond smile over her shoulder at her husband, who was lying in bed in his pyjamas, propped up by pillows piled against the bedstead. She had not yet joined him and was sitting at her dressing table brushing her thick, still golden hair.

'Angus was grinding his teeth when I told him. He said he ought to have thought of it himself. That it was time he was put out to pasture. I tried to tell him I wasn't claiming any credit for what he called my stroke of intuition. That it was only when you mentioned Occam's Razor that the idea occurred to me.'

'Perhaps it's I who should get an award then.' Helen considered the thought for a moment, then shook her head. 'No, I don't want one. I'm happy enough as it is. Did I tell you Rob said they were giving him a fortnight's leave and it might last even longer than that?'

'Yes, my darling, you did.'

'And they don't know yet how long the repairs will take?'

'That, too.'

'Poor Rob. He was so upset. He asked me if I realized it might be weeks before the *Bristol* was fit for sea again and wasn't it awful? I tried to sound sympathetic, but I don't think he believed me.'

Laughing, she turned back to the mirror, but after a few more strokes with the silver-backed hairbrush she set it down.

'I can't be bothered this evening.' She stretched her arms luxuriously, then rose from the low stool she'd been sitting on and went to the window, where she drew the curtains apart a fraction and peered out into the night.

'It's still snowing. We're going to have a white Christmas.'

Madden had returned from London earlier that day to find his wife waiting on the platform at Highfield station for him with a smile and a look in her eyes that had told him what to expect even before she had broken the good news that their son's ship was back in port.

'Rob rang from Hull just an hour ago. They had a dreadful time coming home. They collided with one of the merchant-men they were escorting in heavy seas and started shipping water, and for a while it looked as though they might sink. It must have been horrible, but you know Rob. He's just cross that they're stuck in port now.'

She had poured out the story into his ear while they embraced one another on the platform.

'They docked in the early hours of this morning but he wasn't able to ring us until now. He'll get away as soon as he can. With any luck he'll be home the day after tomorrow. On Christmas Eve.'

Madden's happiness had equalled hers, and in the short time they had spent together while Helen drove him home before leaving to carry on with her afternoon rounds, he had said nothing about his visit to Southwark, feeling his news would keep. It was too late to go to the farm, and on returning to the house he had joined Mary Morris, their maid of many years, in putting the finishing touches to the fir tree that had been installed in the drawing-room in his absence, stringing it with lights and the familiar ornaments brought out of storage each year for display on the drooping green branches. It was a ritual he had come to enjoy, being associated in his mind with past Christmases when his children had been young, and the thought that with any luck this might be the last to take place in time of war had given added meaning to the small ceremony.

Shortly before six Helen had returned, but almost before she had had time to hang up her coat and join them in the drawing-room the doorbell had rung to signal the arrival of the Highfield church choir come to sing carols. It was the group's habit, established by long precedent, to make the Maddens' house the final stop on their round, and as soon as the last notes of 'Hark the Herald Angels Sing' died away, Helen had hustled them inside out of the snow for the hot drink she always had waiting for them. Wartime rationing had imposed its own stringencies on this pleasant occasion, but in spite of a much diminished cellar she'd been able to offer their guests mulled wine spiced with cloves, and in place of the traditional mince pies – missing that year for lack of the necessary ingredients – a tin of sweet biscuits sent to them by an old comrade-in-arms of her husband's, a man who had served with Madden in the trenches more than twenty years before and long since emigrated to South Africa.

Bundled up in their coats and scarves and wearing a variety of headgear, the singers had arrived looking like survivors of a long march, but familiar faces and forms soon reappeared with the shedding of these garments, among them the imposing figure of Will Stackpole, a stalwart of the choir whose rich baritone had made itself heard a little earlier outside. Not having seen Madden for several days, he had greeted him warmly.

'Is it true then, sir? Is Rob's ship back? I had it from Mrs Highway just after Miss Helen called in there.'

Stackpole had known Madden's wife all his life; they had played together as children, and in spite of changing customs and forms of address, to him she would always be Miss Helen.

'He'll be here for Christmas, Will. It's the best present we could possibly have had.'

With the party happily settled before the fire, Madden had drawn the constable to one side and told him briefly about his visit to Southwark and what it had yielded.

'It was a stroke of luck. God knows if the police would have got on to this man Ash otherwise. He's as slippery as an eel.'

They were still huddled together when Helen came over to them.

'You're neglecting our guests, John. And I want to talk to Will myself. I do wish Ted was here,' she had added, pressing the constable's hand. 'Rob always asks about him. It's the first thing he'll want to know. Whether you've heard from him lately? I hope they aren't freezing in that prisoner-of-war camp.'

In the event, and at the urging of both Helen and Madden, Stackpole had remained behind after the others had left to eat supper with them in the kitchen and to listen to the news, which that evening had brought welcome word that the fighting in Belgium was swinging the Allies' way; that the sudden German thrust into the Ardennes had been blunted and much of their armour destroyed.

'It can't go on for much longer.' Helen meant the war itself. 'Surely it'll be over soon.'

When they had finished their meal, Stackpole took his leave, and as Madden closed the front door behind him he heard the telephone ringing. Ten minutes later he joined Helen in the drawing-room. He found her down on her knees with an armful of Christmas presents which she was starting to stack around the tree.

'That was Angus . . .' Madden had stood scowling into the fire. 'I was hoping this business would be over soon. But it doesn't look that way.' Feeling her eyes on him, he glanced down at her. 'There was a new development while I was in London. I haven't had a chance to tell you about it yet.'

The omission was soon repaired, but since Helen had wanted to know all the details, it was not until they had gone upstairs and were getting ready for bed that Madden had completed his account of his evening with Nelly Stover.

'What you said made me realize we'd been overlooking the simplest explanation of how Alfie Meeks might have come to know his killer. Neither Angus nor I had imagined it might date from so far back in his life.'

Quicker to undress than his wife, Madden had lain under the covers watching Helen make her more leisurely preparations for the night. Although he'd been away for less than a week, he had missed this moment of intimacy which dated from the earliest years of their marriage when they had set aside the last hour of each day to share with one another whatever was in their minds. Unused to such openness – he had been reserved as a boy and the habit had grown into one of silence later in life – Madden had been taught by his wife to hide nothing from her, and of the many blessings his marriage had brought him this was perhaps the most precious.

That evening, however, their conversation had stuck to a single subject. Eager to know everything, Helen had questioned him closely, saying little herself, but shaking her head in something akin to despair when he reached the end of his story.

'Poor sweet Rosa. To die at the hands of a creature like that.'

To soften his grim tale, Madden had told her about his suggestion that Nelly send her grandchildren down to visit them.

'They're a lively pair but, knowing Nelly, probably quite well behaved.'

'I don't care how they behave. I'd love to have them.' Helen had smiled for the first time. 'And I hope Nelly will come as well. She sounds like a caution.'

Turning away from the window, now she shed her dressing gown and joined her husband in bed.

'But you still haven't told me what Angus had to say when he rang. Has some new problem cropped up?'

'Not exactly.' Madden's scowl had returned. 'But their hopes of picking up Ash quickly seem to have been dashed. He left his digs a month ago. Right after he killed Rosa, in fact. He could be anywhere now. Anywhere in this country, that is.'

'He can't escape, you mean. Yes, I see . . .'

Helen settled down in bed, moving closer so their bodies were touching. She slipped into the circle of his arm.

'But Angus is worried, and so am I . . . there's something here we don't understand.'

She made no response, but instead drew him down off his bank of pillows until they were lying side by side.

'I don't want to think about that,' she said. 'I'm too happy knowing Rob's back safely and won't be off again for weeks, if then.'

She kissed him and he returned the kiss, more deeply, and took her in his arms. But his brow was still knotted in a frown and Helen saw it.

'You're not giving this your attention, John Madden,' she teased him, running her fingers through his hair, drawing her hand down over his old scar, smoothing out the deep grooves in his forehead. 'I can see we'll have to get this settled before we proceed. What is it you don't understand?'

Smiling himself now, Madden kissed her.

'No, tell me first,' she insisted.

'Well, by rights he shouldn't be on the run, this Ash. He ought to feel he's in the clear. He killed the only witness to the murder he committed in Paris and covered his tracks by getting rid of that French girl as well.'

'But the police know who he is now. Mightn't he have guessed that?'

'He might. But I doubt it.' Madden's brow had darkened again. 'It's possible he's guessed they're looking for Marko, especially now that Paris has been liberated, but not Raymond Ash, surely. Yet the opposite seems to be the case. He's pulled up stakes and gone on the run. So what does he know that we don't? What have we missed?'

22

It was after nine when Fred Poole got home – more than two hours later than he was supposed to knock off – and he was pleased to find Lily working with her Aunt Betty in the kitchen getting things ready for their Christmas dinner in two days' time. He knew their niece was going to stay with them over the holidays, but hadn't been sure whether Lily would arrive that evening or the following morning.

'Blimey, what a night!' he exclaimed when he came through the front door still shaking the snow off his heavy policeman's cape. 'Thought I'd never get away.'

'What was the trouble?' Lily asked as she gave him a hug. She'd come from the kitchen at the back of the small house wearing an apron over her policewoman's skirt, and Fred grinned at the sight.

'Don't often see you in one of those,' he remarked as he shed cape and helmet and then produced an object wrapped in newspaper from under his arm, which proved on inspection to be a bottle of sherry. 'Won it in a raffle at the station,' he announced with a wink when he saw Lily's questioning glance.

Back in the kitchen Aunt Betty was still busy with the prune pudding she and Lily had been making when her husband arrived. Though she was no cook herself, Lily was happy to take orders from her aunt and under her direction had earlier removed the stones from a packet of prunes that Aunt Betty had managed to lay hands on in lieu of the dried fruit she would have liked to have had.

'There'll be no Christmas pudding this year,' she had told her niece when Lily had arrived straight from the Yard after work earlier that evening. 'We'll have to make do with these.'

And a little imagination, as Lily found out when she'd watched her aunt simmer the fruit in a mixture of water flavoured with golden syrup and cinnamon before blending cornflour into the mixture and then pouring it into a damp mould.

'There now, that'll set well. And I'll make a nice custard to go with it, though it'll have to be with powdered eggs.'

A motherly woman who'd been unable to have children of her own, Betty Poole harboured the hope that the cooking lessons she gave her much loved niece whenever the opportunity presented itself would one day take, like a vaccination, and Lily would suddenly blossom into a home-loving body like herself; and once this transformation had been achieved, the acquisition of a suitable young man to go with it would not lag far behind.

Fred Poole himself wisely declined to offer any opinion when these pipe-dreams were aired, as they were quite frequently, and particularly as the end of another year approached. He reckoned he knew their niece better than his wife did, and as soon as he'd poured them all a drink he turned to a subject he knew would seize her interest.

'I've been doing door-to-door, that's why I'm late. Me and half a dozen of the lads. Up and down Praed Street.' He saw the gleam in Lily's eye. 'It'll be on your crime sheet at the Yard tomorrow,' he went on. 'Matter of fact he's an old friend of ours. Remember Horace Quill?'

'That little rodent?' Lily was all ears. 'I thought you put him away. Two years, wasn't it? What's he been up to now?'

'Not a lot.' Fred gave his wife a placatory smile. He knew she didn't like hearing him talk about his work; not the gory details, anyway. 'Fact is, he got himself topped last night.'

'Go on!'

'Up in that rat hole of an office he kept off Praed Street. It must have happened last night, but the body wasn't found till late this morning when a cleaning woman went up. He only had her in once a week, so that was lucky.'

'How'd he cop it?' Lily asked, forgetting for a moment that her aunt was standing beside her.

'Had his head bashed in.' Fred coughed, as if the noise might somehow distract Aunt Betty from the disapproval she was now starting to display. Busy with a sage and onion stuffing, she was stirring the bowl with unusual vigour. 'There was a big brass urn with a plant in it lying next to the body. I heard them talking about it at the station. Gawd knows where it came from; probably nicked off a bomb site, knowing Horace. Anyway, that was the weapon used. They could tell from the blood.'

'Now that's quite enough of that.' Driven beyond endurance, Aunt Betty tried to put her foot down. But to no avail.

'Any idea who did it?' her niece asked eagerly.

'Not a clue. Not as yet.' Fred tossed off his sherry and poured himself another.

'Mind you, with a bloke like that, it could be almost anyone. You could never tell what Quill was up to, except it was likely against the law.'

'He was sent up for selling forged identity cards, wasn't he?' Lily asked.

'That and dodgy ration books and petrol coupons. He and his partners. They had a nice little business going. But he swore when he came out that he wasn't going to touch it again. Said he was going to stick to his profession from now on. At least that's what I heard.'

'His profession?' Lily scoffed. 'He couldn't even do that straight. You remember when he got had up for planting evidence in that divorce case? They should have put him away then.'

She shook her head in disgust. Horace Quill's was a name she remembered only too well from her years at Paddington. A private enquiry agent – so-called – he had dabbled in all kinds of other businesses, including at least one that had caused their paths to cross.

'I had to speak to him more than once,' she recalled now. 'It was about that girl of his, the one he used to send out on the street when he was short of cash. Molly was her name. Molly Minter. A couple of times he knocked her about so bad she had to go to St Mary's. She wouldn't lay a charge, but I warned him if I ever caught him at it I'd see him put away.' Lily shook her head. One of her duties at Paddington had been to keep an eye on the tarts, of whom there was no shortage around the big railway station. 'Silly cow. She thought Quill was going to marry her one day. That's what she told me. Can you imagine – getting spliced to an oily little reptile like that?'

Her words brought a muttered but inaudible remark from Aunt Betty, who was still labouring over her stuffing.

'The trouble is,' she said, speaking aloud now, 'oily little reptiles is the only kind of men you're going to meet, my girl, if you stay at that job of yours.'

'Now that's not true, love.' Fred put an arm around his wife's waist, winking at Lily as he did so. 'There's a nice strapping young copper somewhere just waiting for our Lil to come along.'

His sally brought a snort of disbelief from Aunt Betty which was echoed by her niece.

'That's enough out of you, Fred Poole,' she declared.

'Your supper's been warming in the oven all evening and if you want it you'd better look lively.' To Lily she said, 'I'm almost done here. Why not go up to your room and get into your pyjamas? Then we can all sit by the fire for a spell before you go to bed.'

It was two years since Lily had moved out. Reckoning it was time she left the nest, she had found a place to rent in St Pancras which was nearer to Bow Street, her new place of work. But Aunt Betty had never accepted the move and kept Lily's room as it was, believing that her niece was bound to return one of these days.

Lily took off her apron. But her curiosity wasn't satisfied yet.

'So they don't know why he was murdered?' she asked Fred, who had fetched his plate from the oven while they were talking and was sitting at the kitchen table, eating.

'Horace, you mean?' Fred shrugged. He was making short work of the sausage and mash Aunt Betty had left for him, chewing steadily. 'Like I said, could be any of a number of things. They've been asking around, trying to find out what he's been up to lately. What he's been doing that might make someone want to kill him.'

'Have they asked Molly?'

'His tart?' Fred shrugged a second time. 'Dunno. All I can tell you is what I hear round the station. They're trying to find out if he had a client call on him yesterday. Late. He was topped around eight o'clock. That's what we were doing door-to-door.' He peered shrewdly at Lily. 'Why you asking?'

She hesitated. Then shrugged. 'I was thinking about that business he used to have. False cards. This bloke we're looking for, Ash, they reckon he might have changed his name already. Got himself a new identity.'

'And you think it could have been Quill who got it for him?' Fred chuckled. He popped the last piece of sausage into his mouth. 'I know you want to make your mark at the Yard, love, but you're stretching a little, aren't you?'

'Probably,' Lily agreed with a grin. 'But I'll tell you one thing: if he had got himself a new ID card and there was only one person in the world who knew it – I mean the feller he'd got it from – then it's odds on he'd top him. He's that sort of bloke.'

She saw Fred's eyebrows shoot up in surprise at the bluntness of her words.

'If I was them, I'd talk to Molly,' she went on as Fred rose from the table and took his plate to the sink. 'The CID blokes. I'd squeeze her. Find out what she knows. She was living with Quill the last I heard. He's bound to have dropped a few hints as to what he was up to.'

'I'll pass that along,' Fred said as he rose from the table and took his plate to the sink. 'I'm sure Roy Cooper will be glad of the advice,' he added with yet another wink, referring to a detective-sergeant Lily knew who was stationed at Paddington. 'He's handling the investigation.'

About to go up to her room, Lily paused at the door.

'Tell me, Uncle Fred, do the tarts still meet at the Astor Café?' she asked him.

'So far as I know.' Fred eyed her suspiciously. 'Why you asking?'

'No special reason.' Lily grinned at him from the door. 'But I might look in there tomorrow and wish the girls a merry Christmas.'

23

'To look at them you wouldn't think they were convalescent,' Lord Stratton remarked as the dancers circled one another to the 'Here-we-go-gathering-nuts-in-May' jingle of a Paul Jones, then stopped as the music did and formed pairs again. 'I distinctly remember seeing that young man on crutches only a week ago,' he added as a couple spun by in a brisk foxtrot. 'He seems to have made a remarkable recovery.'

Though confined to a wheelchair after twisting his ankle in a fall the day before, his lordship was in good spirits. The Highfield Christmas party was an annual event he never failed to attend, and he and Madden were watching the dancers from a corner of the church hall decked for the occasion with holly boughs and strung with coloured lights. Not far from where they were was a table supporting two large punch bowls and rows of still empty glasses, but neither man had sampled the concoction on offer, knowing as they did from past years that it took some stomaching. Instead they were refreshing themselves from a bottle of whisky which Madden had smuggled into the hall beneath the blanket covering his charge's knees.

The party had been enlivened by the presence of a batch of young officers still officially recovering from their wounds, but, as Lord Stratton had just noted, remarkably spry when it came to cutting a figure on the dance floor. They had been accompanied by a dozen or so nurses from Stratton Hall, who had shed their uniforms and joined the local girls in providing partners for the unusually large number of unaccompanied males, a patriotic gesture to which the village wives had also lent their support.

'How wonderful Helen looks. She never seems to age.'

Lord Stratton had just caught a glimpse of Madden's wife among the circling couples.

'You ought to be dancing with her yourself, John.' He nudged his companion.

'What? And spoil her pleasure?' Madden grinned. 'I've been told for years I dance like a bear. It's a family joke.'

Lord Stratton chuckled. His gaze continued to wander over the thronged dance floor.

'I can't believe how Lucy's grown up so suddenly. What a beauty she's become. How do you cope with that?'

'I don't. She runs rings around me.'

Madden's smile widened as he watched his lovely daughter sail by – the music, supplied by a gramophone, had changed to a waltz – while the young army officer in whose arms she rested gazed into her eyes with open adoration.

'She arrived from London today in a staff car with an elderly admiral who was on his way to Portsmouth. Somehow she'd persuaded him to offer her a lift. I should have thought it was against naval regulations, but she doesn't seem to pay much attention to those. I just pray the war ends before she's court-martialled.'

The question of their daughter's behaviour in London had provided the subject matter for a spirited family debate at lunch earlier, but though Helen had questioned Lucy closely, she had had to confess to Madden afterwards that she was still no closer to discovering how she spent her evenings in London.

'Late duty. Double shifts. Double talk, if you ask me. But I've got her here for a few days now and I'll get to the bottom of it.'

A portly figure in military garb approached and Lord Stratton hailed him.

'Good evening, Colonel. Or should I call you Doctor? I'm never certain.'

'I'm not sure myself, sir. Some are born great, some achieve greatness and others have it thrust on them. I fall into the latter category. However, as soon as the war's over I expect to return to my humble station.'

Brian Chadwick's moon face glowed with good fellow-ship.

'Hello, John,' he said. 'What's that you fellows are drinking?'

He peered into Madden's glass.

'We smuggled in something less lethal than what they put in those punch bowls,' Lord Stratton replied to the question. 'Would you like some?'

Chadwick reflected for a moment. He studied the dregs in his own glass, then shook his head reluctantly.

'Thank you, sir, but I'd better not. If I mix the two I'll be done for.'

A frown had settled like a cloud on Madden's brow. The appearance of the Stratton Hall medico had stirred a memory in him, and as luck would have it, just at that moment his distracted gaze fell on his wife and the young RAF officer she was dancing with.

'Brian,' he said, 'that fellow dancing with Helen – is he by any chance the pilot you were telling me about not long ago? The one whose face was burned and who had to go off somewhere to have it fixed?'

'That's right,' Chadwick replied after he had peered for several seconds in the direction Madden indicated. 'Tyson's his name. We sent him to Oxford. There's a special unit there. They do plastic surgery. He returned a week ago for further convalescence. Poor fellow, he still looks a bit raw, doesn't he?'

Madden grunted. It was the angry red stripes on the young man's face that had caught his eye. He waited until the gramophone fell silent and the dance ended, then made his way through the milling couples to where his wife was chatting to her partner.

'Have you come to beg for a dance at last?' Helen teased him. Elegant in a simple dark frock set off by a pearl necklace, she had hardly been allowed to leave the floor, and even as they spoke another young officer was positioning himself at a discreet distance away ready to claim her as a partner.

'Not yet. I'm still plucking up my courage.'

Laughing, she turned to her companion. 'Paul, this is my husband, John Madden. John, this is Paul Tyson. His family's from Winchester. They know Luke and Marigold.'

The young pilot had flushed on hearing his name mentioned, and with a gesture that was probably automatic by now had raised a hand to his cheek as he bobbed his head to Madden and muttered 'Good evening, sir.' He was in his early twenties with flaxen hair and pale skin which showed the marks of his ordeal all too plainly. Two livid stripes curving from eye to mouth gave his face an unbalanced appearance, while a further mark the size of a half-crown marred his otherwise smooth forehead.

'Paul's a wonderful dancer.'

Helen slipped her arm through the young man's and Madden saw that she was trying to ease his self-consciousness.

'Can we have another dance later?' She smiled encouragement at him.

While Tyson mumbled an assurance, flushing once more as he spoke, Madden caught Helen's eye and nodded slightly. Then he touched the young pilot on the shoulder.

'Actually, I was wondering if we could have a word, you and I. There's something I want to ask you.'

'Ask *me*, sir?'

Caught off guard, Tyson forgot his disfigurement for a moment. He stared at Madden in open surprise; face to face.

'Yes, it won't take a moment.'

As Helen released the young man's arm, Madden took him by the elbow.

'Why don't we go somewhere where it's quiet.'

'Oh Lord, yes. I remember that afternoon well. I thought about it a lot afterwards – after I'd heard what had happened to the poor girl. It reminded me of the squadron.'

'The squadron?' Madden was puzzled by the remark.

'I mean, how you could be talking to someone one day, just chatting, and the next day they were dead. It happened all the time.'

Tyson flushed. He drew on the cigarette he had a lit a moment earlier.

'The police are curious about that train journey, Paul.' Madden had led the young officer out of the hall into a small ante-room. They could still hear the music and see the dancers through the open doorway, but the noise was deadened to some extent, perhaps by the coats that were hanging on rails all around them. 'They have reason to believe that the man who killed Rosa boarded the train at Guildford; that he may have spotted her then. Do you remember anything out of the ordinary; anything about that trip that sticks in your memory?' Madden paused, and when Tyson failed to reply at once – he appeared to be searching his memory – he added: 'Colonel Chadwick told me you were in the same compartment as Rosa going up to London.'

'Yes, that's right, sir.' The pilot nodded. 'But we didn't really talk during the journey. She met a friend on the train, you see.'

'A *friend*—?'

'A girl. She was Polish, like Rosa. They knew each other.'

'Good heavens!' Madden made no attempt to hide his astonishment. 'How strange that she never came forward.' He pondered a moment. 'Of course, it's possible she doesn't know about Rosa's murder. There was only a line in the paper about it. Who was she exactly?'

'I'm not certain. All I know is what Miss Nowak . . . what Rosa told me . . .' Tyson hesitated. 'You see, I didn't really know her either. I'd only heard her play at that concert, and when I saw her on the platform I went up to her and introduced myself and she told me her name. I said how much I'd enjoyed her performance, but we only exchanged a few words. She was very shy. Withdrawn, rather. When the train arrived I helped her on with her luggage – she had a basket of food besides her suitcase – and found a compartment with a couple of empty seats. The other girl was already sitting there and they recognized one another at once and started talking – in Polish. They were obviously excited to have run into each other.'

'Their meeting was a surprise, then? They weren't expecting it?'

'Oh, no, definitely not.' Tyson shook his head. 'In fact, after a minute, Rosa broke off and apologized to me. She introduced the girl – I'm sorry, I've no recollection of her name – and said they had known one other in Warsaw. They'd been at the same college studying to be teachers. I got the impression they'd had no idea they were both in England. Rosa said she was sorry again and asked would I mind if they talked together – meaning would I mind if she didn't talk to me – and I said of course it was all right and I understood. And that was more or less the end of it as far as I was concerned. We didn't exchange another word other than to say goodbye when we reached Waterloo. I was in a hurry – I was hoping it wasn't too late to catch my train to Oxford – and I left them there still getting their things together in the compartment. The other girl had luggage, too. Anyway, it was the last I saw of them.'

Tyson stubbed out his cigarette in an ashtray. But he appeared to be thinking hard, frowning with concentration, stroking the side of his face where the scars were, as though for a moment he had forgotten about them. Madden stayed silent, waiting for him to speak again.

'You asked if there was anything out of the ordinary, anything I remembered . . .'

'Yes . . . ?' Madden prompted him.

'Well, there was something. It's just come back to me. Only I don't think it meant anything . . .'

'Go on.'

'It's just that they suddenly stopped speaking . . . the two girls . . .'

'Stopped speaking?' Madden frowned in turn. 'What do you mean?'

'They were talking non-stop – in Polish, of course – chattering away as though there was just too much to say, as though they had to cram in everything that had happened to them in the last few years. At least, that's what I remember thinking at the time.' Tyson flushed. 'Of course, you know what happens when people do that in a compartment. Other people get upset, they don't like the noise.' A grin came to his lips. 'An old boy sitting opposite me started coughing and rustling his newspaper, I recall. He was clearly getting fed up

with them, but they didn't realize it and just went on talking
. . . until suddenly they went silent.'

'Why?'

'I'm not sure. We'd stopped at a station, I remember,
so their voices had seemed even louder until the moment
when they stopped. It was as though they'd been struck
dumb. The old boy looked up in surprise, I remember, and
so did I. I was reading a newspaper and when I glanced up
I saw Rosa looking stunned; or surprised, anyway. She was
sitting on one of the seats opposite, so it was her face I saw.
The other girl was beside me and she'd gone silent, too.
Something had happened; but I've no idea what.'

He looked questioningly at Madden; as though he might
have the answer.

'You'd stopped at a station, you said?'

The pilot nodded.

'Could it have been Guildford?'

'Yes, I rather think it was.' Tyson replied at once. 'We'd
been travelling for a while, half an hour at least, and we'd
stopped once or twice already.'

'And presumably people looked into the compartment to
see if there were any free seats? From the corridor, I mean?'

'They must have, sir. As I say, the train was very crowded.
As a matter of fact, Rosa and I got the last two empty seats
in our compartment and it stayed that way until we reached
Waterloo. No one else joined us.'

'Yes, but I'm more interested in who might have looked
in at Guildford. Stuck his head in the door for a moment,
say, and been spotted by Rosa.'

Tyson took a deep breath: it was clear he was trying hard
to be helpful. But after a few moments' thought he shook his
head.

'I'm sorry, sir. It might have happened. People looked in every time we stopped at a station. But I just can't say for certain.'

'I understand.' Madden smiled in encouragement. 'But tell me what happened after that. Did they go on talking as before?'

Again Tyson hesitated.

'Yes and no,' he said, after a moment's reflection. 'They were quiet for a bit, then they started chatting again, but it wasn't like before. The atmosphere had changed. I don't know why. I wasn't watching them exactly, but I did glance at Rosa once or twice and I had the impression something was bothering her.'

'Why was that?'

'It was her manner. I can remember her leaning forward at one point and speaking in a low voice to the other girl. She seemed concerned about something. They were both behaving oddly. They'd gone quiet; they were subdued.' He shrugged. 'I'm only guessing, you understand. Everything they said was in Polish, so I really have no idea what was passing between them.'

Madden rubbed the scar on his forehead; it was a sign of his preoccupation.

'Tell me what happened when you reached Waterloo,' he said.

'Well, I was in a hurry, as I told you, but I helped Rosa get her stuff down from the overhead rack and did the same for her friend and then I rushed off. We'd got in very late and in the event I missed my train to Oxford . . .'

He looked at Madden expectantly, waiting to see if he had anything more to say. As they stood there in silence, a burst of laughter came from the open doorway and a couple lurched in.

'Oops . . .'

The young woman giggled. She was leading one of the officers by the hand and they lingered for a moment, swaying on their feet, uncertain what to do, before backing out.

'Did you happen to learn where this other girl came from?' Oblivious to the interruption, Madden continued. 'Where she'd got on the train?'

Tyson shook his head.

'But she must have been living in the country. When I got her luggage down from the rack I noticed she had a basket of food, just as Rosa did.'

'Can you describe her?'

The young pilot reflected.

'She was about the same age as Rosa, but red-haired. The compartment wasn't heated and she was wearing a coat, so I can't tell you what sort of figure she had. But she wasn't tall, about the same height as Rosa, I should say, but not as pretty.' He flushed again. 'She had a nice smile, though. I remember that.'

'Just one more question. Was the platform at Waterloo crowded when you got off?'

'Packed.' Tyson's answer came promptly. 'With the train so late, everyone was in a hurry to get somewhere. They were piling out of the carriages. There was a proper scrum on the platform.'

Madden smiled. 'Thank you, Paul,' he said. 'You've been a great help. Now you can get back to the party and enjoy yourself.'

He waited until the young man had gone, then followed him back into the hall and stood watching, hands in pockets, while the dancers slowly circled the floor. He was lost in thought, however, and failed to notice Helen's wave as she passed by; nor did he see the kiss his daughter blew him. It was only when a massive figure finally positioned itself directly in front of him, demanding his attention, that he was forced to return to the present.

'Will!' Madden collected himself with a start. 'I was about to come looking for you.'

'Were you, sir?' Stackpole's broad smile belied his tone, which was disbelieving. 'You looked like you were miles away.' Out of his uniform for once, the Highfield bobby was sporting a dark suit of ancient cut fraying a little at the edges.

'No, really. I've a question for you. A problem, rather . . .'

'Let's hear it, then.' Stackpole drained the glass he was carrying in a single swallow.

'How difficult would it be to discover the whereabouts of a young woman living not too far away from here – at least that's my assumption – name unknown, but Polish by origin?'

'An alien?'

'Oh, yes. And in much the same sort of situation as Rosa was, I imagine.'

'Meaning what, exactly?' Stackpole frowned.

'I've just learned they were on the same train going up to London that day. This other girl was taking some food up with her, just as Rosa did. So she's probably living in or near a village rather than a town. And somewhere down the line from here, because she was already on the train when Rosa boarded it.'

Stackpole pondered the question. 'Have you got a description of her?' he asked.

'Not a very good one. She's about Rosa's age, but red-haired. Nothing beyond that.'

'Polish, though – that's the point.' The constable nodded wisely. 'It won't be too difficult. A few telephone calls should do the trick.'

'How can you be so sure?'

'Wherever she is, she must be registered with the police.

She's an alien after all. And if she's living in a village or in the countryside, she'll have done that with the local bobby, same as Rosa did with me. It's just a matter of checking the stations where the train stops and talking to the bobbies involved. I know most of them, by name at any rate, at least as far as Petersfield. I'll start calling in the morning.'

'Would you? I'd appreciate that. It's not something I want to bother Mr Sinclair with, not at this stage. I'm just curious . . .'

'Curious, sir?'

'I've just been talking to that young pilot over there, the one with the scarred face. He was also on the train, in the same compartment as the girls, in fact. I think Ash may have looked in for a moment when they stopped at Guildford. Shown his face. Something happened there. The pilot noticed it. Rosa may have recognized him, and if so it would explain why he moved to kill her so quickly afterwards. What I want to find out is whether Rosa said anything about it to this other girl.'

Stackpole was silent, taking in the information. Then he shrugged.

'Can't see that it'll help much with the investigation, sir, even if you do find out. Nor with the hunt for this fellow Ash.'

'That's true.'

Madden acknowledged the fact with a rueful smile and a nod.

'It's why I don't want to bother the chief inspector. He's got enough on his plate. But apart from the air-raid warden Rosa bumped into in Bloomsbury, this girl was probably the last person she spoke to, and if so, I want to know that.'

He nodded to himself, as if in response to some unuttered thought.

'I want to hear what passed between them.'

24

IT HAD STOPPED SNOWING when Lily woke up the next morning, and after snatching a mouthful of breakfast with Aunt Betty in the kitchen – Uncle Fred wasn't on duty until later that day and was still snoring in bed – she went out with a bowl of beef dripping wrapped in greaseproof paper in her hands and a list of errands in her pocket. The dripping was to be delivered to Ada Chapworth, who had a house in Star Street, fifteen minutes' walk from Orsett Terrace where the Pooles lived, in return for four pig's trotters, which Lily was then to take to the Harwood residence, just across the Edgware Road, in Marylebone, where she would receive in exchange from Ellie Harwood half a pound of sugar, a jar of home-made cherry jam and three eggs.

'And make sure none of them's cracked,' Aunt Betty had told her niece before she set off. 'That Ellie's a sharp one.'

Ever since rationing had been introduced, the trade in bartered goods had grown steadily, and with the shops, despite the approach of Christmas, emptier than ever, housewives had learned to exercise their ingenuity. Lily didn't bother with it herself – she tended to eat her main meal of the day, unappetizing though it usually was, in a police canteen – but she knew how much it meant to her aunt to keep up standards at home and she was happy to do her the favour.

As luck would have it, however, her route to Mrs Chapworth took her down Praed Street, and as she went by the

Astor Café she stopped for a moment to peer through the steamed-up window. Four women were sitting together at a table at the back of the cramped room, and, having paused to check their faces, Lily tucked the bowl of dripping safely under one arm and pushed the door open.

'Merry Christmas, ladies.'

She crossed to where they were sitting, collecting a chair from another table as she went and signalling to the apron-clad man behind the counter with a nod and a gesture that she wanted teas served all round. As she sat down, one of the tarts spoke up.

'Look what the cat dragged in. Where'd you get that coat? Down the flea market?'

The speaker was a heavily built woman whose breasts bulged over the top of her low-cut dress. The garment she referred to was Lily's 'utility' coat. Being off-duty she wasn't wearing her uniform and she ignored the jibe.

'Hello, Molly,' she said, addressing her remark to another of the group, a younger woman with peroxide hair who was sitting by the wall. Red-eyed and tearful, she hadn't looked up at Lily's approach, just gone on staring into her empty teacup. 'I want a word with you.'

'Let her be. Can't you see she's upset?'

The first woman spoke again, her tone more belligerent now. When Lily again failed to respond, she went on, 'What you doing here anyway, Poole? This isn't your patch any more.'

Lily turned her head slowly to look at her.

'What did you call me?' she asked in a tone of disbelief.

The woman slowly went red under her gaze. She shifted her ample body in her chair.

'Constable Poole, I meant . . .' The words were spoken in a mutter.

'And don't you forget it.' Lily continued to stare at her without expression for several seconds. 'Now keep it shut, Dorrie Stubbs, or I'll put you on a charge.'

'For what?'

'Sticking your nose in where it's got no business.'

Lily wasn't short of experience in dealing with tarts, and although she felt sorry for some of them, she'd learned to keep up a hard front. It was true they had a rotten life, but they'd chosen it themselves, or most of them had, and for the same reason: bone idleness. And you couldn't give them an inch, she knew, because they'd take it; and anything else they could get their hands on.

'Now if you want another cup of tea, here it comes – ' she'd seen the counterman approaching with a loaded tray – 'if not, bugger off. I want to ask Molly something and I don't want any interruptions.'

'What you want with me?' In spite of her quiet sobbing, Molly Minter had been listening. The mascara was running down her cheeks from the corners of her eyes as she looked up. 'I don't know nothing.'

'You knew Horace Quill if I'm not mistaken.'

At the sound of the name, Molly burst into a fresh bout of tears.

'There – see what you've done.'

Dorrie patted the hand lying on the table beside hers. The other two girls who Lily didn't know – they must have been new since her time at Paddington – looked uneasy. Their fresh cups of tea stood untouched before them. Ignoring the fuss she'd started, Lily pressed on.

'Have you talked to the law yet?' she asked Molly. 'Have you been interviewed?'

'How could she?' Dorrie demanded before her friend had time to answer. 'She only got back from Streatham last evening. Went to see her old mum, she did. First thing she hears is someone's topped her feller.'

The answer was as Lily had feared, and it gave her pause. She knew she ought to back off now and leave this to Paddington. Roy Cooper would want first bite of any witness and he wouldn't take kindly to her interfering. But she was reluctant to abandon the idea that had prompted her to enter the café and she told herself one question wouldn't do any harm.

'All right, listen now.' She tapped her teaspoon on the table to get Molly's attention. 'This won't take a second. Was Horace dealing in dodgy cards and ration books still? You can tell me. He's dead now, so it won't make no difference.'

Molly delayed her answer while she wiped her eyes; then she shook her head. 'He'd stopped all that. He told me so himself. Said he'd learned his lesson.' She choked back a sob. 'We was going to get married . . .'

Disappointed by the reply she'd got – she was hoping Quill had been up to his old tricks again – Lily rolled her eyes in disbelief.

'It was true.' Molly roused herself. She glared at Lily. 'Just cause you ain't got no one . . .'

'Mind your lip.' Lily scowled. 'And you too, Dorrie Stubbs,' she added, catching the big tart's eye and seeing she was about to add a comment of her own.

'He'd been getting some money together,' Molly continued doggedly. 'He said we was going to get hitched. He'd been working on a job. Proper work, too.'

'What do you mean – proper work?'

'Being a private detective and all.'

'Oh, that . . .' Lily swallowed her disappointment. 'Look, I'm sorry for your loss.'

Feeling she might have been a little hard on the poor cow,

Lily patted her arm and rose to leave. Her idea had turned out to be a dud and she was wishing now she had left Molly Minter to the Paddington CID. Word of this chat she'd had with one of their witnesses was bound to get back to them, and there'd likely be ructions.

'He'd got a client who was paying good money, too.' Molly wasn't finished yet. 'Wads of it, Horace said.'

Wanting to be off, Lily hesitated; her curiosity was piqued.

'What sort of job?' she asked. 'Divorce case?'

'Nah – missing persons.' Molly sniffed.

Well, that was no surprise, Lily thought, as she buttoned her coat and picked up her bowl of dripping. For all sorts of reasons the war had led to people disappearing from their usual haunts. (Some had done it on purpose; flown the coop.) The police didn't have time to look for them, not unless foul play was suspected. From what she'd heard, private detectives were making a mint tracking them down.

'Who was he looking for, then?'

The question came from Dorrie. Lily had already turned away and was heading for the door. But when she heard Molly's reply she stopped dead in her tracks and did a quick about-turn.

'What now . . . ?' Dorrie began in a petulant tone, but Lily cut her off with a fierce gesture.

'What was that you said?' she demanded, fixing her gaze on Molly's upturned face, peering into her wide, tear-stained eyes. '*Who* did he say he was looking for?'

Delayed by a breakdown in the Underground – he had sat fuming for half an hour stuck between St James's Park and Westminster – Sinclair was late for his morning conference with the assistant commissioner. It was nearly ten o'clock by the time he limped down the corridor to Miss Ellis's office with the crime report, and it was plain from the agitated look on Bennett's secretary's face when he opened the door that his absence had not gone unnoticed.

'Oh, there you are, Chief Inspector.'

Middle-aged and fluttery, Millicent Ellis had been a fixture at the Yard for almost as long as Sinclair himself. A small woman with mouse-coloured hair cut to fit her head like a cap and wire-rimmed glasses, she had served as Bennett's secretary for the past dozen years and was devoted to his well-being.

'Sir Wilfred's hoping to get away this morning.' Her tone was accusing. 'He wants to drive down to the country this afternoon with his family.'

Quelling an impulse to remark that it was all right for some – and a temptation to wonder aloud where the assistant commissioner had obtained the petrol for such an expedition – Sinclair had instead gained swift admission to the inner sanctum where, just as Miss Ellis had hinted, he found Bennett impatiently awaiting his arrival.

'I won't take up too much of your time, sir, but there are one or two items you might care to glance at. A V-2 came down in Stepney last night and the firemen had hardly left when the looters started picking through the rubble. Luckily our fellows were waiting for them. They nabbed half a dozen. They'll be up in court this morning.'

'Excellent.' Bennett rubbed his hands.

'And there was a murder over in Paddington. It happened the night before but wasn't reported till yesterday. A private detective called Quill was the victim. I gather he was an unsavoury character. There'll be more on that later.'

While he was speaking, the chief inspector had passed the typed sheets he was carrying across the desk and his superior scanned them in silence for a few moments.

'And what are your plans for Christmas, Angus?' Bennett looked up over the top of his spectacles.

'I was hoping to join the Maddens down in Highfield for a couple of days. They've very kindly invited me. But I don't like to leave London with this Ash business still hanging. I want to be on call.'

With a grunt, the assistant commissioner passed the report back to him.

'So there's been no more progress on that front?'

'None as we speak. That photograph of him we published has drawn no response as yet and we've pretty well checked all hotels and boarding houses in the capital. There's no trace of a Raymond Ash here, so I've ordered the hunt to be extended nationwide. Of course the fact that it's Christmas doesn't help. We're already short-staffed and our men need some time off. But I don't dare let up. He won't.'

The chief inspector sat brooding.

'This is probably the last major case I'll ever handle, and I'd hate it to end in failure. But every day that passes means he's slipping a little further from our grasp.'

Bennett coughed.

'Well, now, I wouldn't . . .' he began, then stopped as the noise of argument sounded from the outer office. Miss Ellis's voice could be heard raised in indignation.

'Now just one moment . . .'

Before either man could react, the door was flung open and Lily Poole stumbled in.

'Good God!' Sinclair stared at her, speechless.

'What on earth—?'

Out of uniform, wearing a coat of singular design, and

with a woollen cap tugged down over her ears, the young policewoman was barely recognizable.

'Sir . . .' Lily gasped out the word as she came to a halt and from habit stood to attention. 'Sir . . .'

It was the only word she managed to utter. Hard on her heels, Miss Ellis appeared brandishing an object wrapped in greaseproof paper in both hands, red in the face and furious.

'Sir, I don't know who this young woman is or how she got up here but she forced her way in . . . sir, I'm sorry . . .'

'Calm down, Miss Ellis, calm down . . .'

Seeing his secretary's distress, Bennett rose from behind his desk, patting the air with his hands to soothe her.

'What's that you've got there?'

'I don't know, sir.' Miss Ellis's throat had turned red and swollen like a turkey cock's. 'This young woman just dumped it on my desk.'

'Remove it if you would.' Bennett spoke gently. 'I'll deal with this.'

He waited until she had gone out, shutting the door behind her, then turned to Lily.

'Now who are you, miss? And what the devil are you doing here?'

'Sir, this is Officer Poole.' Sinclair found his tongue at last.

'Officer Poole . . . !' Bennett gazed at her in seeming wonder. Then, with a shake of his head, he resumed his seat.

'Explain yourself, Constable.' Sinclair had risen to his feet. He confronted the young woman. 'What do you mean by bursting in like this?' He gestured at her attire. 'You're not even on duty.'

'Sir, I'm sorry, sir, but I had to speak to you right away.' Overcome by what she'd done, Lily had been temporarily struck dumb. 'I tried ringing you from Paddington but they said you hadn't got in yet, and then I tried Inspector Styles but his desk didn't answer so I thought I'd better come down to the Yard myself, but when I got here I found you were in with the assistant commissioner and I didn't know how long you'd be.' She paused to take breath. 'But I knew this was something you had to know and right away so I—'

'*Had* to know? What did I have to know?' Sinclair glared at her. The sight of Bennett, whom he was able to glimpse out of the corner of his eye, trying not to smile, only lent fuel to his anger.

'What this bloke was doing that was topped over in Paddington two nights ago, a private detective called Quill—'

'I know all about Quill.' The chief inspector's bark made Lily jump. 'It's in the crime report.'

'Yes, sir, but not what he was doing before he was topped. I know 'cos I got it from his tart only half an hour ago and she hadn't been interviewed yet...'

Lily stopped, realizing what she'd just said. Sinclair's gaze had hardened.

'Are you telling me you've interfered with a CID investigation?'

Lily stood abashed.

'Have you taken leave of your senses, Constable—?'

'Chief Inspector...' Bennett coughed theatrically. 'I'm sure a reprimand is in order, but let's hear what this officer has to say, shall we?'

He turned to Lily, who was still standing to attention.

'I trust you didn't force your way in here without good reason. Just what is it you have to tell us?'

Lily took a deep breath. 'Sir, Molly Minter – she was Quill's tart – she told me he'd been on a job these past few weeks, being paid good money, too, looking for a girl which this client of his wanted found. She knew he was due to meet this bloke that had hired him soon and that he was going to try and get some more money out of him.'

'And why do we have to know that?' Bennett frowned. 'Why is it so important?'

'Because it wasn't just any girl he was looking for, sir.' Lily looked from Bennett to the chief inspector and back again. 'It was a *Polish* girl.'

25

'I'm not sure this is very wise of me, Will,' Madden confessed as they stood together beneath the station awning, taking shelter from the snow that had started falling again a few minutes earlier. 'It seemed a better idea last night. If this girl doesn't know about Rosa being murdered, she won't thank me for telling her now.'

'She'll have to know some time, sir.' Stackpole offered his verdict. 'And if you don't tell her, then it'll be some policeman knocking on her door, and she might like that even less.'

'We're sure it's her, are we?' Madden blew on his fingers. 'The same girl who was on the train with Rosa?'

'No question, sir. Not to my mind. I talked twice to Bob Leonard. He said she came to Liphook, this Eva Belka, about six months ago with a lady from London. A Mrs Spencer. I've spoken to all the bobbies, as far down the line as Petersfield, and none of them has a Polish lass registered who fits the description except Bob. And she definitely went up to London about a month ago, this Eva Belka did. Took the train, I mean. I asked Bob to check and he had a word with the station-master there, who confirmed it. He said he spoke to Mrs Spencer herself that day and another lady. They'd brought the girl to the station and they wanted to be sure she'd reach Waterloo in time to make her connection. And the station-master remembers she had a basket with her as well as a suitcase, which is what that pilot told you.'

Madden grunted. He still wasn't altogether happy.

'Of course, if you wanted to be sure, you could try telephoning this Mrs Spencer. I got a number from Bob . . .'

Stackpole looked questioningly at him, but Madden shook his head.

'What I have to ask this girl – what I have to tell her – can't be done on the phone. I just wish it wasn't Christmas Eve.'

'Why not put it off then, sir? Wait till after the holidays.'

'I thought of that. But with Ash still at large it's not something we can drag our heels on. It sounds as though Rosa may have recognized him that day, and we don't know what she might have said to this girl. Or given her, perhaps.'

'*Given* her, sir?' The constable was perplexed.

'It's just a thought. There's still an aspect of Rosa's murder that's unexplained. Apparently Ash was searching for something after he killed her; there were charred matches found all around the body. We still don't know exactly what happened in Paris that evening. All we know for sure is that Rosa fled the scene. So whatever passed between her and this other girl could be relevant to the investigation. As things stand the police haven't much of a case against Ash. With no corroborating witnesses, what can they charge him with? So every lead matters. At the very least I'm hoping this girl will remember what happened on their journey up to London that day: the incident Tyson told me about. If she could recognize Ash again – if she could place him on the train – it would at least be a link in the chain of evidence.'

'Well, you'll know soon enough.' Stackpole stamped his feet to restore circulation to his frozen toes. They'd been standing there for ten minutes waiting for the train to arrive. 'What's it to Liphook? Half an hour at the most, I'd say.'

It was the closeness of the Hampshire village to Highfield

that had persuaded Madden in the end to make the journey after the constable had rung him shortly after breakfast with the information he was seeking.

'It was no trouble, sir, just like I said. Bob Leonard was the second bloke I rang, and after I'd checked with the others I got back to him. This is our lass, all right.'

According to the Liphook bobby, Eva Belka was married to a young Pole serving with the Allied forces in France, Stackpole told him. Recently he'd been wounded, though not seriously, and she had gone up to Norwich for a few days to visit him in hospital. Her employer was a woman called Mary Spencer, whose home in London had been destroyed by a V-bomb, forcing her to seek alternative accommodation for herself and her young son. Together with Eva, the boy's nanny, they had come down to Liphook six months earlier and taken up residence in a house called the Grange not far from the village.

'Liphook's only taxi has broken down, but you can walk out there easily, Bob said. You'll need a good pair of boots, though, with all this snow.'

Still hesitant about making the expedition – Rob was due to arrive in the late afternoon from London and Madden didn't want to miss his son's return after the anxious weeks he and his wife had passed – he had consulted Helen, who, somewhat to his surprise, had urged him to go.

'Lucy and I will be spending most of the afternoon in the kitchen with Mary,' she had told him after he'd spoken to Stackpole. 'That is, if firstly I can get her out of bed and secondly keep her out of the clutches of her various admirers, who've been ringing up since breakfast asking for her. All that dancing last night seems to have done wonders for the walking wounded. If you're going to go, you might as well do it today. At least you won't have it weighing on your mind over Christmas.'

'I'm sorry, my dear, I've been caught up in this long enough, I know.' Madden had been contrite. 'But I have to be sure I've done all I can. Followed up every lead. I can't explain it exactly, but I feel we owe it to Rosa. To her memory.'

'And so do I.' Helen's kiss had served as a seal on her words. 'But don't be too late back. I want us all to be together this evening.'

Soon afterwards she had dropped him at the station on her way to her surgery and Madden had found Stackpole waiting for him on the platform, with the welcome news that extra trains would be running to cope with the flood of travellers expected over the Christmas period and he would have no difficulty getting back to Highfield once his self-imposed duty was done.

Another figure in a police constable's uniform was waiting on the platform at Liphook when Madden's train arrived, this one considerably shorter in stature than Will Stackpole, but no less portly.

'Bob Leonard, sir.' The bobby touched his helmet. Well past middle age, he sported a grey toothbrush moustache and veined red cheeks. 'We've not met, Mr Madden, but I know you by name. Weren't you with the Yard once?'

'I didn't think there was anyone left who remembered that.' Madden laughed as they shook hands.

'Ah, well, when you've been in this job as long as I have...' Leonard chuckled. 'I was due to put my feet up four years ago, but then the war came along and there was no one else to do it.' He nodded at the train from which Madden had just alighted and which was still disgorging passengers. 'You might have picked a better day. Don't think I've ever seen 'er so full.'

The same thought had come to Madden as he'd sat wedged in a corner seat while they'd crawled along at a snail's pace. Despite the cramped conditions the holiday spirit had been well in evidence and the sound of a sing-song had reached his ears from another compartment a little way down the corridor in the antique carriage. Reprieved by the needs of wartime from the junkyard perhaps, it had been decorated by photographs of straw-hatted girls walking arm-in-arm along a seaside promenade with young men clad in white flannels. Phantoms from another age.

Many of those travelling had belonged to the services and some were still recovering from their wounds. Noticing that an army sergeant standing in the crowded corridor outside was on crutches, Madden had given up his seat halfway through the trip, and when they had finally reached his destination he had paused long enough to help another injured soldier, this one an officer with a bandage covering one eye, who was stepping down uncertainly on to the platform behind him with the help of a cane, oblivious to the salutes which a pair of privates were offering him as they strode by.

Although it had stopped snowing during the journey, the grimy slush covering the platform was deep underfoot and Leonard suggested they take refuge in his office, which was nearby and where he would give Madden directions to the Grange.

'I don't know the young lass myself,' he said as they plodded through the snow, down Liphook's main street.

'Except by sight. Will told me you wanted a word with her, but not why.'

The unspoken question required an answer. The Liphook bobby had done them a favour, after all.

'If it's the right girl, she was on the same train as a young woman who was murdered in London a few weeks ago. Another Pole called Rosa Nowak. She was working for me as a land girl. Apparently they knew each other. Rosa was murdered less than an hour after they parted at Waterloo. I want to have a talk with Eva. I want to know what happened on that journey.'

'You've been in touch with the Yard about this, have you, sir?'

The tone of Leonard's query was polite, but firm, and Madden smiled.

'Yes, don't worry, Constable. I'm not acting on my own. I've been helping the police with this. In fact, I may want to ring Chief Inspector Sinclair from your office later when I come back.'

'You'll be welcome, sir.' Leonard looked relieved. 'In fact it might be easier for you to do it from here than from the Grange, say. The telephone lines are jammed at the moment. It's the Christmas season. But I can get through to the Yard all right, and if you need to ring me from the Grange you'll have no trouble. The village exchange isn't affected.'

Sweating slightly in spite of the frosty air, glad of the boots he'd put on that morning, Madden strode down the narrow lane. Walled on either side by dense woods, the road was more than ankle-deep in fresh snow and the louring sky threatened another fall soon. Since leaving the outskirts of

Liphook he had not seen a living soul; only the cries of a flock of plovers wheeling overhead had broken the silence of the white-clad countryside all around him, and in the deep stillness he had found his thoughts drifting back to the past: to the bitter winter of 1916 when he had huddled with others around flickering spirit stoves in the trenches before Arras, trying to thaw the thick chunks of bully beef in their mess tins. Once a prey to memories of the slaughter, and to the nightmares that had plagued his sleep for years afterwards, he seldom thought of that time now. But on emerging from the woods into a landscape of flat, gently rolling contours not unlike the killing fields of northern France, he found long-forgotten images returning to fill his mind.

He had wasted little time in Liphook, staying only long enough to warm his hands at the small wood fire burning in Leonard's office and to receive directions from the constable on how to reach the Grange.

'There are no signposts up any more. They took them down during the Jerry invasion scare. I dare say it's the same over at Highfield. But if you follow the road to Devil's Lane and turn right at the crossroads, you can't go far wrong. Watch out for a fork in the road when you reach the old mill, though. Left will take you to the MacGregors' farm, and you don't want to end up there.'

There seemed to have been little traffic on the lane recently – he saw no marks of tyre tracks in the virgin snow – but after he had been walking steadily for a quarter of an hour he heard the sound of muffled hoofs behind him, and, turning round, spied a pony-and-trap driven by a broad-shouldered figure well wrapped in winter garments coming his way. He moved to one side of the road to give it passage, but when the trap reached him it came to a halt.

'Where are you headed? Can I give you a lift?'

The voice was a woman's, though it would have been hard to judge her sex by appearance alone: clad in an old army greatcoat, she was also wearing a fur-lined cap whose earflaps, tied beneath the chin, hid most of her features.

'I'm going to a house called the Grange,' Madden replied.

'Are you now?' The answer seemed to interest the driver, and she leaned down from the trap's seat to peer at his face. 'Well, hop on, if you like. I can only take you as far as the crossroads, but that'll save you half a mile's walk.'

As Madden put his foot on the step, she reached down a gloved hand and hauled him up beside her.

'You're not from around here, are you?' The face she turned to him, framed in fur, was fiftyish and weathered.

'No. I came over from Highfield, in Surrey.' He settled himself beside her. 'Madden's my name. John Madden.'

The woman had been on the point of flicking the reins; now she hesitated.

'Not the John Madden who married Helen Collingwood that was?'

'The very same.' Madden grinned. 'And you are—?'

'Elizabeth Brigstock. Bess.' She offered him a hand which he shook. 'I knew your wife years ago, but only slightly. It was when we were girls. Our mothers were friends, but Helen's died young.'

'So she did. Before the war – the last war. I never knew her.'

'We used to be hauled by our mas out to dances in the neighbourhood. In my case, anyway.' She chuckled. 'I was the perennial wallflower. I used to sit watching the couples, thinking the evening would never end. But Helen was such a beauty; she had to fend the young men off. But I did like her; she had such lightness of spirit. One of those people you were always pleased to see. I went abroad after the war and we lost touch, but I was told she'd got married again.' She was still looking at him; but her gaze had lost focus and she seemed to be searching her memory. 'And what was it I heard? There was some story about you . . .'

'About *me*?' Madden grinned. 'I doubt that.'

'No, I'm sure . . . It'll come back to me in a moment.' She smiled in turn and then clicked her tongue. 'Wake up, Pickles.' She flicked the reins. 'Get a move on, you lazy beast.'

Soon they were travelling at a sedate trot.

'I'm the village postlady. One of them. I have to make a circuit of the farms on this side of Liphook. I'll get to the Grange eventually, but only later, I'm afraid, otherwise I'd offer you a lift all the way. You know Mary, do you?'

'Mary—?' Madden looked at her questioningly.

'Mary Spencer.' She returned his glance. Her eyebrows had risen fractionally; in surprise, perhaps.

'No, but I know who she is.' Madden paused. 'Is she a friend of yours?'

'Very much so.' Steering carefully, Bess Brigstock negotiated a dead branch that had fallen on to the road in front of them beneath the weight of snow.

'Actually it's not Mrs Spencer I want to speak to. It's the Polish girl who works for her. Eva Belka is the name I've been given.'

Expecting her to say something more – to question him, perhaps, ask him his business – he waited; but they were approaching the crossroads and Bess slowed the pony to a walk before bringing it to a halt.

'That's your way.' She pointed to her right. 'I doubt you'll find another soul on the road today so you'd better not get lost. Make sure you take the right fork when you reach the mill.'

Thanking her, Madden stepped backwards down from the

seat. When he looked up he found her steady gaze fixed on him. Her face bore an expression he couldn't quite read: half curious, half wary.

'I've just remembered what it was I heard about you,' she said, settling the reins in her hands again. 'My mother wrote to me while I was working in Africa and told me Helen was getting married again and how surprised everyone was.'

'Surprised – why?'

'Because of whom she was marrying.' She looked him in the eye. 'Ma said he was a policeman.'

26

'Well, at last we seem to be getting somewhere, sir.'

Sinclair bustled into Bennett's office with his file under his arm, limping, it was true, but more from habit than anything else. As though in keeping with the festive spirit, the pain in his toe had eased somewhat and he was enjoying the momentary respite from discomfort.

'We've had a sighting of Ash. Tentative, but encouraging. I've just had word of it from Brixton. A local landlady called in at the station this morning and said she was reasonably sure he'd been staying at her boarding house until a few days ago. She said she recognized his face from the passport photograph published in the papers.'

'Reasonably sure?' Bennett paused in the middle of slipping some papers into a drawer to look up. 'What does that mean?'

'Well, bear in mind the snapshot's an old one, taken when he was a young man, so it would have been hard for her to be certain. But in spite of that she seemed to think the resemblance was strong. The detective she spoke to at Brixton pressed her hard, but she stuck to her guns: she said she was ninety per cent sure it was the same man. And there are other factors that seemed to support her story.'

'Such as . . . ?' The assistant commissioner closed the drawer. He was on the point of leaving for his Christmas break, but had asked Sinclair at their meeting earlier that morning to keep him informed up to the last minute.

'His behaviour, in a word.' The chief inspector sat down. 'He was there for a week, but his landlady saw very little of him. He didn't mix with her other lodgers – she served them breakfast and supper – but had his meals in his room. And he always seemed to manage to slip in and out without encountering anyone. Quiet as a cat, she said.' Sinclair's eyes had narrowed. 'The cat who walked by himself, perhaps. My nose tells me it was Ash and I'm acting on that assumption. Especially as we have a name.'

'A name—?'

'A new name. He registered with her as Henry Pratt, which suggests he has a new identity card. He may well have had it all along. A man like him would want to be prepared. He stayed with her only for a week, and that indicates he's been switching addresses since leaving Wandsworth, which is what I'd expect. And thanks to Poole we've also got a ready-made explanation for why he's remained in London. It seems he had unfinished business with this private investigator. I'm having the new name circulated to all stations in the Metropolitan area at once, and if necessary I'll extend that nationwide.'

Lily Poole's dramatic irruption into the assistant commissioner's office two hours earlier had been the prelude to a flurry of action. No sooner had Sinclair dispatched Billy Styles to Paddington to speak to the detectives dealing with the Quill murder than word of Ash's possible whereabouts had reached him via a telephone call from the station commander at Brixton.

'And there's something you can do since you're here,' he had told Lily, who had accompanied him back to his office, still carrying her bowl of what he now learned was beef dripping. 'You say Quill spent time inside recently. Get on to records and find out whether he was banged up in

Wormwood Scrubs and if so whether his sentence coincided with Alfie Meeks's.'

The answer to both questions, it turned out, was in the affirmative. For a period of six months their sentences had been concurrent.

'So Meeks could well have given Ash his name,' he told Bennett now.

'Then you believe Quill's murder is definitely linked to the case?' The assistant commissioner took his glasses off and slipped them into a case. He looked at his watch. Sinclair knew his superior wanted to escape – he had a long drive to the country ahead of him – but saw he was reluctant to leave with a case they were both so deeply involved in coming to a head.

'It's more than a possibility, but we need confirmation. I'm hoping Styles will get that at Paddington. And it's vital we find out who this Polish girl is, the one Quill was paid to search for.'

'Could it have been Rosa Nowak?' Bennett asked. 'Perhaps Ash was looking for her after all.'

The chief inspector pondered his reply.

'I've been asking myself the same question,' he admitted. 'But on the whole I think not. From what Poole said it sounded as though Quill had been employed more recently. Since Rosa was murdered, at least, which suggests there's a second girl involved. We need to speak to this Molly Minter again, find out exactly what it was Quill said to her. We don't know for certain it was Ash who killed him, but reading the facts as I do, the murder bears his mark. He employs a man to do a job and then eliminates him. It's a pattern. Wherever he goes and whatever he does, he slams the door behind him. But we're catching up with him. The net's closing.'

*

Closing, yes, but oh so slowly, the chief inspector thought as he waited in his office for further word from either Paddington or Brixton. Used to the sound of footsteps passing by in the passage outside and to the presence of Lily Poole in the room next to his, he found the silence oppressive. With Christmas a day away only a skeleton staff was on duty at the Yard, and while Sinclair would not have been averse to keeping the young policewoman with him – he'd come to admire her single-minded determination and already regretted the day when he would have to return her to Bow Street – he had turned a deaf ear to her pleas to remain by his side.

'Think of your poor aunt, Constable. She sent you out with that bowl of dripping hours ago. It's time you delivered it to its proper destination.'

But as she was leaving, he had checked her.

'You distinguished yourself today. You used your wits and it won't be forgotten. You have my word. Now go home and enjoy your Christmas.'

He might have said more. Earlier, before they had parted, Bennett had expressed his own appreciation of the young woman's initiative.

'It took some nerve, pushing her way into my office. But she did the right thing. I like her dash. When and if you come to write that report for the commissioner, I'll add a word of my own. She's just the kind of officer the force needs and I intend to make sure he knows that.'

Shortly after one o'clock the sound of heels rapping on the bare wooden floor of the corridor outside heralded the return of Billy Styles from Paddington. He had taken Grace with him, having earlier reported to Sinclair that Lofty Cook was down with bronchitis and would be off for a few days.

'We still don't know for sure whether it was Ash who topped Horace Quill,' he announced even before they had shed their coats and hats. 'But we've got a name for the client who called on him two nights ago.'

'It wasn't by any chance a Mr Pratt?' Sinclair asked in all innocence, and had the satisfaction of seeing Billy's jaw drop in amazement.

'Blimey, sir! How'd you know that?'

When he heard Sinclair's explanation, he shook his head in wonder.

'So he's changed his name again. I don't know how he does it. You'd think he'd get confused. Wake up some mornings wondering who he is.'

While Grace, on Sinclair's instruction, went upstairs to the canteen to order tea and sandwiches to be sent down for their lunch, Billy gave the chief inspector a résumé of what he'd learned.

'They found the name in a pocket diary Quill kept in his flat, which was just a room above his office. The name "Pratt" was jotted down on the 22nd with the time of the meeting, which was 8 p.m. What's interesting was there was no diary found in his office and nothing on his desk to indicate what business he was dealing with. It looks as if whoever killed him took the time to remove anything incriminating. Quill's notes on the case he was handling, for example. Or maybe his report to the client. The desk had been rifled, too, and someone had been through the filing cabinet. Roy Cooper has had the room and the banisters dusted for prints; we're going to compare them with what we lifted at Ash's flat in Wandsworth.'

'Tell me about the murder,' Sinclair said. 'The report in the crime sheet said his head was crushed.'

'That's right. With a brass vase, big as an urn, filled with soil and a dead plant. It must have been standing on a table behind the desk near the window. Quill was sitting at his desk when he was hit – the chair was overturned – and it looks like the vase came down straight on top of his head, which means the killer must have been behind him. He couldn't have done it from in front; the thing was too heavy.'

'Strange . . .' the chief inspector mused. 'Perhaps he was feeling nostalgic.'

'Sir—?' Billy didn't understand.

'That was how Ash killed Jonah Meeks thirty years ago, only he used a rock.'

Billy shrugged. 'I don't know about that. What I thought was he didn't want to use the wire again, give us such an obvious lead. The vase was handy, and provided Quill was otherwise occupied, which he probably was, it would have been a simple way of doing it.'

'Occupied? How?'

'He was obviously at his desk, as I say, and this bloke – Ash, if it was him – must have got up from his chair and started wandering about. Maybe he went over to the window. Anyway he got himself near enough to the vase so that he could take hold of it. All that time Quill was sitting at his desk, and from the evidence it looks as though he was counting some money.'

He was interrupted by the door opening. Joe Grace came in carrying a tray loaded with a teapot, cups and a plate heaped with sandwiches.

'Thought I'd better bring it down myself, sir,' he said to Sinclair as he laid the tray on the chief inspector's desk. 'They're short-staffed upstairs. Didn't know how long we'd have to wait.'

There was a brief pause while they helped themselves from the tray. Not hungry himself, Sinclair accepted the cup of tea Billy poured for him, but waved away the plate of sandwiches. Sipping the hot liquid, he glanced out of the window and saw that it was snowing again.

'We've been going over the murder itself,' he told Grace as he turned back to face them. 'You were just saying it looked as though Quill was handling money when he was killed.'

He looked at Billy, who nodded, brushing the crumbs from his lips.

'They found a blood-stained fiver under the desk. It must have been on the blotter when Quill was hit with that vase. The blotter itself was soaked with his blood. Now it's unlikely to have been a note of his own – his wallet was in his pocket with a couple of quid in it – so it must have been given him by his killer. Along with a wad of them, perhaps. That would have got Quill's attention, all right. Stopped him from looking up to see what his visitor was doing.'

'So you think he was being paid for services rendered?' Sinclair nodded. 'That sounds plausible. Does it mean he'd found this Polish girl, then?'

'That's what we don't know.' Billy glanced at Grace, who was sitting beside him. 'What he was doing was stringing this client of his along. We got that from Quill's tart, Molly Minter.'

'Stringing him along? You'd better explain that.' The chief inspector's brow had furrowed.

'After Cooper had shown us the murder site we went back to the station with him to talk to Molly. They'd been holding her there.' Billy grinned. 'Roy wasn't best pleased at the way Poole had stuck her nose into this, but I told him to let it go. Either that, or take it up with you. Anyway, they'd pulled her in and put her through the wringer and they came up with more details about the job Quill had been on. He seems to have run off at the mouth about it to Molly, mainly because he was so pleased with himself. The girl he was supposed to be looking for lived in the country not too far from London. That's what he told Molly, and he said finding her would be a piece of cake. She knew for a fact that he'd made at least a couple of trips out of London.'

'With what result, though?'

'That's what's unclear.' Billy frowned. 'You see, Molly didn't live with him. She's got a room of her own where she takes her customers. Every now and then Quill would get in touch with her and she'd go and spend the night with him. But her information's patchy. She only knows what he told her, but she gathered he was playing this bloke, this client, making out that the job he'd been given was harder than it was. He'd been paid a fat advance, and according to Molly he thought he could probably get more if he handled him right, plus a final payment when the job was done.'

'Which might have been the case? He could have already found her, but was withholding the information for the time being.'

'That's right, sir.' Billy nodded. 'We just don't know. It's likely the man Quill was seeing two nights ago when he was topped was this same client; it's the only job he was working on. And from what Quill had told her earlier it's quite possible all he was going to tell him was he needed another advance; that he was searching high and low but still hadn't found her.'

'But in that case, why would Ash have killed him?'

'Well, I can think of one reason.' Billy scratched his head. 'He might have twigged he was being made a fool of and decided to cut his losses, look for the girl some other way and close his account with Quill. The way I see it he was always going to top him, Ash was. Quill already knew too much about his business and of course he could identify him by sight. He may have pretended to go along with his request for more money, and then done him when the opportunity presented itself.'

'Alternatively, he may have decided to give Ash the information he wanted and claim his final payment; not being aware, of course, just how final it would be.' The chief inspector rubbed his chin thoughtfully. 'But I take your point: we can't be sure whether he found the girl or not. And the worst of it is we still don't know who she is or why Ash was after her. I take it Quill gave the Minter woman no details.'

'Not her name, that's for certain. Only that she was Polish.'

'And living in the countryside. Just as Rosa Nowak was. We are absolutely sure it wasn't her Quill was looking for?'

Having earlier answered Bennett on this very point, the chief inspector now sought reassurance himself.

'Oh, yes, sir – there's no doubt.' Billy was positive. 'It simply doesn't fit that way. Quill was still supposed to be searching for this other girl weeks after Rosa was murdered. He'd been in touch with his client by phone: he told Molly that. If it was Rosa he'd been hired to track down, Ash would have killed him right after he'd topped her. He wouldn't have waited till now.'

Nodding, Sinclair expelled his breath in a long sigh. He glanced at his watch.

'I'm afraid you're not going to have much of a Christmas, either of you. It's quite possible we'll locate Ash under the name of Pratt today. He has to stay somewhere, and that means either a hotel or a boarding house. They're being checked now: the word's gone out to all stations in the metropolitan area. The process will continue tomorrow if necessary, and you'll have to be on call.'

'That's suits me, sir.' Billy's smile was wry. 'Elsie and the kids are still up in Bedford. I wasn't expecting to see them anyway till this was over.'

'How about you, Sergeant?' Sinclair turned to Grace, who had been silent all this time.

'It's no hardship to me, sir.' Joe Grace's pockmarked face broke into a wolfish grin. 'I want to be there when we catch this bloke. I want to see his face when we put the cuffs on him.'

'The cuffs, yes . . .' The chief inspector nodded. Then his gaze hardened. 'But just as a precaution, I want you both armed from now on. Collect your weapons from the armoury. I'll authorize it. We may get word of Ash's whereabouts at any time and I want you ready to move at once.'

He fell silent and the detectives waited. They saw he had something more to say.

'When you come to approach him, you're to do so with your revolvers drawn. Don't take any chances. If you're in any doubt as to how dangerous he is, cast your minds back to Wapping and what happened to Benny Costa.'

He paused to give his words time to sink in.

'And if he makes any move to draw a gun, you're authorized to shoot him. I take full responsibility. Is that clear?'

Billy nodded. His lips had tightened.

'Sergeant?' Sinclair looked at Grace.

'Oh, don't worry about me, sir.' Grace's grin widened. 'It won't bother me none. Not with a cold-blooded bastard like that. Mind you, shooting's too good for him. I want to see him swing. Or better still, hand him over to the Frenchies. They still use the guillotine, don't they? Now that would go down with me a treat.'

27

'I'M SORRY, MR MADDEN, I really am, but this is something I can't discuss with you, not until Evie gets back. You must ask her. She spoke to me about that incident on the train, but in strictest confidence. You'll have to wait until she's here. It won't be long now.'

Mary Spencer hung her head. Slightly built, and with fine features set off by a pair of expressive brown eyes, she was clearly upset at having to refuse him, but equally determined not to budge from her resolve. Glancing at the kitchen clock, she tugged distractedly at the buttons on the thick cardigan she was wearing. Her eyes met Madden's for a moment, then slid away. She reached for the teapot on the table between them.

'Would you like another cup?'

'Thank you, no.'

Struggling to contain his frustration, Madden glanced at the clock himself. It was just after half-past twelve. He had arrived at the Grange half an hour earlier having walked from the crossroads where he'd been dropped through a flurry of snow, which had lasted only a few minutes and then cleared. The road had led through a small wood before reaching the fork he'd been told about, where the ruins of an old mill stood by a pond and where he had kept to the right as instructed. Shortly afterwards he had seen the chimneys of a house thrusting up above a ridge and then the place itself, a sprawling brick-built dwelling, larger than the average farmhouse and standing a little way off from the road he was on. A narrow, rutted lane had led to a stable yard at the rear of the house, bordered by stalls behind which Madden glimpsed some pigsties and a chicken run. The yard itself was covered with snow out of which a handsome snowman had been erected quite close to the kitchen door. Some five feet in height and broad in proportion, it had conkers for eyes and a carrot for its nose and was sporting a black bowler tilted rakishly to one side.

The yard had been deserted as he'd entered it through a pair of gateposts stripped of the wrought-iron gates they must once have had, but he had taken only a few steps across the snow-covered cobbles when the back door opened and a woman had put her head out.

'Yes . . . can I help you?'

'I'm looking for Mrs Spencer,' Madden had replied.

'I'm Mary Spencer.' Her tone had been friendly.

'How do you do. My name's Madden. John Madden. I live not far away. At Highfield, in Surrey. I took the train over this morning.' He'd walked across the yard to her. 'Actually, the person I want to speak to is Eva Belka. I understand she works for you. Would it be possible for me to see her?'

'Eva . . . Evie?' Her eyes had widened in surprise when she heard the name. 'Yes, of course. But I'm afraid she's not here at the moment.'

Before Madden had had a chance to respond, he'd been interrupted by a sound, the creak of an unoiled wheel, and glancing behind him he had seen the crouched figure of a man emerge from one of the stalls at the rear of the yard pushing a wheelbarrow heavy with cut logs. Elderly by the look of him, he was bent almost double by the load he was propelling through the snow and Madden had moved instinctively to help him.

'Here, let me give you a hand with that,' he'd said.

'Hello—!' Taken by surprise – the old fellow had been plodding forward with his head down – he came to a halt, letting go of the wheelbarrow handles as he did so. Its metal supports rang dully on the snow-cushioned cobbles. Between the scarf he had wrapped around his neck and a cap pulled down low, Madden glimpsed a pair of cheeks covered in white stubble and a rheumy eye. 'Didn't see you there, sir.'

'Oh, Hodge, you really mustn't. That's much too heavy for you.' Mrs Spencer came to life. 'You'll do yourself an injury.'

She had hurried down the steps from the door, but was too late to prevent Madden from taking hold of the handles himself and wheeling the barrow over to a woodbin that stood against the wall of the house near the back door.

'That is kind of you, but you shouldn't, Mr . . . ? I'm sorry, I didn't catch your name.'

'Madden.'

'Mr Madden . . .'

She waited until they had finished tossing the logs into the woodbin, then spoke again:

'Come inside, won't you? And you, too, Hodge. Mrs H and I were about to have a cup of tea.' To Madden she added, 'And you want to speak to Evie, you say?' She smiled. 'It's what my son has always called her and now we all do.'

'If I may.' Madden had followed her up the steps. 'As you've probably gathered, I don't know her, but I believe she was a friend of a young Polish woman who worked for me as a land girl.'

'Really?' Mrs Spencer had looked surprised. 'Well, she'll be back soon so you won't have long to wait. She and my son have walked over to some neighbours of ours.'

Inside the warm kitchen 'Mrs H' was revealed to be a

woman several sizes larger than her husband and occupied at that moment in stoking the embers of an iron range. Down on her knees, she lifted a round, red face lit by a smile when Mrs Spencer introduced them, but continued with her work, prodding the fire vigorously with a poker until she was satisfied, and then carefully inserting logs into it, cut to measure, from a pile lying on the stone-flagged floor beside her.

'A Polish girl, you say?' Having hung Madden's coat and hat on a hook in the wall behind a Christmas tree which stood at one end of the spacious kitchen, Mrs Spencer began to busy herself with the tea things, laying out cups and saucers and fetching a tin of biscuits from a cupboard. 'Eva never told me she had a friend in the neighbourhood.'

'They only met recently,' Madden explained. 'That's to say they didn't know they were living so close to one another, or even that they were both in England. But they attended the same college in Warsaw years ago.'

'Oh, *that* girl . . . !' Mrs Spencer had stood transfixed, a milk jug in her hand. 'Yes, of course – Eva told me all about her. What was her name again?'

'Rosa. Rosa Nowak.'

'I remember now. They met on the train going up to London and Eva said this girl . . . Rosa . . . had promised to get in touch with her. They were both going to be away for a few days, but Rosa said she would ring her when she got back. She had our telephone number, but she never rang and Eva was quite upset. She was hoping they could get together again.'

She had looked at him questioningly, as though hoping that he could supply the missing pieces of the puzzle, but at that moment, deaf to the conversation going on behind her, Mrs H had risen from her knees with an effortful groan.

'There we are . . .'

Dusting off her hands, she had picked up a kettle that was whistling on top of the stove, spouting steam, and brought it to the table.

Aware that he and his hostess were about to embark on a sensitive topic, Madden had decided to delay any further explanation. But during the next ten minutes, while Mrs Spencer poured their tea and the talk had been of small matters, he had twice caught her glancing at him with what seemed to be more than mere curiosity. With a guarded look.

'Come on, Ezra. Up you get.' Mrs H had nudged her husband, who'd fallen into a doze at the table. 'There's lots to do.'

Mary Spencer had escorted them to the door.

'And you will look in on us later this afternoon like you promised?' Mrs H spoke anxiously as she paused on the steps outside. 'We'd like to wish the lad a happy Christmas. You can tell him I'll show him me glass eye if he likes.'

With a chuckle she turned her face in Madden's direction in case he had failed to notice the object.

'They're going over to Mrs H's sister in Liphook for Christmas dinner,' Mary Spencer explained as she shut the door behind them. 'So we won't see them tomorrow. They're such a kind pair. I don't think I would have managed without them.'

Madden had been considering his next words.

'I understand your move down here wasn't voluntary,' he had said finally, and as he'd hoped it brought her up short.

'How on earth would you know that?' she had asked, and when he made no reply she went on, 'Why are you really here, Mr Madden? What do you want with Eva?'

The moment had come to reveal the purpose of his visit, but during the preceding ten minutes he'd become aware of a current of feeling emanating from Mary Spencer: not suspicion exactly, but a wariness which clearly had him as its object. His initial intention, which had been to sit down quietly with Eva Belka and find out what she remembered of the journey she had made with Rosa, now seemed impractical. He realized he would have to deal with her employer first, and in the circumstances frankness had seemed to be his best strategy.

'I'm afraid I have some sad news for her,' he had said. 'Rosa's dead.'

'Oh, Lord!' She had put a hand to her mouth. 'How dreadful. What happened to her? Was it a bomb? Eva said she'd told her she was staying in London for a few days.'

'No, I'm sorry to say she was murdered.'

'Murdered—?'

'That same evening. In fact, only about half an hour after she and Eva parted at Waterloo.'

Mrs Spencer had stared at him dumbstruck. The shock on her face had been unmistakable.

'I think something happened on the train – something Eva was a witness to – and I want to ask her about that. Also, whether Rosa said anything to her about it at the time.'

He had waited for her to respond. To his surprise she'd remained silent.

'Did she talk to you about it, by any chance? Eva, I mean. Since she mentioned meeting Rosa, I wondered if she said anything more.'

While he was speaking Madden had noticed a further change in his hostess's demeanour. For the first time she appeared ill at ease, and he saw that she was keeping something from him.

'Mr Madden, who are you?' Flushed in the face now, she had burst out with the question. 'You say Rosa worked for you as a land girl. But you sound more like a policeman than a farmer.'

'I'm sorry.' He had smiled. 'Old habits die hard. I was a policeman years ago, and funnily enough I met a friend of yours on the way here who asked me about that. Bess Brigstock. She and my wife knew each other once.'

He had deliberately mentioned a name that he knew would be familiar to her, and was relieved to see her face relax a little on hearing it.

'Bess was a friend of your wife's?'

'When they were girls. Helen Collingwood was her name then. She grew up in Highfield.'

'But why are *you* here asking these questions? Surely it's the business of the police.'

'It is, but I've been helping them. I still have friends at Scotland Yard.'

He had paused at that point, hoping she might relent, but after a moment he saw she was still obdurate.

'I don't know how to put it exactly, but I feel Rosa was my responsibility. That I owe it to her to help find her murderer and . . .'

'Yes, yes, I understand now. I see what you mean. But . . .' She had sat biting her lip. 'Oh dear . . . this is so difficult.'

Madden waited. But finally he could contain himself no longer.

'Obviously you know something,' he had said. 'And if that's the case I do urge you to tell me what it is. The man who killed Rosa is a particularly dangerous criminal, one of the worst the police here have ever had to deal with, and though they're on his trail they haven't caught up with him yet.'

She had bitten her lip. 'I suppose they could be connected . . .'

'Connected? What do you mean?' He had pressed her at once, but still to no avail.

'I'm sorry, Mr Madden, I really am, but this is something I can't discuss with you, not until Eva gets back. You must ask her.'

Mary Spencer's eyes strayed to the clock on the wall once more.

'They should be here by now. Let me go and have a look.' She rose from the table. 'Come along if you like.' As if to excuse her stubborn refusal of a moment ago, she smiled an invitation to him.

Madden followed her out of the kitchen and down a short stretch of passage to a sitting-room on the opposite side of the house. A pleasant room furnished with a mixture of pieces of no particular style but all dating from an earlier age, its walls were hung with an eclectic collection of paintings and other adornments that made Madden look twice when his eye fell on them.

'This house belonged to an uncle of mine,' she explained, having seen his expression. 'I never really knew him, only about him, that he was a great traveller. But he certainly had the most extraordinary taste in art, or perhaps no taste at all. If you think all this is peculiar, you should see what I left in the attic.'

Madden had already noted a Chinese silk screen rubbing shoulders with a picture of a wide expanse of prairie across which a lone cowboy galloped, the brim of his hat blown back by the speed at which he was riding. Now he paused to examine a pair of Turkish carpets hung like tapestries on either side of the fireplace and, most unusual of all, a Zulu ox-hide shield crossed with an assegai mounted above the mantelpiece.

'I put those there for safety.' She had caught the direction of his glance. 'My son longs to get his hands on them.'

She had crossed the room, meanwhile, to one of two sash windows facing the door, and when Madden joined her there he found himself looking at a snow-clad garden, formal in design, but much neglected to judge by the unclipped box hedges and pieces of broken statuary dotting the white landscape.

'This is the way they'll come,' she said. 'Eva and Freddie. Look, you can see their tracks going down.' She pointed to a set of fresh footprints running from the terrace in front of them down some shallow steps to a path that led to an open gate at the bottom of the garden. 'They've gone over to the MacGregors'; it's only a mile away. I collected our turkey from them yesterday but forgot to pick up the Christmas pudding Annie MacGregor made for us. Eva said she'd go and get it and Freddie insisted on accompanying her. There are two puppies over there he's fallen in love with, and I dare say we'll be landed with one of them ourselves sooner or later.'

She was chattering, unable to hide her nervousness, and as he looked out over the snow-covered lawns and beds Madden wondered what knowledge it was she was harbouring.

'Oh, Lord – the fire! I'd clean forgotten!'

Clapping a hand to her head Mrs Spencer turned from the window and hurried to the fireplace, where the grate was already laid with twigs and other kindling and a basket stuffed with logs stood ready for use.

'I meant to light it this morning. That friend of mine you met, Bess Brigstock, is coming to spend Christmas with us and I want this room to be warm by this evening so we can sit here. There's a concert of carols on the BBC.'

While she fumbled with a box of matches, Madden turned

back to gaze out of the window and found that the scene he'd been looking at moments before had changed. Two figures had appeared on the path at the bottom of the garden, one of them a small boy. They were moving towards the house, but only by stages, their progress slowed by the snowballs which the child was hurling at his companion, who was hampered by the burden she was carrying: Mrs Spencer's Christmas pudding, no doubt. Finally she held up one arm in token of surrender and having submitted to a final volley from her attacker took hold of his hand and drew him along with her.

'There they are now.' Madden spoke in a quiet voice.

Mrs Spencer made as if to rise, then checked the movement and struck another match instead. 'They're quite useless these days,' she muttered. 'Not like they were before the war.' She had already tried to light two, but both had fizzled and gone out. Now the third one, too, died in her fingers. 'Bother!'

She glanced up at him.

'I'm so relieved.' She smiled guiltily. 'You'll be able to speak to Evie yourself in a minute. You'll see why I couldn't talk to you about it. It's her story to tell.'

As he looked down at her crouched figure – at the way her fingers fumbled with the matchstick she was holding – a thought stirred in the back of his mind. Frowning, he returned his gaze to the two figures making their slow way up the snow-covered path. Both wore coats and gloves, but while the boy was bare-headed, the girl had something over her head, and when they came closer he saw it was a thick woollen shawl. The ends were tucked into the collar of her coat so that they seemed like almost one garment.

At that instant a shaft of memory almost physical in nature sent a shudder through him. Its genesis was an incident that had occurred many years before when he had been a young policeman and recently married. He had come home after a day's work to find his then wife busy with household tasks, and as he saw her figure bent over an ironing board he had realized with the force of revelation that he did not love her as he had hoped he would; that he would never love her in that way and that equally he would never leave her or the daughter born to them a few weeks earlier. In the event, both had died within six months, victims of an influenza epidemic, but the memory of the pain he had experienced at that moment had never left him, and although their causes could not have been more different, it was the same feeling he felt now: the same sickening realization of a truth that could not be denied.

'You say she has a story to tell?'

He turned from the scene outside to look at Mary Spencer again; at the burning match she was holding to the kindling in the grate; to the spent matches with their charred heads that lay on the stones beside her.

'Yes, a quite extraordinary tale. Awful, really.'

'Does it by any chance start in Paris?'

'Good heavens!' The match she was holding dropped from her nerveless fingers; she stared at him in astonishment. 'So you knew all along—?'

He shook his head. 'It was only a guess . . .'

He turned back to the window and watched as hand in hand the two figures mounted the steps to the terrace. The murmured words he spoke were for his ears alone.

'Poor, poor Rosa . . .'

28

'HE KILLED the wrong girl, Angus. He had to decide quickly when they reached Waterloo. He saw two young women dressed much the same, and both with their heads covered, which made it hard to recognize their faces. They both had baskets of food, too, and the platform was crowded. When they got off the train he had to pick one to follow, and as luck would have it he chose wrong: he followed Rosa.'

With the receiver pressed to his ear, Madden stared out at the garden. The phone was kept on a small table by one of the windows, and as he stood there his gaze fell on the straggling line of footsteps which Eva and her charge had left in the snow when they had come up the path from the gate at the bottom of the garden.

'I half guessed it when I saw her walking up to the house; she was wearing a coat with a shawl drawn over her head like Rosa's hood. Then when I saw the matches it was clear to me.'

'Did you say *matches*?' The chief inspector wasn't sure he'd heard right. The telephone line they were using had faded momentarily.

'The charred heads. Mrs Spencer was trying to light the fire and I remembered what Billy had said about finding spent matches around Rosa's body. We thought her killer must have been searching for something. But it was Rosa's face he was looking at. He had to be sure, and it was only then he knew he'd killed the wrong girl.'

'How could anyone do such a thing?' Sinclair was disbelieving. 'Any normal human being would have checked first.'

'We're not dealing with a normal human being, Angus. What was one dead girl more or less to Raymond Ash?'

Even as he spoke, an image of Rosa's face, with its veiled air of sorrow, returned to him with a pang, together with another face, hardly resembling hers in features – Eva Belka was red-haired and fair of complexion – but afflicted now with the same pain and remorse.

'It cannot be so.' Racked by sobs she had kept repeating the words after Madden had revealed to her what had happened to her friend after they had parted. 'It cannot be so.'

Prior to that – and with the eagerness of one who had borne a burden for too long and wanted only to shed it – she had described her brush with a killer in Paris four years earlier, an encounter that had haunted her ever since. In English as fluent as Rosa's, and marked by the same accent, she had poured out her story; still unaware of the tragic chain of events that had led to her compatriot's murder. Judging it better to let her speak first, Madden had kept what he had to tell her until last. But as he listened to her stumbling story and watched as she sat twisting her fingers, her green eyes fixed on his, he had found himself wishing that the sad task had fallen to another.

Still wearing her coat, and with the same shawl covering her hair which had led to Ash's fatal error, she had been ushered into the sitting-room by Mary Spencer, who, though aware of the ordeal facing the young woman and wanting to remain with her, had had her young son to think about. Since he could not be present, she had had to leave them alone, and had paused only to reassure Eva and to tell her she wasn't to worry any longer; that all would be well once she had spoken to their visitor.

When they were done – and before Eva had left him to rejoin her mistress – Madden had made one final effort to comfort her.

'It may seem hard to believe,' he had said gently, 'but even if you had gone to the police earlier it would have made no difference. You and Rosa would still have been on that train together. Nothing would have changed that.'

But his words had gone unheeded; she had continued to weep.

'I was so happy to see her,' she had told him, her eyes filled with tears. 'Sad and happy. I found she was like me, always thinking of the past, of her family. But at least we could talk about the old days. We could share our memories of Warsaw. Now all I wish is that we had never met.'

Once she had left him he had set about the problem of telephoning London, something that had now become a matter of urgency. Remembering the advice he'd received earlier that day, he had got the Liphook exchange to put him in touch with Leonard and had then asked the village bobby to use his authority to get through to the Yard.

'I can't explain now, Constable. There isn't time. You must speak to Chief Inspector Sinclair. Ask him to ring me here at Mrs Spencer's number. Tell him it's urgent.'

'Isn't there anything I can do, sir?'

It had been plain from Leonard's tone that he wasn't altogether comfortable with the request.

'Not at this moment. Later perhaps. You'll have to trust me, Constable.'

Ten minutes later the phone had rung, and Madden, who had not left the sitting-room, had picked up the receiver and found himself talking to Sinclair.

'I'm sorry, John, I was out of my office. They had to hunt me down.'

Calm as his voice was, Madden had realized from his old chief's tone that he was under some stress himself and he would do well not to waste time on preliminaries. Accordingly he had plunged at once into an account of what he'd just learned.

'I'm sorry I didn't speak to you about this before I came over here, Angus, but frankly I didn't think it would amount to anything. I just wanted to find out who this other Polish girl was.'

'Tell me quickly about her encounter with Ash in Paris. Did she see him face to face? Can she identify him?'

'I believe so. The report you got from the French police is substantially correct. Only it wasn't Rosa who went to Sobel's house that evening, it was Eva Belka. She and her husband had been offered a lift to Spain in Sobel's car and told to be at his house on the outskirts of Paris by a certain hour. They went there separately and Eva arrived first. She found the front door ajar, and when she pushed it open he was there. Ash. On his knees by Sobel's body.'

Recounting the scene to him earlier, the young woman had turned pale at the memory, biting her lip.

'Ash must have strangled him moments before. He was busy gathering what Eva said looked like stones from the floor. The diamonds, obviously. She screamed and ran back to the street and he went after her. As she came out of the garden gate she saw a pair of patrolling gendarmes nearby and ran towards them. Ash was coming up fast behind her at that point, but when he saw the police he turned tail and fled. They went after him and one of them called to Eva to wait for them, but instead she carried on and when she reached the Metro station she met her husband, who was coming out of it with their luggage. She told him what had happened and suggested they go back to the house and wait for the police.

But he stopped her. It was as we surmised. He saw at once how dangerous that would be for them. They'd be detained as witnesses by the French police in Paris and eventually fall into the hands of the Germans, and for him that would have meant a death sentence. He'd been part of a resistance group in Warsaw and there was a price on his head. Added to which, Eva's Jewish. The only thing for them to do was to flee Paris at once.'

'How did they get to England?' Sinclair had listened in silence.

'Via Spain and eventually Portugal. Partly on foot. When they got here Eva's husband – his name's Jan Belka – enlisted in the armed forces. He's serving with the Polish Brigade. Some weeks ago he was wounded in Holland and brought back to England to recuperate. Eva went up to Norwich to see him in hospital. That was when she met Rosa.'

'And Ash spotted her, did he?'

'Without doubt. And she saw him, too. But her reaction wasn't what you might expect. The train was standing in Guildford station when the door to the compartment opened and a man put his head in. Eva and Rosa were talking hard and at first they didn't register his presence. This was what Eva told me. But then she looked up and saw he was staring at her. It was Ash. Eva recognized him at once – or thought she did – and it must have shown on her face. The next instant he slammed the door shut. That pilot I spoke to, Tyson, only saw the look on Rosa's face. She seemed startled, but it's clear now that what she was responding to was Eva's reaction. She kept asking her what was wrong, but Eva didn't say. She'd been struck dumb.'

'But surely by the time they reached Waterloo she must have recovered enough to report it?'

'Recovered, yes, but not in that way.'

Madden paused. He was remembering the anguished look on the young woman's face as she had tried to explain the workings of her mind to him.

'All she'd managed to do by then was persuade herself that she'd imagined the whole thing: seen a man who resembled the one she'd spotted for an instant in the hall at Sobel's house four years earlier. You see, this wasn't the first time it had happened to her. On several occasions in the past few years she's seen faces that reminded her of the killer's. I didn't say this to her, but a guilty conscience probably played its part in that. My guess is she's been tormented by the memory and also by her failure to offer herself as a witness.'

'Why on earth didn't she, then? Surely after all this time . . . ?' The chief inspector couldn't contain his chagrin.

'Time was partly the problem, Angus. The poor girl's mortified, but I think I understand the way her mind worked. After all these years, what was the point? For all she knew, the real killer might have been arrested and dealt with long ago. The last place she would have expected to meet him was in England, and that only reinforced her feeling that she was a victim of her own fantasies. But the biggest factor in all this has been her husband.'

'Her husband—?'

'From the very start he'd been against her going to the authorities, not only in Paris, where it made sense, but here in England, too, and it seems he was persuasive. He took the view that there was nothing she could do to help in apprehending the man she had seen, at least until the war was over. She'd achieve nothing by going to the police here except involve them both in a situation from which no good could come. Technically she'd been in breach of the law in Paris, and the only likely result was that she'd be entangled in an enquiry which might well turn out badly for them, given their position as aliens. It's a pity they've been apart so much, Eva and her husband, otherwise I think she might have persuaded him to the contrary. But she seems to have been reluctant to act against his advice. At least until she went up to Norwich.'

'What happened there?'

'She visited her husband in hospital and told him about her experience on the train. He repeated the arguments he'd used before, but something had obviously changed in her. By the time she returned to Liphook she had made up her mind to act, and though it took her a while to pluck up her courage she went to her employer a few days ago and told her the whole story. Mrs Spencer said the authorities had to be informed at once and offered to accompany her to police headquarters in Petersfield. It was agreed they would do so immediately after Christmas.'

'And she had no idea of what had happened to Rosa?'

'None at all. They never see a newspaper down here. Although she had given Rosa Mrs Spencer's telephone number and was hoping to see her again, she had no way herself of getting in touch with her, or of finding out what had happened to her.'

'I take it she didn't see Ash again when they reached Waterloo?'

'Apparently not, though I'm not sure how hard she looked. I think by that time she'd convinced herself it couldn't have been him. We shouldn't overlook how it must have seemed to her: the sheer unlikelihood of him turning up in England after four years of war. What matters, though, is the effect seeing Eva that day had on *him*.'

'Why do you say that?'

'It explains what happened afterwards: what's been baffling us. The speed with which he acted. He'd come face to face with the only witness who could send him to the guillotine, and from the look on Eva's face he knew she'd recognized him. That forced him into recklessness: first, killing Rosa without any forethought; then, once he'd realized his mistake, getting hold of Alfie Meeks, someone he'd have done well to steer clear of. Admittedly the Wapping robbery came off, but he took a huge risk there, as well. The point was, he was running scared. His assumption must have been that Eva had reported his presence here to the police and that with Paris liberated now, word of the Sobel killing would have reached London.'

The chief inspector grunted.

'I won't quarrel with your reasoning, John,' he said. 'It makes good sense. But unfortunately in one respect the situation hasn't changed, and that's what's worrying me now. Eva Belka is still the only witness who can convict him.'

There'd been a change in his tone of voice. Madden had picked it up.

'What do you mean, Angus? Why do you say that?'

'Because he's still after her. I've been waiting to tell you.'

'*After* her . . . ?'

'A private investigator was murdered in Paddington two nights ago. We're fairly sure he'd been working for Ash, looking for a Polish girl on his instructions. A girl who wasn't Rosa Nowak.'

'Looking for her where?'

'Somewhere outside London, in the country. We've no name, but it sounds like the same young woman: this Eva Belka.'

Madden was silent. He was thinking. 'Two nights ago, you say?'

'Yes, but we're not sure yet whether the detective – Quill

was his name – had found her, and if so whether he'd told Ash. There's no time to go into it now, but it seems this Quill was attempting to play Ash. To prolong the inquiry. He'd already been given an advance, and there's a suggestion he was after more of the same.'

'But if Ash killed him . . . ?'

'It could mean he'd been given the information he was seeking. We simply don't know. And since we can't afford the risk, I've decided while we've been talking to take this young woman into protective custody. I'm sending Styles and Grace down to Liphook in a car. They'll have orders to bring her back to London right away. Can you prepare her for that, John? Tell her it's for her own sake?'

'Yes, of course.' It took Madden a moment to respond. He was still coming to terms with the new situation. 'One question: how did Ash know she was Polish?' Then, before the chief inspector had a chance to reply, he went on, 'Of course – it's obvious. He stood there long enough to hear them talking. He may not speak Polish, but he probably recognized the language, and even if he didn't he would have seen that paragraph in the papers about Rosa's murder. It mentioned her nationality. I'm sorry, Angus. I'm rambling. How long will it take Billy and Grace to get here?'

'At least two hours, I imagine. Perhaps longer with the snow.'

'Then you might do me a favour and ring Helen at Highfield. Tell her I'll be late getting back this evening.' Madden's mind was still busy. 'There's also the problem of Mrs Spencer,' he went on. 'She'll be alone here with her son. What if Ash comes looking for Eva?'

'I've thought of that. As soon as we're done I'll ring Petersfield and tell them to send some men over. Armed officers. They'll keep a watch on the house until this is over. In the meantime, what about the Liphook bobby? Should I send him out there?'

Madden hesitated.

'Better not,' he said after a moment's pause. 'He's a good man, but getting on. Past retirement age. He'll be more use staying where he is. He can show Billy and Grace the way out here when they arrive.'

Sinclair grunted his agreement.

'I must say I'd feel easier if I knew whether that private detective tracked the girl down, or whether he was still stringing Ash along. Would it be possible to find out if anyone's been snooping around? I gather Quill was a seedy character. His presence may have been noticed.'

'I'll ask Mrs Spencer.'

The chief inspector cleared his throat. 'I'm sorry about this, John. Truly I am. You shouldn't have been landed with it.'

'Perhaps it'll teach me not to go wandering off on my own without consulting you.'

'There's always that.' Enjoying the joke, Sinclair chuckled. 'Styles and Grace will be in a radio car. I'll keep you abreast of their progress.'

29

'A GREASY LITTLE MAN?'

'That's how Evie described him.'

Bess Brigstock stamped the snow from her boots. Ten minutes earlier, having completed her postal round, she had come clattering into the yard in her trap.

'He called at the Grange one day while Mary was out. Evie had to deal with him and she was upset afterwards. I can see why now. He said he was a detective and made her give him her name.'

As one they turned to look at the young woman who just then had taken Freddie Spencer by the hand to lead him inside. In the last few minutes it had started to snow heavily again, and although the small boy was all for staying outdoors in the yard, his mother had decreed otherwise. Mrs Spencer stood by the kitchen door with folded arms, her resentful gaze fixed on Madden.

'Poor Mary, she's finding it hard to cope with all this.' Bess slapped her gloved hands together. Still bundled up in her coat and fur-lined cap, she stood planted in front of him, oblivious to the flakes that were falling on them. 'She feels you've over-reacted. I'm afraid she's inclined to blame it all on you.'

Madden muttered an acknowledgement. His attempts thus far to convince Mary Spencer of the seriousness of the situation had fallen on deaf ears. Finding her alone in the kitchen following his talk with Sinclair, he had wasted no time in telling her of the forced change in her circumstances.

'This will come as a blow, I know, but the police want to take Eva into protective custody. It's for her own safety. There's a car on its way from London now. She'll have to go back with them.'

Crouched in front of the iron range – she'd been adding more logs to the fire – she had gazed up at him in sheer disbelief.

'Surely that won't be necessary. It means she'll miss Christmas with us. Freddie will be heartbroken.'

Glancing out of the window at that moment, Madden had seen the young woman outside in the yard with her employer's son. The snow had abated somewhat and they were making small adjustments to the snowman they must have built earlier, giving him ears in the shape of turnips and slipping an old clay pipe between his lips.

'I'm sorry, but it can't be helped.' He'd forced himself to ignore her plea. 'The man Eva saw in Paris – the one who killed Rosa – is still at large. In fact, to be on the safe side there are some police officers coming over from Petersfield now. They'll keep a watch on your house in case he finds his way here. Unless, that is, you'd rather move somewhere else.'

'Somewhere else . . . ?' She had put a hand to her head. 'Oh, no, I couldn't do that. That's out of the question.'

'You'll be quite safe here,' he assured her. 'And there's every chance the man the police are looking for will be arrested soon. They're on his trail.'

His efforts to calm her had gone for naught. She'd turned on him.

'But why should this matter so much now? What have you brought on us, Mr Madden?' And when he failed to reply. 'Are you trying to frighten me? Is that it?'

Before he could respond, a cry from Freddie's lips outside

had signalled the arrival of Bess and her trap, and he had turned to watch as, pursued by the little boy, she had guided the pony round in a circle before bringing it to a halt on the far side of the yard near the open doors of the barn.

'Oh, thank heavens.' Mary Spencer had taken heart from her friend's arrival. 'I'm sorry, but I can't discuss this further until I've spoken to Bess.'

Offering no comment – she would find out soon enough that she had little choice in the matter – he had followed her out of the door into the snow-covered yard and then watched as she hastened over to where the trap stood and where Bess was in the process of heaving her heavy body off the seat and down on to the ground. Forgotten by all, Eva Belka had remained where she was, by the snowman, staring off into the distance. Madden had gone over to her.

'I've spoken to the police in London, Eva, to the chief inspector in charge of the case. He's going to take you into what's called protective custody until this man has been caught. It's for your own good.'

She had turned her face towards his and he saw she had barely registered what he had said. Her green eyes were swollen with weeping.

'I'm sorry . . . ?'

'The police are going to protect you. A car is on its way from London now. You'll have to go with them.'

She had nodded dully.

'Don't worry about the rest. It's true, you should have reported this a long time ago. But I think you'll find them understanding.'

She brushed a wisp of red hair off her forehead.

'Rosa . . . how did she die . . . can you tell me . . . ?'

'She didn't suffer,' Madden had reassured her at once. 'It was quick, very quick.' He'd examined her face. 'You must try to get over this,' he had said earnestly, laying a hand on her shoulder. He had seen the depth of her feeling in her eyes; the sorrow that weighed on her now. 'There's no going back. You have your own life to live.'

She had nodded her thanks, murmuring some words that he didn't catch, but before he could say more they had been interrupted.

'Mr Madden . . . ?'

Hearing his name called out he'd turned to see Bess Brigstock striding across the snow towards him. For the past few minutes she and Mary Spencer had been deep in conversation.

'Could we have a word, do you think?'

'When did this man appear exactly?' Madden frowned.

'Oh, a good three weeks ago.'

'And he claimed to be a policeman?'

'That's what Evie said.' Bess reinforced her words with a growl. 'And the MacGregors, too. He went to their farm first. They said he showed them what looked like a warrant card and wrote down their names and the names of their farmworkers. I asked Bob Leonard to find out who he was but he said he couldn't have been a real policeman. He even spoke to his headquarters in Petersfield to make sure. They'd never heard of him. Bob said he might have been a burglar on the lookout for a place to rob.' She saw the expression on Madden's face. 'I gather you don't agree.'

'He was up to no good, all right. But it sounds more like Quill. This private detective. We know he was looking for a Polish girl. That business of taking down names – that was just a front – a way of finding out if they were employing any foreigners. Of course once he'd met Eva he wouldn't have had to search any further. It's odds on he was given a description of her.'

'By the man she saw in Paris that evening? The same one who killed the girl who worked for you.'

Madden nodded again. Bess had come prepared to take up the cudgels on her friend's behalf, but after the brief explanation Madden had given, her attitude had changed and she had listened to him attentively.

'The fact that nothing's happened since may be a good sign,' Madden went on. 'There's some thought on the part of the police that Quill may not have passed the information on to his client. He was trying to extract as much money as he could from him, stringing out the enquiry. If so, he seems to have paid the price. He was murdered himself two nights ago.'

'Good God!' Bess's face stiffened. 'What kind of creature are we talking about?' And when Madden failed to reply – he merely looked at her – she had added, 'Well, I can see now why you and the police are so concerned. Until this man's arrested Evie won't be safe.'

'That's what I've been trying to tell Mrs Spencer. I should have been more direct. Perhaps you could speak to her . . . ?'

'I will. You may depend on it.' She glanced over her shoulder towards the kitchen. 'I'll talk to her as soon as I've seen to Pickles.'

Brushing snow from her cheek, Bess turned to where her pony was standing still harnessed to the trap, frosty plumes issuing from his nostrils, and as she did so the door opened and Mary Spencer put her head out.

'There's a phone call for you, Mr Madden. It's a Chief Inspector Sinclair calling from London. He says he's got some good news.'

*

When he returned to the kitchen ten minutes later, Madden found Bess sitting alone at the table nursing a cup of tea.

'Mary's in the cellar seeing to the furnace,' she said, nodding to a door at the end of the kitchen which stood open. 'She sent Evie upstairs to lie down for a while. The poor girl's exhausted. Mary's feeling guilty herself. Not only wouldn't she listen to you when you tried to explain, but she's failed to offer you anything to eat all day. Do have one.'

She pushed a plate of sandwiches that was lying on the table in front of her towards him.

'She's longing to hear your news,' she added. 'And so am I.'

The smile that accompanied these words softened her rough-hewn features, which Madden now saw in their entirety for the first time. During his absence Bess had shed not only her coat – revealing a pair of corduroy trousers and a seaman's thick sweater beneath it – but her fur-lined cap with its earflaps as well. Her hair proved to be iron-grey in colour and cut short.

'The police have tracked this man down. They know where he's staying in London.'

'Well, that's a relief.' She gave a grunt which to Madden's ears sounded more like a growl. There was a certainty about her solid presence he found reassuring. Her brown eyes held his with a steady gaze.

'They haven't laid hands on him yet. But I'm hoping it's just a matter of time.'

Before he could say more, the sound of Mrs Spencer's voice came to them from below, through the floor.

'Freddie, are you down here?' they heard her call out. 'Are you hiding?'

Glancing out of the window – he'd noticed that the snow

had stopped falling – Madden saw a flicker of movement against the white backdrop.

'He's out in the yard,' he told Bess, who looked over her shoulder and then called to Mary Spencer.

'Freddie's up here . . .'

After a few seconds they heard footsteps and their hostess appeared, brushing aside the branch of a Christmas tree which stood in a corner near the cellar door, puffing from the steps she'd just climbed.

'There you are, Mr Madden.' Her smile was like a peace offering. 'Please have something to eat. I feel I've been starving you all day.'

She opened the kitchen door and looked out.

'Come in at once, Freddie,' she called to her son. 'I've already told you. No more playing outside today. And why haven't you got your coat on?'

After a pause they heard the squeak of Wellington boots on the snow-covered steps and Freddie appeared, flushed in the face and with eyes that sparkled with mischief.

'You didn't see me, Mummy,' he boasted.

'Oh yes I did. You were hiding behind the snowman.'

'Not then. Before.'

'Before when? Oh, you mean down in the cellar. Of course I saw you. I suppose you went out of the door down there, even though you've been told not to. Now I'll have to go down and lock it again. Honestly, you exhaust me.'

She flopped down on one of the chairs.

'I'm so ashamed of myself, Mr Madden. I was quite beastly to you earlier, and all you were doing was trying to help. Please forgive me. Bess gave me a good talking to while you were on the phone.' She smiled. 'I hardly dare to ask, but is it true? Have you got some good news for us?'

'Yes and no.' Madden returned her smile. 'The police have caught up with this man.'

'Thank heavens.' Mary Spencer put a hand to her breast. 'Does that mean Evie can stay with us?'

'I'm not sure. They haven't actually laid hands on him yet. It might be as well not to say anything to her for the time being.'

It was a point Sinclair had stressed when he'd rung to report that the whereabouts of Raymond Ash were no longer a mystery. And to hear from Madden's lips what he himself had learned in the course of the past half-hour.

'I'm sorry if I have to disrupt their Christmas, John, but we can't take any chances. Not after what you've told me. It's obvious Quill found the girl. That must have been him asking questions down there. What we don't know – still – is whether he told Ash.'

Nevertheless, on balance the latest developments had inclined the chief inspector towards optimism and he was now in a far more cheerful frame of mind.

'He's come down to roost in Lambeth this time, Mr Raymond Ash. I've just heard from the station there. And he didn't move far: just up the road from Brixton. He registered as Henry Pratt at a boarding house off the Stockwell Road last Monday and his new landlady swears it's him. She didn't recognize him from the photograph published by the papers, but when they showed her a blow-up of Ash's face she changed her mind. Unfortunately he's out at the moment; he left early this morning. But the place is being watched by the local police and I've got four armed detectives on their way over there.'

'What about Billy and Grace?' Madden asked. As before, he had stood by the window looking out; though now at a changed scene. Gone were the footprints he had seen earlier on the path leading up to the house. The snow that had fallen had covered all trace of them.

'I'd half a mind to recall them,' Sinclair had replied. 'But they were past Leatherhead already and after some thought I decided to let them proceed. If we haven't laid hands on Ash by the time they get to Liphook they'll have to bring the girl back. Let's wait and see, shall we?'

Despite having his hands full, the chief inspector had paused long enough to add a few more details to the brief state of play he'd given his old colleague.

'The detectives I've sent over will wait for Ash inside the boarding house. I don't want him spotting them. I've supplied them with a search warrant and they can have a look at his room while they're waiting. I'm still hoping we'll get our hands on something, some piece of evidence that will tie him to at least one of these killings.'

Sinclair had saved till last his news about the van bringing the Petersfield police contingent to Liphook.

'They went into a ditch, if you can believe it. One of them had to walk to a neighbouring farmhouse to ring head-quarters. Apparently the farmer's going to pull them out with his carthorse. They'll arrive in due course. Oh, and I spoke to Helen. She said Rob had just got back and now you were the only absentee. I told her she needn't worry about there being no trains to get you home: Styles can drop you off at Highfield when he and Grace return to London.'

30

At half-past four, having received no further word from Sinclair, Madden went outside to look at the weather. The fresh snow that had fallen earlier had blanketed the yard and he saw the deep tracks crossing it that Mary Spencer and her son had left when they had walked up to the Hodges' cottage ten minutes earlier.

Persuaded that the crisis was all but over now – the information Madden had relayed to her had done much to lift her spirits – she had decided to pay her Christmas call on the old couple as planned and had taken her son with her.

'Bess will you keep you company,' she told Madden.

In keeping with the festive spirit, before setting out she had got Freddie to turn on the lights of the Christmas tree, and they had all watched as he got down on his knees and crawled underneath the drooping branches of the fir to find the switch.

'Well done, Freddie.'

Twinkling prettily among the green branches, the coloured bulbs had added a further note of cheer to what was now a more relaxed atmosphere.

'I don't want to disturb Evie for the moment,' Mrs Spencer had added before leaving. 'I looked in on her a minute ago and she was fast asleep. Better she gets some rest now, don't you think?'

Madden glanced at his watch. All being well, and provided

the snow held off, the car with Billy and Grace in it would arrive in less than half an hour and from that point on matters could be left in their hands. His own part in the drama of the past few weeks would be over; and none too soon. Not even the imminent arrest of the man they had been seeking, this cold-blooded killer, could assuage the deep grief which the revelations of the afternoon had brought him. The senselessness of Rosa Nowak's death had left him with a feeling of despair, of helplessness in the face of destiny. But could even fate be held to blame, he wondered? No inexorable chain of events had led to the young girl's murder. Chance alone had decreed it. Cruel chance.

Yet black though his mood was, he knew where the cure for it lay, and as he turned to go inside, he took refuge in the thought that his business here would soon be done and that before long he would return home, to the house where he had found his own happiness, and where all those he loved were gathered now under the same roof for the first time in many months.

'You must come over to Highfield in the New Year and visit us,' he told Bess when he went back into to the kitchen. 'Helen would love to see you again.'

'Do you think so?' Left by their hostess with the task of preparing some mulled wine, she was standing by the stove stirring a saucepan, and she flushed with pleasure on hearing his words. 'I've been thinking about her ever since we met this morning, remembering those days.'

'You must come and spend a weekend.'

She smiled and then bent to sniff at the aroma of spices rising from the saucepan.

'Do you know, this takes me back. I was a FANY during the war – the last one, not this one – and whenever we got hold of a bottle of wine we'd gather in one of the tents and warm it up with whatever we could find. Then we'd get tipsy together.'

'A FANY ... I might have guessed,' Madden chuckled. He'd seated himself at the table. 'We thought the world of you ladies. The way you dashed about the Front in your ambulances.'

'Ha!' Bess scoffed at his words. But her glance had turned inward and for a moment she stood lost in memory, her face damp from the steam that rose from the bubbling saucepan.

'We did think of it as an adventure,' she admitted, after a pause. 'At first. We were so determined to be jolly. We kept telling each other these were the best days of our lives. But they weren't really. It's one thing to read about war; it's quite another to see it in the flesh. When it was over, when I came home, I was convinced it would never happen again, the carnage: that men would never inflict such suffering on each other again, no matter what the cause. How wrong I was ...'

She turned her blunt, weathered countenance towards him. Madden saw the question in her eyes before she asked it.

'This man the police are searching for – who is he?'

'Ash is his name, though he's used others in the past.'

'I take it he's no ordinary criminal?'

It was clear she expected an honest reply, and Madden hesitated for only a moment before responding.

'Far from it. He's an assassin. A killer for hire. The police have known about him for years: he left a string of victims on the Continent before the war. Once he broke into a house in France and massacred a whole family. He'd been paid to kill the husband but when the others – the man's wife and daughter – saw him he shot them too. He's gone to great lengths all his life to hide his identity: not to leave any witnesses behind. That's why he wanted to kill Evie, and still would if he got the chance. She's the one person who can send him to the scaffold.'

He paused. Impressed by the strength of character he sensed in her, he'd been carried away and he wondered for a moment if he'd said too much; spoken too brutally. But when he met her level gaze he realized his fears were groundless. She had taken in what he'd said without flinching.

'It's always a shock to find out such people exist.' She spoke after a short pause. She'd been weighing her response. 'And hard to understand how they continue to live in their own skins. To breathe like ordinary human beings.' She shook her head. 'He must have no feelings.'

'None at all,' Madden concurred. 'Only a black heart. That's how a woman who knew him when he was a boy described him to me. He was sixteen when he killed for the first time.'

'Dear God.' She put a hand to her brow.

'But he's come to the end of his rope. They're closing in on him. It won't be long now.'

With a sigh she turned back to the stove. But before she could resume her task the peal of the telephone sounded and she cocked an ear.

'That must be for you.'

'The plot thickens.'

Sinclair didn't trouble to announce himself this time. He began speaking as soon as Madden picked up the receiver.

'No sign of Ash himself yet. He's still out and about. But we've learned that he may have disguised himself. It's possible he's wearing a military uniform.'

The chief inspector broke off to mutter something not

meant for his auditor. Madden caught the words 'be quick' and 'do it now'. Either by chance, or as a result of orders given to the telephone exchange operators, the line was exceptionally clear.

'The detectives I sent over to Lambeth have searched his room. They didn't find anything incriminating, but what they did discover suggests he's up to something. Before we get to that, let me tell you what his movements have been over the past few days. He turned up in Lambeth last Monday. Quill was murdered two days later and Ash's new landlady confirms he was out late that night. The following day he was absent again – she only caught glimpses of him coming and going – and when he got back he had a big parcel with him, contents unknown. But we do have a clue as to what might have been in it.'

Again Sinclair paused and Madden heard him mutter. He waited patiently, the receiver pressed to his ear. The light outside the sitting-room window had dulled since his last call, and already he could see the faint outlines of his own reflection in the glass of the window-pane.

'I'm sorry, John. With Christmas almost on us we're even shorter-staffed than usual. I'm trying to do several things at once. This parcel, then: we suspect it might have contained a military uniform and that Ash may be wearing it now. His landlady's our source for that. Mrs Cully, her name is, and she's a classic of her kind. Not just curious, downright nosy. She can't make head nor tail of this Mr Pratt. He never appears for either breakfast or supper and thus far they've hardly exchanged a word. The best she's been able to do is have a good poke round his room on the pretext of cleaning it, and when our fellows turned up today she was able to tell them she'd seen two suits hanging in the wardrobe when she'd peeped in. Ash had gone out that day wearing another suit, so it was a matter of simple addition to calculate he had three, and they were all there in the wardrobe when our men looked through it, plus the hat which Mrs Cully had seen him with earlier.'

'So he must have been wearing some other clothes, what he had in that parcel, most likely. Yes, I see.' Madden spoke. 'But what makes you think it was a uniform?'

'Again, we've the eagle-eyed Mrs Cully to thank. She was still in bed this morning when she heard footsteps on the stairs. Someone was tiptoeing down them, and that was enough to get her up and over to the window in a flash. She caught a glimpse of an officer going down the steps outside: she only saw his back, worse luck – his greatcoat and cap – but she had no lodger of that description staying there and, as she rather primly put it, no young ladies of the kind who might think of entertaining a gentleman for the night. Which anyway was against the rules. In the course of the morning she observed her other guests departing, but there was no sign of Ash, and later she went upstairs to knock on his door on some pretext and found the room empty. So it looks as though this mysterious officer must have been our man.'

The chief inspector paused, either to catch his breath or to reflect on his own words.

'It's not surprising, after all,' he went on. 'We know he's disguised himself in the past. That was mentioned in the report Duval sent us. What puzzles me is why – why put himself to so much trouble? He'll have to go back to his lodgings at some point and he won't want to be seen dressed up as a soldier boy. Could it be because he's feeling more exposed since we published that picture of him?'

The question was clearly rhetorical: he continued without pause.

'There's not much more to tell. Only a riddle to ponder.

I haven't mentioned this yet, but the men I sent over came on something odd when they searched his room, an item Mrs Cully said wasn't there when she went through it. It was a first-aid kit of the kind air-raid wardens carry around with them in their satchels. They've become war surplus; I'm told you can buy them at any of these markets that have sprung up. The one in Ash's room had been torn open and there was a dressing missing.'

'A dressing?'

'A bandage and so forth. They found the empty packet it had been in. I wondered if he'd been injured. Could he have got into a fight with Quill the other night? There was no indication of it at the scene.'

Sinclair paused, perhaps hoping Madden might offer some suggestion, but when he remained silent he went on:

'I had word from Styles not long ago. He and Grace aren't far from Liphook. But it's slow going. There's a lot of snow on the roads. I haven't heard from Petersfield again, but I dare say the men they sent will get there eventually. Once every-one's assembled we can have another council of war. You can tell Mrs Spencer that. Say nothing's decided as yet. I don't want to drag this young woman up to London unnecessarily.'

'A bandage, you say . . . ?' As though in a trance, Madden had been staring at his own reflection in the window-pane.

'That's right.' It took the chief inspector a few seconds to realize what his old colleague was referring to. 'A dressing from the first-aid kit. Why . . . ?'

'There was a man with his eye bandaged up on the train this morning. An army officer.'

Sinclair grunted. At first he seemed unsure how to respond.

'I take it you didn't recognize him?' he finally asked.

'Oh, no. In fact, I hardly looked at his face. He got off the train behind me and I gave him a hand down.'

The chief inspector cleared his throat. Though his old partner's powers of recollection never ceased to amaze him, his ability to retrieve even the most trivial details from the well of memory, he felt bound in this instance to question the assumption he seemed to be making.

'Aren't you rather leaping to conclusions, John? After all, a wounded soldier is hardly a rarity these days.'

'It wasn't that. It was something else.' Madden spoke in a dead voice. 'I remember it now. He didn't return a salute. Two, in fact.'

'I'm sorry . . . ?'

'A pair of privates walked by as he got off the train and saluted him. He looked right through them. No real officer would do that. You respond automatically. It's drilled into you. I should know – I was one myself.'

Sinclair allowed a few seconds to pass.

'Very well. Let's say for argument's sake that you're right. Why the elaborate disguise?'

'If it was Ash, he would have travelled on that line often, working as a salesman. Perhaps he was afraid of being recognized by one of the ticket collectors. He must know by now that his description's been circulated, that every police-man in the country is looking for him.'

'You're suggesting Quill gave him the information, then? That he knows where the girl's living?'

Madden said nothing. For the past few minutes he had been watching the light fade on the snow outside.

'But that means he arrived in Liphook this morning, when you did, yet there's been no sign of him. What's he been doing all day?'

'I don't know, Angus. I don't even know if it was Ash. But he may have been waiting for dark.'

He broke off to call out loudly over his shoulder.

'Bess . . . ! Bess . . . ! Can you get in here?'

When he spoke again it was to the chief inspector.

'Look, we can't take the risk. I'm going to lock up the house. If you can reach Billy tell him to hurry.'

'Wait a minute, John—'

'No, I can't, Angus, not now.' He heard the sound of Bess's heavy steps approaching. 'There's no time.'

31

SHE BURST IN.

'John—?'

'Ash may be here in Liphook.' He saw her gasp. 'I'm worried about Mrs Spencer and her son. How far away is the Hodges' cottage?'

'About a quarter of a mile.'

'Have they a telephone?'

She shook her head. 'But Mary won't be back for at least an hour. Mrs H will want to serve them tea.'

'I'm going to lock up the house. How many doors are there?'

'Let me see.' She had taken in the situation at once. Her voice was steady. 'Apart from the kitchen and the front door there are two others at either end of the house. You can reach them by the passage. They may be already locked. Mary's careful about that.'

'I'll check them. You fetch Eva. Get her down here.'

They parted at once, Bess heading for the hall where the stairs were, while Madden ran down the passage in the opposite direction to the end of the house, where he found a study with a door giving on to the garden. It was locked, as Bess had said, but he spent a minute shifting a heavy table across the floor and planting it in front of the door to provide an additional barrier.

Running back he stopped at the kitchen, where he first made sure of the door, turning the key in it twice, then switched off the lights. The window above the sink offered a good view of the yard, and he stood there for a few seconds scanning the white-blanketed cobbles outside. The tracks Mrs Spencer and her son had left in the pristine surface were easy to follow: they went from the door to the end of the line of stalls at the back of the yard before disappearing around the corner. His breathing became easier when he realized they were the only footmarks to be seen.

Back in the corridor he stopped in the hall to check the front door. It was locked, but he noticed it also had a bolt higher up and he slid that into its slot. The light on the landing above had been switched on and he could hear Bess's voice urging Eva to hurry. His own destination was now the room at the other end of the passage, which he reached within a few seconds, only to find it filled with unwanted furniture that obstructed his path to the door which was at the side of the house. Having picked his way there, he discovered it was locked, but took the same precaution as he had in the study, this time choosing a bookcase that was standing nearby as a further barrier. Given the cluttered state of the floor, the task was an awkward one, and it was several minutes before he was able to manoeuvre the heavy oak piece into place.

His job done, he hurried back, and when he came to the hall he found that the light on the landing above had been switched off, a sign that Bess and Eva must have come down. But before joining them in the sitting-room, he stopped off again at the kitchen – he wanted to make a further inspection of the yard – and as he entered the room he heard a low rustling noise he could not place at first until he realized it was coming from the saucepan Bess had been stirring earlier: the liquid inside had come to the boil. Stopping by the stove, he paused long enough to shift the heavy pot to one side of the range, first drawing on his gloves so that he could grasp the hot handle, then went to the window and looked out.

What he saw there sent a chill through him.

In the few minutes he'd been away a fresh set of footprints had appeared in the snow. They led from the gate straight to the back door. Whoever had made them had tried to get in. Or so it seemed to Madden as he quickly tested the door and found it still locked. The tracks led off in the direction of the woodbin, but although he leaned over the sink and peered that way he was unable to see how far they went. To do so he would have had to open the door and look out, an act he was unwilling even to contemplate. If it was Ash, and he was lurking just out of sight on the other side of the woodbin, the action might well prove fatal to him.

There was nothing he could do except pray that the police car would arrive soon, within minutes even. But then another thought came to him, a frightening image that sent him racing down the passage to the sitting-room. If Ash was circling the house searching for a way in, he would see Bess and Eva through the window, and if the Polish girl offered him a target he might well take the opportunity to shoot her.

But the room, when he reached it, was empty.

There was no sign of either woman.

Where were they, then? Still on the floor above?

Panting, Madden stood in the doorway, his mind racing.

He wondered if Bess had seen the same tracks as he had from the window of Eva's bedroom – or, even worse, spotted Ash crossing the yard – and decided to stay upstairs. But if so, why hadn't she tried to warn him?

Racking his brains for an answer he switched off the light at the door and went to the window. There was no sign of any footprint on the terrace outside, no indication that Ash had walked round the house.

So where was he now?

What was he planning?

With no weapon of any kind, Madden felt doubly exposed. But as he turned to leave, an idea struck him, and he went to the fireplace and reached up above it to where the shield and assegai were fixed. With a sharp wrench he pulled the spear free, and with its comforting weight now nestling in his hand he returned to the passage and set off in the direction of the hall.

His intention was to go upstairs and find out what had happened to the two women. But he got only as far as the kitchen door, then froze, stopping in his tracks.

Something was different . . . something had changed.

Madden felt the hairs on his neck rise.

Struggling to understand what it was that had made him halt, he caught a whiff of the spiced wine coming from the saucepan on the stove. Steam was rising from the pot. It was being borne to him on a breeze, he realized, a cool wind that brushed against his cheek, and with a flash of insight he knew this couldn't be.

Stepping into the kitchen, he swept the room with his gaze and saw at once where the breeze was coming from: at the far end of the kitchen, behind the coloured lights of the Christmas tree, the door to the cellar stood open.

Madden stared at it. He remembered what Mary Spencer had said: that she would have to go down to the cellar again because her son had left the door to the yard open.

But she'd failed to do that.

Ash was in the house.

The shock was like a physical pain and he turned quickly, half-fearing to find that the soft-footed killer had crept up behind him, his garrotte ready. But the passage was empty: and since he knew that Ash could not have gone in the direction of the sitting-room – or else they would have met – that left only the hall where the stairs were.

He started towards them at once, straining to hear any sound as he tiptoed down the carpeted passage. The hall was in half-darkness: there was a light still burning in the passage and he saw it reflected in a small pool of water on the stone-flagged floor near the stairs, moisture that could only have come from the snow outside.

He paused then. There was still no sound from above, but the silence there was filled with menace and for a moment his heart failed him. He knew the danger that lay in wait for him and how much he stood to lose. In the past, when his life had hung by a thread in the endless slaughter of the trenches, he had learned like others to view his future, if any, with the eye of a fatalist. But those days were long gone. His love for the woman he had married, like some wondrous plant, had flowered into other loves, and now every moment of his life seemed precious to him.

But it was not in his nature to turn from the threat, nor even to wait the few minutes it might take for the police to arrive. Somewhere on the floor above him were two women in imminent peril, and though his fear stayed with him, he put it aside, as he had learned to do when he'd been a soldier. He considered the danger confronting him with a clear mind.

There was no point in ascending the stairs himself. If Ash was waiting in the passage off the landing above, pistol in hand, he would simply provide him with a target. The silence on the upper floor persuaded him that the killer was still searching for his primary victim, for Eva, going from room to room. One or other of the women must have seen him climbing the stairs in his officer's uniform; now both were hiding and it was only a matter of time before Ash found them.

Unless he could be diverted.

At once his strategy became clear to him. He must draw the killer away, downstairs, if possible out into the yard – and then hope that the police car would arrive and Ash would be dealt with. Either way there was no time to lose.

At the bottom of the stairs was a cloakroom where he had seen Mary Spencer hang her son's coat earlier that afternoon. The door was open a few inches, and for a brief moment Madden toyed with the idea of concealing himself there and attempting to seize Ash when he came running down the stairs (as he hoped he would). But the plan seemed rash – he had no idea whether he could overpower the younger man, who in any case was inured to violence – and he dismissed it. Instead he positioned himself at the bottom of the flight, assegai in hand.

'Ash!' He roared out the name. 'Raymond Ash. I have a warrant for your arrest. Drop your weapon if you have one and give yourself up.'

His last words echoed in the empty hall. Expecting his quarry to appear at any moment on the landing above, he prepared to run.

There was silence for several seconds. Then a faint sound reached his ears. The stirring of movement. It came from the floor above and he peered up there.

A hinge squeaked.

This time the noise came from closer at hand, but Madden's attention was so riveted to the scene above, his concentration so fixed on the few square feet of the landing, that only when something like a shadow passed before his eyes – it was no more than a flicker – did he react; and then only instinctively.

He thrust his gloved hand upwards and in that fraction of a second saved his life.

As the wire cut into his palm he realized in an instant what had happened: Ash had been hiding in the coat cupboard behind him and was set on killing him now.

Like two drunks they staggered about the stone-flagged floor, Madden roaring in his chest with the pain and with the effort he was making to fling off the man behind him, who equally clung to his garrotte, growling unintelligibly himself. First they thudded into the wall, then into the front door before ricocheting off that to a table that stood at the side of the hall with a brass tray on it. Knocked off its perch, the tray fell to the floor with a noise like a gong being struck. And throughout the eternity of seconds that passed as they writhed together, Madden kept trying to strike at his foe with the assegai, which he still held clutched in his right hand, thrusting backwards with the short stabbing spear, while his left held the wire at bay. Little by little, though, the pressure was choking him and he felt himself weakening.

Through bleary, tear-filled eyes, he saw two figures appear then, as if by magic, on the stairs, Bess in the lead, her heavy boots pounding on the carpeted runners, Eva at her heels. The sight galvanized him into one last effort. Seeing his attacker's foot on the floor just behind and a little to one side of him, he drove the tip of the assegai into the instep with all his strength and was rewarded with a cry of pain. The band of fire at his throat slackened, and before Ash had time to recover he repeated the action and then threw himself backwards, sending his attacker crashing into the table again. All at once the wire loosened, and as they rolled apart Madden saw that Bess had reached the bottom of the stairs and was coming to his aid.

'Run!' he croaked to her. 'Run!' He had lost his assegai as he tried to scramble to his feet. He saw Ash was doing the same, fumbling in the pocket of his greatcoat as he got to his knees. But his own strength was gone: he knew he couldn't tackle him again. 'To the kitchen—!'

Whether Bess heard his choked cry he never knew, but she turned at once and grabbed hold of Eva's hand. The girl was standing at the bottom of the stairs, paralysed by fright, unable to move, it seemed, until Bess jerked her into motion and then dragged her in the direction of the passage. Unsteady though he was, Madden began to stagger after them, but his feet struck the tray that had fallen to the floor and as he stumbled and almost fell, a shot rang out and he felt the sting of plaster on his face. A bullet had struck the wall beside him and he looked back. Ash had risen to one knee and was taking aim with the pistol.

Madden threw himself forward into the passage as he fired, landing on his hands and knees, then picked himself up and staggered down the corridor to the open door of the kitchen where Bess was waiting like some burly guardian angel. She swept him inside, slamming the door shut behind them as she switched on the light, then cursing when she found there was no key in the lock.

Still gasping for breath, Madden seized one of the chairs by the table. Out of the corner of his eye he saw that Eva had fallen full-length on to the floor. Wide-eyed with shock, she was trying to pull herself up using the edge of the table. As Bess pressed her heavy shoulder to the door he slid the back of the chair beneath the doorknob. Before he could wedge it there, however, there was a muffled report and splinters of wood were blasted inwards from a hole that appeared suddenly. Another shot sounded and Bess clutched at her temple, the blood leaking through her fingers. She stumbled back into the big iron range behind her.

Next moment the door swung open, knocking the chair sideways, and Ash stood there, pistol raised. Seeing Madden, he swivelled to point the weapon at him, not realizing until it was too late that the danger was coming from another quarter. Bess had seized hold of the saucepan of mulled wine off the top of the range and as Ash turned his gun on her she hurled the boiling contents into his face. His scream of agony was accompanied by the sound of another shot and Bess fell to her knees. The saucepan clattered to the floor with her, and without thinking Madden bent and picked it up by its handle, rising in the same movement and swinging the heavy iron vessel around. He caught a glimpse of Ash's face, blistered red and contorted with pain, before the saucepan connected with the side of his head and he reeled back, dropping the gun as he did so and clawing at his face. Grabbing hold of the handle with both hands now, Madden struck him again, bringing the makeshift weapon down on top of his head like a club.

Ash staggered against the door jamb, but did not fall. Instead, snarling through his burned lips, he dropped his head and charged at Madden, butting him in the chest and knocking him off balance. As his feet slipped beneath him on the wet floor, Madden grabbed at the table for support, but missed his hold, falling heavily on his back. Before he could rise he saw Ash bend to pick up the pistol at his feet.

Panting, he came over to where Madden lay. His face had turned scarlet and with his glaring eyes and snorting breath he seemed only half human. Swaying on his feet, he raised the gun and took aim.

The sound of the shot was deafening and it was followed by a shower of broken glass that fell on Madden's upturned face like acid rain, leaving pinpoints of pain. The gun in Ash's hand wavered. He took an unsteady step back. His heavy coat was unbuttoned and Madden saw a bloodstain appear on the khaki jacket beneath. As it spread like a flower opening its petals, another shot sounded, this one even louder in his ears. No longer able to control his limbs, Ash began to stagger backwards, the gun falling from his nerveless grip, and as he landed up against the wall a third shot took him full in the throat and Madden saw the blood leap and spatter on the plaster behind him.

Ash fell where he was, collapsing like a rag doll, ending in a heap on the floor.

Half-stunned and still struggling to comprehend what had just occurred, Madden lay still. He was panting heavily – without realizing it he had been holding his breath – and his limbs felt leaden. Finally, with what seemed like a great effort, he brushed the shards of glass from his face and hoisted himself up on one elbow to look behind him. There were lights in the yard outside: someone was hammering at the door and he heard his name being shouted. It was Billy, calling to him.

Only then did he notice the figure at the window and the unmistakable shape of the heavy Webley revolver that was pointing through the shattered glass. The man outside leaned forward, striving for a better view, and as his face came into the light, Madden recognized the lean, pockmarked features.

'Got you!' Joe Grace hissed, his tone gleeful as he peered at the crumpled figure on the floor. 'Got you, you bastard.'

Madden started at the ring of the telephone – he'd been dozing in an armchair in front of the fire – and he looked at his watch. It was after seven. The phone had been quickly answered: he heard the murmur of Billy Styles's voice, but not what he was saying.

He glanced across at the settee where Bess was lying on her back wrapped in two blankets and with her head bandaged.

She seemed to be asleep. The wound to her temple was slight – the shot through the door had done no more than graze her scalp – but Ash's second bullet had struck her in the side and she had lost a great deal of blood, most of it on the kitchen floor, before Madden, with Billy's help, had stemmed the flow with a dressing made from a clean towel that was later replaced with one taken from Mary Spencer's first-aid box.

Fully conscious all the time, Bess had been scornful of their fussing.

'I was only winged. It's a flesh wound, for goodness sake. Don't carry on so.'

This last had been directed at Mary Spencer, who had been fetched from the Hodges' cottage by Leonard. On the Liphook bobby's advice she had left her son in the care of the elderly couple and hurried back with him, and though appalled to discover what had happened in her absence had rallied quickly, first helping to carry Bess into the sitting-room, then going in search of blankets. Left on his own to build up the fire, which by now was little more than embers, Madden had taken the opportunity while he was alone with Bess to speak firmly to her.

'You know as well as I do how dangerous bullet wounds are. Whether you like it or not, you're suffering from shock. You must lie quietly, and wait for the ambulance to arrive.'

She had smiled at him then.

'That's how I used to talk to the boys I picked up,' she recalled. 'During the war. They were all so young. They used to call me ma'am though I wasn't much older than they were.'

He had sat beside her on the settee holding her hand, waiting until she dropped off to sleep before moving to the armchair.

'I haven't thanked you for saving my life,' he had said. In

truth he had been too busy saving hers as he'd knelt in the mingled blood and wine beside her body on the kitchen floor.

'I thought I'd better.' She'd responded with a smile. 'I could hardly have faced Helen otherwise. Imagine having to tell her after all this time that I'd somehow mislaid her husband.'

For his own part, Madden had wanted nothing more than to talk to his wife: after his desperate fight with Ash and the explosion of violence that followed, the sound of her voice was what he craved above all. But he had refused both Billy's offer and one made a little later by Sinclair to get a call put through to Highfield.

'I don't want to speak to Helen on the phone,' he had told the chief inspector after contact had been re-established between them. 'She'll only worry when she hears my croaking. Better I tell her about this in person.'

Unaware of the drama that had been played out while he was sitting helpless in his office in London, Sinclair had listened in shocked silence to Madden's terse account of his life-and-death struggle with the killer. Most upsetting to the chief inspector had been the hoarse rasp which was all his old friend could manage by way of speech from his still tender throat.

'I plan on spending Christmas in dignified silence,' he had joked.

He had made no mention of his throbbing hand where the wire had left a welt on his palm painful to the touch. Urged by Billy to rest while he and Grace took care of things, he had settled in his chair and then sat for some time gazing at the mark. The agonized minutes when he had grappled with Ash were still raw in his memory: though wounded several times in the war, he had never come so close to death, and recalling the moment when he had lain stunned on the kitchen floor and seen the pistol pointing at him, a mask of scalded flesh behind it, he wondered if the image would ever leave him.

The body of Raymond Ash had been left to lie where it had fallen on the kitchen floor, covered by a dust sheet which Joe Grace had found in one of the rooms downstairs and which he'd tossed without ceremony over the killer's corpse. While Madden and Billy had attended to Bess, he had taken it on himself to see to Eva, who, forgotten by all, had managed to drag herself up from the floor during the last terrifying seconds in the kitchen, but had then sat slumped at the table with her mouth hanging open, seemingly unaware of what was going on around her. Glancing up from his urgent task for a moment, Madden had been reminded of scenes he had witnessed in the past: of men in the aftermath of battle reduced to mere sleepwalkers; shadows of themselves.

It was Joe finally who had taken the girl by the elbow and lifted her to her feet. Surprisingly gentle in his manner, he had coaxed her towards the door.

'You don't want to stay here, Miss,' he had murmured to her, softening his usual grating tone. 'You go somewhere and lie down. We'll bring you a cup of tea in a moment.'

As they'd moved slowly towards the door across the littered floor, one of Eva's trailing feet had caught in the dust sheet, and without realizing it she had tugged the cover off Ash's body, exposing his blistered face with the lips drawn back in a snarl. The sight brought a cry from her and she had turned away sharply. But Grace had steadied her, slipping an arm about her shoulders.

'Now don't you fret, Miss,' he had said as her eyes welled up. 'And don't go shedding any tears either, not for him. Dirt's what he was. No better than scum. And that's God's truth.'

EPILOGUE

'So much for Raymond Ash, then. We can close the book on him. There's nothing more outstanding. We have the diamonds and the money he stole from Silverman. I dare say Sobel's heirs will claim the stones, if they can prove ownership, but that's a problem for the French to handle. We've done our part.'

The chief inspector stretched luxuriously. He was enjoying the way the spring sunshine in Bennett's office made the windows sparkle: windows which for almost five years had been scored by the crisscross lines of anti-blast tape but which now provided an uninterrupted view of the blue sky outside and the glittering river beneath it. Germany's surrender had been announced three weeks earlier and the two men had shared in the joy felt by the whole nation.

'I talked to Duval on the phone yesterday after we'd opened the safe-deposit box. They're definitely Sobel's diamonds: they match the stones on the list.'

'And how much money was there?' Bennett was curious.

'Fifteen thousand pounds exactly. Of course the stones are worth a good deal more, but as an asking price it was just the sort of sum that was guaranteed to get Solly down to Wapping as fast his legs would carry him and no questions asked. He'd seen the list of diamonds that Alfie Meeks had shown him and he must have thought he was on to a good thing. Shrewd of Ash to think of that.'

The cache of money and jewels had been slow in coming

to light. Although every bank in London had been asked to check its records for a Raymond Ash or a Henry Pratt, none had been found holding a safe-deposit box in either name. It had been a chance sighting of Ash more than a year earlier by a fellow salesman employed by the same city firm he had worked for that had provided the vital clue. Like others who had known him, the man had been questioned on several occasions, and over a period of months, as the police had cast their nets wider and wider in the search for leads, and he'd suddenly recalled seeing Ash entering a branch of Barclays bank in Cannon Street one day. The only reason the memory had stuck with him, however unreliably, was because he had heard at the office that same morning that his colleague had called in sick and realized he must be malingering. Contacted by Scotland Yard, the bank manager had tentatively identified Ash from a photograph as one of his customers, Charles Porter by name. Porter had kept a small account at the bank along with a safe-deposit box.

'He opened the account in '40 soon after he got here, using a false identity card.' Details of the discovery had been given to Sinclair that morning by Billy Styles, who was still in charge of the investigation. 'They were easy to come by then, and he was the sort of man who would always need a safe place to hide what he didn't want seen by others. Apart from the stones and the money, there were two sets of false Dutch papers in the box and an American passport which seems genuine and was probably stolen. He may have been planning to use it after the war.'

The chief inspector reflected.

'Duval was pleased to hear about the jewels. It means they can close their investigation as well. But he still wishes we'd laid hands on Ash. Even though we might have had problems making a murder case stick, that wouldn't have been the case with them. Not once they had Eva Belka's statement. The French wanted his head, and given what he did at Fontainebleau I can't say I blame them.'

He sat musing for a moment.

'After more than forty years in this business I thought there was nothing in the way of human nature that could surprise me any longer,' he went on. 'But Ash proved me wrong. What was it like to live inside his skin? I wish I knew the answer: if only for curiosity's sake. But I'm afraid the question will go begging now.'

Bennett grunted.

'By the way, I've some news you'll be pleased to hear yourself. That report we sent to the commissioner regarding the work Poole did here and my recommendation that she be transferred to the CID has borne fruit.' He slid a piece of paper across his blotter to Sinclair. 'As you see, I've been authorized to inform the station commander at Bow Street that the transfer will take effect from next month. I've decided to bring her to the Yard to start her training. What a pity you won't be here to oversee it.'

He sighed audibly.

'But there it is. All good things come to an end. And speaking of which, this is a moment that should be recorded. Angus Sinclair's last case. I feel we should pause for a minute's silence. Those of us who still have to labour on.'

The assistant commissioner had formally accepted his old colleague's resignation only a fortnight earlier, confident that his own would likewise be approved now that the war was over, only to learn to his chagrin that his services would be required for a further six months. Since then his sniping had been relentless.

'Just think, in less than a fortnight you'll be a man of leisure.' Bennett pondered his words gloomily. 'Though I must say I never thought I'd live to see the day . . .'

'What day would that be, sir?'

Determined not to rise to the bait, the chief inspector continued to scan the letter his superior had passed him.

'Why, the day when you would abandon me, Angus. And after all these years we've worked together. Surely a few more months won't make any difference?'

'Alas, I've already made my arrangements, sir. My bags, as the saying goes, are packed.'

He handed the letter to Bennett.

'And what better note on which to end my time here. Lily Poole will make a capital detective.'

He assembled his papers and prepared to leave. Bennett regarded him sourly.

'So your heart's in the Highlands, is it?'

'Sir . . . ?' Sinclair looked up.

'You're off to Scotland, aren't you? You always said you planned to retire there.'

'So I did . . .' Sinclair gnawed his lip. 'But, do you know, I've had a change of heart. Scotland seems a long way off. There's really nothing to draw me back there any more.'

'Well, I'm glad to hear it.' Sir Wilfred's face brightened. 'I'll be retiring myself to our place in Hampshire. It would nice to think we might meet now and again to chew over old times. Are you planning to settle anywhere near there?'

'Near enough.' The chief inspector rose to his feet with a smile. 'In Surrey, as it happens. A mere hop and a skip away. We'll be practically neighbours.'

*

'It'll need some repairs, Angus. So long as the roof didn't leak old Granny Meacham wasn't bothered by anything else. And the bathroom will have to be rebuilt. But you can stay with us while the work's being done.'

Arms folded, head cocked judiciously to one side, Helen Madden surveyed the slate-roofed cottage from the rickety garden gate. It was hanging only by a hinge, and her husband had opened it with care before the three of them went in.

'What do you think?'

'I think it's lovely, my dear.' Sinclair didn't hesitate. 'And I can't thank you both enough for finding it for me.'

The chief inspector looked about him: to one side of the cottage was an apple orchard just coming into bud, on the other an open field dotted with the first wild flowers of spring. Behind them, on the path they had taken along the stream from the Maddens' own house, he had seen daffodils clinging to the banks, and as he looked back now he spotted the blue blur of a kingfisher as it sped upstream.

'You won't be too cold? It loses the sun early in winter. When there is any sun.'

'I shall build large fires and live like a badger in a burrow.'

'You can always come over to us, you know. For a meal, or just to talk. It's only ten minutes by the path.'

It had been Helen herself who had first broached the idea of him coming to join them in Highfield, and once made, the suggestion that he should spend his retirement close to his friends had seemed so logical, inevitable even, that the chief inspector wondered why he had ever thought otherwise.

'You can't possibly go traipsing off to Scotland,' she had declared in her usual forthright manner two months earlier when he had been down on one of his weekend visits. 'What on earth will you do there?'

The chief inspector had replied, tentatively, that he had been thinking of taking up fishing.

'There are plenty of fish in England. The rivers teem with them. In fact, it would be wonderful if you got John interested. He needs a hobby. With George Burrows in charge, the farm almost runs itself. I can see you both setting off in the morning with rods over your shoulders. Do think about it. We'd love to have you here.'

Later, during a walk he had taken in the woods with Madden himself, he had learned from his old friend's lips that he and his wife had had the idea for some time and only been waiting for the right moment to put it to him. Before the day was out he had made up his mind, and lying in bed that same evening, in the room he had slept in so often he had come to think of it as his own, he had felt the burden of his years – for so they sometimes seemed to him now – lift at a stroke.

'Come along, Angus.'

Leaving Madden at the gate – he was still fiddling with the hinge – Helen took Sinclair's arm and they walked up the short path together. Somewhat overgrown with weeds since the death of the previous owner, it was bordered by flower-beds that only awaited new plantings and by a patch of unmown lawn on either side.

'We had Bess Brigstock to stay last weekend – did John tell you? She's become a real friend. I wish we hadn't lost touch for all those years. Her wound set her back for a while and she gave up delivering the post at Liphook. But she's the sort of person who can't sit idle, particularly if she thinks she's needed, and she's talking of working for the Red Cross again. Now that the war's over there'll be a huge problem with refugees and displaced persons. It's the sort of challenge Bess can't resist.'

They had reached the front door of the cottage and they turned to look at the view.

'And you won't have heard either of the invasion we had three weeks ago.'

'The invasion . . . ?'

'John's old friend Nelly Stover brought her grandchildren down for a week, and since I'd been wanting to have Billy and *his* family for some time I invited, them too. We'd forgotten what it was like to have a houseful of small children, and really they behaved very well, at least until Lucy arrived. But she got them going. First she taught them all to play Up Jenkins, then the older ones Racing Demon, and before long there was pandemonium every evening. John and I loved it, but Nelly was most disapproving. For a while at least; until she softened up. She's a wonderful character, tough as old boots, but then she's had to be. I'm hoping we'll see more of her.'

'And what about Lucy?' The chief inspector put the question to Madden, who had just joined them at the door. 'How much longer will she stay in the Wrens?'

'About as long as it takes her to find a way to wriggle out, I should think.' He chuckled. 'She's not cut out for military life, I fear. There's far too much discipline. But I've warned her not to desert. We won't harbour any fugitives here.'

Helen was listening with a smile.

'We probably shouldn't tell you this, but we finally discovered what she's been up to in London all these months. It was a man, of course. I should have guessed.'

'A man?' The chief inspector was taken aback. He wasn't sure how to react. 'But isn't she a little young . . . ?'

'That's exactly what John said.' Helen had seen her husband's scowl. 'You men . . .' She laughed. 'But there's no need to wring your hands, or reach for your shotguns. He was a perfectly respectable naval officer temporarily posted to the Admiralty and now he's safely back at sea. It seems to have been more in the nature of an experiment, at least as far as Lucy was concerned, and anyway it's over. She's an adventurous spirit and there's nothing I can do about that. Except applaud it, perhaps. The best thing was we talked, and that was lovely. It was like finding a new friend.'

She glanced at her watch.

'Angus, dear, I have to dash. I'm going to leave you here with John. I've got surgery in half an hour. Here's the front-door key.' She put it in his hand. 'Stay as long as you like. Have a good look round. You can walk back whenever you feel like it. We'll meet at lunch, if not before.'

She paused on the point of going.

'We're so pleased you've decided to settle here.' She touched his cheek with her hand. 'Though of course things will have to change between us.'

'I beg your pardon.' Caught off balance by her remark, he had failed to catch the teasing note in her voice.

'You'll be my patient from now on, Angus. At least, I assume so. That'll put an entirely new complexion on our relationship. For instance, I noticed you were hardly limping at all when we walked along here. Is your gout better?'

'Not altogether.' Sinclair frowned. The subject wasn't one he liked aired. 'It comes and goes.'

'That's usually the case. There are a number of remedies we can try. But in the meantime, prayer and fasting have been known to work wonders.'

'I'm not sure I fancy either.'

She was already walking to the gate as he spoke, and she turned.

'That's what I was afraid of.'

Pausing to run her fingers through her hair, she shook her head in a gesture that reminded him, with a surge of pleasure, of the young woman he had first known twenty years before.

'I can see already you're going to be a difficult patient. I shall have to keep a close eye on you.'

With a wave to them she went off, and the two men watched as she walked down the stream, her fair hair bright in the sunlight, moving with a grace that was almost a girl's.

Madden grunted. He turned to Sinclair.

'Well? Shall we go inside, Angus?'

'Why not?'

But the chief inspector dallied for a moment. Her last words had sounded a reassuring note and he wanted to dwell on them. There were many reasons for the choice he had made, but one in particular seemed to matter more than any other as he watched her figure disappear round a bend in the stream. He knew now that however long his life lasted, she would always be a part of it.